D1320695

PUT OUT THE FIRES

September 1940—the cruellest year of war for
Britain's civilians as the Luftwaffe mercilessly blitz
their cities. In Pearl Street, near to Liverpool's vital
docks, families struggle to cope the best they can.
A nasty surprise for ever-cheerful dressmaker
Brenda Mahon and flightly Sean's love for little
Alice show how life goes on even when it appears
to be falling apart. Yet while Eileen Costello tries
to hide her ruined hopes of happiness with Nick
and do her best by the husband she hoped had
gone forever, Ruth Singerman returns having
escaped from Austria. Even the joy of seeing her
father again cannot make up for the bitter loss of
her children.

PUT OUT THE FIRES

Maureen Lee

CHIVERS PRESS
BATH

First published 1996
by
Orion
This Large Print edition published by
Chivers Press
by arrangement with
Orion Books Ltd
1999

ISBN 0 7540 1249 2

Copyright © 1996 by Maureen Lee

The right of Maureen Lee to be identified as the
author of this work has been asserted by her in
accordance with the Copyright, Designs and
Patents Act 1988.

All rights reserved

British Library Cataloguing in Publication Data available

And now for Paul, the second one

Printed and bound in Great Britain by
REDWOOD BOOKS, Trowbridge, Wiltshire

In all, Bootle experienced 502 air raid alerts, the final one on 29 December, 1942. Eighty-five per cent of its buildings were damaged, and 1,886 civilians were killed or injured. This small independent borough, hardly mentioned in the chronicles of the Second World War, suffered by far the highest proportion of deaths per 1,000 of the population on Merseyside. It is very difficult to compare like with like in any examination of the statistics of death by enemy action, but it would appear that Bootle suffered more than any other town in the United Kingdom.

The Home Port, by B. J. Marsh and S. Almond

I would like to express my sincerest thanks to Cathy Hankin, not just for her memories of what happened, but for the research she did on my behalf which helped me to write this book.

PROLOGUE

It was in September 1939 that Adolf Hitler despatched his troops into Poland, and Britain and France were drawn into a war for which neither was prepared. One terrible year later, the seemingly invincible German army had swept brutally across Europe, leaving death and destruction in its wake, until almost the entire continent had been conquered.

Now, separated from the advancing enemy only by the English Channel, Great Britain stood alone . . .

CHAPTER ONE

What had happened to the person who had gazed back at her from the chrome mirror over the mantelpiece in the parlour only that morning; the happy woman with sparkling eyes and fresh pink skin, a woman so obviously and radiantly in love?

Eileen Costello stared thoughtfully at her blurred reflection in the window of the Dock Road pub. The glass had been painted dark inside for the blackout, turning the window into a mirror.

The woman had disappeared, gone forever, to be replaced by someone with lank blonde hair and a pale drawn face and dead, expressionless eyes.

And what had happened to the day that had started off as had no other, the day that was going to be the happiest of her life?

You needed to go back a whole year to work it out, right back to the very day war had been declared and Francis had gone off within an hour of the declaration, looking smart and debonair in his khaki uniform, and suddenly, after six years of marriage, she was free!

It was bliss without his domineering presence. Tony blossomed and stopped jumping at the least sound, and she got a job—something Francis had always forbidden—working on a lathe in a munitions factory. Eileen smiled to herself, scarcely noticing she was being jostled by people who came hurrying around the corner. Several glanced curiously at the lovely blonde girl, rather oddly dressed in an old tweed coat that contrasted sharply with her smart straw hat and high-heeled

1

shoes, who was standing on the pavement staring vacantly into a blackened pub window at half past seven on a Saturday evening.

It had been an education working at Dunnings. The conversation that went on between the girls above the sound of the machinery would have made a navvy blush, but she'd grown fond of her workmates and they were almost like a second family.

So, there she was at twenty-six, earning a good wage—more than Francis had ever done—an independent woman in her own right, with control over her own body for the first time in six years. And she was happy, happier than she'd ever been before. In fact, she felt rather guilty that the war, which had brought misery to so many people, had altered her own life out of all proportion for the better.

That was when she decided she didn't want Francis back.

She knew it would cause a furore in Pearl Street. No self-respecting woman booted her husband out, no matter what the blighter might have been up to—not that anyone, even her own family, knew what went on behind the front door of Number 16. A woman was expected to grit her teeth and make the best of things. But Eileen Costello, flushed with freedom and a newfound sense of her own worth, decided she'd had enough.

There was a rumbling from up above as a train ran along the tracks of the overhead railway in the direction of Liverpool, and a sudden tremendous whooshing sound from inside a nearby warehouse as grain was emptied into a silo. On the Dock Road itself, work seemed to be grinding to a halt. There were slightly fewer people about than before, less bustle.

Of course, Francis wasn't exactly pleased when she wrote and told him he was no longer welcome at home—and neither was her sister, Sheila. Sheila thought wedding vows were for life and you should stick by your man 'till death us do part', though Jack Doyle had taken the news his beloved son-in-law wasn't all he was cracked up to be surprisingly well. As for Sheila, she soon changed her mind when, last Christmas, Francis came home on leave and forced his way into the house, and she walked in unexpectedly to find her sister being strangled to death with a towel. That was the day the fateful word 'divorce' had first been uttered, and now even Sheila approved. Sheila, who was in the Legion of Mary, and had a house stuffed full of holy pictures and statues, who went to church whenever she had a spare minute—even she didn't think wedding vows meant you had to spend the rest of your life with a man who'd nearly murdered you. The sisters had decided not to tell their dad about the incident because big Jack Doyle would kill any man who laid a hand on one of his children, and Francis wasn't worth swinging for.

'Penny for them!'

Eileen nearly fainted. If there'd been any colour left in her cheeks, she felt it drain away as she clutched the windowsill of the pub for support.

'Eh, are you all right?'

She blinked as her arm was grabbed by someone who regarded her with genuine concern, a weedy slip of a boy in a sailor's uniform whose round hat barely reached her shoulder. 'I was miles away,' she muttered. 'You gave me a bit of a fright.'

3

'It's Eileen, isn't it? Sean Doyle's sister?'

'That's right. I'm sorry...' She felt uncomfortable that he knew her name and she didn't recognise him from Adam.

He removed his hat to reveal a head of tight carrot-coloured curls. His rather sharp features were a mass of orange freckles, and his eyes the green of tinned peas. His unusual fruit and vegetable appearance tugged a cord in her memory. She realised now she'd definitely met him before.

'I was in the same class as your Sean at St Joan of Arc's. I used to come round to your house in Garnet Street.'

'I remember now,' Eileen cried, for some reason glad of a familiar face just then. 'Ronnie Kennedy!'

'You're almost there.' He seemed gratified she'd remembered. 'It's Donnie. Donnie Kennedy.'

Eileen frowned. 'What are you doing in uniform?'

'I've been called up,' he said proudly. 'I was eighteen last June. I've been down in Portsmouth doing me training. I expect it'll be your Sean's turn soon. He's about six months younger than me.'

'Jaysus! I still think of our Sean as a little boy,' she gasped, horrified. 'It hadn't entered me head he'd be called up soon.'

'Me mam said much the same,' Donnie nodded. 'She nearly had hysterics when me papers arrived.' Despite the fact he looked little more than a child, he seemed very mature and confident. She vaguely remembered he had been a cocky little bugger when he'd come round to the house to see Sean, and the uniform appeared to have added to his idea of his own importance.

4

'Are you sure you're all right?' he asked, concerned again. Donnie Kennedy felt rather chuffed at the idea of making a fuss of Sean Doyle's sister. She was a proper bobby dazzler, and he'd had a bit of a crush on her all those years ago, despite the fact she was so much older and way beyond his reach. 'You looked as if you'd seen a ghost when I first spoke.' Then, with a rush of nerve, he jingled the coins in his pocket and said daringly, 'Would you like a drink?'

'A drink!' She looked down at him vaguely, as if she'd never heard of such a thing as a drink before. 'Not really, but I'd love a ciggie, Donnie, if you've got one. I came out without mine.' She'd just snatched a coat off the rack in the hall, desperate to get out of the house and think things through by herself, leaving the mess behind for her dad and Sheila to take care of for the time being.

'Of course!' Donnie fumbled eagerly in his pocket and held out a pack of Woodbines. She took one gratefully and he struck a match and was about to light it, when she removed the ciggie from her mouth and glanced around uneasily.

Donnie recognised her dilemma immediately. A respectable woman would never be seen smoking on the street. Their eyes met and Eileen smiled ruefully. 'I wouldn't mind a lemonade,' she said, though drinking in a Dock Road pub was almost as bad as smoking in public. Her dad would have a fit if he found out, but if she didn't have a smoke soon she'd burst.

It came as a bit of a relief to find you could scarcely see inside the pub, what with the darkened windows and just two gas jets burning behind the bar. She could feel the sawdust scattered on the

5

otherwise bare wooden floor, and once her eyes adjusted to the dimly lit interior, she saw the place was crowded and ducked her head as she made for an empty table tucked out of the way in a corner. Fortunately, the customers, predominantly male, were too engrossed in their conversation to notice her. She removed her coat and lit the cigarette, whilst Donnie went over to the bar for the drinks.

'Penny for them!'

For one painful, exquisite moment she'd thought it was Nick; that he'd come to Bootle searching for her, demanding to know why she'd hadn't turned up at Exchange Station to meet him as they'd planned. She'd sent Tony along to the station with the news that she couldn't come and why, but today was to have been the start of their life together. He might want to hear from her own lips the reason for letting him down.

'Penny for them!' His first words. She remembered them as clearly as if he'd spoken five minutes ago, not ten months, and not just the words, but the timbre of his voice, the amused expression in it, the warm smile on his long, sensitive face as he looked down at her in the restaurant in Southport. It had been December, and she was sitting alone by a Christmas tree with the sound of carols in the background. At first, she'd thought he was merely trying to pick her up, but it turned out he lived in Melling and recognised her from Dunnings. Nick Stephens was a scientist, and she'd never in all her life met anyone as grand as a scientist before, but somehow that didn't seem to matter as they began to fall in love . . .

The memories flooded back for the umpteenth time that day. The Easter weekend in London

6

when they'd first made love, the last night when they'd danced to *We'll Meet Again*. Nick had decided it was *their* song and every time she heard it on the wireless, she thought of him and London. He'd lifted her up and twirled her round and round and round until she felt as if she would disappear altogether because it was so unreal, because it didn't seem right that anyone should be allowed so much happiness . . .

'Here you are.' Donnie put a glass of lemonade on the table along with a small tot of spirits. 'I hope you don't mind, but you look as if you need it. It's whisky, a double.'

'Oh, Donnie, you shouldn't have,' she protested. 'I didn't bring me purse with me, either, I came out in such a rush, so I can't give you any money.'

'That's all right,' he said modestly. He didn't knock on he hadn't paid for the drinks. Someone at the bar had bought them. Since he'd been in uniform, Donnie had been receiving all the attention he'd always thought he deserved but, owing to his small stature and rather unprepossessing appearance, was aware he never got. Now, not only did he get drinks pressed upon him whenever he entered a pub, but an old lady had actually stood up on the tram into town that day and offered him her seat. 'Here you are, son, sit down and take the weight off your feet,' though he'd refused, of course. A barrow girl outside Reece's Restaurant had given him a big rosy apple and urged him to, 'Give that bloody Adolf a kick up the arse from me,' and all sorts of people wanted to shake his hand and thump his shoulder and tell him what a brave fellow he was.

He lit a cigarette, looked Eileen up and down

and, plucking up his courage, said in his best man-of-the-world fashion, 'You look nice, if you don't mind me saying. In fact, you look like you've been to a wedding.' She wore a pink moygashel suit with a wide belt that accentuated her slim waist.

'I have,' she replied. 'Me friend, Annie Poulson, got married again this afternoon. I was matron of honour.'

Donny's green eyes widened. 'Annie Poulson? Didn't her lads come through Dunkirk?'

'That's right, Terry and Joe. It was in the *Bootle Times*.'

'I don't half hope I see some action like that!' He actually sounded envious.

Eileen puffed on her cigarette, suddenly angry. 'I reckon your mam would do her nut if she could hear you. Poor Annie nearly went out of her mind with worry while the lads were in France.'

'Well, women don't take to war like men,' he said loftily.

'That's 'cos they've got more sense,' Eileen replied in a tart voice.

Instead of being hurt at the put-down, Donny felt a sense of exhilaration at the fact that Eileen Doyle—he couldn't remember her married name—actually considered him mature enough to engage in a proper philosophical discussion about the war. He'd had the same discussion often with his mam, though it usually ended up with her in tears when she was quite likely to give him a swift backhander, uniform or no uniform.

'But we've got to stop Hitler,' he ventured. 'If we don't, the whole world will end up under the heel of the Nazi jackboot.' He felt sure she'd be impressed with that, which he'd read in the *Daily*

8

Herald.

'I know,' she said tiredly and clearly unimpressed. 'But there's no need to get so much enjoyment out of it.'

'I'd certainly enjoy killing a few Germans,' Donny said with relish.

'I'm sure you would. Our Tony's just as bad, and he's only six. He goes to bed every night with a toy gun under his pillow.'

'I won't have a gun of me own, seeing as I've trained to be a signalman.'

He sounded wistful, and Eileen hid a smile as she began to sip the whisky. 'Never mind. Signalman sounds very responsible, probably one of the most important jobs on the ship.'

'I reckon so,' he said, nodding gravely. 'Drink doing you good, like?'

'I think it is.' The whisky felt warm and rather comforting as it slipped down, and she began to relax.

'Take a good mouthful,' Donnie advised, so she did, and he began to imagine telling his mates when he went on board ship next day about the lovely blonde, a real stunner and married to boot, whom he'd taken out the night before. 'We had a few drinks, then...' He stopped, because he couldn't visualise Eileen Doyle doing anything other than finishing the drink and going home. Still, he could make up a good story by tomorrow to impress them all. He began to wonder exactly what was wrong. What was she doing on the Docky when she'd just been to a wedding, and why had she been standing outside the pub looking so lost and alone? She'd nearly jumped out of her skin when he spoke.

9

'I was planning on moving house today,' she said suddenly. 'A friend of mine's got this lovely cottage in Melling—that's where I work,' she explained, 'in Dunnings, the munitions factory. I was hoping to get away from the air-raids.' *I'd hate to come back and find you and Tony weren't here for me,* Nick had said when she protested she didn't want to leave her family.

'Why didn't you?' asked Donnie.

'I missed the train,' she said, then, as if realising this wasn't an adequate explanation, added in a tight anguished voice, 'Something came up.' She finished the whisky in a single gulp.

'Would you like another?'

'No, ta,' she said firmly. 'Me head already feels as if it belongs to someone else.'

Donnie began to run his finger anxiously around the top of his glass. 'I won't half be worried about me mam and dad and our Clare when I'm away at sea, what with the raids getting worse and worse. There were three hundred killed in London last Saturday.' According to his mam, a night hadn't passed without the siren going since the beginning of September. 'That was a right old pounding Bootle got on Tuesday.'

'Well,' said Eileen with a hard smile, 'that's merely another aspect of the war which you men are so fond of.' She didn't wait for his reply, but went on, 'I have a friend, a scientist, who had a good deferred job in Kirkby. He would have been quite safe till the war was over. 'Stead, he insisted on joining the RAF. The last few months he could have been killed any minute...' She broke off. Hundreds, perhaps thousands of young pilots had died as the Luftwaffe tried to wipe the British Air

Force off the face of the earth in a terrible battle of attrition, but not Nick. At least not so far. He was, for the moment, quite safe and sound in Melling, perhaps still hoping she'd turn up.

Donnie had been well to the fore in the queue when brains were handed out, and he began to put two and two together. She had a 'friend' with a cottage in Melling, and another who'd joined the RAF. Some sixth sense told him the friends were one and the same person and Eileen Doyle was almost certainly having an affair, which gave her an added air of mystery and only made her more seductive in his eyes. He glanced at her keenly. The whisky had brought a flush to her smooth cheeks. She was a bit too wholesome to be termed beautiful; there was a touch of the farmer's daughter in her fresh, regular features and creamy hair which she wore in an unusual style, not permed like most women, but dead straight and in a fringe on her forehead, though her dad, big Jack Doyle, had probably been no nearer the countryside than his own. Her soft violet-blue eyes were moist, as if she might cry any minute. He felt a strong rush of sympathy and thought, somewhat wryly, that even if Eileen Doyle undressed on the spot and offered herself to him, he would turn her down, because she was too upset to know what she was doing and probably slightly drunk. He racked his brains to remember who she was married to. What was he like? Well, there was no harm in asking.

'What does your husband do, Eileen?' he enquired casually.

'Me husband?' She looked slightly startled, as if she'd forgotten she had one. 'Oh, Francis was in the Territorials when the war started, like, so he was called up straight away. The Royal Tank Regiment were sent to Egypt last February.'

Francis! Of course, Francis Costello, who worked for the Mersey Docks & Harbour Board and had a seat on Bootle Corporation. Donnie remembered the chap distinctly. He was one of those silver-tongued Irishmen with the gift of the gab who was great mates with Jack Doyle. Everyone spoke highly of Francis, though Donnie, more astute than most, hadn't taken to him much. He seemed a bit of a fake, insincere, as if everything he said was only to impress people.

'I suppose you miss him, like?' he probed.

'I suppose,' she replied listlessly, which Donnie took to mean she didn't miss him at all, though she missed the 'friend', the one with the cottage in Melling who'd joined the RAF. She gave a funny, cracked laugh and seemed to pull herself together. 'I'm not exactly cheerful company, am I, luv? Anyroad, I'd best be going. I only came out for a breath of fresh air, like, and I've been gone for ages. It'll take half an hour or more to get back, and me feet are killing me in these shoes.'

'I'll walk with you,' he said with alacrity, wishing he was big enough to carry her, which he would have offered to do willingly if she'd let him. 'In fact, I might call on your Sean. I haven't seen him since I got me uniform.'

'Well I never!' she said in surprise as soon as they were outside. 'The sun's come out.'

The dark clouds which had appeared when she left the house, as if in sympathy with her mood, had completely disappeared and the sky was a dusky blue. The sun itself was out of sight, but the tops of

12

the ships anchored behind the high dock walls were suffused with an unnaturally vivid light.

A cart passed them, drawn by two horses, magnificent beasts, their sleek bodies as black as coal and with tumbling silken manes. The wooden wheels bumped on the uneven surface of the road, and the driver held the reins loosely in his hands, as if fully confident the animals needed no directions. His shoulders were hunched and he looked tired, as well he might, for he'd probably begun work before the crack of dawn.

'I love the Docky,' Eileen said with a catch in her voice. 'When we were little, me and our Sheila used to come and meet me dad when it was time for him to hand in his tally. I was a bit scared in those days. The high walls made me feel as if we were walking on the very bottom of the world.' She also loved the smells, even if some weren't exactly pleasant; the aroma of oils and spices, of carpets and tea and coal, and all the million and one imports and exports that came from and went to places all over the world. The atmosphere was alien, slightly mysterious, and even now, at this late hour, there were scores of black, brown and yellow faces around, and the gabble of a dozen different tongues.

'Me dad said Liverpool Docks are the next to biggest in the world,' Donnie said, as proudly as if he were the owner.

Eileen nodded. 'That's right, only those in Hamburg are bigger.' They began to walk in the direction of Bootle. 'Have you finished your training, Donnie?' Eileen asked.

'Oh, yes.' He squared his shoulders importantly. 'I take up me first posting tomorrow. I'm on a corvette guarding a convoy of merchant marine all the way to America.'

'Our Cal, that's Calum Reilly, our Sheila's husband, he's a merchant seaman and due back from America any minute, God willing.' She crossed herself briefly, the way his mam often did. It wasn't only in the air that the battle for survival was being fought. The carnage at sea, the loss of life and tonnage of ships being destroyed, was getting more and more horrendous by the day as German U-boats prowled the Atlantic in their search for prey. She looked down at him quickly. 'You'll take care of yourself, won't you, Donnie?'

'Oh, you can bet your life on that!' he said cockily. He couldn't wait to serve his country and give old Hitler the promised kick up the arse. On the other hand, although he did his best not to think about the dangers that lay ahead, sometimes, alone in the middle of the night, he felt quite scared. You had to be devoid of imagination completely, and Donnie had more imagination than most, not to visualise the ship being torpedoed and him tossed into the icy waters of the Atlantic and struggling to stay above the waves. Or, perhaps worse, trapped by fire in the signalroom and roasting, ever so slowly, to death. There were half a dozen of his mates who'd already lost their dads or older brothers at sea, and his man behaved as if Donnie had already had a death sentence passed on him. He was only eighteen, thought Donnie, panicking suddenly, and didn't want to die. There were all sorts of things he wanted to do with his life, and dying young wasn't one of them. One day, he'd like to meet a girl like Eileen Doyle and get married . . .

To Donnie's horror, he felt his eyes fill with tears and he prayed Eileen wouldn't notice. He'd been trying to impress her as a man of the world, and here he was on the brink of crying in the street like a little boy.

'Just a minute, I've got something in me eye.' The tears were by now coursing down his cheeks.

The lie didn't work.

'Oh, luv!' She pushed him into a doorway and took him in her arms and there they were, in the clinch Donnie had been imagining ever since they met, but there was nothing romantic about it as she patted his back like a baby and said, 'There, now. There.'

'I went into town this avvy to buy me mam and dad and our Clare their Christmas presents,' he sobbed, 'in case I was dead by the time it came. Then I walked home along the Docky, because it's where I used play when I was a kid and I thought I might never see it again.'

When he was a kid! He was little more than a kid now, thought Eileen in despair. What a terrible world it had become, when lads of eighteen expected to be dead by Christmas!

'I'll say a special prayer for you every night, Donnie,' she vowed. 'Perhaps you can drop in and see us whenever you're home, just so's I know you're all right, like.' He was a kind lad, and had been a tremendous help that day. 'Come on, now, luv, dry your eyes and we'll go home.'

'I don't think I'll call on Sean,' he sniffed. 'I'll go back to me mam and dad and have a game of Snakes and Laddes with our Clare. It's me last night ...' He stopped and gave his nose a good blow on a rather grubby handkerchief.

'That's a good idea,' she said comfortably. Anyroad, knowing Sean, he'd be out with one of his never-ending stream of girlfriends.

They scarcely spoke again the rest of the way as they turned off the Dock Road and walked passed the Goods Yard and through the warren of narrow streets of two-up, two-down terraced houses where they lived. Eileen seemed lost in thought and Donnie felt too embarrassed to say another word. What on earth would she think of him, breaking down like that?

'This is our street,' he said awkwardly when they reached the Chaucer Arms, and she came to, blinking, as if she'd forgotten he was there. He almost wished he could run away without another word.

'Take care,' she said. 'Don't forget, I'll be praying for you.'

'Ta.' He shuffled his feet awkwardly. 'I hope you come through the raids all right, and . . .' He wanted to say he hoped her RAF friend would come through, too. Instead, just to be polite, he said, 'And I hope your husband comes home safe and sound.'

To his surprise, she gave a little bitter laugh. 'There's no need to worry about Francis, he's quite safe, if not entirely sound. He arrived back unexpectedly this afternoon and they're going to discharge him from the army. He's home for good.'

CHAPTER TWO

Eileen waited on the corner for Donnie to wave goodbye. But she waited in vain, for the small hunched figure merely crossed the street and went into the house without a glance in her direction. No

16

doubt he felt awkward bursting into tears like that, she thought as she continued towards home. She reckoned, somewhat sadly, that she'd probably never see Donnie Kennedy again unless they met by accident.

It had been four o'clock exactly, and she'd been about to slam the door on 16 Pearl Street for the final time, already late for Nick, having missed the train through no fault of her own, when an ambulance turned into the street, bringing Francis Costello home to his family. Eileen was put in the worst predicament she'd ever known; how could you walk out and meet your lover when your husband had returned injured from North Africa?

Sheila thought she should have gone and let Francis look after himself. 'I would have, if it was me.' His head was heavily bandaged and he'd lost the sight of his left eye, but he could walk and talk and indeed had seemed quite cheerful when he arrived. 'You owe him nothing, Eileen,' Sheila cried. 'Nothing!'

By not going, she was letting Nick and Tony down, Sheila added, working herself up into a proper lather. Tony couldn't wait to live in Meiling in the cottage with black beams on the ceiling and roses around the door and apple trees and strawberries in the garden. He'd been looking forward to sleeping in the room with the new curtains which Mr Singerman had made on the window. Most of all, he was looking forward to having Nick for a dad, because his real dad made him feel unhappy most of the time.

'For Jaysus sake, girl,' Sheila said scathingly, 'there's a war on. You should snatch at happiness if it chances to come your way, 'cos by this time next

17

week you might be dead. The most important people are the ones you love,' which all seemed strange to Eileen, because Sheila was the religious one, not her. She *couldn't* have just walked away. She couldn't have lived with Nick, or, more importantly, with herself, if she had. She felt split in two, utterly divided between love for one man and responsibility to another—though if she'd caught the train it might have been different. She would never know how she would have felt, once ensconced in Melling with Nick before she'd learnt Francis was home.

She imagined Nick sitting in the cottage alone. What was he thinking? How was he feeling? She'd slipped along in her dinner hour yesterday and set the table with a new white cloth and freshly polished cutlery ready for today's tea, so the place would look homely and welcoming when they arrived for the start of their life together—not that Nick would be there for long. He had a fortnight's leave due to a broken wrist, but once the time was up, he'd be back to the damn Spitfires he loved so much. In the meantime, there was a tin of salmon in the larder, along with a pound of home-grown tomatoes bought from a woman in the village who grew them in her own greenhouse, plus her and Tony's entire week's butter ration. Unlike them, Nick hadn't been brought up on margarine, and claimed it tasted like petrol.

If only she hadn't missed the train! The thought of what might have been 'if only', of lying in Nick's arms that night, his lovely brown eyes smiling into hers, caused an ache so fierce she felt as if a knife had been driven through her.

She must have been walking in a dream, because

she didn't hear the music, and all of a sudden found herself in Pearl Street, when she'd meant to avoid everyone by going down the entry of the neighbouring street and entering the house by the back way.

Although Annie and Chris had left for their honeymoon hours ago, the reception was still in full swing and most people remained outside as if trying to squeeze as much enjoyment as they could out of the occasion, for Pearl Street loved nothing more than a party. The women wore their best frocks, as befitted a wedding, though the men who clustered around the King's Arms on the corner with their pints of ale had long since loosened their stiff collars and removed their ties. Children playing tick darted in and out of the grown-ups, their voices sounding extra high and extra loud, even above the music, on the still evening air. There weren't so many children about as usual, as quite a few had been re-evacuated to places like Wales and Southport when the air-raids had begun. Eileen noticed Tony wasn't there. When she left he'd been in the back yard kicking a football against the wall with a monotonous regularity that would have got on her nerves had she not known the reason for it. Tony didn't want Francis back any more than she did.

The atmosphere in the street was carefree with an undercurrent of defiant excitement, as if everyone were saying to themselves, 'We know there's a war on, but that's not going to stop us from having a good time!'

In Number 3, the parlour window had been shoved up as high as it would go and Mr Singerman was playing *Tipperary Mary* on the piano. People clapped their hands in time to the music as Agnes Donovan and Ellis Evans did an improvised jig, lifting their skirts as they approached each other with a sort of wary caution, elbows jutting, feet lifting daintily on the confetti-covered cobbles. Ellis was almost twice Aggies's size, yet she seemed the lighter as they joined arms and skipped a circle, changed arms and skipped another. The women's frocks were as familiar to Eileen as the clothes in her own wardrobe; Ellis's blue brocade, bought for a wedding a decade or more ago, was becoming decidedly the worse for wear, as if the creases stubbornly refused to be pressed out for the hundredth or more time. Aggie's brown wool with the turquoise beads like birds' eggs on the bodice, seemed to get bigger the more she wore it; either that, or her already skinny frame was shrinking further in her old age.

Mr Singerman increased the tempo and Eileen imagined his gnarled old yellow fingers skipping over the equally yellow keys of the upright piano with the painted flowers on the front. The pace was too much for Ellis whose face was already bright red, and she collapsed, panting, in an open doorway. Aggie, thirty years older, finished the jig by herself to a burst of applause.

Phoebe Crean's two mongol lads, Harry and Owen, were dancing with each other, their faces the picture of utter happiness as they did a clumsy sort of waltz, whilst Phoebe watched over them, her own face bursting with a mixture of pride and love.

By now, the sun which had reappeared earlier was slithering out of sight for good, so that the chimneys of the fifteen houses on one side of the street were silhouetted blackly against its dark gold

20

radiance and the slate roofs of those opposite had the appearance of melting lead. Eileen tried to slink along to Number 16 unnoticed, but she'd already been spotted. The neighbours crowded round solicitously and several grabbed her sleeve. Pearl Street had already lost two of its own to the conflict. Now another had arrived home with his head wreathed in bandages, and they were full of sympathy for his poor wife.

'Hello, luv. How's Francis?'

'It's a terrible thing for such a handsome chap to be disfigured like that.'

Mr Singerman must have noticed her arrival through the window, and came hurrying out to ask after Francis in the deep, strangely youthful voice which had never lost its Russian accent, despite the fact he'd lived in England for three-quarters of his long life.

'He seems fine,' Eileen assured them. 'He's taken it very well.' Very well indeed, she thought wryly. He'd been quite the proud hero when he first arrived, as if he'd gained a medal, not lost an eye. 'He was about to have a bit of a lie down when I left.'

'Is that Eileen? Is that Eileen Costello?' Paddy O'Hara came towards her, his white stick tapping on the cobbles.

'Here I am, Paddy.' Eileen touched his cheek briefly and he clasped her hand.

'It's a shame, a dead shame,' he said dolefully. 'After all, he didn't have to join up, did he? A man of his age wouldn't be anywhere near to getting his call-up papers yet. He's a fine, brave man altogether, is Francis Costello.'

People always said that about Francis. People

had actually wondered how she'd manage without him when he first went away. If they lived with him a little while, Eileen thought bitterly, if the women spent just one night in the same bed and put up with his disgusting behaviour, they'd soon change their minds.

Agnes Donovan squeezed Eileen's arm hard with her bony fingers. 'Now you mustn't think of giving up that important job of yours. We'll keep a lookout for Francis, and for Tony, too, while you're at work.' She turned to the other women. 'Won't we, girls?'

There was a chorus of agreement and Eileen said, touched, 'I don't know what I'd do without yis all, though I don't think it'll be necessary as far as Francis is concerned. He's already talking about going back to work as soon as he gets his discharge from the army.'

They were the best neighbours in the world, though she was well aware that Agnes Donovan's motives weren't solely altruistic. Aggie liked nothing better than to manoeuvre herself into another woman's house and poke around. Soon, rumours would circulate that so-and-so's bedding wasn't changed as often as it should be or their sink could be a mite cleaner. Eileen reminded herself that Aggie frequently let Sheila have her meat coupons. Deep down at heart, she was kind.

'Anyroad,' said Brenda Mahon, who was Sheila's best friend, 'once Francis is back on his feet, you can still move to Melling. It's a shame you had to put it off.'

'I don't think so,' Eileen said quickly. They knew nothing about Nick, although there'd been rumours she was having an affair. 'I'd better be

22

getting indoors,' she said. 'Else they'll be wondering where I've got to.'

There was no sign of Francis inside. Her dad and sister were sitting in the living room looking glum.

'Where is he?' Eileen asked.

'Still having a kip.' Jack Doyle regarded his eldest girl keenly. She seemed slightly less upset than when she'd left, more grim than unhappy. He was worried sick about her. It had been obvious that she was head over heels in love with this Nick chap. Nick seemed a decent bloke, if a bit poncey, when Jack first met him. At the time, he'd thought, 'Well, what else can you expect from someone who's been to Cambridge University?' But since then, Nick had become a Flying Officer in the RAF, a Battle of Britain pilot, one of a generation of young men willing to forfeit their lives to prevent the Luftwaffe claiming mastery of the skies over Britain. Anyroad, he was Eileen's choice and that was all that mattered. Jack knew what it was like to lose the person you loved. He still grieved for his dear, dead Mollie, despite the fact she'd been gone for more than fifteen years.

The worst thing, though, Jack thought guiltily, was that it was all his fault. Eileen, as soft as a kitten and anxious to please, had only married the bastard upstairs to please her dad. He'd liked the idea of having Francis Costello for a son-in-law, the two were hand in glove when it came to politics; 'He's a good catch, luv, and he really fancies you.' Not only that, she'd put up with him all that time without saying a word.

'I'm sorry I took so long,' she said, 'but I met Donnie Kennedy. You'll never believe it, but he's in the Royal Navy.'

'Weren't he in our Sean's class at school?' You could scarcely see Sheila's plump comely body for children. She was nursing the youngest, Mary, in one arm, and Ryan, nearly two, in the other. The older girls, Caitlin and Siobhan, were draped somewhat uncomfortably over her knees, both half asleep and sucking their thumbs audibly.

'Aye, that's right,' confirmed Eileen. It didn't seem possible that her sunny, good-natured little brother was nearly old enough to fight.

'Someone said the other day the war'd be over by Christmas,' Sheila said hopefully.

Eileen laughed sardonically. 'That's what they said this time last year, and I reckon they'll be saying the same thing next September.'

'However long it takes, however many lives, it's a war that's got to be fought right through to the end,' Jack Doyle said in a tight voice. 'If I were a young man, I'd have joined up like a shot. That Hitler's got to be stopped. As for our Sean, he couldn't be in much more danger than he is now, working for the Civil Defence Messenger Service.' As soon as the air-raid siren sounded, Sean went off on his bike to the nearest ARP Depot, ready to deliver messages if communications broke down. Jack knew if he lost his only son it would break his heart, but so be it, it was a sacrifice worth making. He'd always hated Fascists and everything they stood for. The idea of his country being overrun by Germans with their monstrous creed, of his good friend Jacob Singerman from across the road being carted off to a concentration camp for being a Jew, was an abomination that filled him with horror. He would not just have willingly laid down his own life and that of his only son, but the lives of his entire

24

family, to prevent it.

'Where's our Tony gone?' Eileen asked, conscious that the thumping of the football in the yard had ceased.

'I sent him with our Dominic and Niall for some fish and chips,' said Sheila. 'The poor kids haven't had a bite to eat since the reception, what with all the upset. Now you're back, I'll feed this lot and get them to bed. Give us a hand, the pair o'yis.'

Eileen took Mary, whilst her dad eased his massive frame out of the chair and reached for Ryan. The little girls groaned and rubbed their eyes sleepily when they were dislodged from their mam's knee. 'It's like having a whole bloody school of grandchildren,' Jack grumbled.

'Well, you won't have any more for the time being, Dad,' Sheila said firmly, 'least not off me. Cal's put his foot down; no more kids till there's no more war. He said six kids and a wife is already enough to worry about whilst he's away at sea.'

They carried the children across the street to Number 21. 'Send the boys home if they come back to yours, sis,' Sheila said to Eileen as she was leaving, adding in a whisper, 'Don't forget, there's always room on the sofa in the parlour for you and Tony if there's trouble from you-know-who.'

'Ta, Sheil, but I don't think that's likely.' What was it Francis had whispered as soon as he'd come home? 'I'm sorry about the way things have gone in the past, particularly last Christmas. But I promise I'll be a good husband from now on. You have my word on that, luv.'

As soon as she was back in her own house, Eileen put the kettle on. 'Would you like a cuppa, Dad?' she called when he came in.

25

'No, ta, I'm parched for a pint. I'll be off in a minute. Will you be all right, like?' He nodded upstairs. He was never quite sure what Francis had done to his girl, but it must have been something pretty bad to make her want to leave him, not to have him back. It were nowt to do with Nick at the start. Nick had turned up once the decision had been made. He shuffled his size-twelve boots awkwardly on the shiny oilcloth. 'Y'know, luv, you can still see him.'

She knew straight away he meant Nick, and shook her head emphatically. 'No, I can't, Dad.'

His big, swarthy, handsome face flushed. He wasn't used to discussing intimate matters with anyone, least of all a woman, even if she was his daughter. 'I can't see that it would do any harm,' he protested.

'It wouldn't be fair on Nick,' she said flatly. 'He's only young, twenty-five. We were going to be married, but how can I go ahead with the divorce under the circumstances? No, it's best to set Nick free. He'll soon get over us and meet someone else.' She quickly went into the back kitchen to hide her face, because the thought of Nick with another woman was more than she could bear.

'You know that's not true,' her dad said gruffly. He'd never felt so close to his girl as he'd done that day. There'd been times when it seemed as if his own heart was breaking along with hers. He followed her. 'Anyroad, I reckon nowt'll keep Nick away. He'll be round to Dunnings on Monday looking for you.'

Eileen was already prepared for that eventuality. She'd ask one of the girls to send him away and tell him, for the final time, that it was all over. 'Well,

26

he'll look in vain,' she said briefly.

Jack Doyle persisted, 'What about that card he sent with Tony? What did it say?'

'We'll meet again,' she said in a low voice.

'I reckon you will,' he mumbled. 'I reckon you and Nick were made for each other.'

'Oh, Dad!' She gave him a half laughing, half tearful push. 'Get away with you! Any minute now you're going to turn into a beetroot, you're so red. You're making me feel dead embarrassed.'

Jack Doyle retreated thankfully to the living room. 'Anyroad, as Sheila said, everything might be over by Christmas.' She might feel differently about leaving Francis then.

'D'you honestly think so?'

He wished he'd kept his big mouth shut. He was as straight as a die, was Jack Doyle, and he would never lie to anyone, let alone his daughter. There was no way, as he saw it, that the war would be over by Christmas. He said gravely, 'Well, at least we're seeing some action since Winston Churchill took over the reins, which was more than we ever had with Chamberlain.'

She came to the door and to his relief she was grinning slightly. 'You're a right ould hypocrite, Dad. I thought you always hated Churchill.'

'Oh, I do,' he nodded firmly, 'but it doesn't mean to say he's not a good war leader. Not only that, we've got Attlee as his Deputy, and Ernest Bevin at the Ministry of Labour. Two good socialists at the very heart of power, though it's a pity it took a war to get 'em there.'

She wrinkled her nose. 'All you ever think about is politics.'

'What else is there? What d'you think started the

war if it wasn't politics? Everything's politics.'

'I've heard that before.'

'And you'll hear it again.'

Eileen grinned again. 'I know I will, Dad.' She'd been brought up on politics, listened to him, morning, noon and night, sounding off about inequality and injustice. He'd used her as a sounding board after Mam died when Eileen was fourteen. Sheila, a year younger, was too flighty and never there to listen, and Sean too young. Jack Doyle had been the unpaid representative of the Dockworkers' Union for as long as she could remember, fighting for workers' rights with a tenacity and strength of purpose that were the envy of weaker men and a never-ending bane to management. The local Labour Party still held their monthly meetings in his parlour. To her shame, the politics went in one ear and out the other, but she was proud of her fiery, charismatic dad, and doubted if there was a better known or more respected man in the whole of Bootle.

'What are you going to do about your job?' he asked. He was pleased she'd taken up war work. 'I hope you're not thinking of giving it up, like, because there's no need. Francis seems quite capable to me.'

'Well, I don't want to leave.' It was bad enough losing Nick, without losing her job as well. 'The thing is, what am I to do with Tony now Annie's moved away?' She'd had an arrangement with Annie, who also worked at Dunnings but on a different shift, to look after Tony while she was at work. Now Annie was married, and as from Monday would be living miles away in Fazakerley in her new husband's house. It was one of the

28

reasons that had prompted Eileen to move to Melling where Dunnings was only a few minutes' walk from the cottage. 'I don't want him shoved from pillar to post while I'm at work,' she went on. 'He needs somewhere safe and regular to go when I'm on late shift, particularly when there's a raid.' It was useless to rely on Francis, who would almost certainly return to the old routine of spending his evenings at Corporation meetings or in the King's Arms. Anyroad, she would prefer Tony had as little as possible to do with his dad.

'I'll lend a hand when I can, luv, but I'm on shifts meself, and I've just taken up fire-watching on the docks. 'Fact, I should be there now 'case the siren goes. I'll make me way the minute I've had a quick pint.'

Eileen looked worried. 'I can't ask our Sheila. She'll see to his meals and makes sure he gets off to school with Dominic and Niall, but they're already crammed like sardines in the cupboard under the stairs during the raids.' It had always been her worst nightmare when she was at work and in the relative safety of the underground shelter, imagining Pearl Street being bombed and Tony killed. But it was merely another terrifying aspect of the war shared with all the other men and women in the factory who'd left their families at home.

'We'll try and sort something out tomorrow,' Jack said. 'In the meantime, I'd better be off.' As he was about to leave, he turned, his face once again flushed scarlet. 'By the way, when Francis went upstairs, I suggested he use the back bedroom from now on. I thought that's what you'd prefer.'

'Thanks, Dad,' she murmured gratefully. She'd

29

sworn she'd never sleep with Francis Costello again. In fact, she felt convinced she would kill him if he tried anything now he was back. Even so, she'd been dreading broaching the subject when bedtime came. For over a year, she and Tony had slept in the front bedroom—on the clear understanding he was only there to protect her from enemy attack!

The front door closed and in the ensuing silence she could actually hear the sound of Francis snoring. She put her hands over her ears to shut out the noise. Never, in her wildest dreams, she thought dejectedly, had she visualised living under the same roof as her husband again.

The music in the street had changed. Now it was Paddy O'Hara playing *Danny Boy* on his mouth organ. When Eileen peeped through the parlour window, it was virtually dark and nearly everyone had gone in. One or two remained outside, sitting on their steps, and Harry and Owen were still dancing. As she watched, Phoebe called and they went indoors. Then another door closed, and Paddy began to wander along the street towards the King's Arms, his dog, Rover, faithfully at his heels. Paddy hadn't known whether it was light or dark since 1917, when he'd lost his sight fighting for his country in the trenches of the Somme.

Eileen sighed as she drew the black-lined curtains, making sure the edges touched completely before she turned the light on, otherwise she'd have an ARP Warden banging on the door, demanding, '*Switch that light out!*' which was all they'd had to do until the raids started a few weeks ago.

The parlour mantelpiece looked very bare. The

ornaments and photos were already in the cottage, along with quite a few other personal possessions which she'd been taking along for weeks. She wrestled with the problem of getting them back. She had a key and could collect them in a few weeks' time, when she was sure Nick had gone.

Or should she leave them?

She went into the living room and took Nick's card out of her handbag. He'd bought it at Exchange Station and given it to Tony to bring back; a sepia photo of St George's Hall with just a few words written on the other side in his untidy black scrawl.

We'll meet again, Nick.

Would they?

You never know, she thought with an unexpected surge of tingling optimism, after a decent interval and once Francis had settled in, she could bring up the subject of divorce again—he'd already had a letter from her solicitor. Just because he'd been injured didn't alter the fact he'd done those terrible things in the past. She remembered the way he found fault with every single little thing she did, found dust in places she'd only dusted that morning, and no matter what she cooked for tea, it was either underdone or overdone or something he didn't like. If in a particularly bad mood, he'd squeeze her shoulder or pinch her arm until she felt like screaming and the marks would stay for days, red and angry and painful.

When you thought about it, really thought about it, things weren't quite as hopeless as she'd first thought. In fact, she felt slightly ashamed of the way she had overreacted. She'd behaved as if her life had ended the minute Francis stepped out of

31

the ambulance, whereas perhaps she should have looked upon it more as a delay. It would merely take longer for her and Nick to be together, that was all.

Eileen put the card back in her bag and was beginning to wonder where Tony was when the air-raid siren went. She immediately felt goosepimples rise on her upper arms—it always happened at the sound of the menacing up-and-down wail—and hurried to the front door. To her relief, Tony came running out of Sheila's. She noticed the white shirt which had been bought specially for Annie's wedding was stained with grease and tomato sauce, and his knees were filthy. His wire-rimmed glasses were, as usual, perched on the end of his little snub nose, and his hair, as fine and blond as her own, looked as if it hadn't been combed in days. She felt a rush of love that almost choked her as she stretched out welcoming arms, realising with a pang of guilt how much she'd neglected her son that day.

'Come on, luv. Let's get under the stairs.' She shepherded him into the narrow cupboard which had recently been completely cleared and an old mattress put on the floor. Not many people used the public shelters which were cold, damp and uncomfortable and, incredibly, didn't even have a proper door, merely a curtain hanging where anyone with half a brain knew a door should be.

'What about me dad?' Tony asked.

As soon as Eileen had put a match to the nightlight, she closed the cupboard door and they sat down. The enclosed space was rather claustrophobic, but Tony didn't seem to mind. Indeed, so far he seemed to find the raids more exciting than anything and enjoyed the time spent under the stairs. Secretly, Tony wanted the raids to continue until he was grown up so he could become a fire-watcher like his grandad, or, even better, join the RAF and fly a Spitfire like Nick did.

Eileen said, 'Your dad's in bed. Let's see if he wakes up, shall we? Otherwise, we won't disturb him. Come on, sit on me knee and we'll give each other a cuddle while there's no-one else around. Today's been a day and a half, hasn't it? It's nice to have a bit of quiet to ourselves.'

Though 'quiet' wasn't exactly what they were having. In no time she heard the grim drone of planes approaching, a sound even more menacing than the siren. Then came the answering crackle of ack-ack guns from their side and the thud of explosions in the distance. She hugged Tony close, wondering what on earth the world had come to and wishing Adolf Hitler had never been born.

The raid was surprisingly short. They'd scarcely been there twenty minutes when the All Clear went. 'Well, that wasn't so bad,' she said thankfully. 'The Germans must have got tired and gone home.'

'Mam?' Tony sounded slightly querulous. He made no attempt to get off her knee.

'Yes, luv?'

'Is me dad home for good, like?'

'It looks like it, son.'

'But what about Nick? He didn't half look fed up when I met him at the station and told him you weren't coming.' Tony thought he'd never forget the expression in his beloved Nick's eyes, as if all the happiness had drained out of him and there was nothing left inside.

Eileen said softly, 'He's not the only one fed up,

33

is he, luv? You're fed up, and I am, too. But,' she went on with a determined effort to be cheerful, 'I won't be fed up tomorrer. And neither will you,' she added sternly. 'Tomorrer's another day altogether, and I intend to be as happy as a lark.'

Tony frowned and his glasses threatened to fall off altogether. Eileen pushed them back with her finger and kissed his nose. 'But what about Nick?' he demanded a second time.

'Nick will understand. It'll just take a while longer than we thought before we're all together.'

'Does that mean we will be—one day?' he said eagerly.

'Of course we will.'

'Of course we will,' she repeated under her breath. How could she possibly have thought they would never see each other again? She *couldn't* give Nick up. They were meant for each other. Even her unromantic dad recognised that fact. 'Of course we will.' She pushed him off her knee. 'Come on, I feel as if I'm in me coffin shut in here. I reckon it's well past supper time. I'll make a cup of cocoa. D'you fancy a jam butty?'

'Yes.'

'Yes, what?' She raised her eyebrows.

'Yes please, Mam,' he grinned.

'Turn the wireless on,' she said as she snuffed the nightlight out. She glanced at her gold watch, a present from Nick when they were in London. 'We're just in time for the nine o'clock news.' She almost wished she hadn't listened when the cultured voice of Alvar Lidell announced there'd been another raid on the East End of London. More innocent civilians had been killed, more British planes lost. One hundred and eighty-five

German planes were reported shot down, but she felt no jubilation at this news. It was merely a waste of young lives, no matter whose side they were on.

'Try and find the Forces network,' she said. 'Let's have some cheerful music. And once you've eaten your butty, you'd better get to bed. Your dad would have a fit if . . .' She was about to add, 'if he knew you were still up,' and bit her tongue. Francis no doubt *would* be angry if he knew. He'd always insisted Tony go to bed at half past six, even if it were the height of summer and no matter what day it might be, and even if all his mates were still playing outside. But there'd be no more of that, she thought grimly. Tony'd go to bed when *she* said and Francis could like it or lump it. Anyroad, if he started laying down the law it would be time for his wife and son to make their departure.

*   *   *

The phosphorous fingers on the alarm clock showed nearly half past two. Eileen felt convinced she'd never sleep that night. The ticking of the clock got on her nerves. She'd never realised it was so loud, almost deafening in the dead of night with not another sound to be heard except Tony's light breathing next to her. A floorboard creaked, but there were often strange, slight noises in the house when everywhere was quiet, as if the structure's joints were flexing.

Eileen turned over for the umpteenth time, but her mind felt like the inside of the damned clock, as if there were wheels and cogs whirring away and her brain was ticking just as loudly.

She sat up and wished she'd brought her ciggies

to bed; she could really do with a fag right now, but couldn't be bothered going downstairs to fetch them. The room was brightly illuminated by a clear full moon outside. Before getting into bed she'd drawn the curtains back because she hated sleeping in total blackness; nightlights and candles were becoming more and more difficult to get and best saved for emergencies.

Tony stirred and opened his eyes. When he saw her propped against the headboard, he mumbled, 'What are you doing, Mam?'

'I'm practising sleeping a different way,' she told him. 'Tomorrer night I'm going to stick me legs up in the air and see how I get on. Now go to sleep. You're spoiling me concentration.'

'You're not half daft, Mam.'

He obediently closed his eyes. At least the problem of Tony had been sorted out, Eileen thought with satisfaction. Mr Singerman had called earlier to say Gladstone and Alexandra Docks had been hit and you could see the smoke spiralling into the sky from Pearl Street. Tony had insisted on having a look, despite being in his pyjamas.

'You know, Eileen, I'd be only too happy to look after him when you're at work,' Mr Singerman said when they were back in the house having a cup of tea and Tony was in bed. Francis was still asleep. 'Me and Tony get on famously. He has the makings of a proper capitalist the way he always beats me at Monopoly! I could teach him to play cards and perhaps we could go to the pictures now and then. After he's gone to bed, I could listen to your wireless until you or Francis came home. I know Francis will be a busy man once he's back to normal, what with his job and his Corporation

36

meetings.'

'Oh, would you, Mr Singerman?' Eileen said delightedly. The only thing she'd dreaded about moving was the thought of no longer seeing her friends and family every single day. She was very fond of Paddy O'Hara and all her other neighbours, even Agnes Donovan in a sort of way, but Jacob Singerman was the dearest of them all. He was an excitable, vivacious will-o'-the-wisp old man with a halo of silver hair and a penchant for the pictures, which he visited whenever he had a few coppers to spare. She was certain Tony would be enamoured of the idea of spending the evenings with him the weeks she was at work.

'It would be a pleasure, and I need to start practising my fatherly skills again now it seems my Ruth will be coming home.'

His old short-sighted eyes sparkled over the half-moon glasses which were perched on the middle of his nose. Eileen had never known Ruth. It was more than twenty years since Mr Singerman's only child had gone to stay with his brother in Austria, and he'd never seen her since. Ruth got married, had children, and corresponded regularly, but once Hitler grabbed Austria in his typically ruthless way, her letters ceased abruptly. Her distraught father could only fear the worst. Until yesterday that is, when the good news arrived out of the blue from a most surprising source; a synagogue in Spain had reported Ruth was safe.

'I bet you can't wait to see her,' Eileen said warmly.

The light died a little in his eyes. 'I can't wait, no, but all the same, I keep worrying what has happened to her husband and the grandchildren I have never met.'

Eileen squeezed his arm. 'Let's hope they're all right, too. You'll know soon enough when she comes home.'

'You never heard her play the piano, did you, Eileen? Oh, she was a marvel, that girl. A virtuoso! She was going to be a concert pianist.' He shook his head mournfully. 'She will be annoyed when she finds my old piano so out of tune.'

'She'll be so pleased to see you she won't give two hoots about the piano,' Eileen said dismissively.

After he'd gone, she listened to *Saturday Night Theatre*, but when the play finished, couldn't scarcely remember a thing about it. She'd been thinking of Nick and what they would have been doing if only she hadn't missed the train.

Francis appeared just after she'd put the kettle on to make a final cup of cocoa, and her heart sank. She'd been hoping he might sleep the night through. 'How do you feel?' she asked stiffly.

'Better than I've done in weeks.' He stretched his arms. He'd gone to bed almost fully clothed, having merely removed his battledress top, and his khaki shirt was creased. Francis had always managed to appear rather dashing in the cheap, coarse uniform. Annie always claimed he looked a mite like Clark Gable, handsome, with a devil-may-care look in his brown eyes. The bandage, which had become slightly askew, made him appear rather rakish. 'It's nice to kip down in me own home again,' he said.

'I expect it must be.' The kettle boiled and she went into the back kitchen.

'Y'know, luv,' Francis called, 'I meant what I

said when I first came home. Things are going to be a lot better from now on, I promise.'

I should hope so, she thought grimly. He'd been such a charming man when they first met. She'd been quite carried away by his captivating manner and the compliments which fell from lips which must have kissed the Blarney Stone on more than one occasion.

On the other hand, the better things were, the more difficult she would find it to get away. Her head swam because everything seemed so complicated. Perhaps things would be clearer in the morning, she thought hopefully.

She made two cups of cocoa and gave one to Francis, saying, 'I think I'll drink mine in bed. I've had a busy day and I'm fair worn out, what with Annie getting married and everything.'

'Right you are, princess,' he said jovially. 'By the way, would you mind putting a pair of me ould pyjamas in the back bedroom? I've looked through the drawers, but it's all Tony's stuff.'

'Of course,' she said quickly. 'In fact, tomorrer, I'll change all the clothes around so's you'll have everything to hand when you need it.'

Sitting up in bed at half past two in the morning, Eileen felt an enormous sense of relief that the sleeping arrangements had been sorted out so amicably—not that she would have given in to pressure. Perhaps Francis really had turned over a new leaf. She was halfway out of bed in order to go downstairs and get her ciggies, convinced she'd never fall asleep without one, when a floorboard creaked again, then another. She froze, one foot on the floor. Francis was coming upstairs! He'd probably been to the lavatory at the bottom of the yard.

Eileen jammed a chair under the knob of the bedroom door, just in case, and returned to bed, all desire for a ciggie having gone.

*   *   *

Francis Costello lay staring at the slightly spotted ceiling in Tony's room. There were cobwebs in all four corners and dust on the glass lampshade—Eileen had obviously let things slide since he'd gone away.

From now on, Francis knew he would have to be very clever. It was essential that he get his feet under the table of Number 16 again if he wanted his political ambitions back on course. He'd been rather dismayed at the way Jack Doyle had looked at him with an expression close to disgust, ordering him into the back bedroom in a way that brooked no argument, but Francis was well aware he had the ability to charm the birds off the trees. With a bit of care and some subtle flattery, he'd soon have Jack eating out of his hand again. Jack Doyle virtually owned the local Labour Party and the appointment of a successor to Albert Findlay, the current ailing and elderly Member of Parliament for Bootle Docklands, was within his gift when Albert retired, which he was bound to do before the next election. Jack had promised the gift to Francis, and Francis had never wanted anything in his life as much as the power that such a wondrous gift carried with it. He'd actually married Jack's daughter because a wife and family looked good on a would-be-candidate's record, though he'd never cared much for women, and Eileen in particular irritated him beyond reason, with her feminine ways and feminine smells.

In 1938, he'd even joined the Territorials to enhance his reputation. Military experts were of the opinion that war, if it began, would be over in a few months. But the experts had been wrong, thought Francis sourly. More than a year later, the conflict showed no sign of ending. In fact it was getting more violent by the day.

The Army hadn't been so bad at first. He'd learnt to type and managed to get himself in the Paymaster's office, but once the Royal Tank Regiment had been posted to Egypt, Francis had been petrified. Not that he'd been involved in the fighting: he'd been safe in Alexandria, well away from harm. But say they'd been overrun by the Eyeties? They couldn't be expected to ignore him just because he was a clerk. He'd be taken prisoner, or, even worse, killed, because he was in uniform like every other soldier.

Francis couldn't recall what he'd said to those two youngsters who'd turned on him and beaten him senseless, because he was drunk out of his mind at the time. Newcastle boys they were, arrived only that day, neither more than eighteen. All he could remember was a boot thumping against his head and his head thumping against a wall, and when he came to in the little military hospital he had a feeling he might have made a suggestion that was out of line. Sometimes, when he'd had one over the eight . . .

At first, there'd been a sense of terrible shame, though this was soon replaced with a feeling of relief when he realised he was going to be discharged. It was worth losing the sight in his eye to get out of the Army. He knew nothing untoward would go down on his military record, because no-one had come forward to identify the two lads who'd beaten him, and the reason for the beating was merely rumour. Under the circumstances, the Army would have no alternative but to give Francis the benefit of the doubt.

And now Francis Costello was home, a hero to the neighbours, with his good job at the Mersey Docks & Harbour Board waiting for him, as well as his seat on Bootle Corporation. With a bit of deft manoeuvring, he and Jack Doyle would soon have their heads together working out what they'd do once Francis got to Parliament. Before he knew it, everything would be back as it was before he'd been called up.

No, not everything! He'd forgotten about Eileen. At the bottom of his kitbag was a letter from a solicitor offering him a choice: either he agreed to divorce his wife promptly on the grounds of her adultery, or she would divorce him for cruelty, leaving Francis with no choice, his reputation to consider, but to go for the first option.

Adultery! Francis felt physically sick as rage engulfed his body. How dared she? She belonged to *him*! She was his wife. He'd married her, which meant he owned her, just as he owned his son. A man was nothing if he couldn't keep his wife and child in line.

But, thought Francis, fighting down the rage, from now on, he'd have to be more than clever with Eileen. He'd need to be dead smart. There'd not been the time for divorce proceedings to have got under way, so, no matter how much she riled him, he must keep his temper well under control. If he so much as raised his little finger she'd be off bleating to her dad. He'd buy her little presents the way he'd done when they were courting, make her see a divorce made no sense because she already had the perfect husband.

CHAPTER THREE

Monday was a day of intermittent sunshine and showers with a hint of autumn already in the air. The watery sun had passed its peak in a pale cloudy sky as the Dunnings bus carrying workers for the afternoon shift passed through the heavily built-up areas of Bootle and Walton Vale. When it reached the countryside, it was like entering a completely different world, Eileen thought. The grass on Aintree Racecourse looked particularly green and fresh; it felt ages since she'd seen it, yet it had only been a few days!

They bumped across the little hump-backed bridge over the stream that ran by Dunnings and she looked eagerly through the window, just in case, you never know, Nick might be waiting at the side door where they always met, if only to wave, but there was no sign of him.

Dunnings had produced turbo engines for many years, and the original main building was solid and brick built. Since 1938, when it turned to making parts for aeroplanes, extensions had been haphazardly added, flimsy, rather ramshackle affairs.

Eileen clocked in, then hung her coat in her locker, changed into a pair of navy-blue drill

43

overalls and tied the regulation triangle of material turban-wise around her head, making sure every single hair was tucked inside, even her fringe. The women were frequently warned of the dangers of leaving their hair exposed and the horrific consequences which could ensue if it got caught when bending over the lathe.

She made her way towards the workshop where twenty centre lathes stood in rows of five. The building was one of the newer ones and the high corrugated iron roof turned the place into an oven in the summer. During the cold months, everybody shivered. Most of the women were already standing behind their machines, some having a quick smoke before the hooter sounded, the rest already hard at work. As far as they were concerned, they were working for the Government and therefore against Hitler, and were more than happy to begin work before the official time.

Instead of going to her own lathe, Eileen turned right and walked along a narrow corridor, past a row of glass-walled offices. She paused at the end office, where a woman was sitting at a desk, her head bent intently over her work. In answer to her knock, the woman looked up and smiled, and Eileen went in.

'Hallo, there,' said Miss Thomas. 'I suppose there's no need to ask what sort of weekend you had. I expect it was perfect.'

Miss Thomas was the Women's Overseer, a diminutive, birdlike woman in her early forties. When Eileen had first started, she'd resented her obvious upper-class demeanour, the plummy accent and the way she referred to the women as 'her girls', but as she grew to know her better, she realised Miss Thomas genuinely cared for the women in her charge. Having left her solicitor husband, a man even more violent than Francis, and reverted to her maiden name, she'd been advising Eileen how to go about the divorce.

'I'm afraid the weekend didn't turn out as expected,' Eileen said wryly. 'I thought I'd better tell you—me husband's home.'

'Oh, dear!' Miss Thomas's face fell. 'What happened?'

Eileen described the events of the past two days in detail, finishing, 'He's gone to a military hospital in Runcorn today to have the bandage removed.' On Sunday the house had been more like a station as word got round Francis Costello was back, with neighbours and old friends popping in by the minute to see him.

Miss Thomas frowned. 'I didn't realise he was a fighting man. I thought he had a deskbound job.'

'He did,' Eileen nodded, 'but as he explained yesterday, he volunteered to take some important papers to one of the officers at the front and the car ran over a mine—the driver was killed. I suppose it was a brave thing to do. After all, he didn't have to do it.'

'What happens now? I take it moving to the cottage is out for the moment?'

'Only for the moment,' Eileen said firmly. 'Nick'll be waiting for me at dinner time. We'll decide what's best to do then.' It seemed incredible now to think she'd actually decided to give him up. She couldn't wait to see his face when she told him everything had changed.

'I hope your husband doesn't give you any problems in the meantime.'

Eileen gave a sarcastic laugh. 'He's doing his best to get back in me good books. Butter wouldn't melt in his mouth since he came home. He said me cooking had never tasted so good and he actually had the nerve to call me "princess".'

'What does it say in the Bible about the sinner that repenteth?' Miss Thomas mused.

'I don't know and I don't particularly care,' said Eileen, 'Anyroad, I'd better get down to some work. God! I'm dreading facing the girls. I deliberately sat downstairs on the bus, so's to avoid Pauline on top. I'll get the third degree when they realise I'm still in Bootle, and I've no intention of telling them the reason why.'

'They know about Nick?'

'Of course. It was difficult to keep him a secret when I met him outside every day, but I never talked about Francis if I could avoid it.' She laughed again. 'I feel as if I've been leading a double life. It was the other way round at home.'

'Just be quite firm with the girls,' Miss Thomas advised. 'Fob them off—a little lie wouldn't hurt.'

Eileen was about to leave when Miss Thomas called her back. 'I nearly forgot! I don't know if you've heard, but Ivy Twyford has given in her notice. Her husband has got a job in Sheffield, which means the job of chargehand will be vacant shortly. It's yours, if you want it, Eileen. It means an extra twopence an hour.'

'Chargehand!' Eileen gasped. 'But why me? There's others been here much longer.'

'We, the management that is, decided you had the most responsible attitude. The girls respect you and they'll listen to you. They don't take a blind bit of notice of the foreman.' Miss Thomas smiled.

'Poor Alfie merely gets showered with abuse the minute he puts his nose inside the workshop.'

'Me and Alfie get on fine,' Eileen said. 'I must be the only one who doesn't pull his leg all the time.'

'That's another reason we chose you. You can act as a conduit between Alfie and the girls.'

Eileen left, wondering what a conduit was, and resolving to look it up in Nick's dictionary some time. She felt pleased and flattered at the promotion, though knew it might cause some ill feeling, at least initially, with the women who'd started at Dunnings before she had.

She entered the workshop, where the noise of nineteen lathes functioning at full pelt was almost deafening, to be greeted with a united yell of, 'Morning, Eileen!' With a display of confident cheerfulness she didn't feel, she yelled, 'Morning,' back. If she gave the impression nothing untoward had happened, the girls would be less likely to probe.

The lathe she worked on had already been set up by the woman on the morning shift. She quickly checked what was being made, turned the starting lever, and the machine clanked into action. In no time at all, one-and-a-half-inch distance pieces were dropping into a container underneath, and Eileen felt the fine spray of the nauseous-smelling cooling liquid on her face. When she first started nearly a year ago, she'd thought she'd never get the hang of things, but now the lathe held no more terrors than operating the stove at home.

'How's things, Eileen?' screamed Doris on the lathe next to her, as casually anyone could whilst shouting at the top of their voice.

'Fine!' Eileen smiled back. No doubt Pauline, who worked on her other side, had already reported seeing her on the bus, when, if things had gone according to the plan the girls all knew about, she should have merely walked along the High Street from the cottage. 'I decided to put off the move for a while, that's all.' She changed the subject. 'What did you get up to over the weekend? Meet any nice fellers?'

'If you did, I hope you kept your keks on for a change,' yelled Carmel from behind her lathe opposite.

'I always keep me keks on, if you don't mind,' Doris replied haughtily. 'Eh, what d'you think of me hair? I dyed it a different colour.' She stepped back from the lathe and untied her headscarf to reveal a mop of mahogany-coloured curls.

'Y'look like a bloody toffee apple,' shouted Lil.

'Well, last week she looked like a Belisha beacon with that bright orange.'

'You'd look better, Doris, if your eyebrows matched. One half of your face looks as if it belongs to someone else altogether.' Doris's eyebrows had been shaved off and redrawn with a pencil. She was never able to draw them the same shape and the left was usually higher than the other, ending in a wiggly upwards curve.

'You're dead nasty, you's lot.' Doris pretended to be hurt.

'It looks smashing, luv,' Eileen assured her. 'I like that colour better than the orange.' Doris's wide purple-painted lips clashed less violently than they'd done before. She was a coarse, jolly girl of nineteen, and along with Pauline, who was the same age, spent all her free evenings at dances,

48

being taken home by an endless stream of young men, mainly servicemen passing through Liverpool.

'T'weren't orange,' Doris shouted. 'It were molted gold or something.'

'Molten gold,' corrected Theresa.

'Looked more like mouldy gold to me,' shrieked Carmel.

Eileen grinned. Sometimes, it was more entertaining than the wireless, better even than ITMA, the quips the girls came out with, though some were anything but girls. Carmel was well into her fifties and completely toothless. When she spoke the words came out in a sort of mushy blur, along with a shower of spit. Her false teeth were kept in the pocket of her overalls and only brought out in the canteen. According to Doris, Carmel didn't need cooling liquid, she could provide her own.

Like Carmel, Theresa and Lil, although considerably younger, had been housewives until the war began. Almost overnight, they'd become centre lathe turners and how they managed to run their homes and take care of their large families as well as work an eight-hour shift at Dunnings, was a source of a constant wonderment to Eileen. She had nothing but admiration for their gritty determination to put in a hard day's work, as well as their constant equally gritty good humour—though their language left much to be desired! They turned their worst catastrophes into jokes against themselves. Lil kept them in stitches describing the antics of her drunken loutish husband, and Theresa, a pretty young widow with several children who were looked after by her mother-in-law whilst she was at work, had a fund of stories about her eldest lad who seemed set on a criminal career at thirteen.

Their favourite comment, 'Well, you've got to laugh, haven't you, else you'd only cry,' was usually made when the group in fact had tears running down their faces, but tears of laughter, not of grief.

Most of the women in the workshop were the same: housewives who had depended on their husbands for support, now suddenly wage earners in their own right and immensely proud of the fact. These five, though, the only ones within earshot above the noise of the pounding machinery, had become Eileen's special friends.

'How did your mate's wedding go, Eileen?' Pauline asked. Pauline was a graceful dark-haired girl with a face like a Madonna. She was more serious than the others and also rather vain. Miss Thomas was constantly ticking her off for not covering her hair properly with the turban.

'But it makes me look like an ould washerwoman,' Pauline complained.

'Best to look like an old washerwoman, dear,' Miss Thomas would reply, 'and have a face. You might end up with no face at all if you leave your hair poking out and it catches in your machine!'

'The wedding went fine,' Eileen replied. 'There was dancing in the street till it was dark.'

Someone across the workshop began to sing *Roll out the Barrel* and everyone, including Eileen, joined in. If the women weren't joking, they were singing. Halfway through the foreman came in and they stopped abruptly, and to the tune of Gracie Fields' *Sally*, they warbled, 'Alfie Alfie, show us your thingy', and the embarrassed Alfie turned tail and left, whatever important message he may have

50

brought left undelivered.

The time seemed to crawl by that afternoon, and Eileen kept glancing at the clock impatiently. Work halted at six for the half-hour dinner break, when she would see Nick. She felt sure the clock had stopped, or might possibly be going backwards. It was weeks since they'd met, mid-August, when he'd come home on forty-eight-hours' leave and was so exhausted he'd spent almost the entire time asleep.

Twenty-five to four, twenty to four. The trolley came round with tea and they drank it by their machines. Tea-breaks had been abolished months ago in the national effort to build more planes in order to combat the apparently overwhelming might of the German Luftwaffe.

Ten past five.

'Doesn't your mouth ache without your teeth in, Carmel?' Doris shouted. 'I'm amazed your face stays together, like.'

'It aches with 'em in. That's why I don't wear 'em.'

'What does your ould man have to say? I mean, it must be like kissing a sponge or something.'

Carmel hooted with laughter. 'My ould man's only interested in you know what. He ain't kissed me in a long time.'

'Perhaps he would if you had your teeth in,' said Theresa. 'You must be one of the few women who gives their chap a soft on.'

'I can't think of a better reason for keeping them out,' Carmel leered. 'Fact, I wish I could think of a way of stopping the "you know what". The ould git'll have a heart attack one of these nights.'

'Why don't you put your teeth there, instead,' Doris suggested. 'That'd soon stop him.'

51

By the time Eileen had finished laughing, it was half past five. Only another half an hour to go. The minutes dragged by, but eventually the big hand on the clock jerked to twelve and the hooter went. Eileen switched the machine off and was out of workshop in a flash, dragging the scarf off her head as she ran towards the side door.

Nick wasn't there!

She glanced wildly up and down the banks of the little gurgling stream, half expecting his tall, lean frame to appear miraculously from nowhere.

He must be at home. Perhaps he'd fallen asleep. Perhaps his leave had been curtailed. He might be ill. Eileen mentally listed all the reasons why Nick wasn't waiting as she hurried along the High Street towards the cottage. She'd left her key under a stone beside the door. He would surely have left a message telling her where he was.

She turned off the High Street and down the narrow lane where the cottage was situated, alone and relatively isolated in its large untended garden. It was over two hundred years old, the once wooden exterior now pebble-dashed, with a crumbling red-tiled roof and tiny windows.

The key was where she'd left it and her fingers shook as she unlocked the front door.

'Nick!' she called as soon as she was inside.

There was no answer. Where was he, she wondered desperately?

She went into the low-ceilinged living room and nearly jumped out of her skin. Nick was sitting on the sofa, dressed in his blue-grey RAF uniform, his long legs outstretched and crossed at the ankles. There was an expression on his sunburnt mobile face she'd never seen before, a look of icy disdain.

'Nick!' she cried and took a step forward, expecting him to stand up and take her in his arms.

'Eileen!' The tone was half mocking, as if he were making fun of her own cry of relief. He didn't move.

'Why didn't you come and meet me?' she asked shakily, aware something was terribly wrong.

He raised his eyebrows. 'Under the circumstances, did you honestly expect that I would?'

'Well, yes.' Her blood began to run as cold as the look on his face. This was a Nick she'd never known. He'd had black moods before, when he felt the world was a terrible place, but he'd never taken his bitterness out of her. Indeed, sometimes they'd seemed closer when she tried to coax him back into a good humour.

He smiled and her blood ran even colder. It was a hard, cynical smile, unpleasant. 'On Saturday I was told we could never see each other again. Apparently, your husband was back. Why should you expect to find me waiting two days later as if nothing had happened?'

'I didn't mean it,' she stammered, realising these were inadequate words to use. 'I made a mistake. I wasn't thinking right at first.'

'A mistake? You ditch someone at a moment's notice, but it was all a mistake? I've spent one hell of a weekend, and curiously enough, it doesn't make me feel any better knowing it was all a mistake.'

'But, Nick,' she protested, 'surely, all that matters is we love each other, and . . .'

He interrupted harshly. 'Love? You don't know the meaning of the word, my dear. I thought the

53

same, but it seems I was wrong. The minute Francis was back, I was dispensed with pretty damned swiftly.'

'Oh, Nick!' She half ran to the sofa and sat down, but didn't touch him. Incredibly, she felt too scared. But this was Nick, she told herself, Nick, whose entire body she'd stroked and kissed in the past. 'Didn't Tony tell you?' she said eagerly. 'They brought Francis home in an ambulance. He'd been injured. I couldn't just walk out and leave him, darling. It just wasn't right.'

'But it was all right to leave me?' He laughed sarcastically. 'Leave me for a man who nearly murdered you, or so you told me once.'

'But it was my duty, my moral duty, to stay,' she cried.

He shook his head. 'No, my dear. It was your moral duty to come to me. You promised me, you promised a hundred times we would always be together.'

She hated the way he kept calling her 'my dear' in such a formal way. 'I'm sorry,' she muttered.

'And so you should be,' he said harshly.

'We can still be together...' She briefly entertained the idea of seducing him, of turning his cold tragic face towards hers and kissing him, but felt it wouldn't work. He'd only spurn her, and that would make things even worse.

'It's too late, Eileen.' He turned towards her, and their glances met directly for the first time. She would have given everything she possessed to see his lovely dark eyes light up, to see his warm, quirky smile. 'Can you imagine,' he said, 'is it possible for you to put yourself in my shoes for a moment, and think what it was like when Tony told me you weren't coming? These two weeks were to be a sort of honeymoon, the start of our life together. Oh, God!' he cried hoarsely, showing emotion for the first time. 'I spent hours in the station waiting room trying to digest what had happened. It wasn't just as if the bottom had dropped out of the world, the whole world had disappeared. How could I live without you? Without Tony? I felt like killing myself.'

Eileen whispered, 'I don't suppose you'll believe it, but I felt exactly the same.'

He sighed deeply. 'I don't believe it, no. But I tell you this, Eileen, no woman will ever make me feel like that again. I'll never give my heart to anyone for as long as I live.'

'Please don't talk like that, luv.' She clutched his arm involuntarily but he shook her off, and she felt as if her own heart would break.

'So, what caused the volte-face?' he asked.

She had no idea what he meant. 'The what?' His lips twitched and he was the old Nick for a moment. He always teased her when she didn't understand the words he sometimes used.

The old Nick vanished as quickly as it had come. 'The about turn?' he snapped.

'I realised I'd acted too hastily,' she mumbled. 'I was on the point of leaving the house when they brought Francis home. It would have been different if I'd had some warning. You're not the only one to think the world had ended. It seemed the fairest thing to do was set you free to meet someone else, a woman without all the paraphernalia that comes with me.' If she thought that would mollify him a little, she was wrong.

'Someone else?' he said incredulously. 'You were

55

setting me free for someone else? Well, thanks all the same, but the only woman I've ever wanted is you. It just shows how trite you considered our relationship, that you can visualise me with another woman.'

'It near tore me in two thinking about it,' she whispered. 'Once things had calmed down a bit and I'd had time to think, I realised it didn't have to be the end. Once Francis is on his feet again, I can still leave.'

'You didn't think of telephoning and informing me of your change of heart?' he asked lightly.

'No,' she confessed.

He uttered a sardonic, 'Huh', and she said, angry for the first time, 'Jaysus, Nick! I've never used a telephone in me life until yours. I'm not used to them, it didn't cross me mind.' She stood and began to wander around the room. She noticed the ornaments she'd brought on the mantelpiece, the photo of her family in pride of place on the lace runner on top of the sideboard. This would have been her home. 'Anyroad,' she went on, still angry, 'if you were as upset as you make out, why didn't you come looking for me? I almost thought you had, for a minute, when I went out for a while to clear me head.'

He frowned. 'Perhaps I should have. I thought about it, but by then it was too late. You'd shot your bolt, as they say.'

'What about the card you sent? It said, "We'll meet again".'

'Well, we have, haven't we?'

'I never thought you could be so cruel!'

'Cruel? My dear, the Marquis de Sade has nothing on you when it comes to being cruel.'

She didn't reply. The remark made no sense and she didn't want to make herself appear even more ignorant by asking for an interpretation. Really, she thought dispassionately, they weren't well matched at all. He was highly educated, whereas she'd left school at thirteen. He spoke differently than she did and used all sorts of fancy words. He'd be far better off with a woman of his own—she hesitated to use the word 'class', because her dad would have a fit if he thought she considered herself inferior to any man or woman on earth—a woman on the same level, she decided. A woman who'd gone to university, that's if women did, she'd no idea, who wore elegant clothes and used expensive perfume, not someone in ugly overalls who stank of evil-smelling cooling liquid which took a good brisk scrub to get rid of at the end of the day.

'Have you had anything to eat this weekend?' she asked, suddenly aware that the table was set as she'd left it last Friday.

'No, but I've had plenty to drink.'

'Oh, Nick!' His back was to her. She noticed for the first time the plaster protruding out of his left shirt-cuff. She'd forgotten about his broken wrist. The white plaster contrasted sharply with his slender sunburnt hand. She shivered, remembering the sheer heaven to which those hands had sent her in the past. She no longer felt dispassionate. She wanted him! Her insides throbbed with longing. There was nothing in the world she desired more than for Nick to make love to her at that moment. If they could, if only they could, everything would be all right again. Her hand reached out to touch the little cluster of tight curls at the nape of his lean neck.

'Nick,' she whispered, just as he stood up, out of her reach, 'I love you.'

His face softened as he faced her and she felt a flicker of hope in her heart. 'And I love you, Eileen.' Perhaps he sensed her desire, perhaps he felt it too. He said, 'Do you want us to make love?' When she nodded breathlessly, he went on, 'So do I. Oh, it was great between us, wasn't it? Absolute magic, but,' his face changed, 'it wouldn't work. You see, I can never trust you again, my darling. I would be forever expecting you to let me down.'

She realised it was all over. 'In that case,' she said tiredly, 'we'd best say goodbye, Though don't forget, Nick, it was *you* who left *me* in the first place. You didn't have to join up. You could have stayed in your job for the duration of the war. It's a miracle you're still alive and able to climb on your high horse.'

His face flushed. 'That's a different thing altogether. I had a duty to fight for my country. I couldn't have lived with myself otherwise.'

'And I couldn't have lived with myself if I'd walked out on Francis, but it seems you're the only person allowed to have principles.'

'That's not true, Eileen.'

'I think it is.' She went towards the door. 'You're not going to stay here by yourself over the next fortnight?' Despite everything, she couldn't help but be concerned.

'I'm catching the midnight train to London. I shall stay with friends till my leave's up. I would have gone before, but decided to wait and see if you'd come.'

'So you could tell me where to get off?'

He had the grace to look ashamed. 'I . . . It just

makes me feel a little better knowing I haven't been entirely rejected.'

'You never were rejected. I was in a right ould state when they brought Francis home and I thought I was doing what was best for you. Here's your key.' She threw the key down on the telephone table in the hall.

'No!' He picked up the key and handed it back. 'Keep it. I'll never return to the cottage.' He glanced upstairs. 'It holds too many memories. I couldn't bear to live here without you and Tony. But the raids are getting worse. I'd like you and your family to use it.' His lips twisted wryly. 'You can even bring Francis if you want.'

'As if I would!' she said bitterly. Nevertheless, she put the key in the pocket of her overalls and opened the door. 'Tara, Nick.'

'Goodbye, my darling girl. Give Tony my fondest love.'

From the tone of his voice she had a feeling that he'd cry when she left. He'd cried before because he was an emotional man, perhaps too much so. Someone less sensitive mightn't have taken things so much to heart, but then that someone wouldn't have been Nick and she wouldn't have loved him half as much.

'I will,' she replied with a coolness anything but felt.

*   *   *

She was already working on her lathe when the girls came wandering in from the canteen. They looked rather subdued.

'Eh, Eileen. Have you heard the news?' asked

Lil.

'No,' she snapped, uninterested.

'An entire bomb disposal team were blown up in Liverpool this morning working on this bomb. What sort was it, girls?'

'Delayed action,' said Pauline.

'Jaysus!' Eileen gasped.

'Not only that, you know Myra from the assembly shop? She lost her mam last night in the raid on Norris Green.'

Later on the girls began to sing, but that night they sang only sad songs, *The Old Lamplighter* and *Among My Souvenirs*. How many more sad songs would they sing, thought Eileen, close to tears, before the damn war was over and the world returned to normal? Not that things would ever be normal again for her. Nick had gone, that lovely part of her life had ended. When the time came to leave Francis, she and Tony would have to strike out on their own, she thought listlessly. She did her best to push Nick to the back of her mind and concentrate on work, because it seemed selfish to be preoccupied with her own affairs when people were dying everywhere. At least Nick was alive.

It seemed only appropriate that the klaxon should blare out a warning that a raid had started just after eight o'clock. They trooped down to the shelter, but the raid wasn't a long one. The women returned to the workshop, and for the last hour at Dunnings, no-one sang at all.

*　　　*　　　*

When Eileen got home, she found Francis had a visitor. George Ransome lived across the street and was known as the 'Pearl Street Playboy'. He was a dashing bachelor of about fifty with a pencil-thin moustache, who wore loud pinstripe suits and two-tone shoes, and spent most of his time in the company of various young ladies whose appearance was as flashy as his own. George's parties were frequent and very rowdy, with music and shrill screams coming from Number 17 till well past midnight. When people complained, he would merely wink and say jovially, 'Well, next time I have a party, you're welcome to come.' Before the war, he'd worked for Littlewoods Pools, but when the premises were taken over by the postal censorship service, George had been kept on, his sharp intelligence, not normally apparent to his friends, a useful tool in a vital job. George, conscious of his important contribution towards the war effort, had started to acquire an air of gravitas and the parties and the young ladies were becoming less and less frequent, particularly since he'd joined the ARP. Despite his bad reputation, Eileen quite liked him. Indeed, she secretly found him rather attractive in a seedy sort of way, and although George would have been outraged if he'd known, she also thought his way of life more than a little pathetic.

'Hallo, George.' She was pleased to see him, though would have been pleased to see anyone rather than be alone with Francis.

''Lo there, kid.' He jerked his head and made a clicking noise. 'I've just been keeping the war hero company till you came home.'

'How's your day been, princess?' Francis asked. He looked like a pantomine pirate. The bandage had been removed from his eye and there was a black patch in its place. The left side of his face was the ugly yellow of fading bruises, but for all that, he looked remarkably fit. He was wearing the trousers of his next-to-best suit and a knitted pullover over a collarless blue shirt.

'Fine,' she said, though the day had been anything but. 'What did they have to say at the hospital?'

Francis said, almost proudly, 'They're going to take me ould eye out and put a glass one in its place. According to the doctor, no-one will be able to tell it isn't real.'

'That's good.'

'It's the bloody gear,' George said as he lit a cigarette from the one he'd just finished. He was a chain-smoker and rarely seen without a fag hanging from his bottom lip. 'It'll be dead good having you back in Pearl Street again, Francis. It hasn't seemed the same since you left. Eileen's missed you something rotten, haven't you, girl? Everyone could tell.'

Eileen said quickly, 'I think I'll just pop upstairs a mo and see if our Tony's all right.'

Tony was fast asleep, one hand under the pillow clutching the tin gun he took to bed each night. She kissed him gently on the cheek and whispered, 'Hallo, son,' but he didn't stir.

George was just about to leave when she went down. 'Tara, Eileen.' He threw a pretend punch at Francis. 'See you, mate. Perhaps you'll feel up to a bevvy at the King's Arms by tomorrer night. Oh, by the way, I've arranged for a stirrup pump demonstration on Saturday afternoon. I think we should organise a Pearl Street fire-fighting squad between us.'

Eileen promised she would be there, as she had

no idea what to do with the stirrup pump the government had issued should the occasion arise to use it. She saw George out and when she returned, Francis was in the back kitchen.

'I boiled the kettle for some cocoa earlier on. Would you like a bit of toast for your supper?'

'No, ta, I'm not hungry, but I'd love some cocoa.' She remembered she'd eaten nothing since breakfast, but the thought of food made her feel sick.

'Put your feet up, princess,' Francis called. 'I reckon you need a rest after all that hard work.'

It was strange, really strange, but no matter what a person might have done in the past, even if they'd nearly murdered you on one occasion, it was difficult to remain cold and aloof when the person was making a determined effort to be friendly. Indeed, after the frosty reception she'd had from Nick, it was almost pleasant to have someone fussing around attending to her needs—even if it might only be a pretence, she quickly reminded herself.

'The work's not hard once you're used to it,' she said. 'I really enjoy it. In fact, I was made chargehand today.' Meeting Nick had pushed everything else to the back of her mind and she'd actually forgotten.

Francis came in with the drinks. 'Chargehand, eh?' He chuckled. 'That's quite a responsibility. Y'know, luv, I'm not going to be in hospital for long having me eye done. I'll be well enough for work once me discharge comes through in a few weeks' time. There'll be no need to keep on with your job once I'm earning a wage again and getting a pension from the army. You can take it easy at home.'

Eileen did her best to remain calm. 'I don't want to take it easy, thank you, Francis,' she said coldly. 'I didn't go to work just for the money. I wanted to do me bit for the war effort and I've no intention of giving it up.'

'If that's the way you want it, princess, it's fine by me,' Francis said easily.

Hard luck on you if it weren't, thought Eileen. 'By the way,' she said, 'in case you forgot, the Mersey Docks & Harbour Board have been paying your wages ever since you were called up and I haven't collected a penny. There'll be a nice little windfall waiting for when you go back.'

'Perhaps we can buy something for the house?' Francis suggested.

'There's nothing I need.' The all-embracing 'we' made her squirm inside. 'How's Tony been?' she asked.

For the first time, Francis looked slightly peeved. 'I've scarcely seen him since he came home from school. He popped in a minute about five o'clock to collect something, and I thought he might stay once he saw me. 'Stead, he went over to Jacob Singerman's. Jacob brought him back just in time for the raid and we sat under the stairs till the All Clear. Seemed a bit late to me for a lad of his age.'

'I don't think bedtimes are relevant any more, Francis. No-one's had a decent night's sleep since the bombing started.'

He smiled. It was a dazzling smile, warm and utterly convincing. 'I reckon you're right,' he said. 'Though there's no need for Jacob to look after Tony from now on. I can take care of me own son.'

'I don't think so, Francis,' Eileen said as firmly as

64

she could whilst under the influence of the smile. 'Let's leave the arrangement as it is, if you don't mind. It means you can come and go whenever you please. I don't want Tony left on his own under any circumstances, not with all these raids. It'll only be every other week when I'm on the late shift.'

'Anything you say, princess.'

He was, she thought wryly, like putty in her hands.

'Was the raid a bad one?' she enquired. 'You can't hear much in Dunnings' basement.'

'George said Great Homer Street caught it really bad, and they got the Carlton Cinema in Moss Lane.'

Eileen shook her head. 'I don't see the point in bombing innocent civilians,' she said. 'No-one expected the war would come so close to home.'

Francis had almost wished he was back in the safety of Alexandria during the raid. 'Maybe it'll stop soon. As you say, there's no point.'

*   *   *

But the air-raids didn't stop. As September wore on, the raids lasted longer and became more deadly. At first, it was London's East End that got the brunt of Hitler's wrath, and the poorest of the poor lost what pitiful few possessions they had, as tenements and entire communities were razed to the ground. But it seemed that no major port, no city, was to be spared the terrible carnage, as the Luftwaffe swept across the dark skies to deliver their nightly load of terror.

Incredibly, people actually became used to the eerie wail of the siren. It soon became a part of their lives. Some made for the public shelter, others for the Anderson shelter in the garden, or their own makeshift affairs—under the table or the stairs. There were those who completely ignored the warnings and stayed in their beds and boasted they could sleep through the worst raid, or carried on with what they were doing, determined not to let Hitler disrupt their lives.

No-one, however, got used to hearing the number of people who'd been killed the night before, or coming across an ominous gap in the street where houses had once been, where people had lived and loved, been happy or sad, and where, perhaps, they'd died.

On Merseyside, everyone was in a state of high dudgeon because the BBC made no mention of the suffering they endured. Their city was gradually being blown to pieces before their very eyes, the streets were blocked by rubble and many of the shops, factories and businesses had been forced to close. Central Station had been put out of action, along with the Mersey Underground. T. J. Hughes, a major store, was bombed, and the world-famous Argyll Theatre in Birkenhead gutted by fire. The cathedral and many other churches, along with hospitals and old people's homes, didn't escape the random terror that dropped from the sky and even criminals weren't spared when Walton Gaol was hit and twenty-one prisoners killed, to add to the hundreds of Merseysiders already dead. The docks, the poor docks, the lifeblood of the city, were a particular target and bombed several times a night.

But no-one knew this except themselves; news bulletins merely referred to 'attacks on the North West'. Scousers didn't begrudge the raids on

London being fully reported, but they would have liked recognition that it wasn't the only city being bombed.

'Never mind,' they said stoically. 'It can't get any worse.'

CHAPTER FOUR

The woman stood on the corner of Pearl Street feeling as if her feet were glued to the pavement. She'd come so far, hundreds of miles, yet she couldn't bring herself to take the last few steps home.

It was raining, not particularly heavy, but a steady penetrating drizzle that had soaked right through her coat during the walk from Marsh Lane station. She'd no idea what time it was; eight o'clock, perhaps nine, and felt weary, having spent the entire day changing trains, standing for most of the way in packed corridors.

The cul-de-sac looked narrower and shorter than she remembered it and the houses were tightly jammed together as if they'd been forced down by a giant hand into a space far too small. It was something she'd never noticed when she lived there. On the other hand, the railway wall at the end of the street seemed taller than before. She'd never realised it was as high as the roofs and it looked rather oppressive, like the wall of a prison. The girls used to play ball against the wall when she was a child, though she rarely joined in. She was far too busy practising the piano. On the few occasions she did, everyone had been impressed by her ability

67

to play with three balls, apparently forever, without dropping one. In those days, steam trains had run beyond the wall, and the belching smoke used to cover the washing with little black smuts. Her father had written some years before to say the line had been electrified.

There was no moon that night. She'd already experienced the blackout, and during the journey had been concerned she wouldn't be able to find her way in the pitch darkness. After all, it was twenty years since she'd left the street. But she needn't have worried. An air-raid was in progress and everywhere was lit up as gaily as a carnival. The long thin fingers of searchlights swept across the black sky, and every now and then flares fell like exploding stars and it was bright as daylight for a while. The flares were usually followed by the sound of an explosion, as a bomb was dropped by one of the planes which were occasionally caught in a probing searchlight. Barrage balloons glinted decoratively, like lights on a Christmas tree.

But the greatest illumination came from a fire, a great roaring fire, which was very close, somewhere on the docks, she guessed. She could hear crackling and was sure it must be a timber yard. The woman felt convinced she could even feel the heat from the dancing, twisting flames which leapt up into the sky, though it was probably her imagination, as perhaps was the pungent smell of burning. The area where she stood actually looked quite pretty, the houses with their windows crisscrossed with sticky tape to prevent the glass from shattering, the wet roofs and cobbled steets, all sheathed in a glistening pink glow. Chimneys puffed smoke which made lacy patterns against the fiery sky.

There was the sound of fire engines in the distance and of people shouting, though the area around Pearl Street was relatively quiet. There were voices coming from the public house by which she stood. She tried to remember what it was called and looked up at the sign when the name wouldn't come to mind—the King's Arms! Her father used to go there for a drink on Saturday nights. Perhaps he still did.

The woman regarded everything around her with a curious lack of emotion. Even when a bomb dropped close by she didn't flinch, but remained, as still as a statue outside the pub, as if entirely unaware of the danger she was in. There was only one emotion the woman was capable of feeling at the moment, the same one which had kept her going throughout the last two years, and that was an implacable, all-consuming hatred of Adolf Hitler and every German who had ever lived.

She sighed, and picked a small suitcase up from beside her numb feet. It was time she went home. Even she was able to see she couldn't stand there all night. A flare fell, closely followed by a bomb. It was stupid, if nothing else, to risk her life so near to home considering all she'd been through.

The woman crossed the street and knocked on the door of Number 3. When no-one answered, she knocked again, and after a while, a voice shouted, 'Coming!' She felt shocked when a very old man answered the door and wondered if she'd come to the wrong house. It wasn't until she noticed the familiar dark-red-wallpaper in the hall and the black and red linoleum, that she realised it was the right house after all, and this old man was her father.

'Hallo, Dad,' she said. 'It's Ruth. I've come home.'

*   *   *

The news flashed around Pearl Street the following morning; Ruth Singerman was back, though she wasn't Singerman now, but had a horrible German surname, which her dad said she wasn't to use, so she was going by her maiden name.

As was the custom, the neighbours started dropping in from early morning, out of both curiosity and a desire to offer a warm welcome to one of the street's former residents.

Amongst those who'd known Ruth before, when she was very reserved and extraordinarily ladylike for Bootle, the general impression was that she hadn't changed much. Of course, in the old days, Mr Singerman had spoiled her rotten, what with her mam dying when Ruth was born and her being an only child. Mind you, Jews always spoiled their children and Jacob Singerman, despite the fact he wasn't one of those orthodox ones, was no exception to the rule. Now, Ruth seemed more reserved than ever, indeed rather cold and a mite unfriendly when people called.

As far as looks went, she was still as comely, not a bit like a Jewess with her ivory skin and long brownish-red hair still worn in plaits, though now the plaits were coiled in a bun on her remarkably unlined neck. She'd look even prettier if she smiled, which no-one had seen her do so far, but then, perhaps Ruth hadn't had much to smile about over the last two years, they all decided sympathetically. Everyone had heard the terrible

70

rumours about the things Hitler was doing to the poor Jews.

*　　　*　　　*

Nothing had changed, Ruth marvelled. It wasn't only the wallpaper and the oilcloth that were the same, but every stick of nineteenth-century furniture, every dish, every curtain. Her father even used the tablecloths she remembered; the brown chenille with the stringy fringe which was on all the time, and a cotton cloth with a blue border, so thin you could scarcely feel it, for when they ate. Even her bedroom was exactly as she'd left it, with the waxed lily in a glass case on the tallboy and the homemade patchwork cover on the bed. It was as if the house had been preserved as a shrine, though a shrine to what she had no idea.

Whenever people called, and they still kept coming although she'd been home for two days, her father fussily showed them into the parlour which resembled a museum, the uncomfortable chairs stuffed with horsehair, the ugly sideboard and old-fashioned piano with Lady's fingers painted on the front. There was a hand-operated sewing machine on a small table in the corner. The parlour was even colder than the living room because there was never a fire lit and Ruth dreaded to think what the house would be like in winter. Her father seemed to have become a bit of a miser in his old age, measuring out the lumps of coke for the grate as if they were gold, and keeping the gas light so dim it was far more miserable than it need be with the nights drawing in.

Ruth was surprised at how irritating she found

71

these economies, and even more surprised at the unexpected concern she felt for her bodily comforts. She'd been anticipating a return to the warm comfortable nest of her childhood. Instead, the house was cold and dark and, even worse, the food was meagre. There'd been mincemeat on a slice of dry bread for dinner yesterday, no dessert, and bread and margarine for tea. She wondered what sort of feast she'd be offered today.

So far, she hadn't brought these matters up with her father. To do so, would create an intimacy she didn't want. He would be upset and fuss around, apologising. She wished to remain as distant as humanly possible, even though she could tell from the look in his fading, wistful eyes that he desperately longed for the resurgence of their old loving, demonstrative relationship. But that would never happen, Ruth thought resentfully. She would never be close to anyone again as long as she lived.

The people who came, most of them, also seemed to want something from her, a friendship, a sort of chummy neighbourliness.

May Kelly, for example, who'd been the first to come, had wanted to invoke the spirit of the old days, when they were both girls and occasionally played together in the street. May had grown stout with the years, and her hair had already turned iron grey.

'They were fine times, weren't they, Ruth?'

'I suppose so,' said Ruth, who'd never liked the woman—the girl—and couldn't recall the times as being particularly fine. May, she was told, had never married and neither had her brothers, Fin and Failey. They still lived in Number 18.

'Anyroad,' May said enthusiastically, 'we must

get together for a jangle now 'n' again, talk about the old days. Remember when you were courting our Failey?'

'I only went out with him the once,' Ruth said stiffly. They'd gone to a Beethoven concert given by the American pianist, Gregory Malvern, at the 'Rotunda' in Scotland Road, but Failey had made no secret of the fact he was bored silly and would far prefer to be propped up against the bar of the nearest pub. There'd been no question from either side of them going out again, and Ruth felt mystified as to why she'd gone with him in the first place.

'I've brought you a little present,' May said, 'a quarter of tea, so you'll have plenty for your visitors.' She winked, tapped the side of her broad flat nose, and added tactlessly, 'I've a pig soaking in the bath, so if you want a few slices of bacon you know where to come.'

'Thank you very much, but we don't eat pork.'

Ruth gave her father the gift after May had gone and he wrinkled his face dramatically, though at the same time looked pleased. 'I hope you don't mind drinking black market tea.'

'Is that what it is, black market?' Ruth was shocked.

Jacob nodded. 'The Kellys were criminals before the war, in and out of gaol for shoplifting. They've transferred their talents to the black market, but they're no better at that than they were at thieving. You can get virtually anything from the Kellys— cigarettes, food, batteries—and if you go along with a hard luck story, you can get it for nothing!' He grinned. 'I reckon they pay out more than they take in. They'll be the first black marketeers in the

73

country to go bankrupt.'

'Is that what the pig in the bath is all about?'

He nodded. 'Fin and Failey raid the farms at night. They probably rustled it, like cowboys do in the pictures.'

Ruth watched through the window as the woman went into her house. It was incredible to think May was still living in the place where she was born, whilst she, Ruth, had become a wife and mother and spent half her life in another country. On the other hand, there was little difference between them now; Ruth was back, living in the house in which *she* was born, and as for the husband and children . . .

A young woman carrying a shopping basket came out of the house next to May's, a sad-faced girl with pretty blonde hair.

'That's Eileen Costello,' her father, watching beside her, said eagerly. 'I look after her little boy, Tony, when she works afternoons.'

'She looks very unhappy,' remarked Ruth, noting the drooping shoulders.

'It's strange, but she's been that way ever since her husband was discharged last month from the Army, yet Francis is one of the finest men you could ever meet. A great chap, you're sure to like him.' Jacob Singerman, who still had an eye for a pretty woman, remembered the day of Annie Poulson's wedding, when Eileen Costello had positively radiated happiness and he could scarcely take his eyes off her dazzling face.

'I don't see anything strange about it,' Ruth said flatly. 'She obviously doesn't want her husband back.'

This was something Jacob had begun to suspect

74

himself, but fond of Eileen though he was, he was more concerned with his own flesh and blood at the moment.

Throughout the two years during which he'd received no word from his daughter, he'd been on tenterhooks, expecting to hear she was dead, her husband was dead, as well as the grandchildren he'd never met. Even worse would be to hear nothing at all, to die himself without ever learning what had happened to his Ruth and her family. Jacob knew all about the Fuhrer's concentration camps, even if the British Government tried to pretend they didn't exist.

Now, miraculously, Ruth was back and at least one of his prayers had been answered. But although Ruth's body might be there, her spirit was somewhere else. She was cold and uncommunicative. It wasn't so much that she refused to answer his many questions, she simply ignored them. It was as if he hadn't spoken when he asked about Benjy and the children. His heart ached for the bright-eyed girl who'd left to stay with his brother in Graz, and ached even more fiercely for the woman who'd come back. What terrible things had happened to his dear Ruth?

'I expect you will want to play the piano,' he said hopefully, 'though I'm afraid it's terribly out of tune.' He was longing to hear her play something, but she hadn't touched it, not that there'd been much time. He lifted the lid and struck a few notes. 'C sharp is completely off key.'

'Why don't you get a tuner in?' she asked in an uninterested voice.

'I keep meaning to.' Even tuned, the piano was nothing like the one she was used to, he thought miserably. She'd had a Steinway, a baby grand, at home in Austria.

Jacob Singerman felt wretched that he could offer his precious daughter so little. What sort of home was this to come back to after 143 Blumenstrasse, a double-fronted house with a big garden and a garage for the cars? There was a snapshot of the house in the album he'd begun to keep when he realised she wasn't coming home. It was a rare day he didn't look through the pictorial history of her life, starting with a photo when she was two, then older at the piano, her wedding, numerous snapshots of Simon and Leah growing up. There was even a photo of the cook, Gertrude, in the album. After all, Benjamen Hildesheimer was a professional man, a dentist, patronised by the great and the good of Graz.

'I'm sorry,' he said brokenly.

'For what?' Ruth wondered why he looked close to tears.

'This!' He spread out his arms. 'This is not much to come back to.'

'There's nothing wrong with it. Though I find it odd nothing has changed.'

'What was there to change?'

Ruth shrugged, feeling as if the conversation was going nowhere. He was staring at her soulfully and she sensed he wanted to take her in his arms and comfort her, or possibly for her to comfort him. Their only physical contact had been a perfunctory kiss on the cheek when she first arrived. She'd escaped from his embrace then, and felt the same urge now to get away from his grief-stricken face.

She left the room, saying, 'Let's have a cup of tea. Ever since I arrived in England, the old desire for tea has returned, yet I scarcely drank it at home. We preferred coffee.'

Ruth filled the kettle, though it took forever to boil on the range in the living room with the fire being so low. 'Is there any more coke, Dad? I don't feel like waiting half an hour for my tea.'

'I'll put the last bit on. I need to buy some more.'

'You'd best get some groceries in, too. Surely you're allowed more than this on rations?' When it came to fresh food, there was merely half a loaf and a small piece of cheese in the larder and nothing at all in the meat safe. They'd had fried bread for breakfast.

He looked slightly uncomfortable. 'I'll do some shopping later on.' He went out into the yard and came back, puffing slightly, carrying a shovel of coke.

'Who lives next door?' Ruth asked. 'They had a terrible row last night. It must have been midnight before they finished shouting. It sounded like a foreign language.'

'That's Ellis and Dai Evans,' he explained. 'They have what you would call a stormy relationship and fight in Welsh. Dai works on the docks and drinks his wages. They have two daughters and poor Ellis has a struggle to live on what is left, though things are a little better now the eldest girl is working.'

'How old are the girls?'

'Dilys is fifteen. Do you remember the Adelphi, the big hotel in town?'

When Ruth nodded, Jacob continued, 'That's where Dilys works as a chambermaid. Myfanwy is still at school and the apple of her mother's eye, but for some reason noone has been able to identify, Dilys gets nothing but the lash of her tongue.'

'This Ellis sounds horrible.'

'She's not so bad,' he shrugged. 'It's just her way of staying alive.'

Ruth was standing over the fire, waiting for the kettle to boil. Her glance strayed impatiently to the mantelpiece.

'I remember this!' she exclaimed. She picked up the little musical box which had stood in the middle of the mantelpiece since the day Jacob had moved in. 'I used to play with this as a child and you were always worried I would break it.' She opened the box and the *The Blue Danube* tinkled out.

'Your Uncle David sent that from Austria as a wedding present. It was always your mother's favourite possession.'

Ruth examined the pink and blue enamel box with its fancy gold trimming. 'The gold looks real. It's probably worth something.'

'Is it?' he said, slightly amazed. 'Well, David was a far better businessman than I was. I suppose he could afford to send gold.'

Jacob Singerman knew if he closed his eyes, he would be able to see his dear wife, Rebecca, standing with her ear to the box as their daughter was now. Rebecca had died within an hour of Ruth's birth. He recalled fondly that in the past, opening the box had been a signal to talk about Rebecca, to describe her funny little habits, the way she dressed, how she'd never quite got the hang of English and made embarrassing mistakes, how once in a shop she'd requested, 'Black buttons for my goat'.

But Ruth was examining the box as if it brought back no memories at all, Jacob noticed sadly,

78

looking at it with the cold eye of a pawnbroker offered a pledge.

The following day, her father was out shopping and Ruth was in the house alone when there was a knock on the door. She considered briefly not answering, but supposed she must. So far, she'd hadn't been outside the house, so everyone in the street knew she was in. They seemed to know everything about everybody, as if they were a large extended family, not thirty entirely separate households.

Eileen Costello, whom Ruth had by now met, stood outside holding a brown paper bag.

'I won't come in,' she said quickly, as if sensing she wasn't welcome, 'it's just that I've been baking this morning and your dad's always partial to a bit of bunloaf. Mind you, it'll probably taste like concrete, what with only one egg and half the fruit.'

'Thank you very much,' Ruth said with less enthusiasm than she felt. In fact, she was starving and the bunloaf was more than welcome.

'Are you settling back in?' Eileen asked politely.

'Sort of.'

'I hope our Tony's not being a nuisance. If he talks too much, just tell him to shut up.'

'He's no trouble.' In fact, Tony was the only person whose presence Ruth didn't mind. He asked no questions and expected nothing from her except her occasional admiration when he won at cards.

'I expect you'll be looking for a job of work soon?' Eileen said.

Ruth frowned and wondered what the woman was talking about. She said coldly, 'Why should I?'

Eileen, aware of the coldness, pulled an embarrassed face. 'I'm sorry! It's nowt to do with

79

me, is it? I'm always poking me nose into other people's business. Anyroad, I'd best be off. Tara!'

She was about to leave, when Ruth called, 'Eileen?' She didn't like the first-name intimacy, but only a few of the older people were referred to as Mr or Mrs. 'Why did you ask if I'd be looking for work?'

'As I said, it's nowt to do with me. I wouldn't have brought the subject up, except we need women in the factory where I work.'

'But I'd like to know.'

'Well,' Eileen shuffled her feet uncomfortably. 'It's just that your dad has enough struggle living on the rent from his ould tailor's shop, I didn't see how the two of yis could manage.' She bit her lip. 'Look, it's your dad's place to tell you this, not mine.'

'I'd prefer you did,' Ruth insisted. 'I promise I won't say we've talked.'

Eileen shrugged. 'There's nowt else to tell. Your dad never has two ha'pennies to scratch his arse with. That's why I have him in our house so much, so he can sit in the warm and listen to the wireless. Not that I don't love having him,' she added hastily. 'Look, I'll have to go, else I'll miss me bus.'

'Thanks again for the cake,' Ruth said, closing the door. She went slowly back into the house, feeling slightly stunned. After a while, she began to root through the drawers of the sideboard, then in the cupboard underneath, until she found what she was looking for: a rentbook, a building society pass book and a little pad of receipts, all kept together in an elastic band.

It didn't take long for Ruth to establish her father's financial situation. It had been failing sight that caused him to sell the tailor's business just before she went away, and the pass book showed the £150 he received for the goodwill. But almost immediately more than half had been withdrawn. Her fare to Austria, she realised with a shock, her spending money, the new clothes. The trip had been her twenty-first birthday present—'I want to show you off to my brother and his wife.'

Thereafter, his capital had been taken out in tiny dribs and drabs until five years ago, when there was nothing left at all. Fortunately, he'd had the good sense to retain the lease of the shop. The receipts showed he received fifteen shillings a week rent. On the other hand, he paid nine and sixpence for the house, which meant he was left with a few shillings a week to live on! Yet he'd never said anything in his letters. She'd always assumed him to be relatively well off.

The key sounded in the door and Ruth hastily put the books back, just as Jacob came bustling in with his shopping bag, looking a trifle self-important she thought.

'I've got some nice steak and kidney,' he said breathlessly, 'though the queue was a mile long, and they'd just got Brussels sprouts in the greengrocer's, so we can have a stew with some potatoes, I even managed to find coffee.' He smiled happily. 'We can have a feast today. Put the kettle on, love, and we'll have a cup of coffee straight away.'

Ruth wordlessly fetched water from the back kitchen, wondering where the money had come from to buy all this stuff. As she leaned over the range to stand the kettle on the hob, she noticed the musical box was no longer on the mantelpiece.

She went out into the other room where he was putting the groceries away and humming a tune, *The Blue Danube*.

'Where is it, Dad?'

He stopped humming immediately and his face fell. For the first time since she'd come home, Ruth saw her father properly. What a dear face he had! As dear and as kind as a face could be, so gentle, with those silly half-moon glasses on the middle of his nose, quite useless to see through. He was the sort of man who wouldn't hurt a fly. She thought of all he'd done for her in the past, the piano lessons, the pretty clothes—not just for Austria. She remembered him sitting under the gaslight in his tailor's shop, his eyes screwed up as he stitched. 'You'll damage your eyes, Dad,' she used to say, and she'd been right.

Most of all, Ruth recalled the devotion, the love which had no boundaries; there was nothing, absolutely nothing she could do wrong. The stories he told came to mind; stories of old Russia and of Liverpool when he first arrived. He'd brought her unknown mother to life, turned Rebecca into a real flesh and blood person.

He was staring at her strangely, as if aware she was going through some sort of inner turmoil.

One part of Ruth, a small part, wanted to burst into tears, to cry on his shoulder that she was sorry, sorry she'd been so frigid since she returned, sorry that he was poor and she hadn't sent money when she had it, and that she'd thought him a miser, when in fact he was the most generous man in the world. He'd sold the musical box, her mother's dearest possession, in order to buy his daughter food.

But to another part of Ruth, the very thought of an embrace or a kind word was repellent.

'Where's the musical box, Dad?' she asked again.

He let out a long, slow breath. 'I pawned it. I never knew it was worth anything until you said.' As if expecting her to protest, he spread out his arms and shrugged expressively. It was a gesture she remembered clearly from the past. 'Possessions aren't important. Memories are what matter, and you can't pawn them.'

'How much did you get?'

'More than expected, nine pounds.'

'It was probably worth five times that.'

He smiled. 'Not in Bootle.'

'I'll look for a job tomorrow,' Ruth said firmly.

'No, no!' he protested. 'We can't have you working.'

'Then what else will you pawn?' Ruth shrugged and flung out her arms, unaware the gesture was exactly the same as his own. 'The waxed lily in my bedroom? You might get half a crown for that. Or your old sewing machine? What's that worth, five shillings, ten? I don't know about these things. And when everything is pawned there is to pawn, what do we live on then?'

He hung his head. 'I don't know.'

'I have nothing but the clothes I stand up in and a few spare things in my suitcase.'

Jacob wondered what had happened to the fine jewellery she used to own, but said nothing. He'd already noticed she didn't wear a wedding ring.

'I'll go upstairs and take a look in the wardrobe,' she said, 'and see if any of the clothes I left behind are fit to wear.'

The wardrobe reeked of mothballs. Ruth took the frocks out one by one. They were well preserved, but much too old-fashioned to wear now. Not, only that, they were childish, with puffed sleeves and sashes and too many frills. Still, the material was good. It might be less expensive to have them altered than buy new. She was hopeless with a needle, always had been—perhaps her father knew of a dressmaker she could use. Indeed, Mrs Waterman, who'd made the frocks in the first place, might still be in business.

Ruth closed the door on the wardrobe and pulled out the drawer underneath. It was full of underwear, neatly folded. She'd taken little baggage to Austria, as the plan had been to stay only three months. There were more things in the tallboy, a pretty shawl she'd worn when she went to concerts with her father and several cream flannel nightdresses. She took one out. Incredibly, it was as good as new, with its high lace-trimmed neck and long gathered sleeves. It meant she would be warm in bed that night; the one she'd brought with her was as thin as the table cloth her father still used.

In the top drawer, she found a heart-shaped chocolate box containing her old jewellery, and drew out a long colourful string of beads. It was all cheap, mostly bought from Woolworth's, and some pieces had tarnished, but somehow it felt more precious than all the expensive stuff she'd acquired since. She inserted a pair of drop earrings that matched the beads and looked at her reflection in the spotted wardrobe mirror.

It was incredible, truly incredible, but it was as if the old Ruth Singerman were staring back—no, she corrected herself, the *young*. She undid the plaits

84

coiled on her neck and let them hang loose. She felt that if she tried really hard, she could erase the last twenty years from her mind and become the young Ruth again.

Did she want to? She leaned forward and asked her reflection quite distinctly, 'Do I want to?' But the reflection provided no answer. One of their friends in Graz, a psychiatrist, had used hypnotism to treat his patients. She wondered if she could be hypnotised to forget she'd ever had a husband and two children.

She closed her eyes and had an immediate vision of Benjy hanging from the stairwell. She quickly opened her eyes again. It was guilt she felt more than anything when she thought about Benjy, because she hadn't loved him for a long time. She found his middle-aged paunch and the ridiculous mutton-chop whiskers he'd affected quite repugnant. Even in death, it was easy to feel guilt, but hard to feel sympathy for a man who'd taken his own life rather than stand up to the German monsters.

By then, the house had been stripped bare. The hated Huns had taken everything of value: the pictures, the Steinway, the furniture, even her furs. The children had gone the same day as Benjy. That's what had tipped him over the abyss into despair. Ruth arrived home to find she no longer had a family. Benjy was dead and the children had disappeared.

'Where?' she asked faintly. Jews seemed to be vanishing daily off the face of the earth. There would soon be not a single one left in Graz. It could only be the barbarians who'd taken her children. They'd left the most precious things till last. But no, to her relief it wasn't as calamitous as she'd first thought, not quite.

Gertrude Bruening, wonderful, loyal Gertrude, more like an angel than a cook, who had hidden her in her own home for the next two dazed and wretched years, was sitting on the bottom stair, rocking to and fro and wailing like an animal which had returned to its lair and found someone had stolen all its young.

'A group of Simon's friends came from the University,' Gertrude said breathlessly when Ruth calmed her down. Both ignored the body swinging overhead. 'Oh, you should have seen them, Frau Hildesheimer, their eyes were fever bright and they were bursting with excitement. They were planning to escape to America. But Simon and Leah had to make their minds up there and then if they wanted to go with them. There was no time to wait for you to come home. Mr Hildesheimer, poor man, he tried to stop them. Me, I insisted they go, I knew it's what you would have wanted.' She burst into tears. 'At least I hope so. If not, you'll just have to give me the sack.'

'It's what I wanted, Gertie,' Ruth whispered. 'Let's hope they'll be safe.'

Perhaps they were, perhaps they weren't. That was two years ago and Ruth had received no word from her children.

There was a noise from the yard and she got up and went to see what was happening. Her father was dragging a sack of coke into the yard. He must have bought it from the coalyard across the street. He looked happy again, as if the money from the musical box had changed the course of their lives forever. At least, Ruth thought dispassionately, she

86

could make sure he lived comfortably from now on. But she could never love him as she used to. He was old. One day he would be taken from her, and losing another loved one would be too much to bear. She would keep him at a distance, keep the whole world at a distance. From now on, Ruth Singerman would have a heart of stone.

She went back to the mirror, and for some reason she was never able to explain, she picked up a pair of nail scissors which had been in the box with the jewellery and began to hack away at her plaits. She'd had them for as long as she could remember, and it took ages to cut through the thick browny-red hair.

It looked terrible when she'd finished, as if her head had been attacked with a pair of garden shears. Tomorrow, before she went to look for a job, she'd go to the hairdresser's and have a perm.

The plaits themselves looked pathetic now they were no longer part of her. Shivering, Ruth put them out of sight in a drawer. They made her think of dismembered limbs.

'The kettle's boiling,' her father called, 'and I've no idea how to make coffee.'

'Coming!'

Ruth took a final glance at herself in the mirror. She could never be the old Ruth Singerman again, and Ruth Hildesheimer no longer existed. From now on, she would be an entirely new person altogether.

She squared her shoulders and went downstairs.

CHAPTER FIVE

Tony Costello had found a kitten, pure white with a black patch over one eye and three black paws. It came crawling out of the wreckage of a bombed house one Saturday morning when Tony was out searching for shrapnel—the jagged metal remnants of bombs. His mam complained bitterly about having such horrible reminders of the war on the sideboard as if they were ornaments, but Tony was proud of his collection and the bigger the pieces the better as far as he was concerned. One day, he might have enough to build a bomb of his own.

The kitten came tripping purposefully over the rubble towards Tony, mewing loudly as if it recognised a friend.

'Can I keep him, *please*, Mam?' he pleaded when he took it home. He'd die if she said no.

'Oh, I suppose so,' she said reluctantly. 'But you'll have to see to it yourself. I've enough to do without having a cat to look after on top of everything else.'

'It's not a cat, it's only a kitten.'

'In case you haven't noticed, kittens turn into cats, just like little boys turn into men.' She poured milk into an old saucer and as they watched the kitten lap up the drink greedily, Eileen ruffled her son's fine blond hair. She found it hard to refuse him anything nowadays. Although he appeared quite happy, she felt she'd let him down as badly as she had Nick. 'What are you going to call him?'

'Snowy?' he suggested after an earnest think.

'That's nice. There's an old shoebox in the

washhouse along with the waste paper. If you crumple a bit of newspaper inside, it'll do for a bed.'

'Ta, Mam,' Tony said blissfully. 'I suppose I'd better make him a gas mask.'

Eileen grinned. 'Aren't you the clever clogs! Anything to keep you busy. Now, get from under me feet, else I'll never get this pie done before your dad's home for his dinner.'

Tony trotted away contentedly clutching the kitten and Eileen rolled a circle of pastry out and placed it carefully on a plate which contained a mixture of stewing steak and potatoes, fluting the edges with a knife. She marked off the section containing most of the meat for Tony.

After putting the pie in the oven, she collected the remaining pieces of pastry for a jam turnover. It would do for tomorrow's pudding with custard. In previous days, the turnover would have been eaten for supper or cut in slices for anyone who might drop in for a cup of tea, but nowadays you couldn't be as generous with your food as you used to be, tea in particular. Two ounces a week for each person wasn't nearly enough, though it was more than anyone's life was worth to let Sheila hear you complain, not with so many merchant seamen losing their lives in the effort to keep the country's belly full—well, half full!

Francis often brought home little treats which she suspected were black market. Last week, for instance, he'd turned up with a lovely piece of ham for Sunday dinner which had lasted through to Tuesday sliced cold. Eileen felt uneasy about getting more than her fair share of rations. She would far sooner live on the same amount of food as the rest of the street—not counting the Kellys, next door, who ran a thriving black market business—but it was awfully difficult to turn down half a dozen eggs or a couple of pork chops when they were put in front of you. She never mentioned the gifts to her dad. Jack Doyle would do his nut if he thought any of his family were eating food that hadn't been acquired completely above board. Eileen salved her conscience a little by giving a lot of stuff to Sheila; five of the eggs had gone her sister's way, and Tony had the sixth.

She wondered, it being Saturday and Francis's half day, what sort of present he would bring? After being home for nearly two months and back at work for the best part of that time, it had become a sort of ritual; he always turned up with sherry or a box of chocolates. Once, he'd brought a pair of silk stockings, though the intimacy of the gift made her feel uncomfortable and she'd given them away.

Sheila was becoming increasingly impatient, accusing her of being too nice to Francis. 'Before you know it, everything will be back to normal and Nick might never have existed.'

'But what else can I do?' Eileen asked helplessly. 'We're living under the same roof together. If he's nice to me, it's awful hard not to be nice back.'

It was relentless, the charm, the presents, the way he offered to do things around the house when she was at work—the other day he'd distempered the back kitchen a lovely duck-egg blue. Now he was talking about using his accumulated wages to have a bath put in the wash-house, which would save fetching the tin tub indoors and bathing in front of the fire.

'What do you think, princess? Let me know when you've made up your mind and I'll get someone in to do it.'

What else could she say, but, 'Yes, please, Francis?' A proper bath seemed the very ultimate of luxury to Eileen; imagine not having to hump in pail after pail of water from the back kitchen!

Mind you, he'd always liked the house to be smart so he could show off when people came round on Corporation business. Number 16 was one of the few houses in the street to have electricity, and Eileen had a proper stove in the back kitchen to cook on—there was a green tiled fireplace in the living room where the old range used to be. Francis could always work miracles. Even in wartime, she marvelled, he was able to find a plumber and a new bath, though it would probably be one of the Corpy workmen doing the job as a foreigner.

She sighed and cursed herself for being so weak-willed and easily influenced. It was ironic to think that Sheila and her dad were able to resist her husband's charm offensive, and even Tony seemed wary of his dad, yet she, the chief victim, was gradually being drawn back under his spell.

The other day a letter had come from the solicitor dealing with the divorce, wondering why he hadn't heard from her. She took the letter into work and showed it to Miss Thomas.

'I've no idea what to do,' she confessed.

Miss Thomas didn't answer for a while. Eventually, she shook her head. 'I don't know how to advise you, Eileen. Is it definitely all over with Nick?'

Eileen winced. 'It seems like it,' she muttered.

'But you still love him? I can tell by your face.'

'I'll love Nick all my life, but it's nowt to do with him in a way,' Eileen said. 'I'd made up me mind about the divorce long before things got serious between me and Nick, but Francis is all sweetness and light. He can't do enough for me. He even sends his white shirts to the laundry to save on the washing. Once or twice, I've found meself calling him "luv". I'd feel dead mean walking out. Anyroad, where would I go?'

'Oh, Eileen! You're in a right old mess.'

'I am that,' Eileen said ruefully. 'Y'know, when I'm on the afternoon shift, it's nice to go home and find the cocoa made. He asks how the day went, all concerned like, and we end up having quite a pleasant little chat.'

Miss Thomas leaned forward, her chin cupped in her hands. 'You know, I'd very much like to meet Francis Costello. He sounds a remarkable man.'

'What do you mean?'

'Since I came to work here, one of my most vivid memories is being called to the First Aid Room by Sister Kean. Apparently, you'd fainted at your machine and when she undid your blouse, your neck was red raw and bruised.' She gave a wry smile. 'You wouldn't tell me what had happened, but subsequently I learnt your husband had tried to kill you the day before, the same husband with whom you are now having pleasant little chats!'

'Jaysus!' Eileen groaned. 'You must think I'm dead stupid.'

'Of course I don't,' Miss Thomas said quickly. 'I probably understand more than most women would.' Miss Thomas had walked out of her marriage for the sake of her sanity, with no

92

alternative but to leave her three daughters behind. 'My own husband behaved abominably, but on the rare occasions he treated me like a human being, I felt supremely grateful even though I knew it wouldn't last. Do you think it will last with Francis?'

'I don't know. Sometimes, I wonder if the accident has changed him for the better. Other times, I think he's just putting it on, the way he did when we were courting.'

'But even if it's the latter, it's hard to resist, isn't it?'

Eileen nodded fervently. 'Awful hard! I've got meself into a terrible muddle.'

Miss Thomas stared down at the solicitor's letter. 'What I think you should do,' she said slowly, 'is ask yourself this question: if Francis stays the way he is, if he never returns to being the person he was before, do you want to spend the rest of your life with him?'

Eileen's smooth cream brow creased into a frown. 'I never think about the future,' she confessed. 'At the moment, I just treat each day as it comes, what with the raids and losing Nick. All I want is for the war to stop and the killing to end.'

'And when that happens, where does Francis fit in?'

'Nowhere,' Eileen said simply.

'In that case,' Miss Thomas said crisply, 'I think you should reply to this letter by saying you still wish to proceed, but would like matters held in abeyance for the moment.'

'Would you mind writing that down?'

As Miss Thomas began to scribble on a notepad, she said, 'You're a softhearted person, Eileen, and probably feeling very vulnerable at the moment, but I think in a few weeks or months your head will clear and, who knows, you might see Francis for what he really is. He probably hasn't changed at all.'

'That's what I keep telling meself when I'm at work. Once I get home, I don't know what to think.'

Miss Thomas ripped the sheet out of her pad and handed it to Eileen along with the letter. 'Continue to treat each day as it comes, my dear. I think that's what we're all doing at the moment.' She smiled sadly. 'After all, none of us can be sure if we or our loved ones will be alive by tomorrow.'

Which was only too true, thought Eileen, as she began to scrub the rolling pin. Only the other day, the Harrisons, who ran the coalyard at the end of the street, had learnt another of their grandsons had died in the fighting in North Africa, and a girl she'd gone to school with had lost her husband at sea.

'Snowy doesn't want a gas mask,' Tony said disappointedly, as he came in from the yard carrying a shoebox and a recalcitrant kitten struggling to get a brown paper bag off its head.

'I'm not surprised, poor little thing! Perhaps a gas mask isn't such a good idea, you're suffocating him. He'll go back to the bomb site where he came from if you don't leave him alone.'

'I'll take him over to me Auntie Sheila's to show Dominic.'

'No!' Eileen said sharply. 'Let Snowy be for a while. He's probably tired. Anyroad, your dinner'll be ready in a minute.'

'Can I just go and *tell* Dominic, then?'

'All right, but don't be long.'

Tony raced out of the back way. Eileen put the shoebox in front of the fire and placed the kitten inside. The tiny furry body was no heavier than a feather. 'Now, you go to sleep,' she said sternly. 'I bet you've been through a lot recently, but you've found a good home so don't blot your copybook by making a nuisance of yourself straight away.'

Snowy promptly tipped the box on its side and began to play with a scrap of paper. Eileen sat on the floor and picked him up. She placed him on her chest, where he stared at her fixedly with huge blue eyes.

'You're a pretty little thing for a feller,' she told him. For the next ten minutes she played with the kitten, forgetting all about the housework which still had to be done. A key sounded in the front door and she scrambled guiltily to her feet.

'You're a terrible time waster, Snowy,' she whispered.

There were voices in the hall. Francis had brought someone home. Eileen's face fell when a young man with heavily brilliantined blond hair and a fresh cherubic face entered the room. Rodney Smith was a rent collector with Bootle Corporation and Eileen had always loathed his smarmy, ingratiating manner. It was with Rodney that Francis had gone drinking to some club or other in Liverpool every Saturday night, Francis, at least, returning dead drunk and completely unbearable. She'd rather hoped the friendship had died the death once Francis was home again. But it seemed it hadn't!

Francis came in beaming and carrying a bunch of magnificent bronze chrysanthemums which he

95

handed to her with a flourish. He'd had his glass eye for several weeks and you'd never know it wasn't real except when he looked sideways and only one eye moved.

'They're lovely, Francis,' she murmured dutifully. 'Thank you very much.'

'Thought they'd brighten the place up a bit, like,' he said. 'I met Rodney on the way home. There's no need to make us a cup of tea. We'll go in the parlour in a minute for a glass of Johnny Walker and a chat about old times.'

'How are you, Eileen?' Rodney asked in his squeaky voice that never seemed to have broken, despite the fact he was well into his twenties.

'Fine,' she answered briefly. 'I thought you'd have been called up by now.'

'I failed me medical. It appears I've got pigeon toes.'

'He's not A1,' her husband said jocularly. 'Not like me.'

'That's a shame.'

Francis suddenly snarled, 'What the hell's this?' He was staring down at Snowy, who'd begun to attack the laces on his shoes. He moved his foot out of the way irritably.

'Our Tony found him on a bomb site,' Eileen explained. 'He's called Snowy.'

'You know I don't like cats.' His handsome sallow face twisted into a scowl. It was the first time she'd seen him scowl since he'd come back, and she wondered if Rodney Smith wasn't already having a bad influence.

'I didn't, actually, but I'm afraid he's here to stay, Francis,' she said firmly. 'I've already promised Tony.'

96

'Have you now!' He sounded more than a little annoyed.

She took the flowers into the back kitchen and began to hunt for a vase. There were times when she almost wished Francis would do something or say something which would disgrace him forever in her eyes and she would no longer be in this peculiar state of limbo, not knowing whether she still detested him or not. Perhaps Snowy would be the catalyst which would push him over the edge and give her an excuse to end the marriage once and for all.

On the other hand, perhaps not. When she went into the living room with the flowers in a vase, Francis had recovered his good humour completely, and both he and Rodney were throwing balls of paper for the kitten. There was no way of knowing whether Francis was doing it to impress her, or had Snowy now captured the hearts of the entire family?

'He's quite a nice little thing,' Francis said. 'I suppose he might have been put down if someone else had found him. So, how's your day been, princess?'

'Busy.' Saturdays were always busy, trying to catch up on the work there hadn't been time to do all week.

'A woman's work is never done, eh?' Rodney said with a smarmy smile. Eileen ignored him.

'The plumber's coming Monday with the bath,' Francis said. 'Rodney's offered to arrange it for us.'

'What time? I'm on mornings.'

'In that case, I'll ask one of the neighbours to let him in. I'll sort the washhouse out tomorrow and give the walls a lick of distemper. There's plenty

97

left of that blue I did the kitchen with.'

'Thank you, Francis.'

'Don't thank me, princess. I'm doing it for all the family. By the way, I've got another present for you.' He took an envelope out of his pocket. 'There's a dinner dance at the Blundellsands Hotel on Christmas Eve. I've bought us two tickets.'

'Oh, I don't know about that!' she said quickly. She had no wish to go out with him socially. 'I wouldn't like to leave Tony, not on Christmas Eve,' she added by way of excuse.

'Tony can go to your Sheila's, and we needn't stay late,' he said coaxingly. 'We can be home by midnight.'

'But what if there's a raid?'

'Everyone thinks the raids'll be over by Christmas. We won the Battle of Britain, didn't we? According to the papers, we've nearly turned the corner.'

'That's right,' Rodney concurred.

'I'm not sure, Francis,' Eileen said hesitantly. Yet it seemed churlish to refuse when he was doing his damnedest to please her.

'Come on, princess. Buy yourself a new frock, or get Brenda Mahon to make you something really posh. Get your hair done! It'll be a nice change. After all, you work really hard all week. It's about time you had a bit of enjoyment out of life.'

Oh, he knew how to get round her, did Francis Costello! He was smiling at her with genuine warmth, as if making her happy was more important to him than anything else in the world.

'All right,' she said grudgingly, though wished she could take the words back when Rodney Smith said, 'I've got tickets for me and me mam. That

98

means we can all go together.'

She dreaded to think what Sheila would say when she found out. On the other hand, it *would* be nice to have a new frock, and she might well ask Brenda Mahon to make it.

Sheila was wrong about one thing, though. The day would never come when it would seem as if Nick had never existed. Eileen thought about him every single day, but it wasn't the wonderful times they'd had together that she remembered—the weekend in London, the night in the cottage before he went away when they'd made love on the grass—it was the last time she'd seen him that she couldn't get out of her mind. It hadn't been her darling Nick sitting on the sofa looking at her with such hard, unsympathetic eyes, but someone else altogether, a man she'd never known. Apparently, she didn't come up to this man's exacting standards. But, Eileen argued to herself, she'd done what was right and proper for *her*. Surely he knew her well enough to realise she had no choice in the matter?

Every time she heard *We'll Meet Again* on the wireless, she switched it off, feeling a mixture of resentment and terrible sadness. If only she hadn't missed the train! She and Tony would be living in the cottage, miles away from Francis Costello, the Irish wizard, who was gradually drawing her back into his sticky, silvery web.

Francis was about to go into the parlour with Rodney. He paused. 'What's the matter, princess?'

'Nothing,' she replied. 'Why did you ask?'

'You just sighed, that's all.'

'I didn't mean to,' Eileen said. 'After all, what's there to sigh about?'

*   *   *

Brenda Mahon's parlour always reminded Eileen of Aladdin's cave. A treadle sewing machine stood in the middle of the room and every surface was covered with great swathes of sometimes quite glorious material. Numerous garments in various stages of completion hung from the picture rail. Boxes of thread, pattern books and several pairs of scissors were jumbled together on the mantelpiece and women's magazines scattered all over the floor. A full-length mirror reflected the colourful chaos, making the room appear bigger and even brighter.

Brenda was a dressmaker who made clothes for some of the wealthiest women in Liverpool. They came from far and wide to be measured and fitted by someone who'd never had so much as a sewing lesson in her life, yet the clothes that emerged from the chaos of her parlour not only fitted perfectly, but they were beautifully made; the seams double stitched, the lining perfect, the collar lying better than anything bought from a shop. Sometimes, little extra individual touches were added, such as a flower made from the same material sewn to the waist, a scalloped neck, an embroidered cuff.

The rates Brenda charged were variable, depending on where the client lived. Those from 'toffy-nosed addresses' paid double what she charged her friends and people from less salubrious places. Even then, she was far cheaper than most dressmakers, but Brenda didn't just sew for money, but for love. She was never happier than when she sat at her machine, treadling away as she made a dance frock for some posh lady from Calderstones, or something out of a piece of leftover material for one of her friends.

Brenda was equally good with knitting needles or a crochet hook, and she'd turned out scarf and glove sets too numerous to count for the Red Cross during the air-raids—she could turn a thumb in the dark.

'That's lovely,' Eileen said when she went into the parlour. A length of maroon panne velvet was being rapidly fed through under the foot of the machine.

'It's for a cloak. I'm going to line it with cream satin.'

'It should look lovely. I expect you're booked up till Christmas.'

'Till next February, actually,' Brenda said through the row of pins she kept conveniently in her mouth. 'But not for me mates. What are you after, Eil?'

'I'm not sure. I just wanted to look through your pattern books.'

'Here's the Simplicity. The Vogue's on the mantelpiece.'

It was something of a mystery how Brenda had acquired the books, because she never bought a pattern, being able to cut the material out by merely looking at the picture. Eileen moved a length of bottle-green taffeta out of the way and began to leaf through the pattern book.

'Is it for a special occasion?' asked Brenda.

'Francis has got tickets for a dinner dance in Blundellsands on Christmas Eve,' Eileen replied, knowing this news would reach her sister before the day was out.

'Xavier and me took the girls to Blundellsands once,' said Brenda. 'I remember there was a tent on the beach.' She cocked her head sideways and said thoughtfully, 'I've fancied making a tent ever since.'

There was a lifesize head-and-shoulders portrait of Xavier Mahon on its own specially crocheted mat on top of the wireless in the other room. He was the handsomest man in Pearl Street, or possibly the whole of Bootle, with exquisite matinee-idol looks. The picture showed him staring romantically into the far distance, his smoky dark eyes brooding, his lips curved in a mysterious smile. The film star impression was slightly marred when you met Xavier in the flesh, because he was short, barely five foot four inches tall, and spoke with a pronounced and rather unattractive nasal twang, as if, people said nastily, he had an ollie stuffed up each perfect nostril.

Xavier was either unaware or unbothered by any criticism of his voice and stature; everyone agreed he was the most conceited man who ever lived and seemed convinced the sun shone out of his own miniature arse.

Brenda openly adored him. If she could have sewn herself a husband, she said frequently in his hearing, he would have turned out looking exactly like the one she already had, which only bolstered Xavier's already massive ego even more. She waited on him hand and foot. Xavier didn't need to strike a match before Brenda had struck it for him. He preened himself in a never-ending variety of Fair Isle and complicated cableknit pullovers, with sleeves and without, which his wife had lovingly made, for Xavier was a dandy, the Beau Brummell of Pearl Street, whose collection of hats—eleven at the last count—was a source of amusement to most people and of envy to a few.

Six months ago, Xavier had been called up and was now garrisoned on a wild, remote island in the Orkneys. Although she missed him, Brenda was already used to his frequent absences, as he used to work for the London, Midland & Scottish Railways as a guard, and often spent nights away.

'Found anything?' Brenda enquired through the pins.

'Not yet.' Eileen realised she was merely enjoying looking at the fashions rather than choosing something for herself. 'Trouble is,' she said, 'I don't know what I want. If I have something dressy, it might be ages before I have the opportunity to wear it again.'

'True,' agreed Brenda, 'but y'know, Eil, nowadays, with so many women going to dances in uniform, not everyone gets dressed up like they used to. You could have something plain, like a costume or a cocktail dress.'

Eileen grinned. 'I can't see meself in a cocktail dress!'

'You know what I mean,' Brenda said placidly. She was the happiest and most contented person Eileen knew and never lost her temper, not even with her most irritating customers who changed their minds after the material had been cut or didn't buy enough for their chosen pattern. Or, even worse, put on weight, or lost it, in between being measured and the final fitting. Her mouselike plainness was perhaps accentuated by the lovely tumbling material she was surrounded with, and her looks were in direct contrast to those of her husband, though everyone agreed that Xavier Mahon wouldn't have wanted a pretty wife. He couldn't have stood the competition.

It was the remainder of the house that reflected Brenda's rather prim and proper self, being as neat as the pins that were so often in her mouth, almost unnaturally so.

'I'd quite like a costume,' Eileen conceded. She eyed the maroon velvet. 'How much a yard would that cost? I wouldn't mind it in blue.'

Brenda pursed her lips, losing several pins. 'Nine and elevenpence, I reckon.'

'Jaysus! Nine and eleven a *yard*!'

'You'd need four yards for a suit, and I charge seventeen and sixpence. That's less than three pounds for a velvet suit. I reckon it'd cost seven guineas or more in George Henry Lee's.'

'I'm not sure, Bren. It's nearly a week's wages.'

'It's up to you, girl.'

'I might go to the Co-op on Monday and take a look at their material.'

'Don't take too long, now,' Brenda warned. 'I've already got a rush on to finish stuff for Christmas.' She finished a seam, cut the thread, and started on another. 'Did you see the King and Queen when they came to Bootle last week?' she asked.

'Nah!' Eileen said dismissively. 'I was at work, anyroad, but you know what me dad's like. According to him, he came out of the womb a republican and he reckons us three kids should feel the same. He'd have a fit if he thought I'd hang about just to get a glimpse of royalty. Did you go?'

'I took the girls,' said Brenda. 'It was an excuse for them to wear their new frocks.' Brenda's daughters, Muriel and Monica, were always

104

identically and impeccably dressed. 'She looked nice, the Queen. Wore a lovely hat tilted on the side of her head and three rows of pearls. The King seemed a pleasant enough chap, though a bit shy. It were good of them, y'know, Eil, to come all the way to Bootle just to see the folks who've been bombed out.'

'Maybe, but it's only what they're paid to do out of our taxes.'

'Your dad'll never be dead while you're alive, Eileen,' Brenda said with a smile. Jack Doyle's position as a socialist, trade unionist and sworn enemy of the establishment, was well known and mainly respected throughout Bootle.

Eileen took the remark for what it was meant to be, a compliment. 'In that case, forget about the velvet. I'd feel uncomfortable wearing something that cost more than some men earn in a week to keep their family. I'll look for something cheaper.'

'It's all the same to me, Eil,' Brenda Mahon said cheerfully. 'It's still seventeen and sixpence, whether it's sacking or gold lamé.'

*   *   *

'Is anyone going down the High Street today?' Carmel screeched. 'If so, I'd like a jar of home-made tomato chutney off that woman by the Post Office.'

'What did you say?' Doris yelled.

Carmel repeated the request at an increased decibel.

'I can't hear you. Say it again.'

'Have you gone deaf or something?' Carmel frowned suspiciously. 'They say too much of the other affects the hearing.'

'I'm not deaf,' Doris grinned. 'It's just that every time you say "tomato chutney", a shower of spit comes out. I just wondered if the louder you shouted, the further it went.'

'Cheeky bugger!' Carmel looked affronted.

It was only then that Eileen remembered she'd left a pound of tomatoes in the cottage, along with a loaf of bread, a tin of salmon and quite a few other groceries. It wouldn't have entered Nick's head to throw the fresh food away. He said he hadn't eaten and almost certainly hadn't noticed it was there.

She decided to forgo her dinner, which was no hardship, as she rarely felt like a full blown meal at ten o'clock in the morning, despite the fact she'd been up since five.

'I'll get you some chutney, Carmel,' she called.

'Ta, luv. You're a dead good sort.'

'Huh!' said Doris scathingly.

Eileen ignored the comment. Although most of the women had taken kindly to her promotion, a few, Doris in particular, resented the position of overseer being given to someone who hadn't worked at Dunnings for as long as they had.

'I wouldn't have wanted to be overseer,' said Carmel in the ensuing row, during which Eileen had been accused by Doris of sucking up to Miss Thomas. 'It would have been no use asking me. I couldn't cope with the responsibility.'

'Me neither,' echoed Theresa. 'Anyroad, if it was the person who'd been here longest, it wouldn't be you, Doris, but Mona Dewar, and I wouldn't want *her* telling me what to do, not in a million years. Mona's a right ould cow.'

'Not only that, you're too young, Doris,' said Lil. 'No one wants to be bossed around by a chit of a girl.'

'Thanks very much!' Doris tossed her head haughtily.

'There's nowt wrong with being a chit of a girl,' Lil said reasonably. 'We've all been chits at one time or another. I think Eileen's got the right . . .' Lil regarded Eileen thoughtfully. 'The right air of authority.'

Eileen began to wish she'd never accepted the promotion as she was scrutinised for the appropriate air of authority by half a dozen pairs of eyes, particularly when Doris said, 'You mean the right creepy-crawly attitude.'

'I don't know what you're talking about, Doris,' she said weakly. 'I've never creeped or crawled to anyone.'

'No! You were forever in Miss Thomas's office sucking up.'

'How can you say that when you weren't there?' Eileen began to lose her temper. 'If you must know, Miss Thomas was sorting out a domestic problem for me.'

'I don't believe you,' Doris said flatly.

'Well, I don't bloody care,' Eileen flared back. 'Now, get on with your work. That batch is supposed to be finished by going home time and you've scarcely started.'

With ill grace, Doris turned back to her machine, and Pauline said, 'I wish you'd shurrup about it, Doris. I don't give a toss who's overseer. As long as I get me wages at the end of the week, that's all I care!' There was a murmur of agreement from the other women.

The job made little difference to Eileen's own work. It merely meant consulting with Alfie, the foreman, at the beginning of the day and getting a schedule of work in hand. Then, as each woman completed a batch of work, it was Eileen who assigned the next job on the list. She was scrupulously fair, unlike Ivy Twyford, the previous overseer, who, everyone suspected, kept the simplest jobs for her friends. As everyone was paid on piece work, a string of complicated work assignments could seriously affect the level of wages received at the end of the week. Gradually the women grew to accept Eileen as overseer and the tension eased. Doris was the only one who continued to make life unpleasant.

As soon as the hooter went, Eileen slipped into her coat and made her way down the High Street to the cottage. It was a glorious day for November, brilliantly sunny and unseasonably warm.

The first thing she noticed was that the windows needed a good clean. She longed to attack them there and then with the new window leather which was in the cupboard under the sink, but there was no time. Inside, the table was still set, ready for tea, and it looked rather ghostly, Eileen thought, with the cutlery and condiments full of dust and the flowers in a bowl in the centre completely dead. She forced herself not to mope and feel sad as she put everything away, though it was hard not to compare the dead, withered flowers which turned to dust when she touched them, with the end of her love affair with Nick.

The tomatoes were in the larder, squashy and full of mould. She put them in an old newspaper to throw away at work, and flung the loaf, which had turned completely green, out to the birds. The remaining groceries, the salmon, a few jellies, tins of custard and gravy powder, she decided to take home, even the butter, which smelt more than a bit off, but it was silly to waste food during a war.

'I think that's it!' she said aloud.

She was about to leave when she noticed the family photograph on the sideboard; her dad looking like a martinet with his hand on her dead mam's shoulder, Sean a mere baby, the girls standing one each side, Sheila coyly gazing at the camera, and Eileen looking rather awkward. There were other things; little ornaments people had given her for birthdays or Christmas, including a set of lace doilies Brenda Mahon had made. Eileen wasn't quite sure what prompted her to leave everything where it was. Maybe it was because doing otherwise meant there would be no reason for her to visit the cottage again.

On the way back, she almost forgot Carmel's chutney, and had to return to the house by the Post Office, where she bought a jar for herself at the same time. Worried she'd be late, she began to hurry towards Dunnings, but as she approached the factory, realised there was plenty of time. The men who usually went for a drink in the pub across the road were still sitting on the bridge which passed over the narrow stream. She could hear the occasional wolf whistle, which meant the girls must have come outside for a breath of fresh air on such a lovely day.

When she arrived at the bridge, she saw them sitting on the path, their backs against the factory wall. Most were having a last minute smoke before the hooter went. Doris, hands outstretched, was wiggling her fingers wildly in the air—she'd probably been painting her nails with that hideous purple polish she used. All the women were staring as if fascinated at something in the sky and when Eileen followed their gaze, she saw a plane making acrobatic turns in the far distance. It looked no bigger than a fly as it looped and twisted. There was a lazy, idle air about it, as if the pilot had merely gone up to play. If you listened hard, you could just about hear its distant drone.

The plane began to approach, growing larger and blacker by the second, and the men on the bridge started to wave and cheer.

'Come on, mate!'

'It's a Battle of Britain pilot, I reckon.'

The plane was almost upon them by the time the German crosses on the wings and tail could be seen, and the pilot, in his leather helmet and goggles, was clearly visible. As it zoomed downwards, little spurts of fire came from underneath the cockpit, accompanied by a sharp repetitive noise, a rat-tat-tat.

No one moved, no one spoke. The only sound to be heard was the noise of the engine as the plane appeared dead set on crashing into the wall where the girls sat. Then, at the very last minute, with a deafening roar it veered sharply upwards and completely vanished out of sight.

It was only then that everyone emerged from their state of frozen shock.

'He's shot the women! He's shot the fucking women!' a man yelled.

Eileen dropped her bag and scrambled down the bank.

The girls were sitting transfixed against the wall,

open mouthed, but very much alive. About two feet or three feet above them, a neat row of bullet holes had been chipped out of the brick wall.

'He missed!' screamed Doris. She stood up and shook her fist at the sky. 'I caught that bleedin' Jerry's eye, and I *willed* the bugger to miss.'

'Oh, Doris!' Eileen flung her arms around the defiant girl. 'You're so *brave!*'

Doris said hoarsely, 'No, I ain't, Eil. I was bloody terrified.'

Stunned members of management began to emerge from the side door of the factory, and the shaken women were ushered inside. The canteen was hurriedly re-opened to provide cups of tea.

'If anyone wants to go home, I'm quite happy to take them,' Miss Thomas called.

But no one went home. In less than half an hour, everyone was back at work, though the narrow escape was the only topic of conversation for the rest of the shift. No one could be quite sure if the German pilot had meant to kill them or had deliberately missed.

'I suppose there's one or two decent Jerries about,' reckoned Theresa. 'Maybe he just wanted to give us a fright.'

'Well, he succeeded,' Carmel said with a leer. 'I nearly shit me keks, I can tell you.'

'I think it was dead exciting,' said Doris boastfully. 'I can't wait to tell me mam. If I had a choice, I'd sooner be shot at than not shot at. It makes me feel sort of special.'

'You deserve a medal, the lot o'yis,' Eileen told them proudly.

One good thing to come out of the incident was that from that day on, Doris stopped making catty

111

comments about Eileen's promotion. Indeed, the women grew closer than they'd ever been before.

CHAPTER SIX

The screams coming from next door had become so ferocious that Ruth Singerman, lying in bed with no alternative but to listen—no-one within earshot could possibly sleep through such a noise—began to worry for Ellis Evans' sanity. It sounded as if the woman was rowing with herself in Welsh. Her voice was the only one that could be heard, a terrible, endless, piercing shriek. If Dai was at the receiving end of the diatribe, he was making no attempt to answer back. The row, if that's what it was, had been going on for nearly an hour.

There was a raid in progress and Ruth could hear planes overhead and the occasional screech of a bomb to vie with Ellis, followed by an explosion and the terrified whinny of the horse in the coalyard opposite. Both she and her father preferred to ignore the raids, or at least pretend to ignore them, and remained in bed if they'd already gone up by the time the warning siren sounded.

'If I'm going to die, I'd prefer to die in comfort,' Jacob chuckled, though he kept his underwear on. 'So I can get dressed quickly in case of an emergency.'

Ruth found it astonishing how quickly the air-raids seemed to have become part of everyday existence. So much so, it was the nights there was no raid at all that were remarked on.

'See bloody Hitler had other things to do with

himself,' people would say the morning after they'd had an uninterrupted night's sleep.

Even when folks they knew were killed, everyone seemed to take the loss of a neighbour or a friend in their stride. 'What else can they do?' Jacob shrugged when Ruth remarked on this phenomenon. 'Run around in a panic screaming their heads off like Ellis? People are very brave under the most trying of circumstances. Londoners are having it far worse than us, but according to the papers, they're taking it like the proverbial bricks.'

Ellis!

Ruth pulled the bedclothes over her head to shut out the sounds, but it was useless. The screaming persisted and the bedclothes were no help. She wondered if there was something genuinely wrong. Perhaps the entire family were being murdered? If so, Ellis had cried wolf for too long, because no-one in Pearl Street seemed interested.

Another bomb came screeching earthwards and Ruth felt the hairs rise on her neck, though according to Jacob, 'If you can hear the bomb coming, it means it's not meant for you.' Perhaps he was right, because the subsequent explosion sounded several streets away. It was strange how the urge to stay alive persisted, no matter how many times you tried to convince yourself that life was no longer worth living. Even stranger was the fact she felt a sense of immediate danger much more strongly than during the two years spent hidden in Gertrude's house. In fact, there she'd actually felt quite safe, but in Bootle the bombs weren't searching for any particular victim; death and destruction was applied quite randomly. Any target, rich or poor, Jew or Gentile, would do.

Ruth decided to go down and make a cup of tea. She'd never fall asleep until the row next door—and the raid—was over.

The living room was warm and the remains of the fire still glowed in the grate. Ruth raked the coals into life, filled the kettle and put it on the hob to boil. She didn't bother lighting the gas mantle. The coals gave off sufficient light to see by and the room seemed cosier that way. Everywhere looked quite different from when she'd first come home; there were new curtains on the window which Jacob had made himself, a proper mat in front of the fire to replace the tattered rag rug, new tablecloths. Ruth got surprising satisfaction out of making life more comfortable for her father. It made up for not loving him as much as she should.

'You spoil me,' he protested when she came in laden with groceries, including the ginger marmalade and shortbread biscuits which she remembered were his favourites.

'It's only our rations, Dad,' she told him.

'But I wish you didn't have to work.' He continued to fret, as if she was above work, too genteel to earn an honest crust.

'I love it, Dad, honestly.'

Which was true, in a way. Playing the piano had always been her favourite occupation, and now she was being paid for doing what she liked best. Soon she would have saved enough to redeem the musical box from the pawnshop.

She had decided not to apply for a job in Eileen Costello's factory, although the pay was good and, apparently, the work not too tiring once you got used to it. Ruth wanted to work in a place where no one knew anything of her history, a place where

114

she was a total stranger, because people might feel sorry for her and pity was something she couldn't have stood—or prejudice; after all, Ruth been married to an Austrian, the country that had spawned the monster, Hitler. Perhaps Eileen would have kept quiet, but *she* would have known.

It had been for that reason, to get away from people who knew her background, that weeks ago Ruth had caught the train to Liverpool city centre in search of work.

Liverpool had scarcely changed since she last saw it. The sights she loved were still there, solid and eternal; St George's Hall, Lime Street Station, the Walker Art Gallery, though here and there a bomb-scarred shop, the burnt out remains of a building, an ugly heap of debris, reminded her that the world had changed, if not the city.

Ruth wandered around the shops and bought two pairs of stockings, a lipstick and a box of Ponds face powder out of the money from the musical box. She justified the extravagance by telling herself she'd soon be earning money of her own.

'You're lucky,' said the girl on the cosmetics counter in Lewis's department store. 'We've just had a delivery.'

'Is powder difficult to get? I didn't realise.'

'All make-up's difficult to get.' The girl laughed. 'Where have you been? On the moon, or something?'

'It's a long time since I bought any,' Ruth muttered. Despite everything, she was still concerned with how she looked, though in a cold, detached sort of way, because at the back of her mind there was always the image of Benjy's body swinging in the stairwell and an aching void left by her lost children. For instance, she was quite pleased with her hair. Instead of a perm, only a trim was needed to tidy up the ends. Once washed, her hair had turned quite wavy.

'You were curly as a baby,' Jacob said when she returned from the hairdresser's. He'd been shocked to the core when she came downstairs that morning minus her long auburn plaits. 'I must admit it looks very nice. Modern, like that film star, what's her name—Laraine Day.'

Ruth was amused to find he went to the pictures nearly every week, his single indulgence.

'It's only threepence at the front. I'd sooner go without a meal than miss the pictures.'

He knew the names of all the stars and enthused over Fred Astaire and Ginger Rogers, Myrna Loy and William Powell, his favourites. Perhaps, thought Ruth, he'd like to see *Gone With The Wind*, which she'd noticed was showing at the Odeon. They could go together as a special treat one Saturday. Presuming she got a job, of course, which wasn't likely if she merely wandered around buying stockings and make-up; spending money rather than finding a way of earning it. She was, she confessed to herself, at a loss where to look.

A familiar shop came within view when she turned the corner at the bottom of Ranelagh Street: Cranes in Hanover Street, where she used to buy most of her music.

Ruth hurried across the road, drawn somewhat inexplicably by the sight of a white baby grand piano in the window. There were no customers inside and no sign of an assistant when she entered, though plenty more pianos, all upright. The sight of so many brought back the urge to play. She hadn't played a piano since the Hun took the Steinway. There'd been a reluctance to use the one at home once her father told her it was badly out of tune. Remembering how he'd cared for his beloved piano, it would have made her feel even more guilty for neglecting him when she found the old mellow velvet notes off key. She'd never realised how poor he was. In fact, it was only over the last two years at Gertrude's that she'd given him much thought.

The baby grand's lid was propped open and there was music for a collection of Chopin waltzes on the stand, just waiting to be played. Unable to resist, Ruth sat down and opened the music. She played hesitantly at first, then with growing confidence. Her fingers flew over the keys. Chopin was glorious!

She was approaching the end of the second page and was preparing to turn the music over, when a wizened liver spotted hand reached out from behind and turned the sheet for her. Without pausing, Ruth played on. The sheet was turned again and again, until she finished with a flourish and looked up.

A very old lady, well into her eighties, was standing directly behind. She wore a black ankle-length dress and several rows of jet beads, and her deeply lined face was as liver-spotted as her hands. Her blue eyes belied her age, bright and full of life.

'That was beautiful.' She nodded approvingly. 'You're Ruth Singerman, aren't you? I recognised you straight away, more from the way you sit, than anything. Your back is incredibly arched when you play.'

'You recognised me?' gasped Ruth. The

woman's rather clipped, well modulated voice was as youthful as her eyes.

'You gave two concerts at Crane Hall. I recall them distinctly, even though it must be more than twenty years ago. Everyone thought you would be a great pianist one day, but . . .' She paused.

Ruth raised her eyebrows. 'But not you?'

'No, if you don't mind my saying. You were brilliant, but not brilliant enough.'

'I haven't got the span.' Ruth spread her hands. 'See? They're not big enough.'

The old lady nodded. 'Even so, you could have made a living giving concerts to the masses, the ones who can't recognise brilliance from genius. What happened?'

Ruth shrugged. She rather liked the woman's blunt candour. 'I got married and had a family. That seemed a better thing to do than earn my living as a second-rate pianist—not that I felt I was making a choice at the time.'

'You did the right thing,' the woman said approvingly.

'Do you play?' asked Ruth.

'Not very well. I suppose you could say I was adequate.'

'This is a beautiful instrument!' Ruth ran the back of her hand along the milky-white keys. 'It has the tone of a harp.'

The old lady smiled for the first time. 'I don't suppose I can persuade you to buy it?'

'I couldn't afford the music, let alone the piano!' Ruth got to her feet, suddenly embarrassed. 'What a terrible nerve, walking in off the street and taking over your most expensive piano! I'm so sorry.'

'Please don't apologise!' The old lady squeezed

Ruth's hand. 'I enjoyed the Chopin immensely.'

'I don't suppose you need staff?' Ruth said hopefully. 'That's what I'm doing in town, looking for work, but I've no idea where to start.'

'The *Echo*'s the best place, dear. There's a whole list of vacancies every day. We're fully staffed, I'm afraid. Some of our assistants were called up, which is why I'm here part-time, along with one or two others who retired many years ago.'

'I'll buy a paper later on.' Ruth glanced around the showroom, grateful for the woman's good manners or lack of curiosity in not demanding a detailed explanation of why she was in need of work. 'It's just that selling pianos is the thing I'd most like to do.'

'*Playing* would be better, surely?'

'Of course it would! But I need to earn some money, and who will pay me to do that?'

The blue eyes twinkled. 'Reece's Ballroom will, my dear,' the woman said swiftly. 'They need a pianist for their Afternoon Tea Dances. Wednesday to Saturday, three o'clock until five thirty, with a fifteen minute interval at a quarter past four. The pay is ten shillings a session and the tips are good. Most customers throw a threepenny bit or a sixpence in the saucer by the door on their way out.'

'How on earth do you know all this?' Ruth asked, amazed.

'Because I'm the current pianist! I was talked into doing it as a favour. I can't *wait* to get away!' The old lady clasped her hands together fervently as if she was about to pray. 'People can't dance to classical music, and I detest these modern composers: Irving Berlin, Jerome Kern, Cole

119

Porter—their songs will never stand the test of time. In another few years, no one will have heard of them.'

'I don't know about that! *Night and Day* is quite beautiful, and I couldn't get *They'll Never Believe Me* out of my head when I first heard it. *There's A Small Hotel* was . . .' Ruth paused.

'Was what?'

'My daughter's favourite,' Ruth said abruptly.

'Well, my dear, the job's there waiting if you want it. Do you?'

'Yes, I do,' Ruth said without hesitation.

'Wonderful! What day is today?'

'Tuesday.'

'Then I shall write a note of introduction which you can take with you tomorrow.' Her sigh of enormous relief was followed by a hearty chuckle. 'I expect Reece's will be glad to see the back of Edith Hollingsworth. It's obvious to everyone I don't enjoy what I do, and they'll be pleased to have someone young and attractive for a change. I've joined the Women's Voluntary Services, so I've far more important things to do with my afternoons whilst there's a war on. I don't need the money as you so obviously do.'

'You remind me of my father. He's in his eighties, yet still full of life.'

Ruth felt uncomfortable when the woman looked slightly annoyed. 'People are always surprised if the older generation don't take to their beds and prepare to die once they're past sixty. You are only as old as you feel, and I feel like a young woman—most of the time.'

'I'm sorry,' Ruth murmured.

'No matter.' The blue eyes regarded her

searchingly. 'You feel very old, don't you, Ruth Singerman?'

'Very old,' Ruth said slowly. 'Very, very old.' She began to pick out *There's A Small Hotel* with her right hand, and gradually extemporised the bass with her left. 'Have you got a compendium of modern songs? I don't know all that many.'

'I thought you didn't have enough money for music?' The old lady said with a smile.

'I was going to treat myself to a coffee in the Kardomah if I found a job. I'll go without.'

*   *   *

Armed with the note from Edith Hollingsworth, and dressed in one of her old frocks which Brenda Mahon had quickly stripped of frills and shortened, altering the high neck to a more fashionable V, Ruth turned up at Reece's, just across the road from Cranes, the following day.

She wasn't at all surprised to be met with indignation by the manageress.

'But we don't know anything about you! Oh, that Edith Hollingsworth is an arrogant woman! To think she can just give the job up without a moment's notice and send a complete stranger along in her place.'

'Would you like me to audition?' Ruth asked humbly.

'What good would that do?' the woman said in high dudgeon. 'People will be arriving in fifteen minutes.'

'In that case, do you mind if I put in a spot of practice?'

'Practice? You need to practice?'

121

Ruth had practised for hours the night before, much to her father's delight, though he was uneasy about the job. 'It seems a bit degrading, love, getting tips off people,' he said doubtfully.

'I meant I'd like to see what your piano is like,' Ruth explained, entirely sympathetic to the woman's anger.

'My piano is every bit as good as anything they've got in Cranes,' the manageress said, even more indignant.

'I'd just like to get used to it—that's if you want me to play. I perfectly understand if you prefer to cancel this afternoon's dance.' She prayed the suggestion would be rejected. It was.

'I can't possibly cancel this afternoon's dance,' the woman said scathingly. 'You'll just have to do for today. At least you look a bit more pleasant than that Edith. Bloody old bat, you'd think she was playing for a funeral, not a dance where people have come to enjoy themselves.'

The dancers were mainly middle-aged and middle-class, though there were several servicemen who looked lost without any young women to partner them.

Ruth started off feeling more nervous than she'd done as a child when taking an exam, but she soon relaxed and the piano became an extension of herself. She'd never minded what sort of music she played; Beethoven and Bach might well be far superior composers to Berlin and Porter, but in the end, no matter who wrote it, it was merely a combination of notes on a keyboard, and she had always played everything to the furthest extent of her talent.

She put everything she had into the last waltz, *I'll*

Be Seeing You, and whispered underneath her breath, 'Will I; will I, be seeing you, my dear Simon, my darling Leah?'

'Here's your tips. You've got twice as much as that old bat Edith.'

Ruth came to. She was still sitting at the piano, miles away. Everyone had gone and she hadn't noticed. The manageress was offering her a plateful of threepenny bits and sixpences. Amongst them, Ruth noticed several shillings.

'Thank you.' Her heart lifted. She'd brought the ration books, just in case, so she could buy groceries on the way home and order some more coal.

'You can stop for the interval, you know,' the manageress was saying. 'You played right through.'

'I didn't want to stop, though I will if you'd prefer.'

'Oh, no!' the woman said with alacrity. 'Whatever it was, the customers really loved it.'

'It was Brahms' Lullaby.'

'Well, I'll see you the same time tomorrow.'

Ruth had a job!

*   *   *

The kettle boiled, a high-pitched whine which briefly drowned the screams still coming from next door. Surely, Ruth thought impatiently as she made the tea, the woman would have to stop sometime? She was amazed she hadn't lost her voice by now.

'You filthy whore! You dirty, filthy little whore!'

Ellis spoke—yelled—in English for the first time. So, it was one of the girls in receipt of this epic tongue-lashing! Almost certainly Dilys, a

123

pathetic spotted pudding of a girl, as quiet as her mother was voluble.

Poor kid! Ruth had never shouted at her children, though there'd been plenty of rows with Benjy over the last few years. She felt a surge of anger against Ellis. The woman was lucky to *have* her children. She was abusing her position as a mother, screeching at poor Dilys like a mad woman.

Anger rising, Ruth went into the parlour and lifted the lid of the piano. It had been tuned and cleaned and sounded as mellow and velvety as it had ever done. She pressed her feet down on both pedals, and began to play *Alexander's Rag Time Band* as loudly as she could.

Three things happened in quick succession: the All Clear sounded, Ellis stopped screaming, and a door slammed with such force in the neighbouring house it must have shaken the entire street.

'What's going on?' Her father came in, a coat over his pyjamas, looking more intrigued than anything. He loved drama. Any unusual happening was apt to cause him much enjoyment. He'd gone to bed in exceptionally high spirits, having beaten Tony Costello at Monopoly for the first time in weeks.

'I was merely trying to remind Ellis there are people living next door. It seems to have worked.'

'That was a row to end all rows. I wish I could speak Welsh. I would have loved to have known what it was all about.'

Ruth closed the piano lid. 'Would you like some tea, Dad? I've just made a pot.'

'A midnight feast!' He did a little jig. 'I'd love a cup.'

As they went into the living room, he said blissfully, 'Oh, it's lovely having the house so warm. I think I'll have a short bread biscuit with my tea, that would be luxury indeed!'

Such little things seemed to please him out of all proportion, thought Ruth sadly.

They sat drinking their tea in the dark, the room lit only by the glowing embers of coal in the grate. 'This is nice,' Jacob sighed contentedly.

Ruth didn't answer.

'I'm sorry, love.' His moods could rise and plummet within the space of seconds. Suddenly, he sounded close to tears.

'What for, Dad?' Ruth asked, mystified.

He beat his brow dramatically. 'Ah! I am such a selfish old man. Here I am, so happy you are home, flaunting my happiness, and forgetting entirely that you can't possibly be as delighted to be with me as I am with you.'

'That's silly, Dad. It's lovely being home.' Which was true, in a sort of way. Her main worry when she was in hiding was what would happen to Gertrude if the Germans discovered her sheltering a Jew. This was the reason she'd risked her life to escape, but deep down inside she felt an urgent need to be with her father. She'd been too busy even to think about him over the years, but suddenly she'd become aware he was the only family she had left.

'But you're not happy!'

It was more a statement than a question, but Ruth recognised a question did indeed lurk behind the apparently innocent remark. He was probing. He wanted to know what had happened to Benjy and the children. Perhaps this was the time to tell him, in the dark where he could scarcely see her

125

face, nor she his. He had to know some time.

'Benjy's dead,' she said softly.

There was a long silence.

'Oh, my dear!' his old voice quavered eventually.

'He killed himself,' Ruth went on, 'because he couldn't stand what the Germans were doing. Even worse, what they were likely to do in the future. They put us Jews out to work like slaves, Dad; cleaning the streets, scrubbing the steps of the public buildings. The soldiers laughed and kicked us. I could stand the humiliation, but not Benjy.'

'And your children, Simon and Leah, my grand-children?'

Ruth could scarcely hear, his voice was no more than a whisper. 'I've no idea whether they are dead or alive,' she said hopelessly. 'They planned to escape through Switzerland and France to Spain, then to America. I've had no word since, but then, how could I? They are as ignorant of my fate as I am of theirs.'

'That is a long journey to make,' Jacob said gravely. 'But why America?'

'I don't know, Dad.' Incredibly, she actually managed a smile in the dark. 'Perhaps, like you, they'd seen too many pictures!'

She'd made the first part of the journey herself two years later, sold everything she still possessed, her wedding and engagement rings, every scrap of jewellery. Together with Gertrude's life savings, there'd been enough to buy forged papers and bribe someone to drive her to Spain. No, not quite enough; the 'someone', an acquaintance of Gertrude's husband, had wanted more than money once they'd set off, a typical Austrian couple going on holiday. Ruth, past caring, made no objection. It

126

would have been dangerous to do otherwise. The man held her fate in his fat little hands. She let him have his way, it meant nothing.

She gave her father the bare bones of her own escape, leaving out the part that would have upset him.

'I arrived in Barcelona,' she concluded. 'Gertrude had discovered, God knows how, a synagogue there acted as a kind of sorting house for refugees. They wrote to tell you I was safe and arranged for my sea passage to England.'

'This Gertrude, she sounds like an angel sent from heaven,' Jacob breathed.

'She is indeed,' Ruth said fervently. 'Some day, when this is all over, I shall repay Gertrude for all she did for me.'

'You must also go to America to search for Simon and Leah. There must be similar places keeping a check of refugees.'

'I intend to one day, Dad.' Ruth felt as if a load had been lifted from her shoulders. 'Will you do me a favour?' she asked.

'Anything, you know that.'

'I don't want to talk about it again.'

'Then we shan't,' he said gravely, 'though I have one question. Your Uncle David and his family, what happened to them?'

'I don't know. We'd had no contact for years.'

'Nor me.' He sighed. 'Now, I shall go to bed, though first I must go to the lavatory. My old waterworks aren't what they used to be.'

'Can you see all right in the dark?'

'My dear, I have been going to the lavatory in the yard for over fifty years. I have gone through mists and fog, through thunderstorms and

127

snowdrifts. I could find my way blindfolded.'

He returned, minutes later, sounding slightly alarmed. 'There's someone crying in the yard!'

'In *our* yard?'

'No, next door's. It sounds like Dilys.'

'Oh dear!' Ruth bit her lip. 'You go to bed, Dad. I'll see to her.' He'd had enough excitement for tonight.

'Are you sure?'

'Quite sure,' she said firmly.

As soon as he'd gone, Ruth went outside. A curious stillness hung over the Bootle night air, as if the dust was settling from the raid and suffocating the small town into silence. The sky over the docks was a brilliant pink from the fires burning below.

At first, Ruth could hear nothing from next door, but after a while she became aware of a dull, miserable snuffling sound which was interrupted by an occasional sob.

'Is that you, Dilys?' she called.

The snuffling stopped. After a while, a hoarse voice said, 'Yes.'

'What's the matter, dear?'

There was another pause before the girl replied, 'Me mam's thrown me out.'

It was Ruth's turn to pause. She couldn't very well conduct a conversation through a six-foot brick wall in the middle of the night. 'You'd better come in a minute.'

She half expected the girl to refuse. Instead, the latch was lifted on the Evans' back gate. Ruth opened her own gate to let the girl in.

Once inside the house, she lit the gas mantle and told the girl to sit down. 'Oh, you poor thing!' she exclaimed when she turned round. Dilys's podgy face was black and blue and there was a cut under one eye.

'Did your mother do that?' she asked, shocked.

The girl nodded. 'She hit me with a coat hanger.'

'But why?'

Dilys frowned. Already plain, her injuries only added to her unattractive appearance. Her face was covered in spots and there was a suppurating boil on her chin.

'She says I'm having a baby.'

Ruth swallowed hard. '*She* says!'

'I haven't had a period for ages and I'm getting fat.' The girl frowned again and looked down at her stomach. She pulled her black skirt smooth. She was already plump, but under the skirt there showed a definitely pregnant bulge.

'But, Dilys,' Ruth said reasonably, 'women don't just have babies out of thin air. You have to . . .' She stopped, unable to find the words. 'I mean, you have to have been with a man to have a baby.'

Dilys looked vacantly at Ruth. 'What do you mean?'

Ruth felt completely out of her depth. 'Has your mother ever told you the facts of life, dear?' she asked wildly.

The girl shook her head. She looked quite stupid, as if the entire situation were beyond her comprehension. Her eyes glazed over, and she appeared to concentrate hard as if trying to remember. 'There was a man,' she said eventually. 'But even so, I can't possibly be having a baby.'

Ruth blinked. 'Who was this man? What did he do?'

'He was a guest. I thought the room was empty,

but when I went in to clean, he was still in bed. He asked me to get in with him.'

'So you did?'

'Well, I had to, didn't I?' Dilys answered, faintly indignant. 'You must never argue with the guests. The guests are always right, according to Mrs Haywood. She's the Domestic Supervisor,' the girl added by way of explanation.

'I doubt if Mrs Haywood meant you to go *that* far, Dilys,' Ruth said faintly. 'When did this happen?'

'Last summer some time,' the girl said vaguely.

'Did you tell your mother this?'

'She didn't want to listen. She called me a whore and threw me out.' Dilys glanced around the room. 'I like your hearthrug. Is it new?'

Ruth glanced at the girl in astonishment. She'd stopped snuffling as soon as she came in, and had seemed more sullen than upset to begin with. Now, she appeared quite calm and entirely unfazed by the whole episode. Perhaps, Ruth reasoned, she was so used to her mother's hysterical tantrums that they'd ceased to have any effect. She appeared unable to realise the seriousness of the fact she was almost certainly expecting a baby.

'I'll go and have a word with your mother,' Ruth sighed.

'She won't take any notice,' Dilys called as Ruth went down the hall.

Dilys was right. Ellis opened the front door, a huge bulky figure in a tattered nightdress, her red face even redder in the glow of the vermilion night sky.

'Dilys is next door,' Ruth began, but was rudely interrupted before she could say another word.

'Well, she can stay there,' Ellis said brutally.

'May I speak to Dai?' Ruth, realising the situation was hopeless from the start, decided to try another tack.

'I sent Dai and Myfanwy to bed. It's nothing to do with them and Dilys is nothing to do with me. I've disowned her. She's a sinful girl expecting a sinful baby. I won't even pray for her when I go to chapel on Sunday.'

'But, Ellis . . .'

The door was slammed in Ruth's face, shaking Pearl Street to its foundations for the second time that night.

Oh, God! What on earth was she supposed to do? Ruth was about to return home when a figure came hurrying around the corner. Eileen Costello!

'Eileen?' Ruth called urgently. 'Can I have a word with you?'

The woman jumped. 'You gave me a fright! What on earth are you doing, wandering around in your dressing gown? What's up?'

'Can you come into the house a minute?'

To Ruth's relief, Eileen didn't hesitate. 'I'll just pop indoors and tell me husband I'm home, else he'll be worried,' she said breathlessly. 'I'm terrible late, it must be gone midnight, but the bus was held up in Walton Vale, then it had to go on a detour to avoid a crater. I won't be long.'

She was only in the house a minute before she came out again. 'Is your dad all right?' she asked in a voice full of concern.

'He's fine, it's Dilys Evans.' Before going inside, Ruth quickly explained the situation, finishing, 'I don't know what to do with her.'

'Poor kid,' Eileen said sympathetically. 'I expect

she's in a right ould state.'

'Not really. She's far calmer than I am.'

'I'll have a word with her.'

'Mrs Costello!' Dilys's podgy face lit up when Eileen entered the room.

'Hallo, luv,' Eileen said gently. She knelt in front of the girl and took her hands. 'I understand you've got yourself in a bit of a mess?'

Dilys nodded earnestly. 'So me mam says.'

'How d'you feel, luv? Have you been sick, like?'

'Oh, no. I feel fine. Fact, everyone at work has been saying how well I look lately.'

Ruth dreaded to think what she must have looked like before.

'You mean, no one at work has guessed about the baby?' Eileen asked.

The girl merely looked confused. 'How could they? I don't understand what me mam's on about. She just took one look at me when I got out the bath, then made me get dressed so she could throw me out.'

Eileen and Ruth exchanged worried glances.

'You'll understand soon enough, luv,' Eileen said. 'Is it all right for you to go to work tomorrer?'

'Oh, yes,'

Eileen looked up at Ruth. 'I think that's best, don't you? She can say she just walked into a door or something to explain away the bruises.'

'I suppose so.' Ruth had no idea what was best. 'But where's she going to live? Is Ellis likely to take her back?'

Eileen shook her head. 'I doubt it.' She patted the girl's hand. 'We'll have to find somewhere for you to live, won't we?'

Quite out of the blue, Dilys said childishly, 'I

132

want to join the Navy.'

'The Navy!' exclaimed Ruth.

'She's always wanted to be a WREN,' Eileen explained.

'But she's not nearly old enough!'

'She's old enough to dream,' Eileen said. She got to her feet with a sigh. 'Anyroad, I'd best be going. Can you put Dilys up for tonight, Ruth? Perhaps the two of us can sort things out tomorrer morning. In the meantime, I want to go round to me dad's and see if him and our Sean are home yet. They weren't there when I called on me way home, and I'm worried about the pair of them, what with me dad fire-watching, the docks up in flames, and our Sean riding all over the place on his bike during the raids.'

Ruth nodded and hoped Eileen didn't notice her reluctance. She wasn't very keen on having to give up her bed for Dilys, but she couldn't very well put an expectant mother on the lumpy, overstuffed sofa in the parlour—nor could she expect Eileen Costello to take complete charge of the situation, as she'd rather hoped she would.

'The Jerries got Costigan's in Stanley Road tonight,' Eileen was saying, 'and a woman told me the public shelter in Garfield Street was hit, but she didn't know if anyone was killed. It's like a horrible game, isn't it? Like Tick, except you can't run away. Oh, well!' She chucked Dilys under the chin. 'Tara, luv. Don't worry now. Ruth and me will see you're all right.'

After Eileen had gone, Ruth took Dilys upstairs, gave her a nightdress and showed her where to sleep. The girl bounced up and down on the edge of the bed. 'This feels nice and comfortable.'

133

'It is,' Ruth said dryly, thinking about the sofa. She stared at the girl, noting her red chapped hands and thick legs. She had scarcely any ankles. If she was going to help the girl, she wished she were more attractive with a more appealing personality. Someone, for instance, like her own daughter, Leah.

On the other hand, she thought as she carried the only spare blanket downstairs, there was absolutely no chance of becoming fond of Dilys, which was a good thing, because Ruth had no wish to become fond of anyone, man, woman or child, again.

*　　　*　　　*

'I've been thinking,' Ruth said when she called on Eileen next morning. 'The most sensible thing is to find Dilys a place in a home for unmarried mothers.' She'd thought of little else all night as she'd struggled to get to sleep on the sofa. It was a way of shifting the onus for Dilys entirely onto other people—people who were trained to do it, she thought virtuously.

But to Ruth's dismay, Eileen Costello dismissed the suggestion entirely out of hand. 'Absolutely not!' She shook her head vehemently, as she ironed a small grey flannel shirt on the living room table. Her sister, Sheila, was there with two toddlers, and a white kitten slept peacefully, perched somewhat precariously on the back of an easy chair. 'They're dead awful those places. They treat the girls like fallen women and have them praying for forgiveness all the time. No, we'll find her somewhere to live, like we promised. If Francis

134

wasn't home, I'd put the kid up here.'

Ruth felt she might be exaggerating about the homes, but didn't argue. Nor did she remind Eileen that *she* had promised nothing. It was all Eileen's idea that Dilys be looked after, but she seemed to take for granted that Ruth felt the same as she did, and Ruth was too ashamed to admit she didn't. 'What about the rent?' she asked.

'Dilys can pay the rent herself for the time being and she'll have to put every spare penny aside for when she stops working. I'll have a word with Dai on the quiet and ask him if he can contribute a few bob—I mustn't forget to get her ration book.'

Sheila handed Ruth a cup of insipid tea.

'If necessary,' Eileen finished, 'I'll pay any shortfall meself.'

'You can count on me,' Ruth felt bound to add. She couldn't help but feel a sneaking admiration for Eileen. There hadn't been any suggestion that Dilys should be left to get on with things alone, nor any criticism of the girl's actions or apportioning of blame, merely an instant, positive response to help. Eileen Costello, Ruth decided, would be a good person to have as a friend if you were in trouble.

'You do realise,' Sheila said, 'that Dilys Evans is a penny short of a shilling?'

'I didn't until last night.' That morning, Dilys had gone off to work at six o'clock quite happily as if nothing untoward had happened and she'd always lived in Number 3 and not the house next door.

The back door opened and five children came pouring into the house, arguing fiercely. Tony Costello was amongst them.

'Our Caitlin's found a big piece of shrapnel and

135

she won't give it to us,' one of the boys said hotly.

'I wish you wouldn't play on bomb sites,' Sheila said fretfully. 'It's dangerous. There might be unexploded bombs.'

'But, Mam, our Caitlin's found . . .'

'I heard you the first time. Why should Caitlin give you the shrapnel if it was her that found it?'

'Girls aren't supposed to have shrapnel. Shrapnel's for boys.'

'Oh, sod off, the lot o'yis,' Sheila said irritably.

Caitlin stuck her tongue out at her brothers, and the children left. Sheila shouted, 'And keep your clothes clean for school!'

Eileen had gone into the back kitchen to change the iron. Ruth noticed the way she ruffled Tony's hair affectionately as he passed by. The two seemed to share a special rapport, Ruth thought wistfully, feeling suddenly lost without her own children.

There was a yelp from the yard and a girl's voice screamed, 'Me mam said it was mine!'

'Jaysus!' Sheila groaned as she went outside. There was a note approaching hysteria in her voice as she scolded her sons.

'She's not normally so bad-tempered,' Eileen whispered as she came back with the fresh iron, 'but she's out of her mind with worry about Cal, her husband. She never normally shows it, but Aggie Donovan was round first thing this morning to say two of his ould shipmates had died when the *Mayberry* was sunk.'

Sheila returned, looking harassed. 'I'll be glad when they're back at school full time.'

'They've closed St Joan of Arc's down, with it being so close to the docks, like,' Eileen explained to Ruth. 'The kids have to go all the way to St Monica's, and then only for a half a day.'

Ruth, anxious for the subject to return to Dilys, listened impatiently whilst the sisters complained to each other about the inconvenience this arrangement caused.

'About Dilys,' she said after a while.

'I'm sorry, luv,' Eileen said penitently. 'Here we are, yacking away, and you'll be wanting to get to work this avvy, won't you, same as me? I think the best thing is for me to have a word with this woman at work, Miss Thomas. I reckon she'll have a list of rooms to let, because some of the girls come from far afield and she has to find them accommodation. So, if you wouldn't mind putting Dilys up for one more night, Ruth, we can sort something out tomorrer. Is that all right with you, luv?'

Ruth's heart sank as she thought about another night on the sofa. 'Of course it is,' she said firmly. How could she possibly refuse?

CHAPTER SEVEN

By the end of November the war seemed to be poised at a particularly cruel stalemate, with no battles won, no battles lost, merely an orgy of death and destruction on either side, the main targets being innocent civilians, both British and German alike. Whilst the RAF pounded Berlin, the Luftwaffe meted out similar punishment to Britain.

'It seems daft,' Eileen Costello said bitterly. 'Why don't we just agree to bomb ourselves, at least it'd save the fuel? We're going nowhere at this rate.'

'Everyone says we've turned the corner,' Francis remarked.

'So you said before, but what bloody corner?' Eileen demanded. 'The Italians have attacked Greece, our ships are being sunk like nobody's business, and the other night the Jerries virtually wiped Coventry off the face of the earth!' Bombs had dropped every two minutes for five whole hours and the city had been reduced to rubble. 'Seems to me we're going round in circles, not turning corners.'

'The raids can't last forever,' Francis muttered, more to comfort himself than his wife. George Ransome kept hinting he should join the ARP, but Francis was too frightened.

'Here we go again,' Eileen groaned one Thursday night when the siren went at twenty past seven. Francis was out. He seemed to be out a lot lately, she thought. She saw little of him, even during the weeks she was on morning shift. Some nights she'd gone to bed by the time he arrived home, but at least he was always sober, so she didn't mind in the slightest how long he spent away.

'Tony,' she called, 'come on, under the stairs.'

Tony went in search of Snowy. 'I wonder what Nick's doing?' he said as they settled down on the mattress. The kitten hated the raids and was already curled up, shivering, on Tony's knee.

'I've no idea, luv.' It was ages since he'd mentioned Nick.

'Spitfires fly over to France and strife the enemy.'

'Strafe, luv, not strife. Then I expect that's what Nick's doing,' she said in a tight voice.

She did her best not to think of Nick. There were times when she wondered if he was still alive—he could die and she'd never know. It would be his next-of-kin who would be informed, in other words, his mother in the USA, not Eileen. It was hard to put him out of her mind for a while, but soon awareness came that tonight's raid was like no raid before and Nick was forgotten. It sounded as if the entire Luftwaffe had been sent to bomb the living day-lights out of Liverpool.

In wave after wave they came, for hour after hour. Eileen thanked God she was on mornings and could be with her son. She did her utmost not to show her fear, though every now and then she ducked and clutched him in her arms whenever a bomb screamed to earth close by. Tony, incredibly, didn't seem bothered.

'That was a near miss, Mam,' he'd say excitedly every time the house shuddered.

There was a lull around midnight. Eileen emerged to make a cup of tea, along with Snowy, who scratched at the door to be let out. She was just filling the kettle when Francis came in.

'Where on earth have you been?' Eileen asked.

'Just having a drink with a few mates,' he explained briefly. 'Jaysus! It's bedlam out there.'

'Is there much damage?' Eileen asked.

'Quite a bit, but mainly on the docks. According to a warden I spoke to, the other side of Liverpool has caught the worst of it. I reckon this is the longest raid yet.'

'And the heaviest!' Eileen shuddered. 'Now as you're here, I'll just pop over the road and see if our Sheila's all right.'

It was as clear as daylight outside. The silence

139

seemed ominous, as if a promise were hanging in the air that the carnage was likely to begin again any minute.

Eileen drew the key on its string through the letter box of her sister's front door and went inside, but stopped halfway down the hall. The children were singing in their shelter under the stairs.

> *'Sing a song of sixpence*
> *A pocketful of rye.*
> *Four and twenty blackbirds,*
> *Baked in a pie.*
> *When the pie was opened . . .'*

Their young voices sounded pure and innocent as they rang through the house. Sheila had given birth to all her six children in the double bed upstairs, brought them into the world full of the hope, as all mothers were, that they'd grow up into a better and more prosperous world than she and Cal had known. Instead, Eileen thought bleakly, Cal was sailing the treacherous waters of the Atlantic, with death in the form of German U-boats poised and ready to pounce at any time of the day or night, whilst at home, his entire family were equally at risk.

The children had finished the nursery rhyme. 'That was the gear,' cried Sheila. 'I reckon your dad might well have heard it if he'd been listening hard enough. Now it's your turn to pick a tune, Siobhan.'

Incredibly, Sheila's voice was steady and quite cheerful. Eileen turned on her heel and left the house, closing the door as quietly as she could. She felt it wiser not to intrude on her sister and the children just at the moment.

She was walking back when Mr Harrison emerged from the coalyard at the end of the street. He usually spent the raids in the stable comforting Nelson. The sounds drove the poor horse hysterical.

'Look, Eileen!'

He was pointing up into the sky behind her. Eileen turned. Some distance away over the docks, a parachute was drifting silently to earth. She felt her heart turn over. Was the heavy raid a lead-up to the invasion everybody had been expecting for months, ever since France had fallen?

They both watched as the parachute disappeared behind the black roofs, then came a blast louder than anything heard before. Eileen felt as if the ground were about to open up beneath her. Nelson whinnied, terrified, and Mr Harrison hurried back to calm him.

'There, boy!' Eileen heard him say as she ran indoors.

Francis was white-faced and shaking. 'What the hell was that?'

Eileen explained what she'd just seen. 'It was a bomb on a parachute.'

As if the enemy planes had signalled to each other it was time to re-start, the bombardment began again with a vengeance. Eileen opened the back door and Snowy shot into the house like a bat out of hell. 'I'm going to bed,' said Francis.

'You'll never sleep through this,' Eileen warned.

'I know that only too well.' He preferred to be by himself so there'd be no witness to his terror. Anyroad, if the house was hit he reckoned he'd be no safer under the stairs than in the bedroom.

Tony had fallen asleep, which was a blessing.

141

Eileen lay beside him, partially covering his sleeping form with her own body, whilst the raid continued.

It wasn't until four o'clock that the All Clear sounded and she emerged from the shelter feeling dog-tired. She hadn't slept a wink all night and was due to leave for work in an hour's time. She went into the new bathroom, ran a few inches of warm water, knelt in it, and splashed her body from head to toe in an effort to wake herself up.

Francis appeared just as she was about to put the kettle on. He looked red-eyed and equally weary.

'You should have stayed in bed and tried to catch up on your sleep,' she said. 'Tony's been asleep for hours.'

'I wanted a cup of tea.' Francis looked at her in surprise as she combed her hair. 'What are you doing?'

'Getting ready for work.'

'Surely you can give it a miss for once?' he said testily. He resented the fact she thought her work so important.

'I couldn't possibly. Everyone else will have been up all night, same as me. What would happen if we all decided to give it a miss?'

He shrugged churlishly. 'Suit yourself.'

'Why don't you go back to bed and try to snatch a bit of shut-eye,' she suggested sympathetically, feeling he was entitled to be grumpy under the circumstances. He'd been rather preoccupied of late and she wondered why.

'I might well go back once you've gone,' he said.

She made herself a slice of toast. Francis refused anything to eat, but gratefully accepted a cup of tea. He seemed to have recovered his good humour.

'I'm sorry if I was short with you, princess. It's just that it's been a terrible night.'

'Don't give it another thought, luv.' She glanced at the clock. 'I'll have to be off in a minute.

'Eileen?'

There was something in his voice that made her stiffen. 'Yes, Francis?'

'I don't suppose you could lend me a few bob, like?' There was a shamed expression on his face she'd never seen before.

'But you only got paid yesterday,' she said, astonished.

'Yes, but I owed some cash and I've nowt left for the week ahead.'

'How could you owe a whole week's wages?'

She'd never questioned him in the past, not about anything, because she knew that doing so would only bring quick retribution in the form of a savage pinch which would leave her bruised for a week. Perhaps Francis remembered the old days when she did what she was told, because he no longer looked ashamed, but swallowed impatiently, as if doing his utmost to keep his temper. 'The truth is I lost a bit of money playing cards,' he muttered.

'Is that where you were last night, playing cards?'

Francis nodded. 'I got a bit carried away, that's all.'

'More than a bit, it seems to me. And where did this card game take place?'

'Rodney Smith's,' he said through gritted teeth. If she asked him another question, so help him, he'd wallop her.

'I might have known!'

143

With an effort, Francis said, 'Don't worry, princess. It won't happen again.'

'I should hope not!' she said severely. 'I can let you have ten bob, but don't forget, Francis, it's me who pays for the housekeeping. I don't take a penny of yours. All you have to do is pay the rent and settle the bills. I'm not prepared to subsidise gambling.'

It was hard, awfully hard, not to lash out and send her flying for daring to speak to him as if he was a schoolboy. 'Ta, luv.' Francis did his utmost to sound grateful.

She handed him a ten-shilling note out of her purse. 'That should see you through the week.'

'There's another thing, princess . . .'

'What's that, Francis?'

'I keep bringing it up with your dad, but he seems dead evasive. It's this matter of the Labour Party picking a successor to Albert Findlay when he retires at the next election. Your dad always promised it would be me, but he doesn't seem prepared to commit himself when I bring the matter up nowadays.' He hated having to ask her, it was demeaning, but Jack Doyle didn't appear nearly as willing as expected to be wrapped around Francis's little finger. In fact, Jack seemed reluctant to talk to him except when he had to.

'There won't be an election till the war's over. There's no need, not with a coalition Government.'

'I know that, princess, but it wouldn't hurt to have someone ready in place to take over from Albert.'

'I'll have a word with me dad,' Eileen promised. 'I'd better go, else I'll miss the bus.'

Everyone at Dunnings was full of the previous

144

night's raid. Despite the fact that, like Eileen, no one had slept, they were remarkably chirpy and full of beans. The mood was one of defiance. There was no way Hitler and his new-fangled parachute mines would prevent them from doing their job.

'Where's Theresa?'

The women had already started work when they noticed Theresa's lathe was standing idle.

'Perhaps one of her kids is ill,' someone suggested.

But Theresa's mother-in-law looked after the children, Eileen recalled, feeling worried.

'Maybe she's missed the bus. She'll probably be along any minute.'

'She's never missed the bus before.'

Every time the workshop door opened the women looked up, expecting Theresa to come bustling in, full of excuses as to why she was late. As the morning wore on, they kept glancing uneasily at her lathe. The conversation was forced.

'Just think,' Doris shouted, 'it'll be the first of December on Monday. We'll have to start thinking about Christmas presents soon.'

'Aye,' yelled Carmel. 'It seems no time since it was last Christmas. The year's flown by.'

'It has that.'

The girls were having their dinner when Miss Thomas came into the canteen and sat at the end of their table. They could tell by the expression on her face that she was the bearer of bad news.

'I've just had a phone call from Theresa's sister. It seems the entire family were sheltering underneath the Junior Technical School in Durning Road. The school got a direct hit and more than a hundred and fifty people were killed.'

Miss Thomas took a deep, shuddering breath. 'I'm terribly sorry, girls, but Theresa and her children are dead.'

* * *

Next morning, Eileen collected the ration books for the week's shopping, which could well take up the entire morning by the time you'd stood in all the various queues. She was dreading coming face to face with the evidence of Thursday night's raid. It was horrible to see the wreckage of people's homes, the heaps of dusty bricks and slates and smashed chimneys, all jumbled together with precious furniture and ornaments and personal possessions that had taken a lifetime to collect. She could never understand those people who made a special journey merely to gawp at their fellow citizens' misery.

She called on her sister first, because it was wise to take Sheila's ration books with her just in case the shops had some unexpected luxury in stock. Last week she'd managed, somewhat miraculously, to buy sausages—not that there'd been anything luxurious about *them*, she thought, remembering their anonymous taste and sawdust texture. Still . . .

Sheila was in the living room stirring something in a pan over the fire, all flushed and starry-eyed. Calum Reilly was due home that afternoon, and she'd been over the moon all week. The younger children were playing house underneath the table.

'Cal's already here,' she sang. 'His ship docked earlier than expected. He turned up at five o'clock this morning.'

'Where is he?' Eileen asked.

146

'Still in bed having a lie in. He's fair worn out, poor Cal.' She had the satisfied, satiated look of a woman who'd recently been well loved. Eileen used to feel envious of her sister—until she met Nick. She wondered if it was the Merchant Navy who'd worn Cal out, or Sheila.

There was a peculiar and rather unpleasant smell emanating from the pan Sheila was stirring. Eileen sniffed and pulled a face. 'Whatever it is you're cooking, Sheila, it don't half pong!'

'It's jam!' Sheila said smugly.

'Jam? Where on earth did you get the fruit?'

'It's pineapple jam.' Sheila looked even more smug. 'Would you like a taste? I've got a bit on a saucer. It's nearly set.'

'Pineapple! You're codding me, sis. I never saw much of pineapple before the war, let alone since.' All fruit was difficult to get, even apples, and oranges had disappeared altogether.

'Have some.' Sheila thrust the saucer at her. The mixture looked remarkably like chunky pineapple jam. 'What does it taste like?' she enquired eagerly.

Eileen licked her finger warily. 'Have you had a taste?'

'A bit.'

'What do *you* think?'

Sheila collapsed into giggles. 'It tastes like turnips! I made it out of turnips. Brenda found the recipe in a woman's magazine.'

'To be honest, sis, it's dead awful! I hope you didn't make me any.'

'I did, actually, but me feelings won't be hurt if it's not wanted.'

'That's good, because it's not!'

'Never mind,' Sheila said contentedly, 'the kids

like it.'

'Don't give our Tony any. I don't want him poisoned.'

The sisters looked at each other and burst out laughing. 'Isn't it funny,' Eileen mused, 'the way you can laugh, no matter what happens? Yesterday morning, after Miss Thomas told us Theresa and her entire family had been wiped out, I thought I'd never laugh again, but before the day was out, the girls were making jokes, and we were all laughing fit to bust, though none of us could get the news out of our minds. Everyone kept saying, "Theresa would have appreciated that!"'

'It's a way of coping, I suppose.'

'I suppose,' Eileen sighed. 'Anyroad, I've come for your ration books. I'm off to do the shopping.'

'They're on the mantelpiece behind St Anthony. By the way, Brenda said your frock's ready for the final fitting.'

'I'll pop round later on.' Eileen had decided on a relatively plain-styled dress in fine lavender-coloured wool.

'I asked her to make our Sean a Fair Isle pullover for Christmas,' Sheila said, 'and she did nearly all one side during Thursday night's raid. Sean was saying the other week how much he fancied one, so it should be a nice surprise.' Her face lit up. 'Talk of the devil!'

The back door opened and Sean Doyle came in. People had joked Mollie Doyle must have had it off with the coalman when Sean was born. He was a throwback to some wild Gaelic strain in the family, a dark-eyed, dark-skinned, good-looking gypsy of a boy, with a natural, outgoing personality.

''Lo there!' he said easily.

148

The sisters watched fondly as their young brother threw himself gracefully into a chair, whilst the object of their gaze basked in the affection which he only regarded as his due. He knew one of them would get up and offer him some food, which was why he'd come. His dad wasn't home and he was too idle to feed himself.

'Would you like something to eat, luv?' Sheila asked.

'Wouldn't say no,' Sean grinned. 'Got any bacon?'

'You must be joking! And I've no eggs, either, to save you asking. There's cornflakes, porridge or toast. Take your pick.'

'Cornflakes, please, with lots of sugar.'

'It'll be cornflakes with hardly any sugar,' Sheila said briskly.

'You're a lazy bugger, our Sean,' his other sister complained. 'Surely you can help yourself to cornflakes at home?'

'You know I don't like eating by meself.'

'You're a bloody liar, as well.'

The words were uttered with a smile, because lazy though Sean was, and a liar to boot, the sisters' love for their brother was largely uncritical. He was spoilt, not through being showered with worldly goods and allowed to do as he pleased—Jack Doyle had always been strict, a stern, uncompromising man to have as a dad—but there was something engagingly attractive about Sean, which, taken with his unusual looks, made him irresistible to family, friends and strangers alike. Everyone liked Sean Doyle. They either didn't notice, or didn't care about, the many weaknesses in his character. He was training to be a motor

149

mechanic and led a charmed life; made a fuss of by his sisters, and enjoying the special glory of being 'Jack Doyle's lad'. Eileen and Sheila muttered disapprovingly about the numerous girlfriends, the numerous broken hearts he caused, 'But if the girls are daft enough to fall for him, there's nowt we can do about it,' they remarked to each other.

'I got me call-up papers this morning.' Sean knew this would be a bombshell, and was gratified when both his sisters reacted with appropriate shock, though it was no more than he expected. 'They want me in the RAF.'

Sheila screamed, and Eileen groaned, 'Oh, no!'

'When do you have to go?'

'I'm to report at Warrington in a fortnight's time.'

'Does our dad know?' asked Sheila.

'Not yet. The postman only came as I was leaving.'

'Jaysus!' Eileen glanced at Sheila. 'It doesn't seem right, does it? It feels like only yesterday he was a little boy.'

'Well, it isn't right, is it?' Sheila cried angrily.

Sean looked quite unconcerned, but Eileen remembered Donnie Kennedy, who'd appeared so proud and full of himself, yet was inwardly petrified.

Calum Reilly appeared in the doorway, in the process of buttoning up his thick flannel shirt. A youthful looking man with clean-cut boyish features, Cal bore himself with a quiet dignity that commanded respect. He was loved to distraction by his family, and the love was wholeheartedly reciprocated—Sheila and his children were all Cal thought of when he was away at sea. His eyes locked with Sheila's for a second before he said, 'I thought I heard voices. Hallo, Eil.' He kissed Eileen on the cheek and gave Sean a playful cuff around the head.

'He's had his call-up papers,' Sheila said tearfully. 'They want him in the RAF.'

'I reckon that means we've lost the war for certain,' Cal smiled. 'Is there a cup of tea going, luv?'

'In a minute. I think this jam's just about ready.'

'Is that what it is? I thought you were boiling some of me old socks.'

'Don't eat it, Cal,' Eileen warned. 'It tastes worse than it smells.'

Cal carried the heavy pan into the back kitchen and Sheila went with him to fetch the water for the tea.

'Don't forget me cornflakes,' Sean shouted.

Eileen regarded him worriedly. 'Are you scared about joining up, luv?'

Sean said flippantly, 'I'm not scared a bit.'

Eileen felt convinced there was a undercurrent of fear in his voice. 'Have you heard from Donnie Kennedy?' She'd been meaning to ask him about Donnie for ages.

'No,' Sean said lightly. Insensitive he might be, but even Sean Doyle knew this was not the right time to inform his sister that only the other day he'd heard his old classmate had been killed.

*   *   *

It looked as if it was going to be a raid-free night, Brenda Mahon thought thankfully as she began to sew the hem of Eileen Costello's dress by hand

151

with neat, symmetrical stitches. It was a nice style, classically plain, and would suit Eileen's tall, shapely figure to perfection.

This was her favourite time of all, when Muriel and Monica were in bed, and she was free to sew all night if she wished. She frequently stayed up well into the early hours if she had a load of work to get through. Brenda smoothed her hand over the soft material. She loved the feel, though velvet was the nicest, with silk coming a good second. Taffeta she liked least, so harsh and stiff.

The lavender thread came to an end, so she back-stitched, snipped the remainder off, and threaded another length. Most women used far too much cotton when they sewed by hand—sheer laziness, because they couldn't be bothered threading the needle frequently, though more time was wasted in the end, because the cotton only became knotted if it was too long. Brenda never used more than about fifteen inches.

She began to sew again, humming *Whispering Grass* underneath her breath. Xavier sometimes sang it at parties and weddings when he did his Hutch impersonation. Brenda began to plan the letter she would write him tomorrow. She always wrote to Xavier on Sundays, reporting in detail on the week's events, though she wouldn't tell him how bad Thursday night's raid had been, else he might worry. He'd never get the news from the wireless or the newspapers. They still seemed intent on pretending there'd never been an enemy plane anywhere near Liverpool, let alone that the city had been bombed.

Brenda had bought a postal order for two pounds ten shillings to include with the letter.

There was no way her Xavier could possibly live on the shilling a day allowed him by the Army. Even when he was home, she'd always subsidised her husband—not that she minded. Xavier was a man in a million, and pandering to his expensive tastes made her feel necessary and needed, as if he wouldn't shine so much if it weren't for her. She was secretly proud he preferred whisky to beer and always bought good cigarettes. His collection of hats was way beyond the means of any normal LMS employee—he had a penchant for headgear of all different styles and colours. She smiled fondly, recalling the time he took deciding on which hat to wear whenever he went out.

As soon as Eileen's hem was finished, she'd make herself a cup of cocoa, then start on that navy-blue costume for the woman from Hunts Cross. Brenda felt a little anticipatory thrill at the idea of cutting out the serge material. That was the best part, the beginning; a length of smooth, virginal cloth and knowing that it would shortly turn into a beautifully finished garment, something *she* had created.

The sharp rap of the knocker on the front door made Brenda jump. Glancing down, she saw she'd pricked her finger and drawn blood, which fortunately hadn't touched the frock.

She looked at the clock. Half past eleven! It could only be someone like Sheila Reilly at such an unearthly hour. Perhaps one of the kids had been taken ill and she needed a hand.

On the other hand, it could be Xavier, home without warning in order to surprise her!

With this exhilarating thought predominant, Brenda hurried down the hall and opened the door.

A young woman stood outside, a grubby child of about eighteen months in one arm, and a cheap cardboard suitcase in the other. The child, a boy, was crying pitifully and his nose ran, to such an extent that the sight made Brenda feel slightly sick. She resisted the urge to reach out and wipe the mess away with her hand-embroidered hanky.

'Yes?' she said politely, convinced the woman had come to the wrong house.

She felt even more convinced this was the case, because the woman was frowning, as if she'd expected someone else to have answered the door. 'Is Mrs Mahon in?' she asked.

If she's come for dressmaking, I'll kill her, thought Brenda, I could have been in bed by now. On the other hand, the woman didn't look as if she had two ha'pennies to rub together, let along the money for new clothes. Her coat was too tight across her noticeably buxom breasts, and her thin flowered frock hung several inches below. She wore a black felt hat that looked as if it had been used as a football, it was so full of dust. The baby was even more shabbily dressed. He'd stopped crying and was watching Brenda warily, eyes like saucers, whilst he sucked on a dummy. He was a handsome little chap, all the same, and reminded Brenda of someone. She couldn't quite put her finger on who.

'Well, is she in or not?' the woman said impatiently.

Brenda was never sure afterwards why it should happen, but warning bells began to ring inside her head. 'Is who in?' she asked, playing for time. Why should the woman automatically assume *Brenda* wasn't Mrs Mahon?

154

'Mrs Mahon, of course.' She was quite pretty in a tartish sort of way, with blonde curly hair protruding from underneath the battered hat, and big brown eyes. She must have only recently renewed her lipstick, which was a greasy and startlingly vivid crimson. Despite the fact she looked worn out, she had a spunky, tenacious look, as if life had been tough, but so far she was still on the winning side.

'Oh, I know,' she cried as she hoisted the baby upwards with her arm, 'I expect you're the lodger, Brenda, ain't you?'

'The lodger?' Brenda said weakly. The woman was a cockney. Why should a strange cockney woman come searching for her in the middle of the night, and what on earth was she on about—the lodger?

'*Put that light out*!' a voice thundered from out of the darkness.

Brenda realised she'd left the parlour door wide open and the light was clearly visible outside. 'You'd better come in,' she muttered.

She showed the woman into the living room, where she threw the suitcase on the floor and plopped down on a chair with a sigh of relief.

'Christ! It's good to get the weight off me plates o'meat.'

'Y'what?' asked Brenda, mystified.

'Me plates o'meat—me feet.'

'Wanna drink, Ma,' the little boy whined.

'In a minute, Sonny.' She looked up at Brenda, who was standing in the middle of the room feeling dazed—the lodger! 'Well, if you wouldn't mind telling Mrs Mahon I'm here. I'm sorry it's so late, but I set off from Stepney at ten o'clock this

155

morning and we've been travelling all day. Poor Sonny ain't had a bite to eat, poor little shrimp.'

'Who shall I say it is?' hedged Brenda.

There was a horrible smell in the room; perspiration and dirty underclothes and that cheap perfume you could buy by the pint in Woolworths for three pence ha'penny, and something else. Brenda sniffed. Sonny had dirtied his pants.

The woman smirked. 'It'll probably come as a bit of a shock, but say it's Mrs Carrie Mahon, her daughter-in-law.'

The warning bells in Brenda's head stopped merely ringing and began a thunderous clang. 'I think there must have been a mistake . . .'

But there was no mistake. Before Brenda could say another word, the woman pointed across the room at the photo of Xavier on the wireless, crying, 'There he is, the darlin'! Look, Sonny, it's your daddy!'

* * *

Sheila Reilly was savouring the first raid-free night in weeks, though she'd got so much into the routine of spending hours wide awake under the stairs that, despite the fact she was dead tired, she just couldn't get to sleep. Fortunately, the children had dropped off straight away. Mary was breathing easily in her cot in the corner. It seemed strange, not having a baby to breastfeed during the night. For the first time in nearly eight years she hadn't a child under twelve months to nurse.

Cal had gone back to sea that morning and she felt lonely in the bed without him; one night they'd had together, just one night, and that had been rudely interrupted by a raid. She laid her hand on the pillow where his head had rested, when the front door opened and someone came running up the stairs. Sheila sat up, heart racing. The last time this had happened, it had been her dad and her sister coming to tell her Cal's ship had sunk. He'd survived on that occasion, but to be sunk a second time was tempting fate . . .

A figure rushed into the room and began to shake her furiously.

'I'm awake, I'm awake,' Sheila whispered hoarsely.

'Sheila! Oh, Sheil! The most terrible thing has happened.'

It was Brenda Mahon, her best mate. They'd been friends since they started school together more than twenty years ago, had been bridesmaids at each other's weddings, and each given birth to their first child the same week, though Brenda had stopped at two, whilst Sheila had gone on to have another four.

'Is it Xavier?' Sheila cried.

'You bet your bloody life it's Xavier, the bastard!'

Sheila gasped. She'd never heard Brenda swear. Not only that, Brenda had never come bursting into her house like this before, not even during the day, let alone the middle of the night. It must be midnight, at least.

'What's he done?' Sheila had never taken to Xavier. He preened himself too much, took all Brenda's money from the dressmaking, and let her wait on him hand and foot, unlike Cal, who would never take a penny off a woman and always gave a hand when he was home.

157

'He's only gone and married someone else!'

'He's *what*?'

'He's married someone else, the bastard. She's in our house now; Carrie. She's got a horrible smelly little boy called Sonny.'

Mary stirred fretfully in the corner.

'We'd best go downstairs.' Sheila got out of bed and took Cal's old overcoat which she used as a dressing gown from behind the door.

'I'm sorry, Sheil,' Brenda said when they were in the living room. 'But I just had to talk to someone. I couldn't possibly have waited till tomorrow.'

'That's all right, luv.' Sheila patted her metal curlers. 'I must look a sight. It's just that me hair's a mess and I didn't put me curlers in last night with Cal home.'

Brenda couldn't have cared less if her friend had shaved her head. 'If I could get me hands on Xavier now, I'd throttle him.'

'But what's happened, luv?'

'Well,' Brenda explained as calmly as she could, 'this woman, Carrie, turned up asking for Mrs Mahon, her mother-in-law. Xavier told her she lived in Bootle and wouldn't take kindly to him getting wed, so he'd kept the news a secret—they got married two years back, by the way. But, and this is the worst part, Sheil,' Brenda's eyes glittered with rage, 'he also told her his mam had a lodger living downstairs, a dressmaker called Brenda who had two little girls. That's who Carrie thinks I am, the lodger!'

'Have you told her the truth yet?' Sheila asked, wide-eyed.

'Not yet. I've let her do most of the talking so far.' Brenda struck a fist into the palm of her hand.

158

'Jaysus, Sheil! I wish Xavier was here so I could scratch his eyes out.'

'You'd better tell the poor woman, luv,' Sheila advised.

'Aye, I suppose so.'

'What made her turn up now, right out of the blue?'

'Because she wasn't getting any money off the Army—that's because it's me who's been getting it, being Xavier's real wife. She last saw him six months ago just before he was called up, and she hasn't heard a word since.' Brenda twiddled her thumbs in her lap. 'The thing is, Sheil, I quite like her in a way, poor lamb, though she's as common as muck and a real flamer. She don't half look poor. She's only nineteen, and Sonny's not all that horrible, but the spitting image of Xavier, if the truth be known—I knew he reminded me of someone the minute I clapped eyes on him.'

'Oh, Bren!' Sheila squeezed her friend's hand.

'Isn't it awful, Sheil? He didn't even tell her where his mam lived, only Bootle. If she hadn't found his union card or something, she wouldn't have known where to come.'

'You must be dead upset, luv.'

'Upset?' Brenda shook her head. 'I'm not upset, but I'm so bloody angry, I could *spit*! I used to wonder why he spent so much time in London. The other guards came home, even if it meant using the milk train, but Xavier said he needed his sleep. There was a cheap hotel by Euston Station, or so he said. To think, Sheil, he was keeping another woman on *my* money! He'll never get another penny off me, I'll tell you that much, the slimy, two-timing son of a bitch, I could kill him!'

'I'm sure you could,' Sheila said sympathetically. 'I'd feel the same if it was Cal,' she added, though the possibility of her darling Cal doing such a thing was beyond the bounds of her imagination.

Brenda said nothing. There were no words to express the rage she felt. Her body, every single little bit of it, was pounding so violently, she felt as if she might explode.

'What's this Carrie doing at the moment?'

'Searching the house from top to bottom looking for her mother-in-law by now, I reckon.' Brenda laughed sarcastically. 'I made them a cup of tea and bite to eat, they were both starving. Then I told her I was going to borrow a cup of sugar, which she must have thought funny at this time of night.' She sighed. 'I suppose I'd better put her up for the night, she'll have to leave first thing tomorrer morning.'

'You'd better get home and see to her, Bren.'

'I suppose so. You won't tell anyone about this, will you, Sheila? I couldn't stand everyone knowing.'

'I won't tell a soul, I promise.' There was a wistful note in Sheila's voice.

'Oh, all right,' Brenda said grudgingly. 'You can tell your Eileen, but that's all.'

'I hate having secrets from our Eileen.'

'I know you do.' Brenda suddenly wished she had a sister of her own to confide in. Her only brother was far away in Plymouth and they rarely corresponded. 'I'd better be off then.'

'Do you want me to come with you?'

'No, I'll manage on me own.'

The smell in Brenda's living room was even worse by the time she got back. Carrie and Sonny

160

had finished eating and the little boy was fast asleep on the floor.

'I've got something to tell you,' Brenda announced.

'I reckon you have,' Carrie said spiritedly, 'and that's the whereabouts of Mrs Mahon, my ma-in-law. I've been upstairs and she ain't there. I hope you haven't murdered her or something.'

'*I'm* Mrs Mahon.'

'But you ain't old enough!'

At that moment, Brenda felt old enough to be Xavier's grandmother, let alone his mother. 'Xavier's mam died twenty years ago. I'm his wife. I married him in nineteen thirty-two.'

Carrie laughed contemptuously. 'You bleedin' liar! You're making it up. Xavier always said you fancied him.'

Brenda felt her blood boil. 'I'll show you me wedding lines, if you like.'

'You do that!'

'And while we're at it, I wouldn't mind taking a look at yours.'

As Brenda searched in the sideboard drawer for the envelope containing her most important papers, Carrie rooted through her cheap red handbag.

'Here they are!' Both women spoke together as they each brandished a piece of white paper.

Both paused before taking the paper from the other.

'I believe you,' Brenda said eventually.

'Same here.' Carrie sank back in the chair. 'Strike a bleedin' light!' She beat the arm of the chair with her fist. 'I'd like to cut the bugger up into little pieces and fry them!' She got up and walked up and down the room several times, snapping her fingers angrily, then sat down again. 'With my luck, I might have known someone like Xavier was too good to be true.'

'I'm sorry.'

Carrie's big brown eyes widened. 'Why should you be sorry? It ain't your fault, no more than it's mine. He's double-crossed the both of us, the bleedin' swine.' Her voice, which was low and slightly hoarse, cracked with venom.

Brenda had been expecting hysterics, tears at least. She quite admired the way Carrie had taken the news with anger and resentment, much the same way as she'd taken it herself.

'Though it's worse for you in a way, me turning up like this,' Carrie was saying. She looked at Brenda curiously. 'I feel as though I should hate you, but I don't.'

'I don't hate you, either,' Brenda said quietly. 'But I hate Xavier.'

The two women were silent for a while, both lost in their own thoughts. What on earth had Xavier seen in the girl, Brenda wondered? He was so fastidious, and although Carrie was pretty in a coarse sort of way, she wasn't exactly clean—or hygienic. She'd made no attempt to clean up Sonny, and the room was beginning to smell like a lavatory. You never know, she thought dryly, Carrie might be thinking much the same, wondering what Xavier had seen in such a plain little woman. Brenda had no illusions regarding her appearance.

'I expect you'll want to go home tomorrer,' she said. 'I can let you have the fare.'

Carrie shook her blonde wavy head. 'There's no point in going home. I lost me ma in the raids, then

162

me flat went the same way. Me brothers are both away in the Army, and me mates are scattered all over the place, so's I've nowhere to live.'

'I'm sorry about your mam.'

'Don't be,' Carrie said laconically. 'It was no great loss. She was a right old bitch, me ma, but she looked after Sonny when I was at work, least pretended to. She was pissed rotten most of the time. I wouldn't have come here if I hadn't been in such a hole. I had to give up me job because there was no one to keep an eye on Sonny, and I was at me wits' end knowing which way to turn next. When I wrote to the Army to ask why I wasn't getting an allowance for me and Sonny, they didn't bother to write back.' She smiled ruefully. 'Throwing meself at the mercy of me ma-in-law was the very last resort. I was worried I'd give her a heart attack, just turning up like a bad penny, as they say.'

'You don't get much off the Army, anyroad,' Brenda explained, 'just twenty-five bob a week, plus seven which is stopped out of your husband's pay. Servicemen are only left with seven bob of their own to live on.' Except Xavier, that is, she thought darkly, the man with eleven hats, probably the only private in the entire British Army to get an allowance off his wife.

'That would have done me with knobs on,' Carrie said.

'What'll you do now?'

Carrie shrugged. 'Can you put me up for the night? I don't mind if me and Sonny sleep on the floor.' When Brenda nodded, she went on, 'I'll look around for somewhere to live tomorrow and find a job. It'll be nice to get away from the bombing for a

163

change.'

Brenda didn't bother to illuminate her on the situation in Liverpool with the raids.

'And who'll look after Sonny?' she asked, glancing down at the little boy. He would look quite nice once cleaned up, but what a pity he looked so much like Xavier.

'I'll sort something out.' Carrie grinned cheerfully. 'After all, I've been fending for meself since I was fourteen.' She pulled a face. 'God! I wish this time it hadn't all turned so sour.'

It's turned even sourer for me, Brenda thought bleakly, because it was so unexpected. Until tonight, she'd always considered herself one of the luckiest women in the world.

'I don't suppose you've got anything to drink?' Carrie asked hopefully.

'I'll make more tea . . .' Brenda offered.

'I meant a drop of the hard stuff; whisky, gin, something with a bit of bite in it?'

'I'm sorry, I don't drink. Xavier finished off the whisky last time he was home.'

'How about a cigarette? I'm aching for a gasper.'

'I'm afraid I don't smoke, either,' Brenda said apologetically. She took a deep breath. 'Look, I've been thinking, you can stay here if you want.' Brenda was never sure why she made the offer. Perhaps it was because she thought the two women Xavier had deceived should stick together. 'I'll look after Sonny and you can go to work. But you must promise, on your heart, not to tell the neighbours who you are. Just say you're a friend of a friend or something.' Carrie would have to change her ways, though, wash more frequently and keep Sonny clean.

'Strike a light, Brenda, you're a proper good sort, you really are!' Carrie looked genuinely grateful. 'But what happens when Xavier comes home?'

Maybe *that* was why Brenda had asked Carrie to stay.

'We'll cross that bridge when we come to it,' said Brenda. 'But I can't wait to see his face when he finds the two of us together. Can you?'

CHAPTER EIGHT

Dilys Evans seemed to settle down quite happily in her room over an off-licence in Spellow Lane. The couple who ran the shop were elderly and childless and let several rooms to young girls who'd been billeted in Liverpool for reasons concerning the war.

Eileen Costello bought Dilys a wedding ring from Woolworths. 'Say your husband's in the Army, luv,' she advised. 'According to Miss Thomas, they're a nice couple, but very straitlaced. They keep a strict eye on the girls and I doubt if they'd be pleased if they knew you weren't married.'

'I'd sooner he was in the Navy,' said Dilys.

'The Navy, then.' Eileen smiled over the girl's head at Ruth. The two women had accompanied Dilys to 'settle her in'. The room was rather dark and over-furnished, but Dilys didn't seem to mind. Indeed, she appeared thrilled to bits at the idea of living by herself, far away from the sharp tongue of her mother, and with a bed all to herself. In Pearl

Street, she'd had to share with her sister.

'It's like a lovely big adventure!' she declared gleefully as she unpacked the few possessions which Eileen had coaxed off Dai. 'I'm glad me mam threw me out. I've even got me own ration book.'

'You must give it to the landlady,' Ruth told her. Breakfast and an evening meal were provided at the all-in price of fifteen shillings a week.

'All right.' Dilys suddenly clutched her side. 'Ouch!'

'What's the matter, luv?' asked Eileen in concern.

'Nothing. Just a bit of a pain, it felt like cramp.'

Eileen and Ruth glanced at each other warily. 'Have you seen a doctor yet?' Ruth enquired.

'Why do I need a doctor?' Dilys looked at her blankly. 'I don't don't understand why I need a husband, either.' She sat on the bed and kicked her heels playfully on the floor. 'Never mind, it's all dead exciting.'

'I wonder when it's due, the baby?' Ruth said as she and Eileen made their way home on the tram. 'She was vague about the incident with the man, just said it was "last summer", which could mean any time between May and September.'

'She don't show much,' Eileen said. 'Though a girl at work felt sickly one morning, and before the shift was over she'd had a baby boy weighing over five pounds. No one had guessed, and even the girl herself didn't know she was expecting. I showed quite a bit when I was having Tony, but not as much as our Sheila. She always puffs up like a balloon.'

'I looked like an elephant each time I was

166

pregnant.' The remark came out quite naturally, when Ruth had sworn she'd never talk about the past to anyone.

'Did you have a hard time, like? People with small bones often do. Me and our Sheila are lucky. We're big-boned like me dad.'

Ruth swallowed. 'I did with Simon, but not with Leah. She was a week early and much smaller. Simon was late.' Simon had been late for everything ever since. She felt she had to change the subject away from herself. 'She'll miss the build-up, won't she? Dilys, I mean. You know, buying things for the baby, wondering whether it will be a boy or a girl? Perhaps the penny will drop one of these days and she'll realise she's pregnant.'

'Perhaps. On the other hand, even when she's had it, she may find it difficult to accept it's hers. We might end up with a bigger problem on our hands, though I'll have a word with Miss Thomas at work. She'll know what to do. She always does.'

'Would Ellis take it?' suggested Ruth.

Eileen looked doubtful. 'I don't think so. Anyroad, she's not a fit person to have a baby. She bullied Dilys something rotten. Imagine how she'd behave with a kid who was born "out of wedlock", as they say.' She looked rueful. 'But then who am I to have an opinion? I've already made enough mess of me own life, without passing judgement on other people's.'

Ruth glanced surreptitiously at Eileen. Her lovely fresh face looked unbearably sad. 'Not according to the street,' she ventured. 'Everyone seems to think you and Francis are the perfect couple.' Ruth had met Francis and had been impressed with his easygoing charm.

'Aye, I know,' Eileen said dryly. 'But the street don't know what goes on behind closed doors, do they?'

'I'm sorry,' Ruth said quickly. 'I didn't wish to pry.' Nothing had irritated her more since she'd come back than people asking questions, questions, and more questions, yet here she was, doing the same thing herself, or at least, gently probing into another woman's affairs.

'It's all right, luv. I don't suppose you know anyone proper till you're married and have lived with them full time.'

'I suppose not. My own husband, Benjy, was a darling man when we were courting, but once married, he turned into a real stuffed shirt, concerned only with appearances.' Ruth grimaced. 'He even grew a set of mutton-chop whiskers. I couldn't stand the sight of them.'

She'd done it again! Imparted a confidence without intending to.

Eileen rolled her eyes. 'Husbands, eh!'

They both laughed.

*　　　　*　　　　*

From then on, Eileen called on Dilys a few evenings a week when she was on the morning shift, taking a collection of the latest women's magazines from the girls at work. During the week when it was her turn to keep an eye on the girl, Ruth hung round in town once the Afternoon Tea Dance was over, and met Dilys outside the tradesman's entrance of the Adelphi Hotel. She took her to Lyon's for a cup of tea and an Eccles cake, and had difficulty persuading her that one was enough for a girl in her condition.

'What condition?' Dilys would enquire blankly.

Ruth spent the intervening time buying presents in the shops which were all dressed up for Christmas. Amazingly, there were quite a few people to choose presents for. Apart from her father, there was Tony Costello, whom she'd grown quite fond of, and his mother, because Ruth and Eileen had become sort of friends through their shared sense of responsibility for Dilys, and of course, Dilys herself, plus odds and ends for the forthcoming baby.

One evening, as she wandered round whiling away the time before she was due at the Adelphi, Ruth noticed a Somerset Maugham play, *The Circle*, was showing at the Royal Court Theatre, and impulsively went in and asked for two tickets for Saturday, one for herself and the other for her father. She loved the author's novels, but had never seen one of his plays. It would be a nice Christmas treat for them both. They could meet Dilys beforehand and take her somewhere more salubrious than Lyon's for tea, which would be a Christmas treat for her at the same time. It was safe to go out again at night; the air-raids had been almost non-existent during December.

Unfortunately, Ruth was informed at the Box Office, Saturday, being the last night, the theatre had sold out, so she bought two for Friday, instead.

Feeling rather pleased with herself, she met Dilys later by the side of the hotel. The girl came out looking puzzled and upset.

'What's the matter?' Ruth asked.

'I've got the sack,' Dilys said indignantly. 'Mrs Haywood said I'm having a baby.'

169

'But Dilys, you *are!*'

Dilys shook her head stubbornly. 'It's not possible.'

The Lime Street pavements were packed with people, either just finishing work or arriving for a night out on the town. It was pitch dark. At twenty past five, when the blackout began, the Christmas and street lights had been switched off and the city plunged into darkness. Ruth said no more as they struggled through crowds until they'd queued up for their food in Lyon's and found an empty table.

'Dilys, love, what about the man you told me about, the one last summer, the one who invited you into bed with him?' she hissed.

'What about him?'

Oh, Lord! The strange thing was, plain and spotty though Dilys was, as well as incredibly stupid, the more Ruth got to know the girl, the more she liked her. It was hard to do otherwise. She was so naive and innocent, so utterly unspoilt, like a five-year-old in a fifteen-year-old's body.

'I can't understand why people keep going on about it,' the girl said peevishly. 'Me mam was just the same. How can I *possibly* be having a baby when I'm not married?'

*   *   *

Jacob wasn't in when Ruth arrived home, slightly later than usual. He must still be in the Costellos', having taken Tony home to bed. She slipped across the road to tell him she was back.

'I was beginning to worry where you were,' he said when he opened the door. 'Come in. I'm just listening to Moura Lympany on the wireless. What

170

a wonderful pianist she is, though not as good as you,' he added loyally. 'It's a pity you gave it up.'

Ruth smiled as she followed him down the narrow hallway. 'They say love is blind, Dad, not deaf. I was never a patch on Moura Lympany.'

He shook his head. 'That's a matter of opinion. Why are you so late, love?'

'I've been having a long talk with Dilys,' Ruth answered with a sigh. 'It turns out it was her who thought we were stupid. I spent a good hour explaining that you can still fall pregnant even if you're not married. She thought it couldn't possibly happen to single girls, they had a special dispensation.'

'Poor child. Did you manage to convince her that there is no such dispensation?'

'Only halfconvinced. Maybe Eileen can have a talk with her. I think she trusts her more than me.' Ruth sat on the edge of a chair and glanced around. She always felt curiously surprised that Eileen's house was almost completely devoid of ornaments and photographs.

'Next week will be Christmas,' said Jacob. 'What will happen to Dilys over the holiday? She's always welcome in our house, you know, for her Christmas dinner.'

He'd half forgotten he was Jewish, had Jacob Singerman. Having lived amongst Gentiles for most of his life, he had come to celebrate the Christian festivals of his neighbours.

Ruth smiled. 'Christmas, Dad? Yet there was no Rosh Hashanah or Yom Kippur.'

Jacob blushed and beat his brow with considerable force. 'Oh, what a terrible Jew I am! Your mother would turn in her grave if she knew

I'd brought you up with nothing to believe in.'

'You brought me up with principles, Dad. Perhaps that's all that really matters in the end.' She recalled that Benjy had been slightly ashamed of being Jewish, and affected Christian habits in order to ingratiate himself with the high and mighty of Graz.

'We will go to the synagogue over Christmas,' Jacob promised. 'I meant to go in September to thank God when I heard you were safe.'

'Whatever you like, Dad.' Ruth stood. 'I'm starving and the meal at home smells good. What is it?'

'Stew with lentils and broad beans.' They always had stew on the days she worked because it was all he could cook, though he usually managed to make each one slightly different.

Ruth remembered the tickets for the Somerset Maugham play and showed them to her father. 'I asked for Saturday, but they were sold out,' she explained when Jacob fretted he wouldn't be there to look after Tony.

'Francis is here less and less of a night-time. As you know, last night Eileen was the first to arrive.'

'Surely Francis can take care of his own son just for the one night?' Ruth argued.

'I suppose so, though I mustn't forget to tell Eileen. Anyway, love, you go home and start on your tea. I'll be back as soon as I can.'

After she'd eaten, Ruth wondered if Brenda Mahon would alter another of her frocks for Friday night. It would be nice to wear something new for the theatre—well, sort of new. She decided to pop along the street and ask her.

'I'm sorry, Ruth,' Brenda said, 'but I'm not taking on any more work at the moment.'

'It would only be a small matter to remove the lace on the bodice and take the hem up a few inches, and perhaps the collar would look better without a frill,' Ruth said persuasively. She held the dress up by the shoulders, hoping Brenda might feel inspired by the challenge to turn it into something modern.

'I'm sorry,' Brenda said again. She ran her hand through her short dark hair which looked rather tousled, as if it hadn't been combed that day, which wasn't at all like Brenda. She was usually as neat as ninepence, as Jacob would have said. 'I just don't feel in the mood for sewing at the moment. It's taking me all me time to finish off the work I've got to do for Christmas.'

'Oh, well, never mind.' Ruth folded the dress. 'I hope your mood soon changes, otherwise you're going to have a lot of disappointed customers at Christmas.'

*   *   *

'Did you get married in a church or a registry office?' Brenda asked when she returned to the living room, which was hazy with smoke.

'Registry Office,' Carrie answered. She had a cigarette in one hand and a glass of gin and orange in the other.

'That means you're only married in the eyes of the law. With us, it was in church, which means we're married in the eyes of God as well.'

173

'I'm not married in the eyes of anyone, am I, darlin'?' Carrie puffed. 'I'm back to being Carrie Banks again.'

'Lucky old you!' said Brenda gloomily.

She was still mad, more than two weeks later, spitting mad. She hadn't written to tell Xavier about Carrie turning up, because she wanted to see his face when he turned up himself, even if it meant waiting months. She hadn't sent him any money, either. He could live on seven bob a week, like all the other men. Xavier rarely wrote, but she was expecting a letter any minute remarking on the fact there'd been no postal orders in her last two letters.

'Have some more gin,' suggested Carrie.

'I wouldn't mind.' Brenda handed over her glass. There was a crashing sound from the parlour, where the girls and Sonny were playing. Normally, Muriel and Monica would have been in bed hours ago, but Brenda had forgotten what normal was. Both women ignored the noise.

'Have a fag. It'll calm your nerves. I couldn't live without me gaspers.'

'So I've noticed. I don't want to start smoking.'

'You didn't want to start drinking, either, but you did, and you enjoy it, don't you?'

'Aye, I suppose I do. It gives you a nice dizzy feeling.'

'Have a fag, come on! You might enjoy that, too,' coaxed Carrie.

'Light it for me. I don't know how.'

'You just strike the match, see! Then take a deep puff in, and lo and behold, you've got a lit fag. Here you are, gal.'

'Ta.' The cigarette was smeared with lipstick, but Brenda didn't care. She coughed and spluttered a

174

little over the first few puffs, but smoked the rest without too much difficulty.

Carrie refilled her own glass.

'You're drinking too much,' Brenda warned. 'Not so much the gin, but the orange. You're turning yellow.'

'I would have turned yellow a long time ago if it were the gin and orange. No, it's these shells I'm working with. Everybody in the factory's yellow. It's something in the gunpowder.'

Carrie had got a job in a chemicals factory in Chorleywood, a long way to go, but the wages were unbelievably high. Six quid a week and meals thrown in, which was compensation of a sort for turning yellow.

'Are you sure it's safe?' Brenda asked worriedly.

'Safe? Of course it's safe,' said Carrie dismissively. 'Mind you, I wouldn't stay if you turned green or purple or something. Yellow looks quite attractive, like a suntan.'

'I suppose it does in a way.' Brenda brooded briefly. 'Were you expecting Sonny when he married you, if you don't mind me asking?'

'I don't mind a bit. Yes, I was, as a matter of fact. Were you expecting Monica?'

'Jaysus, no! We didn't do anything until after we were married.'

'Did he do it twice a night with you?'

'Not bloody likely! Did he with you?'

'Well, yes, but then he only saw me a couple of times a week. I mean, it was more with you on average,' Carrie said. Both women were anxious not to score points off each other. 'D'you know, I'm starving? I don't half fancy some chips.'

'I'll make some if you like,' Brenda offered.

'Nah! It's shop-bought chips I fancy, not home made. Shall I go and buy some?'

'I wouldn't say no.'

Carrie departed, but not before nearly falling headlong over a beautifully embroidered cushion which had been left on the floor.

It was terrible, Brenda reflected, the way everything was being neglected; the house, the children, and even worse, her work. Women kept calling wanting to know why their frocks weren't ready as promised, and Brenda had to keep fobbing them off with a lie.

'I don't feel at all well,' she would explain.

'You don't look it,' the customers would reply when they noticed the dishevelled figure standing in the doorway. Brenda didn't ask them in because everywhere was in such a state.

Things had all gone entirely the opposite way to what she'd planned when Carrie first turned up. Instead of Sonny becoming clean, Monica and Muriel were growing dirtier and dirtier by the day. It seemed too much trouble to do the washing and tidy the house and all the other household tasks which Brenda had automatically done in the past.

It was all Xavier's fault. The lodger! The dressmaker who lived downstairs and fancied him!

The morning after Carrie came, Brenda had gone into the parlour, and instead of the excited little thrill she always felt when she surveyed the work in progress, the cloth just waiting to be cut out and made into beautiful things, she felt sick. The lodger! The dressmaker who lived downstairs . . .

The bastard!

Carrie had gone marching off in search of work

and didn't return till late that night, armed with a bottle of gin, twenty fags, and a fruit cake.

'I got this marvellous job,' she sang joyfully. 'They were so desperate, they asked me to start straight away, right after the interview. They even gave me a sub when I explained I was skint. Three quid! There was a queue on the way home, so I joined it and bought this cake. Fortunately, I had me ration books.'

She seemed oblivious to the fact that the house was a tip and there was no meal waiting. 'Let's have some fish and chips,' she said airily when Brenda began to make excuses.

Now Carrie was turning yellow, the house was even more of a tip, and Brenda spent the days listening to the wireless, reading books and looking after Sonny. Not that the poor little lad needed much looking after. He was used to being ignored, and seemed quite happy to play on the floor with the girls' toys and be fed with jam butties and sweets when Brenda remembered he was there. She'd attempted to wash him once, but he'd screamed blue murder, so she didn't try again.

Yet the funny thing was she felt quite happy in a peculiar way. The money from the Army was enough to pay the rent and buy the groceries, and Carrie gave her two pounds board and lodging and for taking care of Sonny, so there was no need for Brenda to work now she no longer had to support Xavier. She quite enjoyed her lazy days and couldn't wait for Carrie to arrive home with a fresh supply of gin and full of funny stories about things which had happened at work. They'd sit for hours swopping memories of their husband and calling him every name under the sun.

'He used to talk about you a lot,' Carrie had said the other night. 'It was Brenda this, and Brenda that. I think that's why he made you into the lodger, so he could talk about you. Sometimes, I used to feel quite jealous.'

'Huh!' Brenda snorted, not the least bit flattered.

'We could have him sent to jail, you know.' Carrie flicked her cigarette and the ash landed in her glass. 'It's a crime, marrying someone else when you're still married. It's called bigamy.'

Brenda chewed her lip. 'Do you think we should?'

'I ain't sure. I'd have to think about it.'

'Me, too. It'd be in the *Echo*. I'd never be able to hold me head up again. I'd have to move away.'

'Perhaps it'd be best to leave it, then.' Carrie nodded her wavy blonde head. 'Not for his sake, but for yours.'

Brenda jumped when a voice shrilled from the parlour, 'Mam! Our Muriel's gone asleep.'

She leapt to her feet, feeling guilty and slightly dizzy from too much gin. It was ages past the girl's bedtime.

The parlour was a mess, one corner piled high with pieces of material and half-finished clothes. There was dust on the sewing machine and the children had been rolling spools of thread all over the floor. Sonny was chewing the handle of the pinking shears. Brenda quickly grabbed them out of his grubby little hands.

'Come on, off to bed the lot o'yis,' she said.

'My face is all sticky, Mam,' Monica complained.

'Go in the back kitchen and I'll give it a wipe over.'

178

She helped the sleepy Muriel upstairs, cleaned Monica's face, and persuaded Sonny it was time he also went to bed. The girls' old cot had been unearthed from the washhouse and installed in their room. He went uncomplainingly for once. Sonny seemed used to keeping the most unearthly hours and rarely went to bed before midnight.

Downstairs again, Brenda sank into the chair, exhausted after the slight exertion. Carrie came in carrying a large bag of chips.

'Never mind, there's all the more for us,' she said, when Brenda explained the children were in bed. 'Y'know, Bren, I've been thinking. Us two could go dancing over the holidays. It'd be nice to get out of the house for a change.'

'Dancing! I can't dance.'

'Didn't you go dancing with Xavier?' Carrie asked, astounded.

'No, why, did you?'

'Often, the Hammersmith Palais, mostly. He couldn't half trip the light fantastic, could Xavier. What the hell did you do with yourselves all the time?'

'We went for walks and we used to go to church a lot. I didn't even know he could dance.' It seemed so tame, going to church, Brenda thought resentfully. She had a mental picture of Xavier swooping across a dance floor with Carrie in his arms and could have strangled him all over again.

Carrie, however, looked equally hurt. 'He never went to church with me,' she pouted.

*　　　*　　　*

Francis Costello sat on the train on his way home

from work feeling as if he'd come to the end of his tether. He'd lost over five pounds at cards that week and if he didn't win some back he'd have to ask Eileen for money again. Every other source of borrowing had already been exhausted. Indeed, it had become embarrassing asking the chaps at work if they'd lend him a few bob and the excuses were growing thin. How many times could you explain, 'I seem to have left me wallet at home,' without people realising it was another lie? Before you knew it, he'd have a reputation and his job might be at risk if it got back to those on high. The chaps had probably already guessed it was gambling of some sort, either the horses or the dogs or cards. Quite a few were still owed money and expected to be paid back before Christmas. Even his old mate, George Ransome, had flatly refused to lend him a penny when he realised what it was for.

'You're mad to play for money,' he said disparagingly when Francis asked him for a loan. George had actually been quite shocked when it was suggested he too might like to come along to Rodney Smith's one night for a couple of hands of poker. 'I like a good time more than anyone, but losing me hard-earned wages isn't my idea of fun.' He gave Francis a funny look. 'Anyroad, I'm busy with the ARP, aren't I? I've more important things to do with me time than play bloody cards for money. Believe me, Francis, it's a mug's game.'

It was odd, thought Francis, how he'd completely lost the knack since he'd left the Army. He'd rarely played cards before joining up, but there was little else to do when you were shut inside a barracks. He'd taken to poker like a duck takes to water, winning pounds a night with ease. But nowadays he was completely out of luck, a consistent loser. Perhaps, he thought hopefully, if he took some memento from the Army with him tonight it might act as a good luck charm?

Francis scowled. There shouldn't be any reason to feel any reluctance about asking Eileen for money. She was his wife, dammit, and her wages were every bit as much his as they were hers, in fact more so. If only things were as they used to be in the old days when she was firmly under his thumb, he would have demanded her wage packet, unopened, and doled out the housekeeping the way a husband should. He would have known what to do if she refused. He could have kicked himself for spending all that back pay on a bloody bathroom. Just think what he could have done with the cash now!

The train stopped at Kirkdale and quite a few people alighted. He'd been counting the stations automatically, otherwise you'd never know where to get off in the blackout.

Francis lit a cigarette, puffing the smoke out angrily. The eye that was no longer there began to ache with a pounding, gnawing throb, which it had begun to do a lot lately. It always happened when he thought about his terrible predicament and the fact his wife brought home several quid a week, far more than was needed for the housekeeping. What a pity, he cursed again, that the days when she did what she was told were over.

Or were they?

He was sick to death of kowtowing and being nice to her. There were times when it was all he could to do keep his hands to himself when she looked at him with her big blue eyes, smelling of

181

scent and talcum powder and all the sickly things women used. There were other times, mainly Saturdays after he'd had a few drinks, when he longed to get his hands on her, to drag Tony out of the bed and give her what it was a husband's right to give.

She'd never liked the way he did it. Sometimes she'd cry afterwards, but the crying gave him a sense of perverse satisfaction, made him feel like a big strong man inside.

He wondered jealously what it had been like for her with this other man, the one she'd committed 'adultery' with, according to the letter from the solicitor? Francis had searched the bedroom high and low until he'd found a bundle of letters from someone called Nick underneath a newspaper lining the tallboy drawer. He read them, often, when she was on afternoons.

'Who's this Nick?' he asked Tony once, but the lad just blinked vaguely and said, 'I dunno.'

He was lying, Francis could tell. He'd probably been told to keep quiet. Francis would have liked to shake the truth out of him, but he'd be bound to tell Eileen, and then . . .

Then what?

There was no way Jack Doyle was going to get him the promised nomination, not now. Eileen had probably told her dad all sorts of lies. It was obvious that Francis was flogging a dead horse.

So, when you looked at it clearly, there was no reason for him to go on being 'clever' as he'd planned, because he was getting nowhere and never would. He was wasting his time.

When the train reached Marsh Lane, Francis threw his cigarette stub on the floor and stamped on it with such force that the woman sitting opposite nearly jumped out of her skin. He stepped onto the platform feeling like a new man. Today was Friday, Eileen's pay day. When she came home, he'd demand her wage packet and give her what for if she refused.

He walked towards Pearl Street feeling jubilant, his confidence growing with each step. As soon as he'd had his tea, he'd take whatever was in the tin in which Eileen kept the money for the gas and electricity meters, and go round to Rodney Smith's and win back everything he'd lost that week. It wasn't just at home that things were going to change. He could feel a dead certainty in his bones that he was about to have a winning streak. This was going to be the first of many lucky nights. Once he'd got his five pounds, he'd clean the lot of them out. He wouldn't need Eileen's wages, but he'd still take them as a matter of principle. He thought briefly about Tony, but knew Jacob Singerman would never leave the lad by himself when he brought him home and realised Francis wasn't in.

There was a meal waiting for him in the oven, though the peas were hard and the gravy had virtually dried up. Francis ate it, feeling bitter. It was no sort of meal for a man who'd put in a hard day's work. Once his finances were sorted out and he was on the expected winning streak, he'd make Eileen give up that damn job she thought so much of and concentrate on looking after her family at home.

Francis pushed the plate away, the meal half eaten. There was a time when he would have gone to Sheila's for his tea, but his sister-in-law hardly spoke to him nowadays. Thinking about this only made him feel even more angry with his wife. It was her fault; she'd turned Sheila against him, just like she'd turned her dad.

Francis rubbed his hands together fiercely, as if he were rubbing out the recent past. He'd no intention of washing the plate, as he usually did. 'Things are going to change around here, Eileen Costello,' he crowed out loud. 'There'll be no cocoa waiting for you tonight, even if I'm home in time to make it.'

He was on his way upstairs to change his shirt when the air-raid siren went, but Francis didn't pause. There'd been scarcely any raids throughout December. It might be just a false alarm. Anyroad, the card school usually ignored the bombing and played right through. Everyone was too taken up with excitement to notice what was going on outside.

The front door opened and he heard his sister-in-law shout, 'Are you there, Francis?'

'I'm upstairs,' he shouted back.

'I've brought Tony home. There's no room for him in our shelter. I just wanted to make sure you were in. Tara, then.'

Francis swore under his breath as he came down the stairs. His son was standing in the living room, his hands stuffed in his pockets and his glasses perched on the end of his nose. He looked awkward and stared uncomfortably at his dad. The two had spent little time alone together since Francis had returned.

'Where's Mr Singerman?' Francis demanded. 'Shouldn't you be with him?'

'Me mam told you the other day, he's gone to town.'

Francis swore again. His son was his flesh and blood and he loved him in his own strange way. It didn't seem right to walk out and leave him by himself, not whilst there was a raid on. On the other hand, he just *knew* his luck was in tonight. There was no way he was prepared to miss the game. He cast around in his mind for someone he could leave Tony with. Aggie Donovan would take him, but she might have already left for the public shelter around the corner.

'We'd better get under the stairs, Dad.' Planes could already be heard overhead.

Francis made a quick decision. Perhaps this was the way fate had meant it to be. Tony would be the good luck charm. Jacob often said how good he was at cards.

He nodded brusquely at his son. 'Get your coat on, lad. We're going out.'

*   *   *

Everyone at Dunnings was just finishing their dinner when the klaxon blared at twenty past six to signal a raid had started. No one bothered with the shelter; too much time had been wasted and production lost, and nothing had been dropped as far out as Melling—at least, not yet.

As the evening wore on, word began to circulate from department to department and from worker to worker, 'The raid's a bad one. It's the worst so far.'

'It can't be worse than that one in November, surely?' Doris shouted when the news reached the workshop.

'Seems like it.'

185

Eileen and Pauline stopped their machines and went outside to look. They'd get into trouble if they were found, but neither cared.

'Jaysus!' Eileen gasped.

The sky over Liverpool was crimson and black, as if the entire city was on fire, and searchlights raked to and fro like swords. The sheer horror of the scene was only made more awful because, although they could hear the dull thud of explosions in the distance, the sound predominant was the delightful gurgle of the stream at their feet as the water rushed over the stones. There was an air of unreality about the whole thing, as if they were watching it in the pictures.

'I wish we could go home!' Eileen said fervently.

'So do I.' Pauline put her arm around Eileen's shoulders.

'This is the worst part, knowing there's a raid on and being so far away.' Eileen shook herself impatiently. 'I'd best pull meself together. It's the same for everyone, isn't it? You've got your mam and dad to worry about.'

'Perhaps we shouldn't have come,' Pauline murmured.

The two women stayed watching for a while, silent and horrorstricken.

'I wish we hadn't. Come on, let's go back.'

They cast a last look at the red sky over Liverpool before returning to their lathes.

*   *   *

Whether you got home or not if there was a raid on depended on the whim of the driver of your particular bus. Some drivers parked on the fringes

186

of the city and refused to budge until the All Clear sounded; sitting safely in their cabs, they were immune to the insults hurled in their direction by their passengers who called them lily-livered cowards or worse. Other drivers forged blithely ahead as if nothing of significance was happening outside the bus.

On the Friday before Christmas, when the whole factory had been on tenterhooks all night, and people had been in and out to see if things were calming down and coming back to report in shocked voices that things seemed to be getting worse, everyone emerged at ten o'clock ready to kill the driver of their bus if he refused to take them home.

One lucky vehicle turned left as it left the factory on its way to Maghull and Ormskirk, away from the raid. The rest turned towards Bootle and Seaforth, Everton and Spellow Lane, and the centre of the city.

There was no sing-song that night on the bus that went to Bootle, no carols as there had been all December. Instead, no one could take their eyes off the sinister red umbrella that hung over Liverpool, and they silently prayed their loved ones had come to no harm.

Perhaps their driver was as anxious to get home as they were. He stopped only to let people off, then drove on, even faster than usual.

Eileen and Pauline were sitting together on the top deck. They'd not long passed through Walton Vale when an explosion rocked the bus.

'Oh, God!' Pauline giggled hysterically. 'I can't believe this is happening!'

'Don't worry, luv,' Eileen said automatically. Her

187

entire body was tense, rocking slightly as if willing the driver to go even faster than he already was. The closer they got to Bootle, the more it seemed as if the entire town was in flames. There were fires everywhere. Every now and then a bomb would drop and debris could be seen being blown into the air, black and terrible against the red sky, then it would quickly subside; a house, a street blown to pieces.

It wasn't right, she thought savagely. The heavens were supposed to be a tranquil place, a peaceful blanket over the world. Instead, they'd become a threat, a source of danger, the place from which death was delivered upon people who'd done no harm to anyone.

'I'll see you Monday, Pauline,' she said when her stop approached. She didn't add, as she usually did, 'Have a nice weekend.'

It was relatively calm when she began to walk down Marsh Lane. Funnily enough, things didn't seem quite so bad when you were in the thick of them as they did from a distance, though the sky was crimson in every direction and she felt as if she were walking through hell, particularly as there wasn't another soul in sight. Almost immediately, a fire engine came racing around the corner, its bell clanging furiously, closely followed by two ambulances.

She darted into a shop doorway when a bomb landed close by. There was the sound of breaking glass and falling rubble, followed by a woman screaming. A dog began to howl, and Eileen wondered briefly if Snowy was all right as she set off again.

'For Christ's sake, woman, get under cover!' An

ARP warden ran past, pushing her aside with considerable force. 'What d'you think the shelters are for?'

Eileen ignored him. Another few minutes and she would be home. She began to run when she turned off Marsh Lane, down Garnet Street, where the houses stood in rows of regimented neatness, their windows glinting crimson. At least her dad's house was safe, though that was no guarantee he was safe himself as he was firewatching.

She became aware of the pleasant smell of baking bread and noticed that the bakery on the corner of Opal Street was on fire. Several firemen wielded their hoses on the gaily crackling flames, to little apparent effect. Incredibly, there was singing coming from the public shelter opposite the King's Arms. Someone was playing the harmonica— almost certainly Paddy O'Hara. 'Bless 'em all, Bless 'em all,' they caroused cheerfully.

Eileen was never quite sure later whether there was an explosion or not, but suddenly a wall collapsed directly in front of her and she stumbled and fell on a heap of broken bricks.

A man's voice shouted, 'Are you all right, luv? Anyroad, you should be in the shelter.'

'I'm fine.' She struggled to her feet. She was almost home, but the wall that had just fallen belonged to the end house in Pearl Street, Number 29. Her sister lived only a few doors along.

At last! She rounded the corner, breathless. Her own house and all those on the far side stood untouched, but the windows of several opposite were shattered, and the door of Number 29 had been thrown across the street and lay smashed to pieces against the pub.

'Phew!' She gave an audible sigh of relief as she hurried into her sister's. It was obvious that Tony and Francis were all right.

'Sheila!' she shouted.

'Is that you, sis? What's happened? I'm too scared to come out.' Sheila's voice was shaking.

Eileen went into the living room. The rear window had completely disappeared. She nearly stepped right on it, lying in the middle of the floor in one large shattered piece, still glued together with criss-cross sticky tape. The fireplace and the hearth were heaped with soot and all the furniture had moved slightly across the floor. The burning sky outside illuminated the entire room a shade of ghastly crimson. 'Everywhere's in a hell of a state, Sheil, but the house is still standing.'

The cupboard door opened and Sheila peeped out. She was clutching Mary, who was fast asleep. 'I thought we'd had it for a minute or so then.'

'Are the kids all right?'

'They're fine, considering. There's only Dominic and Niall awake.'

'Is there any shrapnel, Auntie Eileen?' one of the boys shouted.

'If there is, you won't catch me looking for it,' she answered sharply. She attempted a smile in the direction of her sister. 'What do you want to do, Sheil?'

'What else can I do, 'cept stay where we are till it's all over, then clear up the mess?' Sheila said simply.

She was right, Eileen reckoned. Anyroad, lightning never struck twice, and the family were probably safer in a house that had already been hit, albeit slightly, than anywhere else in Bootle.

190

'I'll bring you over a cup of tea as soon as the All Clear goes,' Eileen promised. 'There's no way you'll light a fire in the grate till the soot's been cleared. Our Dad'll see to the winder tomorrer. I'd best be off home, or Francis and Tony'll will be worried where I've got to.'

'All right, luv. Thanks for coming.'

'Tara, sis.'

When Eileen let herself in, Snowy came running down the hall and leapt into her arms, mewing piteously. 'You poor little thing,' she cried as the kitten snuggled into her neck. 'I expect you're terrified in all this noise.' She frowned. It wasn't like Tony to shelter without his precious Snowy. Eileen rushed into the living room and opened the cupboard door. The space was dark and empty and she felt her blood run cold. Where were they?

Perhaps Francis had gone out and left Tony with one of the neighbours. Who, she wondered, doing her best not to panic. She ran out into the street, still clutching the kitten, and hammered on Mr Singerman's door. As she half expected, there was no reply. He and Ruth had gone to the Royal Court and were probably sheltering in town.

Eileen stood in the middle of the street, glancing around wildly as she wondered whose door to knock on next. Several people used the public shelter. Perhaps that's where Tony was.

Her legs were shaking as she ran back down the street, even more conscious now of the dull roar of the planes overhead, the constant scream of bombs, explosions, the smell of burning. Instead of being safely in her arms, her son was somewhere out in all this chaos.

The shelter was dimly lit and crowded and the

191

people inside were still singing at the top of their voices, *We're going to hang out the washing on the Siegfried Line . . .*

'Is Tony Costello here?' Eileen yelled.

The singing faltered to a halt. 'Y'what, luv?'

'Tony Costello, is he here?'

'Is that you, Eileen?' Aggie Donovan pushed herself forward.

'I'm looking for our Tony,' Eileen explained. 'I just got home from work and he's not there, nor Francis.'

'Has anyone here seen Francis Costello?' Aggie shouted.

There was a chorus of 'no's and murmurs of sympathy. 'It must be awful,' a woman said loudly, 'for those that have to be at work during a raid.'

Eileen's heart sank. 'Thanks, anyroad.'

'D' you want me to help search for them, like?' Aggie asked.

'No, ta. I'll go and knock on a few doors.'

But although she knocked at every conceivable house, no one had any idea where Francis or Tony were—no one, that is, until George Ransome came lurching down the street in his ARP uniform.

Eileen grabbed his arm. 'Have you seen Francis?'

George's eyes were red-rimmed and sore and his face was covered with black smears. 'I've just come for a pack of ciggies,' he muttered.

Eileen grabbed his arm and shook it. There was nothing dashing about George tonight. He seemed to have aged a decade since she last saw him. There was a funny, dazed expression on his face and his eyes were empty, as if he were in some sort of trance. She wondered if he was drunk.

'Have you seen Francis, luv?' she asked again, trying to keep her voice calm.

'I've seen everything there is to see tonight, girl,' he said dully. He'd seen things that he'd never get out of his mind for as long as he lived; dead bodies were bad enough, but bits of people, arms and legs and heads, were more than he could stand. 'I've come home for more ciggies, that's all. I need a smoke really bad.' And a break from all the horror, a moment alone with a fag to try and forget what was going on outside.

'Have one of mine, George.' Eileen lit a cigarette, amazed her hands were so steady. She put it in his mouth and they both ducked when a bomb exploded on the far side of the railway line and a small shower of debris descended on them. Nelson neighed hysterically in his stable next to the wall and Snowy clawed Eileen's shoulder in fright. She'd actually forgotten she was still carrying the kitten clutched to her neck whilst she'd searched frantically for her son.

'About Francis,' she reminded George, though he looked in too far gone a state to remember anything at the moment.

He was taking long dragging puffs on the cigarette and jumped when she spoke as if he'd only just realised she was there. 'Eileen!' he said in surprise. Then his heart sank. Eileen Costello! Was it his place to tell the woman she was a widow? George Ransome pulled himself together and decided it was.

'I'm sorry, girl. Jesus Christ, I'm so sorry!' He began to weep.

'Sorry about what, George?' Eileen felt as if her voice was coming from a long way away.

193

'About Francis, girl. He's dead. He was at Rodney Smith's in Rimrose Road. The house got a direct hit.' That had been the most terrible thing of all, pulling the broken body of his old mate out of the rubble.

'But what about Tony?' Eileen screamed. 'What about Tony?'

George covered his face with his hands. The hands smelt of blood and dead flesh. 'Oh, Christ!' he moaned. It was even worse than he'd thought. So *that's* who the dead kid was. Tony Costello.

CHAPTER NINE

On the day after the worst raid inflicted on Liverpool so far, Sheila Reilly took her family to the cottage in Melling long before the air-raid siren wailed to warn more death and destruction was on its way. At Eileen's insistence, Brenda Mahon and Carrie Banks and their children also went. What did it matter, six kids in the big bed and three in the little one, and the adults sleeping, or trying to sleep, on the chairs downstairs? Even if you woke up aching all over, at least you woke up, which was more than many people had done the night before.

The raid on the second night was even longer than the one before. On the third night, three days before Christmas, the bombardment persisted for twelve whole hours. Sheila kept looking out of the front window at the red sky over Liverpool. 'I hope our Eileen's all right,' she said more than once. Eileen had refused to come with them and Sheila knew full well the reason why. Her sister was hoping to be killed, like Tony, though she hadn't put the hope into words. Sheila didn't blame her sister for wanting to die. She might well want to do the same if she lost her entire family. The thought of the emptiness without someone close to love, not a single person to call your own, seemed so horrendous that Sheila buried her head in the curtain and began to weep.

'What's the matter, Sheil?' asked Brenda.

'What d'you think? I can't get our Eileen out of me mind.'

'Oh, she'll get over it,' Carrie said offhandedly. 'People get over everything in time.'

Sheila dried her eyes on the curtain but didn't answer. She detested Carrie Banks with her couldn't-care-less attitude to everything. The woman was a bad influence on Brenda, for one thing. The two of them were standing in front of the mirror, giggling together, as Carrie showed Brenda how to apply eyeshadow and mascara. They were going to a dance on New Year's Eve. The pair were smoking and flicking ash all over the polished floor. Despite the fact Brenda had given up dressmaking, she'd managed to make them a frock each for the dance, though she looked ridiculous in the creation she'd run up for herself, a bright green crepe de Chine affair which was too tight, too short and too low in the neck. Brenda was dead plain and she'd never look anything else, no matter what finery she got decked up in.

'Would you like a drink, Sheila?' Carrie asked, waving a bottle of gin in her direction.

'No, ta, though I wouldn't mind a cup of tea.'

Neither woman made any attempt to go into the back kitchen, so Sheila went herself to put the

195

kettle on. As far as she could make out, no one would have eaten for three days if it had been up to Brenda and Carrie. Sheila had done all the cooking, and the cleaning, too.

Sheila sighed as she waited for the kettle to boil. She'd drink the tea out here, just to get a bit of peace away from the giggling which got on her nerves. She crept upstairs to make sure her children were safe and sound. They were still there, tucked together like sardines in the double bed. There'd been a terrible row each night whilst they arranged their legs around each other and adjusted their arms. Now they looked like little angels, all six of them. Six children, she thought breathlessly, all hers!

She went down, made the tea and drank it leaning against the sink. Outside, the wind was howling through the tall trees that bordered the large garden. Sheila opened the door to watch and listen. The sound was strange and rather eerie to someone who came from a town where there were few trees about, and those mainly in the park. She wondered how on earth her sister could have visualised living in such an isolated place, miles away from her family. The bare trees were waving madly, like devils against the pink sky. Sheila quickly shut the door. It was frightening.

On the other hand, she thought sadly, if Francis hadn't come home and Eileen had been living here, Tony would still be alive.

*   *   *

On Christmas Eve the women went back to Bootle. The previous night Liverpool had been let off

196

relatively lightly and it had been the turn of Manchester to endure the main brunt of the heavy raid.

Sheila would have returned, raids or no raids, because Francis and Tony Costello were being buried that day.

What a terrible day for a funeral, Sheila thought; Christmas Eve and the sky overcast and grey and the wind whipping like razor blades through the wide open space of Ford Cemetery. She stood holding the arm of her white-faced sister, her dad on the other side, with Sean behind like a guardian angel, looking grown up and important in his blue-grey uniform. He'd only been in the RAF a fortnight and had been allowed twenty-four hours' compassionate leave.

The neighbours were all there, every single one, except Jacob Singerman who was too ill. George Ransome stood on the far side of the open grave, as stooped and grey-faced as an old man. He was weeping openly, as were Aggie Donovan and Ellis Evans and many of the other women. Paddy O'Hara's eyes wavered sightlessly over the crowd. Even Rover seemed aware there was something unusual happening. He lay with his nose on his paws, whimpering softly every now and then.

Tony's little coffin looked so pathetic when it was laid on top of the bigger one of his dad. Sheila took a long shuddering breath, determined not to cry because Eileen wasn't crying. Her sister's face was frozen, completely expressionless, as if she were beyond grief, and when it was time for her to throw a handful of soil into the grave, she put her hand in her pocket and threw something else in at the same time, Tony's wire-rimmed spectacles.

'Someone found them,' Eileen said in a strange husky voice. 'You never know, Tony might need his glasses wherever he might be.'

*   *   *

People couldn't possibly have been more kind and sympathetic, but it was *her* son who'd been killed, not theirs. You couldn't expect them to grieve as she was doing, not over Christmas, and she couldn't stand the sight of women coming happily home laden with last-minute shopping, particularly the toys, nor the sound of carols and hoots of laughter coming from the King's Arms. It would be even worse on Christmas morning when the kids played out in the street with their presents, particularly with Sheila living with her whilst her own house was being repaired. On Christmas Eve, after the funeral had taken place, Eileen knew she had to get away, and there was only one place to escape to, and that was the cottage. She yearned for its peace and quiet.

'But you *can't* go there!' said Sheila, horrified, when Eileen told her of her intention. 'It's so lonely.'

'That's why I want to go,' Eileen said simply. Her dad and Sheila had been towers of strength, as had Sean for the short time he'd been home, but that was only another reason to leave her family behind. Like everyone, they'd had a tough time lately and she didn't want to spoil their holiday merely by being there. They'd have to tread round on tiptoe, terrified of saying the wrong thing and hurting her feelings.

Ruth Singerman was the only person who

198

seemed to understand, though even she wasn't quite sure if it was the right thing to do. 'I know it must get you down, the constant distractions when all you want is to be alone with your grief, but perhaps it's not such a bad thing to have people around.'

Eileen shook her head stubbornly. 'I can always come back if I need company, can't I?'

'As long as you do,' warned Ruth.

'Is your dad any better?'

Ruth shook her head worriedly. 'He would have been upset anyway, because he loved Tony, but he regards himself as entirely responsible. If we hadn't gone to the theatre, none of this would have happened.'

'That's stupid!' He was such a dear silly old man, Jacob singerman.

'It may be stupid, but it's true,' Ruth said flatly. 'To tell you the truth, I feel terrible myself. It was my idea to buy the tickets, not his.' She searched Eileen's drawn face for absolution. The sensible part of her head told her it was indeed stupid to feel guilty over such an innocent act, but another part insisted she was far more responsible than her father. She felt even more guilty about laying all this on Eileen at such a moment, wanting her forgiveness when the poor woman was already totally distraught.

Forgiveness was instantly forthcoming. 'I don't blame anyone except the Germans,' Eileen said firmly, 'not even Francis.' It would have been easy to blame Francis for taking Tony with him, too easy, but he'd only been doing his duty as a father. In fact, she blamed herself for not realising how badly he'd caught the gambling bug, for having

199

gone to work at Dunnings in the first place. She sighed. 'If you don't mind, Ruth, I'd like to get away soon.'

'Are you sure you'll be all right?'

'Positive.'

Positive! Positive she'd be all right! How strange that you could talk so coherently and sensibly when you were tearing apart inside. She couldn't imagine that she'd ever be all right again. Part of her had died along with Tony, and each night since she'd lain on the bed, and although she wished no harm to fall on the neighbours, she'd prayed one of the bombs screeching downwards would come through the ceiling and blow her to pieces as another bomb had done her little son. But the weapons had chosen other victims, other mothers, other sons.

There was a couple with two children on the Melling bus, taking presents to their grandma.

'Will she have mince pies?' the little girl asked.

'Aye, and crackers,' said the father.

'The sort you pull?'

'That's right, luv, the sort you pull.'

'Merry Christmas!' the children called as Eileen got off at the Post Office. The driver and conductor shouted the same thing.

'And the same to you,' she said.

She walked down the silent, unlit lane which led to the cottage. The sky was black for a change; no moon, no searchlights, no red clouds. In fact, it was so dark she missed the gate, and walked right past before she realised she'd gone too far.

Sheila had told her the house had been left in a state. 'I'm sorry, luv, but Brenda and that Carrie didn't lift a finger. I did me best to clear it up before we left, but as fast as I did it got messed up again.'

Eileen swept the floor, made the beds and washed the dishes. It seemed important to have the place looking as she'd left it weeks ago. She lit the fire with rolled-up newspaper and one of the firelighters she'd bought when she thought she was moving in, gradually adding a few of the logs which were neatly stacked in the garden shed, until there was a roaring blaze. Then she made a cup of tea and switched on the wireless.

She sat there, warm and comfortable in the soft chair, with music swelling throughout the black-beamed, low-ceilinged room. The fire crackled and popped in a friendly fashion.

It looks pretty, she thought idly, so pretty. It would have been a nice place to live, particularly with Dunnings just along the road. Miss Thomas had said it would be all right to disappear about half past eight in the morning and make sure Tony was up, give him his breakfast and take him to school. He'd been really looking forward to playing football in the garden. Eileen stared deeply into the fire and tried to cry, because she hadn't cried once since she learnt he was dead. Someone had said you felt better once you'd cried. But no matter how hard she concentrated, the tears wouldn't come. Anyroad, there was no way she'd ever feel better. Her life was over, no longer worth living without her son. All that was left was an empty, aching shell of the person who'd once been Eileen Costello.

At a quarter to twelve, she put her coat on and went to Midnight Mass in St Kentigern's, the little church in the High Street. By the time Mass began the church was crowded and the aisles were packed with worshippers forced to stand. The priest reminded them in his sermon that hundreds of people had died in Liverpool over the last few days and offered up prayers for them and their relatives.

Eileen told herself that she was not the only bereaved parent in the country, that there were others who'd also lost sons and daughters, but it didn't seem to make any difference. The gnawing ache persisted and grew like an enormous lump of grief inside her.

She returned home and lay on the settee, watching the fire as one by one the logs collapsed, showering sparks, into a heap of glowing ash which slowly turned grey and then there was nothing. She began to shiver, not just because she was cold, although she was freezing, but because she suddenly had no control over her body. The shivering became violent and she could hear a woman screaming and realised it was herself.

'I want to die! *Please* let me die!' she pleaded.

At some time during the night, she fell into a fitful wretched sleep, but was woken by a car driving down the lane, its engine roaring. Dawn was just breaking and a slit of grey light showed through the curtains. It was Christmas Day and Tony would have found his presents by now; the jigsaw of a Spitfire, the Enid Blyton book, the box of soldiers. The nagging ache inside her hurt so fiercely she felt as if she might burst. She jumped up quickly and went out into the garden where she plunged into the ankle-high wet grass and began to run, waving her arms like a madwoman.

'Please let me die!' she screamed.

'Eileen!' a voice called loudly and urgently, but she ignored it because it could only be part of her

202

nightmare, but the voice called again, even more loudly, 'Eileen!'

She stopped running and looked back at the house. Nick was standing in the kitchen doorway looking at her in astonishment. 'Have you gone mad?'

Eileen walked towards him. Nick! What on earth was he doing here? She was conscious of the fact that she felt nothing, absolutely nothing, yet this was Nick, the man she'd thought she'd love forever.

'You've got no shoes on!' he said irritably when she came near. 'You'll catch your death of cold.'

Eileen looked down at her stockinged feet. They were soaking. 'I didn't realise,' she said vaguely.

'There's no fire lit inside, it's freezing.' He frowned. 'What the hell's going on? Where's Tony?'

Eileen pushed past him into the kitchen. 'Tony's dead,' she said.

Nick's frown disappeared. His face seemed to collapse in front of her eyes. 'Jesus Christ!' he groaned. 'Oh, no!' He turned away as if he were about to cry, then turned back just as quickly. 'My dearest girl, no wonder you wanted to die,' he cried hoarsely. 'Come here.'

He picked her up bodily in his arms and carried her into the front room and laid her on the settee, where he removed her wet stockings and fetched an eiderdown from upstairs and tucked it around her.

'There!' he said gently. 'There!'

He cleared the grate, relit the fire and made a cup of tea. Whilst she drank it, he knelt on the floor and stroked her hair. 'When did it happen?' he whispered.

'Friday night during the raid.'

His brown eyes glistened with emotion. 'I loved Tony as a son,' he said softly.

'I know you did.'

'What on earth are you doing here all by yourself?' he demanded. His face twisted in alarm. 'Please God, don't tell me your family have come to any harm?'

'I just wanted to be alone, that's all,' she assured him. 'Me family are fine.'

'Including Francis?'

She shook her head. There were times when she completely forgot about Francis. He was dead, unmourned by his wife, but not by the neighbours, who thought the world had lost a great man.

'I can't say I'm sorry,' Nick muttered.

'He didn't turn out too bad in the end,' she said, feeling Francis should get the credit he deserved. 'He was quite a good husband over the last few months. He never did either me or Tony any harm.'

Nick made a face but didn't answer.

'What made you come?' she asked curiously. 'You said you'd never return to the cottage.'

He stretched his arms and she noticed how tired he looked. He'd probably been driving all night. In fact, she supposed it was the sound of his car that had woken her.

'I intended staying with friends in London for a few days,' he explained. 'I lost my way in the blackout and found myself going towards the Great North Road. Then, the most peculiar thing happened. I felt as if I was being drawn towards Liverpool, towards you. I felt convinced you needed me.' He looked sideways at her. 'Do you?'

She couldn't be bothered being tactful. 'I don't

know,' she said bluntly. 'To be frank, Nick, I've scarcely thought about you over the last few days.'

He nodded understandingly. 'That's not surprising. But are you glad I'm here?'

Although she remembered clearly how hurt he'd been when she hadn't turned up in September, even so, she wasn't prepared to lie and say things she didn't mean no matter how much he might want her to. 'I'm glad *someone*'s here,' she said. 'On reflection, it was a daft idea to come to the cottage by meself. I think I might have ended up in the loony bin by the end of the day if you hadn't come.'

'So, you *do* need me!' he said eagerly.

She lay back and closed her eyes and tried to decide if she needed Nick, but the inside of her head was too woolly to decide anything and she fell asleep with Nick sitting on the floor beside her holding her hand. She dreamt that Tony was calling her. He sounded frightened, wanting his mam.

'Tony!' She sat upright and glanced wildly around the room. 'Where's Tony?'

Nick had fallen asleep with his head on her knee. He woke, instantly alert. 'It's all right, darling, I'm here.'

'But I want Tony!' Her body heaved as she began to cry, and Nick wrapped his arms around her.

'That's good,' he whispered. 'Let it all go. Cry all day if you want.'

Her body felt as limp as a rag by the time she'd finished weeping in Nick's arms. 'I'm sorry,' she moaned. 'What a way to spend Christmas Day when you could have been with friends.'

He shook her gently. 'As if I'd want to be

anywhere else!' he chided. 'Shall I make more tea? Are you hungry?'

She shook her head. 'There's not much food out there, anyroad.'

'I bet you've hardly eaten over the last few days. Why don't you wash your face and comb your hair and we'll go to the pub for a meal? Your stockings are dry, I hung them from the mantelpiece.'

She shook her head again, because the idea seemed grotesque, but after a great deal of persuading, Nick managed to convince her it would do her good.

The pub was packed and they had difficulty finding two empty seats at a table. Eileen felt entirely divorced from the other customers, who seemed to be having a wonderful time. Her body was numb and empty and she couldn't visualise ever being part of the real world again.

'I can't stand it here,' she whispered the minute Nick had finished eating. She'd hardly touched her own meal.

'Then we'll go home, but before we do, I'd like you to have a good stiff drink.' He went over to the bar and returned with a double whisky and she recalled Donnie Kennedy had brought her the same thing in the pub on the Dock Road all those months ago. Now poor Donnie was dead, like Tony.

'Did the drink do you good?' Nick asked as they were walking home.

'That's what Donnie asked,' she said. She felt slightly dizzy, as she had done then.

'Who?'

'It doesn't matter.'

They'd only been inside the cottage a few

minutes when the telephone rang. 'It must be for you,' Nick said. 'No one knows I'm here.'

'For me?' She picked up the receiver and said, 'Hallo.'

To her amazement, it was her dad. 'We're worried sick about you, girl. Are you all right? I'll come and fetch you if you like.'

Her heart softened as she thought about his huge frame stuck in a telephone box. He'd probably never been inside one before. 'As all right as I'll ever be, Dad,' she answered. 'Nick arrived this morning.'

'That's good!' There was relief in his gruff voice. 'Tara then, luv.' He rang off before she could say goodbye herself.

When she went back into the living room, Nick said, 'I think you should go to bed.'

She nodded obediently. 'All right.'

'In fact, I'll come with you. I'm completely exhausted. I can't remember when I last had a good night's sleep.'

Eileen said quickly, 'Nick, I don't want to . . .'

He kissed her forehead. 'I know you don't, darling. I just want to hold you, that's all.'

She went to bed in her petticoat because it hadn't crossed her mind to bring a nightdress, and was fast asleep by the time Nick got under the clothes. When she woke up it was pitch dark outside and his arm was heavy on her hip and his breathing steady and even. She lay there, thinking for the first time in days about someone other than Tony. She was glad Nick had come. There was no one else in the world she'd sooner have with her at the moment. It was just so hard to deal with anything outside her immediate grief. She turned over carefully so as not to dislodge his arm, until they were facing each other. It had been light when they came to bed and the curtains were still open. She could just make out his face in the dark. He was beautiful, she thought, beautiful in the way men sometimes were, with glossy olive skin and long dark eyelashes she'd always envied. His hair was black and curly and remained curly, no matter how short it was cut. It was his eyes she loved most, a lovely liquid brown that turned her stomach inside out when they looked at her in a particular way. His nose—well, his nose could have been a better shape, a bit smaller and slightly less crooked.

Impulsively she leaned across and kissed him. His eyes opened. 'Darling!' he whispered.

'Make love to me,' she said urgently.

'Are you sure?'

'I'm not sure at all. I just thought I might lose myself in you for a minute.'

'Let's see!' He began to touch her and, incredibly, she no longer felt empty, but full of desire. It was every bit as good, perhaps better, than it had ever been before. There was an added desperation inside Eileen, as if the more passionate she became, the more it would lessen, temporarily at least, her aching misery.

When it was over and they lay in each other's arms, Nick murmured, 'I don't think a day has passed since I last saw you when I've not thought about us, about making love and wondering if it would ever happen again.'

'Nor me.'

'Honest? I thought you might forget all about me once you were back with Francis.'

'As if I could forget you, Nick! And I was never

really back with Francis, not properly. I was merely put in the position where I had no choice.'

He stroked her face. 'I was horrible, wasn't I?' he said in a small voice.

'You were,' she confirmed.

'Selfish, too. I couldn't understand how you could put him before me.'

'But I didn't, Nick,' she began, but before she could go on, he laid his finger on her lips.

'I know, I know. Afterwards I realised I'd done precisely the same thing when I joined up. There are certain things that make you the person you are. I *had* to fight, and although you thought it meant I didn't love you, you stood by me and gave me the benefit of the doubt. I was too impatient to understand you had to stay with Francis. I let you down.'

'I let you down, too, although I couldn't help it.'

'You know,' he mused, 'on the last day we were here together, that terrible day, I kept praying you would try to seduce me. If only you had, I would have been lost.'

'I thought about it, but I was too frightened. Say you had rejected me?'

'I'm sorry, darling,' he whispered. 'I nearly wrote to you loads of times since, but I was worried it might land you in trouble.'

'Never mind. It doesn't matter now, does it?' The wretchedness was gradually returning. Everything that had happened with Nick seemed trite and unimportant compared with her recent loss.

Normally acutely sensitive to her feelings, to the slightest nuance of expression in her voice, for once he didn't seem aware that she had changed. 'No, it doesn't matter, not now,' he said. 'In a few months' time, after a decent interval has passed, we can get married, can't we?

'Can't we?' he repeated urgently when she didn't answer.

'I don't know, Nick,' she said tiredly.

'Christ!' He threw back the clothes and got out of bed. She could just about see his long, smooth, naked body gleaming in the dull light. 'Why not?'

'You'll catch your death of cold. Get back into bed.'

'Not until you've told me why we can't get married.'

She sat up and dragged the eiderdown around her shoulders. It was freezing in the unheated bedroom. 'Nick,' she said impatiently. 'I'm not in the mood for this sort of thing.'

'Neither am I. Why can't we get married? I thought that's what we both wanted more than anything in the world.'

'Get back into bed, please.' She patted the space beside her. There'd often been times when she thought of him as a little boy, not much different from Tony. 'Please?'

'Oh, all right!' he said sulkily.

His skin was like ice and she pulled the eiderdown around him. 'I'm not sure why I don't want us to get married just yet, Nick. It's to do with Tony, I know that much. I used to feel as if you were marrying the pair of us, not just me.'

'I know, I know, I felt the same.'

'It's different now, entirely different without him. It doesn't seem right . . .' Eileen struggled for the words. 'I mean, I can't *contemplate* being happy for a long, long time, if ever.' She touched his face.

210

'Please say you understand, darling?'

'I think so,' he said grudgingly.

'What are you wearing?'

He actually managed to laugh. 'That's a bloody stupid question. Nothing!'

'I mean, did you come in uniform or civvies?'

'Uniform, of course. Didn't you notice?'

'No.' She shook him. 'That's what I'm trying to get at, don't you see? I didn't even take in how you were dressed. I'm all switched off, Nick. I don't want to marry you feeling like a zombie. It wouldn't be fair.'

'I don't give a hang what's fair. All I want is for you to be my wife. That's all I've ever wanted since the day we met in Southport. You could come and live by the base in Canterbury. It would do you good to get away.'

For a brief moment, she was tempted, but more by the thought of getting away than being married. 'No, Nick,' she said firmly. 'I want us to be married, but not yet.'

'I'm beginning to think this relationship is doomed,' he said bitterly. 'Every time we're about to get together something happens to prevent it.'

'Jaysus, Nick!' Her voice was raw and hoarse. 'Tony's *dead*!'

'Aah!' He slid down the bed and buried his face in the pillow then beat the pillow with his fist. 'I'm sorry! I'm so besotted with you I can't think of anything else.'

She lay over him, her cheek against his back. 'I understand.'

'You understand everything. You're too good for me.'

'Let's go to sleep,' she said, 'and we'll talk about

it in the morning.'

*   *   *

Nick left soon after breakfast, as his leave expired at midnight. 'Do you want me to write?'

Eileen nodded. 'Often, and I'll write to you,' she promised.

He pulled a face as they embraced for the last time. 'You know I love you, don't you?'

'I know, and I love you.' It was just that at the moment the love was buried underneath mounds of grief.

He hugged her so tightly she could scarcely breathe. 'One of these days we'll be together for always.'

'I promise, Nick.'

After he'd gone, she began to tidy up, feeling numb. It would be wise not to spend another night at the cottage, though she dreaded the thought of returning to Pearl Street. The house would never be the same again without Tony there.

There was a knock on the front door. She felt convinced it must be her dad, but it was Miss Thomas who stood outside, a moth-eaten fur coat over the inevitable costume and an old-fashioned felt hat on her head.

'Eileen!' The two women embraced briefly. 'I'm so sorry, dear, though "sorry" is such an inadequate word, isn't it?'

'Come in. I'm afraid it's a bit cold. I'm leaving soon and I've let the fire die. I was just about to go home.' Eileen led the tiny woman into the living room. 'How did you know where I was?'

'I called at Pearl Street earlier and your sister

told me you were here. I intended coming to Melling, anyway, as there's some work I'd like to catch up on.'

'Trust you to find work to do on Boxing Day!'

'I'm going away tomorrow on a long deserved holiday, although I say so myself, and there's something I must do before I go.' Miss Thomas perched herself on the edge of the chair like a bird. 'Forgive me if it seems a silly question, but I feel bound to ask—how are you?'

Eileen shrugged. 'Bearing up,' she lied.

'Everybody bears up remarkably well considering. Virtually every single worker turned up for both shifts on Monday, yet some of them had been through hell over the weekend.'

'I forgot all about work. Anyroad, it was the funeral.'

'I know, dear. I was there, along with Carmel representing the girls.'

'That's nice of you,' Eileen said awkwardly. 'I'm afraid I didn't notice.'

'I would have been surprised if you had.' Miss Thomas smiled warmly. 'I've come to offer my condolences and say that I completely understand if you don't want to return to work for some time. If you need a week or two off, then take it.'

'A week or two?'

'Oh, my dear!' the woman said hastily. 'I'm not suggesting you'll get over it that quickly, not for a moment!'

'I know.' Eileen played with the material covering the arm of the settee, plucking at the threads where it was bare. 'I'm not sure if I want to go back to Dunnings,' she said hesitantly. 'I'm not sure if I want to do anything I was doing before. I definitely don't want to return to me old house. Yesterday, Nick turned up and I didn't want to marry him and I always thought that's what I wanted more than anything in the world.'

'What do you want to do then? Have you any idea?'

'No.' Eileen shook her head. 'I thought a bit about joining up, y'know the WRENs or the ATS or something, but I imagine the girls all being a bit like Doris, man-mad and only interested in having a good time. I'd probably feel a bit old and out of things.'

'You may be right. I've no idea.' Miss Thomas frowned, having immediately assumed Eileen's problem was her own. 'Why don't you come away with me?' she suggested eagerly as if this was a solution. 'I'll be gone a fortnight. It'll be a break and might help you make up your mind what you want to do with your life.'

Eileen looked at her in astonishment. 'Where to?'

'Norfolk. I've friends there. It's very bleak and lonely, but I love it. You can go for long walks all by yourself, if that's what you want.'

'But what about your friends, won't they mind?' Eileen found the idea of long lonely walks in strange countryside rather appealing.

'Of course not. They have this massive house and half the time they don't know who's staying. You have to see to yourself for most meals—get your own breakfast, at least. Why not come with me, Eileen,' Miss Thomas said persuasively. 'I hate the thought of leaving you like this.'

Eileen managed to smile. 'But I'm no longer your responsibility, am I?'

Miss Thomas smiled back. 'I'm asking because we're friends. You're the only person I've told about my husband. Anyway, it's partly selfishness on my part. I hate driving long distances alone.'

At that point Eileen nearly refused. Miss Thomas was an appalling driver and her nerves had been in tatters on the one occasion she'd been given a lift in her little battered car. But what did that matter, she thought bleakly? It was like waiting for a bomb to come bursting through the ceiling. It didn't matter at all.

'All right,' she said. 'I'll come.'

CHAPTER TEN

It wasn't fair, Ruth thought passionately, it just wasn't fair. She hadn't wanted anything to do with other people. She hadn't wanted involvement in any lives other than her own, yet here she was heartbroken and stricken with guilt because a little boy she scarcely knew had died, worried about her father, about Eileen, about Dilys. She'd thought, she'd hoped, she was beyond compassion.

Although Jacob was well enough to get up, his mind still seemed hazy. 'Where's Tony?' he kept asking.

'You know where, Dad,' Ruth would answer patiently.

'He's in the kitchen, I can hear him.'

The white kitten came wandering in. Eileen had asked Ruth to look after him whilst she was away. It jumped on Jacob's knee and he smiled and began to stroke its arched back. 'Hallo, Tony,' he murmured. Ruth sighed despairingly. It was too much!

She was also worried about leaving her father whilst she was at work. It was then she began to appreciate the neighbours.

'I'll pop in and keep an eye on ould Jacob,' Aggie Donovan offered eagerly. 'Y'know, we moved into the street the same month, and my ould man popped his clogs not long after your mam popped hers.'

Even Ellis Evans, who'd not spoken to Ruth since the night Dilys left home, offered to listen out for him, and May Kelly came over with half a bottle of rum when she heard he was out of sorts. Sheila Reilly suggested Dominic and Niall would love to play Monopoly, she never had the time to spare herself, but Jacob flatly refused when Ruth brought up the idea.

On New Year's Eve, the tea dance at Reece's was an exceptionally merry occasion, with Ruth having to play a succession of last waltzes, finishing with *Auld Lang Syne*, so it was late by the time she called on Dilys on her way home.

Dilys had sunk into the throes of a deep depression once she realised the reality of the situation she was in. 'But I don't want a baby,' she said repeatedly. 'I want to be a WREN. As soon as I was sixteen, I was going to pretend I was older and join up. Some lad from the Adelphi joined the Army and gave the wrong age.'

'Maybe you still can, Dilys,' Ruth would say, more to comfort the girl than anything. Without Eileen, she was unable to offer any sensible advice. How on earth did you go about having a baby adopted?

216

'I *am* a sinful girl, just like me mam said,' Dilys wailed, 'and I'm having a sinful baby. I don't want a baby born out of sin.'

'Oh, Dilys, love, that's a silly thing to say,' Ruth remonstrated. 'Babies bring their own love. Once you've had your baby, you won't be able to resist him, or her. Women never can.'

'That's what worries me,' Dilys moaned in a rare moment of astuteness. 'I don't want to be stuck with a baby, whether I love him or not. I'm already fed up being tied to this room and not having any money to go out. It didn't seem to matter while I was at work.'

'Have you got sufficient for your board and lodging?'

'Enough to last a few more weeks,' Dilys said sulkily. She'd been quite good about putting her wages away. 'Another thing,' she continued, 'Mrs Furlong keeps asking about me husband. She wants to know why he never writes. He didn't even send a Christmas card.'

Mrs Furlong was the landlady who, Ruth remembered, had been described as 'straitlaced'. She cast wildly around for something which would put the woman off. 'Say he's thousands of miles away off the coast of . . . Russia!'

'Where?'

'Russia.'

'Where's that?'

'Thousands of miles away,' Ruth said jokingly, but the joke didn't work as Dilys merely grimaced.

'I'll try and remember the name.'

Ruth wished the girl a Happy New Year, saying, 'I hope it won't be too miserable all by yourself.'

'The Furlongs have asked all the girls downstairs

to let the New Year in.'

Which was something, thought Ruth as she caught the tram home. At least she wouldn't have Dilys to worry about tonight. She hurried down Pearl Street wondering what state her father would be in when she arrived.

To her relief, the sound of male voices came from the living room when she entered the house and she recognised one voice as belonging to Eileen's father, Jack Doyle, a man she admired because he seemed so uncomplicated and straightforward. He got on well with her father, who always perked up considerably when Jack arrived.

Jack, unrehearsed in the niceties of what was considered polite behaviour in the circles which Ruth had not long ago inhabited, made no attempt to stand when she entered the room. He merely nodded his head and grunted, 'Hello, there,' in his almost churlish way, but to her surprise another man immediately jumped to his feet. He was almost as broad as Jack and just as tall, though considerably younger, with a thatch of crisp blond hair and eyes that were a bright startling blue. His almost perfect regular features were weatherbeaten like Jack's, as if he spent a lot of time outside. Ruth frowned. He reminded her of someone, she wasn't sure who.

Jack Doyle said, 'This is Matt Smith, who works alongside me on the docks. He wants to meet you.'

Why, Ruth wondered, as she held her hand out for the newcomer to shake.

Matt Smith clicked his heels together in a military fashion and said, *'Ein gluckliches neues Jahr, Frau Singerman!'*

218

A Happy New Year, Mrs Singerman! Ruth felt herself grow hot, then cold, and her legs threatened to give way. She glanced at Jacob, but he was playing with the cat and had noticed nothing. To think she was hearing the dreaded language again in her own father's house! To think that this man was clicking his heels like a member of the Gestapo whilst he shook hands! She remembered where she'd seen him before, not the man personally, but men like him; on posters and paintings and in films. He was a perfect specimen of Adolf Hitler's German master race: a tall, blond, blue-eyed Aryan. She felt almost physically sick as she snatched her hand away and ran into the back kitchen.

'Ruth!' Jack Doyle had followed her. 'I'm sorry, luv. We never dreamt . . .'

'What's his name?' Ruth demanded. 'His real name?'

'Matthew Schmidt.'

'Is he German?'

'Yes, but . . .'

'I have no wish to meet Germans. I hate them all,' Ruth said angrily. 'I would be glad if he would leave my father's house.'

'That's not fair, luv,' Jack said reasonably. 'Y'can't tar all Germans with the same brush. Matt's a communist. No one could hate Hitler more than he does. He was a wanted man in Germany before the war because of his activities, that's why he left, but not till after he'd lost his wife in one of them there camps. As if that wasn't enough, the British authorities stuck him in prison when the war began for being an alien. He's only been out a couple of months.'

But Jack might as well have talked to himself. 'I have no wish to meet Germans,' Ruth repeated stubbornly. She made no attempt to keep her voice down. A few seconds later the front door slammed as Matt Smith left.

Jack Doyle looked at her reproachfully as the sound echoed through the house. 'You're making a big mistake, luv, if you can't admit there might be a few good Germans about—and the good 'uns have to be exceptionally brave.'

He went into the other room and she heard him say, 'Well, Jacob, have you made your mind up yet? A drink'll do you good and it doesn't look as if there's going to be a raid tonight. We can see in the New Year in peace.'

'Well, it'll be a nice change,' Jacob answered, sounding more like his old self than he'd done since Tony Costello died, much to Ruth's relief. 'I'll just get my coat.'

Jack reappeared in the doorway and said to Ruth, 'I'd like you to keep that business about Matt to yourself, if you don't mind. I'm the only one he's told. He thought you and he might have something in common, that you might like to talk.'

'Don't worry,' Ruth said sarcastically. 'His secret is safe with me.'

'Y'know, luv, it's nowt but prejudice to damn the entire German race. Isn't that we accuse them of when it comes to the Jews?'

Ruth tossed her head and didn't answer.

'Oh, well,' Jack sighed. 'By the way, we're all going to our Sheila's to let the New Year in. You're welcome to come.'

A few minutes later, Jack Doyle and her father gone, Ruth was left to smart and gnaw her fingers alone. Prejudiced! Ruth Singerman, prejudiced! Perhaps if she'd had some warning she might have felt differently, but to click his heels like that, speak in German—it had come as a terrible shock. She'd begun to feel safe and protected in Pearl Street, despite the raids. It had felt as if the enemy had invaded her very home.

She decided not to go to Sheila Reilly's, because Matthew Schmidt—Matt Smith—might be there, and despite everything Jack Doyle had said, she had no wish to be in the same house as a German. Instead, she listened to the wireless which she'd bought Jacob for his Christmas present, opened the rum, and when clocks all over the country struck midnight, Ruth Singerman was in bed and dead to the world.

*   *   *

Brenda Mahon couldn't help but notice that, whilst Carrie was always one of the first to be asked to dance, she was one of the last. She was always asked, because there were more men than women, far more, mainly in uniform, but Brenda wondered if she'd dance at all if it were the other way round. Carrie had disappeared about half an hour ago and Brenda felt a little frightened on her own. Perhaps the dance wasn't such a good idea—or the frock. At Carrie's insistence she'd made the frock too tight and cut too low at the bust and it was hurtful to think that, despite showing off so much of her rather limited figure, she was still only danced with as a last resort. For the very first time she missed Xavier. They'd started courting when they were both fourteen, so she'd never been out with

221

another man, and her plainness had never bothered her before. In fact, she'd always felt rather special being married to the best-looking man in Bootle, if not the whole of Liverpool. Between dances she began to wonder what was going to happen in the future. She was still Xavier's wife. Was she prepared to have him back after the terrible thing he'd done?

'Wanna dance, queen?' The band started up again and a young man stood before her, eyebrows raised expectantly.

'I can't dance very well.' She felt bound to explain this to all her partners as she tottered after them onto the dance floor. The high-heeled shoes which Carrie had loaned her were too big and she'd had to stuff the toes with tissue paper.

'Don't matter. Fred Astaire himself would have a job in this crowd.' The Orrell Park ballroom was packed to capacity on New Year's Eve. Carrie had bought the tickets well in advance. 'What d'you do, queen?' the young man asked as they joined the throng.

'I'm a dressmaker,' Brenda answered. 'And you, I mean what do you do?' She'd become a little bored with the routine, the same old questions and answers with everyone she danced with. So far, no one had asked her to dance a second time.

'I'm a fitter on the docks. Only escaped death by the skin of me teeth during last week's raids.'

Brenda did her best to look impressed. 'Lucky you,' she murmured.

He slid his arm further around her waist and said in her ear, 'Can I take you home?'

'I'm sorry, but I'm going home with me friend,' Brenda answered, feeling panicky.

'Is your friend the one with the fair wavy hair, wearing a red dress?'

Brenda nodded.

'I thought as much. In that case, she's already promised to go home with me mate, Dave, which means we can make a foursome.'

So he was only asking because his mate had attached himself to Carrie! Brenda desperately wished the last six weeks would melt away and everything be the way it used to be. If Carrie hadn't turned up, she'd be at home sitting in front of her sewing machine, the girls in bed, and waiting for it to be quarter to twelve so she could pop along to Sheila Reilly's and let the New Year in.

'Me name's Dougie, by the way, Dougie Fox.' He pressed his cheek against hers and slid his other arm around her waist so she was left with nothing else to do with her right arm other than put it on his shoulder. He was a rather unpleasant looking young man, she thought, with a narrow mean face, and his breath smelt like a sewer. She cursed Xavier for putting her in such a position, but knew if he came through the door at that moment she would have taken him back like a shot, no matter what he'd done. She didn't want to be single. This was what it must be like all the time if you wanted to meet men, having to go to dances and put up with unpleasant individuals breathing all over you and assuming they only had to ask and you would let them take you home.

When the dance finished, the young man led her back to a corner where Carrie and his mate were snuggled together in a passionate clinch, much to Brenda's disgust. Carrie came up for air and winked. 'Dougie found you, then?'

223

'Seems like it,' Brenda said shortly. 'Excuse me a mo.' She couldn't stand it another minute, she decided as she pushed her way through the crowd, praying Carrie wouldn't follow, and collected her coat from the cloakroom in the foyer. She wasn't cut out to be a single woman. Outside, she waited at the first bus stop she came to, but when no bus arrived after about ten minutes, she began to run, somewhat clumsily in the too-big shoes, towards the next stop. She was halfway towards Bootle and halfway between stops and feeling tearful, when a bus finally turned up and the driver kindly stopped the already packed vehicle when she waved at him frantically.

'Come on, Tilly Mint,' the conductor shouted. He put his hand under her elbow and helped her on board.

'Ta.' Brenda stumbled on the platform when a heel twisted sideways, and she nearly fell. The conductor picked her up and placed her inside the bus where she squeezed herself onto the long seat by the door. She wondered why such a strong young man hadn't been called up, but noticed he wore spectacles, really thick, so his eyes looked like pebbles behind the glass.

'Had one over the eight, have you?'

'No, I haven't had a drink all night.' She closed her coat where it had flapped open at the bottom so he wouldn't see her horrible, too short frock, and stuffed the matching dolly bag in her pocket. Carrie said you needed an evening bag to take dancing, just big enough to hold your ticket, a hanky, some money, and your identity card. She'd never wear the dress again. Perhaps she could turn it into something for one of the girls, presuming

224

she ever felt in the mood.

'You're never going to get us home before midnight, are you?' the woman beside Brenda said accusingly to the conductor.

'Don't look like it, missus. Fact, it don't even look like you'll be home this year.' He winked at Brenda. 'But it's ould Adolf you should blame, not the bus. There's so many roads closed, we've been wandering all over the houses and the timetable's been knocked for six.' He took a large watch out of his waistcoat pocket. 'Another five minutes and it'll be nineteen forty-one.'

The passengers chatted amiably together, wondering what the New Year would bring, and after a while the conductor began to shout a countdown, 'Five, four, three, two, one—Happy New Year, everyone!'

'Happy New Year,' the entire bus shouted back, and they all began to sing *Auld Lang Syne*. Brenda shook hands with the conductor and the people sitting on the seats nearby.

'Happy New Year, Tilly Mint.' The conductor winked again. 'May all your troubles be little ones.'

Brenda laughed. She would sooner have been on the bus any day than in the Orrell Park ballroom with Dougie whatever-his-name-was. 'It's too late for that,' she said, 'I've already got troubles, and believe me, they're big!'

*   *   *

The house was very old with beamed ceilings—a bit like the cottage except that it was about twenty times as big. It was also very cold and draughty and the wind whistled in from the North Sea, through

225

the gaps around the windows and up through the floorboards and around the doors. It was situated only about five hundred yards from the sea, and in between the house and the icy grey water there were flat muddy marshes that glistened wetly, particularly in the mornings when the sun rose and turned them into blank mirrors that stretched either way for as far as the eye could see.

Now, at nearly midnight, with no moon visible, the marshes merely glinted dully here and there, as if there were an odd dusty jewel in a muddy setting.

Eileen Costello was sitting alone on the trunk of a fallen tree looking out to sea. Although well wrapped up in a borrowed coat, borrowed woolly socks and someone else's Wellington boots, she was still freezing cold. There was an untidy cloakroom by the front door of the house full of coats and gloves and scarves and boots which didn't seem to belong to anyone in particular. You were supposed to help yourself when you went out.

'No one comes prepared for the weather,' Miss Thomas—Kate—told her. She had to call Miss Thomas 'Kate' from now on. 'So Laura and Conor provide for all emergencies.'

Laura and Conor Kinnear were their hosts, the owners of the draughty old house, though Eileen had been there several days before she'd managed to establish this for herself. When she arrived, she'd been introduced to dozens of people, young and old, and five minutes later had no idea who they were. The Kinnears had five children who seemed to range from their mid-teens to early twenties, and all had friends to stay. Then there were other guests like Eileen and Miss Thomas— Kate.

The strange thing was, the Kinnears made no attempt to look after the people staying with them. Laura was a windswept woman with short untidy hair cut like a man's, who wore clothes that Eileen wouldn't have been seen dead in—jumpers with the elbows out and tweed skirts full of threads and holes. Conor was little better and seemed to live in the same tatty pullover and a pair of baggy trousers that were about two sizes too big. No one dressed for dinner, something she'd always assumed the upper classes did, but perhaps she'd seen too many films. In fact Eileen was probably one of the best-dressed women at the table—she'd brought with her the lavender wool dress which Brenda Mahon had made for the dinner dance on Christmas Eve, probably one of the last things Brenda had done before she'd gone off dressmaking.

As Kate said, you looked after yourself, and Eileen usually helped herself to breakfast and took it back to eat in her cold bedroom, rather than in the company of a score of young people who had either been to university, were currently there, or planned on going in a year or so's time. One of the boys wore an Army officer's uniform. They made her feel tongue-tied and ignorant as they talked of things about which she knew nothing, or in an intellectual and knowledgeable way about the war.

No one bothered to sit down to lunch, which was another help-yourself affair, and the evening meals were uneatable: usually mashed swedes and potatoes, and meat you could have soled your shoes with. Why, Eileen wondered initially, did people come? After a while, she realised they came for the conversation. They came to talk. Wherever you went, whichever room you entered, there were

227

people in little earnest groups just talking.

'What does Conor do?' Eileen asked Kate. If he hadn't talked so posh she'd have taken him for a binman.

'He's a Professor of English Literature at Cambridge University,' Kate said. 'And a playwright, very famous. Have you never heard of Conor Kinnear?'

'I don't go to the theatre much,' Eileen muttered. She'd only been to pantomimes at the Metropole in Bootle, and once to see George Formby in town. If it hadn't been for the scenery she might have wished she hadn't come, because she felt uncomfortable amidst so many formidably clever and talkative people, but she'd felt drawn to the flat desolate beauty of the landscape straight away. She walked for miles and miles alone, inland down long bare paths lined with black brittle hedges, and along the narrow road that ran parallel with the marshes, and on some days she never saw another single soul. From time to time, the peace was shattered when planes took off or returned to an airbase some distance inland, leaving the resultant silence only more palpable, and Eileen feeling as if she was the only person left in the world.

Once, she'd come to a village with just one shop and the smallest pub she'd ever seen, surrounded by a few tiny cottages. It seemed incredible to think that people actually lived there, so completely cut off from the rest of humanity. She'd considered the cottage in Melling to be isolated, yet it was a mere bus ride from the thriving metropolis of Liverpool. She bought a postcard in the shop to send to her dad, a view of Norwich Castle, though when she got back she had trouble knowing what to write. She couldn't very well say, 'Having a lovely time,' which people usually wrote when they were on holiday, because she wasn't having a particularly nice time at all; it was merely interesting, and so far she had scarcely spoken a word to anyone except Kate. In the end she merely wrote on the card, 'Happy New Year to one and all,' and signed it, 'Eileen'.

She slept well at night, but woke up every morning with the memory of a strange dream which always had the same theme: she was wandering alone through unfamiliar countryside, a strange city, or a house where she'd never been before. It was never quite light and never quite dark, and a disembodied voice kept calling urgently, 'Eileen, Eileen Costello.' She always woke before discovering whose voice it was or what it wanted, with the unpleasant, niggly sensation that she'd left something very important undone.

Now it was New Year's Eve, and the Kinnears had clearly attempted to make an effort for the occasion. Laura wore a grey georgette frock that looked as if it had been used as a duster, and a double row of jet beads. She'd combed her hair and applied a touch of lipstick and Conor wore an evening suit and looked relatively smart. He was very thin and gaunt with deepset eyes and a large nose which Kate had said was 'Roman'. He seemed to have trouble remembering which children belonged to him, which was hardly surprising seeing as there were so many there. The children had all disappeared earlier in the evening.

'They've gone dancing,' Kate explained. 'There's an RAF camp a few miles away. You've probably heard the planes.'

229

The adults sat down to dinner in a long room lined with shelves which were crammed with books and all sorts of other strange paraphernalia, such as a collection of shells, a stuffed bird in a glass case, some ravelled knitting, and several pairs of shoes. Everything was full of dust, marvelled Eileen, which was another strange thing she'd noticed about the upper classes. *They didn't give a damn what people thought!* If it had been her or anyone else in Pearl Street expecting visitors, the house would have been scrubbed from top to bottom beforehand and every surface polished till it shone. She turned away, embarrassed and slightly ashamed for noticing. It was exactly what Aggie Donovan would have done. The food, as usual, was unpalatable, a sort of mutton stew served in two big dishes which were passed around so people could help themselves, though everyone else seemed to be eating heartily. Perhaps they were too busy talking to notice what was on their plates.

The man beside her said, 'So, do you think the Americans will come in with us?'

At last, a subject which she knew a little about, because her dad had been pinning her ear back for weeks, calling the Americans every name under the sun for not joining in the war on the side of the British.

'Well, Roosevelt got re-elected in November, didn't he?' she said, trying to sound knowledgable. 'And he did it by promising the USA wouldn't enter the war.'

'In that case, you don't think they'll come in with us?'

'I think they might find it difficult not to when it comes right down to it, particularly if Japan joins in on the side of Germany.' She hoped he wouldn't ask why this was significant. If only she'd listened more closely to her dad! It was something to do with Indo-China and oil . . .

'True, very true.' The man nodded. To her relief, the woman on his other side demanded his attention and Eileen was left free to chew her piece of mutton until it was tender enough to swallow.

After dinner, they played charades, but Eileen, her eye on the clock, went out to the cloakroom at half past eleven, wrapped herself up in borrowed clothes, and left the house to sit outside on the log where she'd sat many times before. Every now and then the moon peeped out from behind a cloud and the wet marshes glistened briefly.

What was to become of her, she wondered despairingly, now that she was no longer a mother, no longer a wife? She could be Nick's wife if she wanted, but she had no idea if she wanted to or not. The deep yearning ache she felt for the loss of her son returned in full force and she almost cried out with the pain.

'Tony,' she whispered. 'Dear God, Tony!'

'Who's that?' a man's voice called, and a figure she didn't recognise loomed up out of the darkness.

'Eileen Costello,' she said, trying to keep her voice steady. She resented the figure, whoever it might be, intruding on her grief. Why hadn't he stayed indoors and played charades and sung *Auld Lang Syne* with everyone else?

The man came over and sat down beside her on the log. It was Conor Kinnear, all muffled up in scarves, a woolly hat and an ankle-length overcoat, which disguised his almost skeletal frame. Eileen felt slightly apprehensive. They hadn't exchanged a

231

word since Kate had introduced them and she wondered if he'd remember who she was. She prayed he wouldn't think her another academic and start talking about things she didn't understand.

'I had to get out,' he explained. 'I can't stand the false emotion when everyone falls weeping into each others' arms at the stroke of midnight. It's so bloody hypocritical.'

'I always liked it meself,' Eileen said.

'Really? I suppose it depends whose arms you fall into. I'm not the least bit fond of that lot in there and have no intention of pretending I am.' He took a cigarette case out of his pocket, offered it to her, and lit both cigarettes with a lighter, rather clumsily with his hands in thick gloves.

'Why have them to stay,' Eileen asked curiously, 'if you don't like them?'

'I didn't say I didn't like them, I said I wasn't fond of them, which is an entirely different thing.'

Eileen shrugged. 'I suppose so.'

'Kate told us about your child,' he said. 'I'm so sorry.' He didn't sound particularly sorry. His voice was more conversational than sympathetic.

'Ta,' Eileen said briefly.

'I suppose you think you'll never get over it?'

'I suppose you're going to tell me I will.' She didn't care if it sounded rude. On the other hand, she reckoned he wouldn't care, either. She'd no intention of taking advice from a man who couldn't remember the names of his own children.

'I wasn't, actually. You never will get over it. When you're an old woman on your death bed, you'll still be mourning your lost child. On the other hand, you'll learn to live with it. One of these days, it might take weeks or months or even years, but one day the tragedy will take second place to other things which will seem more important.'

'You're sure of that, are you?' Eileen said sarcastically.

The moon came out for a second and she saw him smile. 'Relatively sure. There are a few people, a tiny few, who buckle under and wilt away, but most of us have sufficient will to survive. You're one of the survivors. You wouldn't be here if you intended to allow your child's death to dominate the rest of your life.' He threw the remainder of his cigarette away and it sizzled on the wet sand. 'Coming here means you've already taken the first step back onto the road to normality, and the day will come, I promise, when you'll be able to laugh and enjoy life again.'

'Are you speaking from personal experience, or have you just read all this in books?' She felt convinced he was talking through his intellectual hat, and was even more sure this was the case when he didn't answer her question, but merely stood up and slapped his sides.

'It's freezing!' he exclaimed. 'I've lived here for twenty-five years, but I shall never become accustomed to Norfolk winters. I think I'll go indoors and secrete myself in my study. If anyone wants to kiss me, I shall convince them they already have.' He extended his hand. 'Coming? I reckon we're well into nineteen forty-one by now. I don't want any of my guests catching pneumonia. It takes Laura all her time to look after the healthy ones.'

'I suppose I'd better.'

He pulled her upright, but immediately released her hand. 'Happy New Year, by the way.'

233

'The same to you.'

*   *   *

Kate was alone in the vast, untidy kitchen when Eileen entered in search of a cup of tea the following morning. 'What happened to you last night?' she enquired. 'I searched everywhere to wish you a Happy New Year, but you'd completely disappeared.'

'I preferred to be by meself,' Eileen explained. 'Did anyone else notice? I hope they didn't think I was rude.'

'Of course not! Nobody here gives a hang about that sort of thing. Anyway, Conor disappeared, too, but then he always does on New Year's Eve.'

'He was outside with me. We had quite a long talk.' Eileen poured tea out of the cracked, half-fullpot. 'This is a bit cold. Is it all right if I make some more?'

'Anything goes in this house, dear. The kettle's about to boil for my coffee. Empty the pot and make a fresh lot. Would you like some bacon and egg? I'll do yours with mine.'

'No, ta. I'll make some toast.' She cut a slice of bread and held it by a fork in front of the blazing fire. The kitchen was usually the only warm room in the house. 'Where is everyone?'

'Still in bed except for Conor. He lit the fires and went out for a walk. The young ones didn't come back until a couple of hours ago. In fact, it was they who woke me up.' The kettle boiled on the peculiar looking stove that had its own fire glowing behind a thick glass door and Kate made herself a cup of coffee and poured water in the teapot. She cleared a space on the bare scrubbed table which was heaped with last night's dirty dishes and began to eat. 'What did you and Conor talk about last night?' she asked.

Eileen found the butter dish amidst the mess on the table. 'Life, I suppose,' she replied, adding rather sarcastically, 'He was full of good advice. He told me I'd get over losing Tony in time. You'd think he was some sort of expert on getting over things.'

'Well, he is in a way,' Kate said surprisingly. 'Conor lost his twin brother in the last war on the very first day they went into battle. They were identical twins and had a special bond. He was bereft without Christopher. At the time he thought he'd never get over it.'

'Oh!' Eileen felt uncomfortable. 'I didn't know.'

Kate smiled. 'How could you? I'll tell you something else you didn't know. Conor and I were childhood sweethearts. We were to be married when the war ended. Instead, after Christopher died, he called it off and a few years later he married Laura.'

'But why?'

'I've no idea,' Kate shrugged. 'We remained great friends, but we never talk about the past. I told myself it was because he loved me too much, and was scared I'd be taken from him as his brother was. In other words, he was casting me out of his life before it could happen again.'

'But he appears happy now, doesn't he?' Eileen needed to know if Conor Kinnear was happy. It seemed important, she wasn't quite sure why. Perhaps because it proved what he'd said last night was true. He'd never got over losing his twin, but

235

the loss had come to take second place to other things in time.

'Perfectly happy,' Kate assured her. 'He loves Laura and his children, even if he does get them confused occasionally. Everything turned out well for Conor in the end.'

'But not for you?'

'No, not for me. Though I don't know,' Kate mused. 'I had a Christmas card from my eldest daughter, Celia. She'll soon be eighteen and is starting to ask questions. One of these days perhaps I shall tell her why her mother left.' She smiled. 'I've been happier than I've ever been at Dunnings, despite the longing to see my girls. You sort of live life on two layers and it's the top layer, the immediate one, that seems the most important.'

'Conor said that one day I would laugh and enjoy life again, but I can't imagine that happening, not ever.'

'It will, my dear, it will.' Kate leaned across the table and briefly held Eileen's hand. 'That's enough deep thoughts for now. I think I can hear Conor coming back.'

Conor entered the kitchen along with a tall, bluff, red-faced man of about fifty in mud-stained boots and carrying a basket of eggs, still matted here and there with straw. They both nodded briefly at the women at the table.

'Are you sure the Ministry have had their proper allocation?' Conor asked anxiously.

'Yes, sir,' the man replied with an air of tried patience. 'They've had their six dozen. This is what's over.'

Conor looked worried. 'It doesn't seem quite proper having more than our fair share.'

'Well, you've got a lot of guests, sir,' the man said reasonably. He spoke with an attractive Norfolk burr.

'I suppose I have.' Conor rubbed his chin thoughtfully. 'But once my guests have gone, Ted, I want you to take the surplus to the local hospital.'

Ted shuffled his feet and looked slightly annoyed. 'That's what I've always done up to now, sir.'

Conor turned to Kate and Eileen. 'The farm's become a worry since the war began,' he complained. 'We're inundated with inspectors from the Min of Ag telling us what to grow and how much milk and eggs they want. Every time I eat a piece of meat, I worry that I'm breaking the law.' He turned back to the farmhand. 'How's the new land girl making out?'

Ted's red face grew even redder as he expostulated, 'Bloody hopeless, sir, if you'll excuse the language. She's even worse than the last one and don't know one end of a cow from the other. She was a typist back in Ipswich.' His voice rose in disgust. 'A *typist*!'

Eileen longed to butt in in defence of the poor typist who'd come all the way from a town to this isolated place in order to do her bit. The girl had to learn, she thought.

Ted had begun to complain even more bitterly. 'Not only that, Mr Kinnear, sir, but now Bob's had his call-up papers and he'll be off in a couple of weeks. We're going to have to get another of them damned Land Army girls.'

'Oh, dear!' Conor looked crestfallen. 'Never mind, Ted. You manage the farm wonderfully. No one could do a better job than you.'

237

Ted departed, slightly mollified, and Conor smiled. 'Flattery will get you everywhere, it seems.'

'I didn't know you owned the farm,' Eileen said. She'd noticed it about half a mile away from the house.

'I'm beginning to wish I didn't,' Conor said, 'but I don't suppose there's a hope of selling it at present.'

*　　　*　　　*

After breakfast, Eileen wandered over the fields to the farm, a long two-storey red brick building which looked as old as the Kinnears' house. The front garden was neatly tended, but when she pushed through the five-barred gate at the side, she found the vast rear a dreary sea of mud surrounded by a series of ramshackle sheds. Chickens pecked their way through the mud and one fluttered down beside her and hopefully pecked the toe of her boot. Pigs grunted, cows mooed, and a large dog eyed her balefully. She was about to depart hastily when she noticed the animal was tied to a stake.

'What do you want?' A short stubby woman in a white overall had opened the back door and was looking at her even more balefully than the dog.

'Nothing really. I just came to look at the farm. I'm staying with the Kinnears.'

'Huh!' The door was slammed shut without a word.

'Isn't she a bitch?'

Eileen glanced round in search of where the voice had come from. A woman about her own age was leaning on the bottom half of a split doorway, the top part of which was open. 'She was a bit

238

rude,' Eileen said. 'Who is she?'

'Ted's wife, Edna. Ted's the farm manager. I'm afraid he's gone into Norwich, if you've come to see him.'

Eileen made her slippery way across the farmyard towards the woman, nearly falling headlong in the process. 'I've never been on a farm before,' she explained when she arrived. 'I just came to see what one looks like. I'm staying at the big house over there.'

'Oh! So, you're one of the upper crust, are you? And here was me thinking you might be the new land girl, though it would have been awfully quick.' She was an attractive woman, fine-featured, with long dark curly hair tied back with a blue ribbon. Eileen had never seen a member of the Land Army in the flesh before, either. Despite the rather mannish uniform—the Aertex shirt and tie, thick green jersey and felt hat worn at a jaunty angle on the back of her head—the woman managed to retain an air of elegance.

'I'm not one of the upper crust,' Eileen informed her firmly, 'I'm merely a guest, that's all. Back in Liverpool, I'm a centre lathe turner, at least I was until recently. How are you getting on? I understand you're new here.'

The woman pulled a face. 'Abysmally! I worked in an office until a month ago, and, like you, I've never been near a farm in my life. Ted doesn't have any patience with me. He acts as if I've been sent to try him, not help him. You wouldn't think I'd given up a well-paid Civil Service job to help feed my starving country.' She leant her elbows on top of the door and looked around her gloomily. 'Isn't it depressing? I had visions of lying in fields of

239

sunkissed swaying corn and the smell of baking bread wafting from the farm kitchen. Instead, all I can smell is pigshit, and all I can see is mud.'

Eileen smiled. 'Perhaps you shouldn't have come in December! As for the farm, I suppose it is a bit basic.' In fact, the scene might well have been the same a hundred years ago. There was nothing to suggest this was the twentieth century; no trucks or tractors, no neatly paved yard or concrete buildings, merely the collection of tumbledown wooden shacks which looked as if they'd been stuck forever in their sea of mud. Conor Kinnear had clearly not thought it worthwhile to invest money in his farm. Even so, Eileen rather liked it, just as she liked all the scenery on this part of the Norfolk coast. It was completely natural and unspoilt, untouched by anything modern. 'I'd better be getting back,' she said. She wanted to see Conor because she'd just had the craziest idea. 'What's your name, by the way?'

'Peggy Wilson.'

'I'm Eileen Costello.' You never know, she thought as she began to make her unsteady way out of the farmyard, if Conor went along with her crazy idea, she'd be seeing Peggy Wilson again pretty soon.

CHAPTER ELEVEN

A fist hammered on the bedroom door and Eileen shouted, 'I'm awake.' The floor on the landing creaked under Ted's heavy tread as he walked away. Eileen pulled the bedclothes around her shoulders and groaned. What she wouldn't have given for a cup of tea first thing! The room was freezing, so cold it hurt to breathe and she touched her nose to make sure it was still there, in case she'd caught frostbite during the night. After a while, she sat up and lit the oil lamp on the bedside table and began to get dressed, struggling into as many garments as she could whilst still underneath the clothes. She'd no intention of getting washed; a quick splash of the face with the icy water in the pitcher on the washstand would do until tonight. As she pulled on a pair of knee-length woollen socks, Eileen wondered if she was completely mad to have joined the Women's Land Army—not that she was a member yet. Her application was 'in hand', and would be processed swiftly under the circumstances, in that she was already working on the farm that would employ her. In the meantime, she was living in the farmhouse with Ted and Edna Wright—much to the latter's disgust—and, until she got her uniform, wearing clothes borrowed from the Kinnears: drill overalls, long socks, several of Conor's old jumpers and a lumpy sort of duffel coat.

She'd approached Conor with her proposition on New Year's Day, straight after her visit to the farm. He'd looked at her as if he'd never seen her before, as if they hadn't had an intimate conversation about life and death the night before. He was in his study typing and seemed irritated by the interruption.

'Have you spoken to Ted about it?' he enquired brusquely when she asked if she could work as a land girl on his farm in the place of the man about to be called up.

'He's gone to Norwich,' she explained uncomfortably. Perhaps she was disturbing the writing of a great master-piece.

'Of course, I forgot. I'll have a word with him when he returns.' He turned back to his work and Eileen was dismissed, feeling slightly let down. She'd thought he'd jump at the idea. She sought out Kate to ask her opinion.

Kate chewed her lip and looked doubtful. 'It's frightfully hard work, Eileen.'

'Well, I'm used to hard work at Dunnings, aren't I?'

'Yes, but it's entirely different sort of work; backbreaking, and rather lonely. You're used to crowds and having your family around.'

Which was exactly what Eileen *didn't* want at the moment. 'I think I'll give it a try,' she persisted. 'Even if Conor doesn't want me on his farm, I can join the Land Army, anyroad, and work somewhere else. I don't care where it is, though I like it round here.'

'In that case, I'll drive you into Norwich,' Kate said in a matter-of-fact voice. 'If there's a local recruiting office, Norwich is where it will be. I'll make some enquiries on your behalf.'

'You always seem to be doing that,' Eileen said wryly. 'When I asked about getting divorced, you said, "I'll make some enquiries on your behalf".'

'Did I?' Kate looked at her keenly. 'I hope you're doing the right thing. We're not due to leave for a few days. Perhaps you'd like to think about it a bit more?'

Eileen shook her head. 'No. Me mind's made up. To be frank, I don't really give a damn what I do, but I've got to do something, haven't I? All I know

242

is, I don't want to go back to Pearl Street, not yet, anyroad.'

To Eileen's surprise, Sheila didn't seem the least bit shocked when she returned home to Bootle a few days later to collect some things and told her what had happened. 'I've applied to join the Land Army, Sheil. I'm going to work in Norfolk.'

Sheila looked as if she might cry. She took her sister in her arms and hugged her tightly. 'I understand, sis, though I'll miss you terrible. It was bad enough when you were only going to live in Melling.'

'And I'll miss you, Sheil.'

Her dad was equally understanding. 'Good idea, luv,' he nodded approvingly. 'You need a change. But what about your house, just in case it doesn't work out, like?'

'I'm keeping the house on, Dad,' she informed him. Sheila was already back in Number 21 now that it was repaired. 'There's droves of people without a home to go to since the Christmas raids. I've been in touch with the Billeting Office and some other family is going to rent it for a few months until their own place is put right.' George Ransome had offered to store her personal possessions in his boxroom. Sheila would sort everything out once Eileen had gone.

'Do us a favour, sis,' Eileen implored. 'Take Tony's things, his clothes and toys. I can't bear to look at them. You can keep whatever you want.'

'All right, Eil. I'll keep the clothes, but not the toys. I'll hand those into one of them Rest Centres. I'd only nag our kids soft in case they got broken.'

Before leaving, Eileen went to see Ruth and Jacob Singerman and apologised for leaving the

243

responsibility for Dilys Evans entirely on Ruth's shoulders. 'How's she coping?' she asked. 'I hope you can manage on your own?'

'She's coping well,' Ruth assured her, which was the opposite of the truth. Dilys was growing more and more hysterical by the day, so much so, that when Ruth had visited her yesterday the landlady had complained as she was leaving, 'She cries all day long. It disturbs the other girls and upsets my husband. Has she no family of her own who can help?'

Ruth couldn't very well explain Dilys' family had thrown her out, else the woman would want to know why. 'No,' she lied. 'She's all alone, an orphan.'

The landlady looked sympathetic, but doubtful. 'It wouldn't be so bad if she'd let me help, but she locks the door and won't answer when I knock.' She went on to ask when the baby was due.

'About the middle of February,' Ruth guessed wildly. 'She got her dates mixed up so she can't be positive.'

'You realise she won't be able to stay once the child arrives? The other girls have to be up early for work and I don't want their sleep disturbed by a crying baby. I did tell the woman from Dunnings that when she first enquired.'

'I realise,' Ruth sighed.

Eileen was saying, 'If you have any problems, Ruth, get onto Miss Thomas. She'll know what to do.'

'I'll bear that in mind.'

'How's your dad?' Eileen whispered as Jacob went into the back kitchen to feed the white kitten, which seemed to have grown considerably since she'd last seen it.

'Much better, thanks. Almost his old self again.'

'That's good,' Eileen felt relieved. 'I was dead worried about him when I was away.' As Jacob shuffled back into the room, she said, 'I hope you don't mind looking after Snowy for a while longer?'

'Not at all, Eileen. In fact, I've grown so fond of him, I'm dreading the time coming when you'll want him back.'

In that case, please keep him,' she said quickly. 'Tony loved his kitten dearly, and I feel guilty about leaving him behind. He would have wanted you to have him more than anyone.'

Jacob's old face twisted in a mixture of sadness and delight. 'Are you sure, Eileen?'

'Positive.' She'd no idea when she would be back in Pearl Street, if ever, and Snowy was merely another haunting reminder of her lost son.

Ruth came to the door with her when it was time to leave. 'I envy you, in a way.'

'*Envy* me?' said Eileen, astonished.

'Oh, not the circumstances,' Ruth said hastily, 'though I know exactly how you feel. I've lost two children, but I suppose with me there's always the chance they might still be alive. No, I meant I envy the fact you've joined the Land Army. I wish I could do something worthwhile and adventurous towards the war effort. I'm fed up with Reece's, it seems such a trite way to spend my time, but the pay's good and the hours are short which means I don't have to leave my father on his own for very long.' Jacob was undoubtedly better, but he seemed fragile of late, and frequently fell asleep nursing the kitten in his chair. There were times when he seemed so still that Ruth was scared to touch him in case he was dead. 'I'm sorry, Eileen.' She involuntarily clasped the woman by the shoulders. 'I shouldn't be burdening you with this. You've more than enough worries of your own.' There was something about Eileen that always made Ruth want to confide in her.

'Don't give it a second thought, luv.' Eileen smiled warmly. 'I think I know what you mean—I'd probably feel the same way meself.'

'I've started a bank account,' Ruth said shyly. 'As soon as I can, I intend to go to America in search of Simon and Leah.'

Eileen paused, then kissed Ruth impulsively on the cheek. 'I'll give you my address, shall I? Then you can write and tell me all the news.'

*   *   *

As Eileen pushed her legs into the stiff overalls, she wondered if Ruth would still be envious if she could see her now. She was almost fully dressed by the time she got out of bed. She put an extra cardigan on, then the duffel coat, tied a woollen scarf around her head and went downstairs.

Her boots were in the back porch. The soles leaked and the fleecy lining was still damp from the previous day. She'd scarcely had them on a minute before her feet felt cold despite her thick socks. She stamped on the coconut mat to try and warm them before going outside into the blackness of the morning, where she found the mud had frozen into solid ridges during the night. The dog gave a muted 'woof', but she said firmly, 'It's only me, Rex,' and he subsided with a muffled growl. He was beginning to get to know her. As she made her stumbling way across to the cowshed, the wind howled and she could feel flecks of snow whipping against her face. Ted was already at work in the end stall. Several oil lamps were suspended from the rafters casting a yellow glow over the scene. Despite everything, her cold feet, her desperate need for a hot drink and her general misery, Eileen always found the cowshed rather welcoming. It seemed to have an almost religious significance, reminding her of cribs and Bethlehem and the birth of Baby Jesus.

'Morning,' Ted said shortly.

'Morning.' She picked up a stool and carried it into the stall furthest away from Ted. Ten days ago, when she'd first started and after some brief instruction, she'd barely managed to milk two cows by the time Ted had done the other twelve. Yesterday morning, she'd managed six.

'You're not too bad at this,' Ted conceded. He seemed quite pleased. 'Much better than that bloody Peggy woman.'

'Peggy's a far better worker than you give her credit for,' Eileen said defensively, but Ted merely grunted in reply. Poor Peggy was driven to distraction by his constant criticism. She could do nothing right in Ted's eyes. Perhaps it was because he thought Eileen was a friend of Conor Kinnear's, or maybe he felt sorry for her—she'd discovered on her first day he knew about Francis and Tony—but he was always friendly and encouraging.

'Morning, Norma,' she whispered, patting the cow's rump before proceeding to pump away at her icy swollen teats with equally icy fingers. It was no use trying to milk a cow with gloves on. A satisfying gush of milk poured into the metal container underneath. When she'd finished, Eileen stroked the animal's soft neck. 'Thanks, Norma,' she murmured. 'You've been a very good cow today.' Norma was inclined to be frisky if she was in a certain sort of mood, and once had Eileen off her stool and into the straw with a sudden flick of her tail.

She carried the stool into the next stall. 'And how are you today, Daphne?'

'Humph!' There was a grunt from the far end of the shed. 'I've never known cows given names and talked to before.'

'The horses have names and you talk to them. Anyroad, they respond better if you have a little chat.'

'Who said?'

Eileen didn't answer, but wished Ted's cordial attitude was shared by his wife. Until officially a member of the Land Army, she wasn't entitled to live in the hostel along with Peggy and the other local land girls. Initially, she'd thought Conor and Laura might accommodate her in the big house. Instead, it had been arranged that she live on the farm.

'I hope you get on with Edna Wright,' Kate said worriedly when everything was sorted out. 'I've always found her a frightfully difficult person. It's a pity, in a way, you've got to stay with them. It would have been much nicer to have gone straight into the hostel, but then it would have meant waiting, and I know you're desperate to start straight away.'

Eileen remembered the woman who'd stared at her more balefully than the dog on the day she'd visited the farm. Maybe her bark's worse than her bite, she'd thought hopefully.

But she was wrong. Edna Wright was the rudest and most unfriendly person Eileen had ever met. She seemed to regard their temporary lodger as an intruder. If circumstances had been different, if Eileen had cared about being happy, she might not have stuck it out at the farmhouse after the first night.

She'd been on and off freezing trains and waiting on freezing stations since leaving Liverpool at six o'clock that morning, and as she was expected, hoped someone would be at the station to meet her. But there was no one, and she was forced to walk down miles of dark country lanes carrying her suitcase which grew heavier with each step. Fortunately, she'd come across the station during her long walks and more or less knew the way.

There'd been no sign of Ted when she reached the house. A surly, hatchet-faced Edna showed her to her room without uttering a single word, not even in response to Eileen's polite attempts at conversation as they made their way upstairs.

'Well, if that's the way you want it . . .' she muttered when the woman left after drawing the blind and plonking the oil lamp she was carrying on the bedside table, leaving Eileen alone in the white painted room with its sloped ceiling and brass bedstead. It was quite a pretty room in a bare, almost spartan sort of way, with plain white curtains and a lovely old-fashioned jug and pitcher set on the washstand above which a faded sampler was embroidered with *Oh Lord, Welcome All They Who Reside Under My Roof*.

'Huh!' Eileen said aloud. She unpacked her clothes, put them away in the curtained alcove, and wondered if she was supposed to go downstairs for something to eat. As usual, she was dying for a cup of tea, but surely Edna would have said if there was going to be a meal?

She sat on the bed and waited and waited for Edna to call. Whilst she waited, it got colder and colder. She glanced around the room for a fireplace, but there was none, and no electricity, either. She shivered. How was she supposed to keep warm?

After about an hour of waiting, she realised she wasn't going to be fed. There was a wireless downstairs and she could hear music, voices, laughter. The sounds made her feel isolated and very alone.

What on earth was she doing here, in this strange cold room, desperate for a cup of tea and hundreds of miles away from the people who loved her? For a while, she briefly contemplated packing her suitcase and going back to Bootle, even if it meant waiting on the station all night until a local train arrived to take her as far as Norwich. But there was nothing for her in Bootle now, merely memories, she thought sadly. The people who loved her had their own lives to lead. There was nothing for her anywhere. Anyroad, this was what she wanted, to be alone. It was why she'd applied to join the Land Army, to get away from people and places she knew, things that reminded her of what she'd lost. Eileen realised she'd entirely forgotten about Nick.

She sighed, and decided to go to bed, though she did a Mr Singerman and left on most of her underclothes underneath her nightdress. The sheets were crisp and fresh and seemed to be made of ice, though after a while she began to feel warm and fell asleep more quickly than expected.

During the night, she was disturbed twice by the sound of aeroplanes passing overhead, but as there'd been no siren, she assumed they were from the nearby RAF camp on their way to Germany and back with a load of bombs.

Ted woke her by banging on the door and shouting, 'Mrs Costello, Eileen.'

Grey daylight filtered through the white curtains. Eileen got out of bed and hurriedly put a coat over her nightdress before opening the door. Ted looked harried as he stood frowning down at her. 'I'm sorry,' she muttered. 'Have I slept in?'

'I deliberately left you, seeing as how you'd had such a long journey yesterday, but it'll be half past six from tomorrow on. Put your working clothes on and I'll show you what's to be done. Breakfast'll be in about half an hour.'

'Ta.' They were going to feed her!

In fact, the breakfast was delicious. Thick slices of crisp fried ham, two eggs and tomatoes, followed by toast and marmalade.

'Where on earth do you get the tomatoes from at this time of year?' she asked. They were in the kitchen, and Ted, who appeared to have already eaten, was sitting with her smoking a cigarette.

'Edna bottles 'em.' He nodded towards the silent figure at the sink with her back to them. Edna had made no attempt to acknowledge Eileen's friendly 'good morning'. 'And she made the marmalade and the bread.'

'It's lovely, Edna, all of it,' Eileen said warmly. 'I was never able to make bread as light as this.'

Edna gave no indication she'd heard. Eileen felt her heart sink. It was going to be very difficult over

251

the next few weeks, living in the same house as someone who seemed unwilling to exchange the basic courtesies.

'It's a lovely room, too,' she said to Ted. 'Very homely.' Like the rest of the house, the big kitchen was painted white. There were copper pans hanging on the walls, along with several other utensils that Eileen had never seen the likes of before. The room had a comfortable, lived in look. There were two plump armchairs in front of the blazing log fire and a battery wireless on a shelf nearby. Three cats dozed on the hearth, one heavily pregnant.

'Edna keeps the place looking nice,' Ted murmured. Eileen noticed Edna's back stiffen and was aware of a tension between the two. 'Now, as soon as you've finished, we'll get down to work. I don't normally stop for a break at this time of day.'

'I'm sorry.' Eileen gulped down the remains of her second cup of tea. She wouldn't have minded a third. 'I didn't realise I was keeping you.'

'It's what you call a mixed farm,' Ted said later as they tramped through the mud. 'We have a bit of everything, 'cept sheep, and it's not what you'd call big. Three of us managed it afore the war, Horace, Bob and me, but the Ministry insist on every single inch being cultivated and we're still at work clearing the scrub—that's why we took on an extra hand—not that you'd call that bloody Peggy much help.' His bluff red face creased in disgust. 'She's less than useless, that girl.'

Eileen stopped at the sty to look at the pigs. She'd never realised pigs were so nice. You could almost cuddle the little ones. She kept her thoughts to herself, feeling Ted wouldn't take kindly to pigs being described as cuddly.

They came to the stables, which contained two fine black and white horses with well-groomed manes and massive fluffy hooves. 'This is Bessie, and that's Warrior,' said Ted. He patted Bessie's neck affectionately. 'They're the best workers we have.'

'They're beautiful,' Eileen said admiringly. 'I love horses. We have one living a few doors away down the street. He's called Nelson. He can't stand the raids.'

Ted was looking at her with astonishment, and she realised it probably sounded strange, a horse living in a street. 'Nelson pulled the coal cart,' she explained.

'Where's that bloody Peggy?' Ted frowned. 'I put her to work cleaning this place up earlier on.'

Peggy Wilson came bouncing into the stables, her cheeks and the tip of her fine nose pink with cold. Dark curls spilled out from underneath the felt hat which was set somewhat precariously on the back of her head. She wore dungarees underneath her fawn overcoat, and hobnailed boots. 'I've just been to the loo,' she said breathlessly. 'I've nearly finished here.' She noticed Eileen and her eyes lit up. 'Oh, hallo! Ted told me you were coming. I've been dying for you to arrive so that I'd have some female company.' She glanced at Ted. 'It's horrible working with nothing but men.'

'If you could call it working,' Ted said cuttingly. 'Well, I'll leave you in Peggy's hands. Once the stables are finished, you can help Horace out with the beet on the west field.'

'Yes, sir!' Peggy saluted smartly and Ted's red

face turned even redder as he marched away.

'He hates me purely because I'm a woman and we aren't supposed to work on farms,' Peggy said as soon as Ted was out of earshot. 'I do my best, really I do, but he always finds something wrong.'

'No one can do more than their best.'

'Tell that to Ted!' Peggy put her hands on her hips and looked Eileen up and down. 'Are you warm enough in that get up?'

'Not particularly, but it doesn't matter. I'll have a proper uniform soon enough.'

'You must be keen to start work if you're willing to live with that awful Edna. What's she like at close quarters?' She began to sweep the floor vigorously with a rush broom.

'Horrible!' Eileen told her of the reception she'd got the previous night. 'I was dying for a cup of tea, at least.'

'Bitch! Most of the locals hate us land girls, Edna's worse than most.'

'Why should they hate us? We're all on the same side.' Eileen asked in surprise.

Peggy shrugged. 'Dunno. They're awfully old-fashioned here, and we seem like liberated women. We go in pubs by ourselves which women aren't supposed to do, and the young men like us better than the local girls. Whenever there's a dance, we always get asked first, particularly if we're in uniform.' She put the broom away and slung a khaki haversack over her shoulder. 'Come on, we'd better get going. Ted'll have a fit if he finds we're still here.'

Once outside the farmyard enclosure, the wind lashed even more keenly across the fields, which were surrounded by bare black hedges offering no

254

protection at all. The marshes could be glimpsed in the distance, and beyond the marshes, the North Sea glinted dully, like unpolished pewter. Eileen shuddered as she stuffed her hands in her pockets and reminded herself that only very recently she'd found herself drawn to this bleak scenery. But it seemed different today, bleaker, more desolate and not in the least appealing. As they trudged over the broken, frozen soil, Peggy began to get on her nerves. She had a juvenile, gushing manner and chattered unceasingly, mainly about her mother. Eileen felt she would have preferred to be alone with her thoughts. Her heart sank for the second time that morning. Was it going to be like this every day?

She was an only child, Peggy informed her, and her widowed mother wouldn't let her out of her sight for a single moment when she wasn't at work. 'Mummy's only young, forty-nine,' she complained in her breathless, rather childish voice, 'and I could see myself stuck with her for the rest of my life. Ever since the war began, I kept wanting to join up, the WRAF or the WRENs or something, but she practically had hysterics whenever I suggested leaving. In the end, I put my foot down and joined the Land Army. At least it means there's no chance of being sent abroad—not that I would have minded. Unfortunately, we're less than an hour away from Ipswich by train, which means she keeps nagging me to come home for weekends.'

'I suppose she's lonely,' Eileen said reasonably.

'So was I,' Peggy said bluntly, 'stuck at home all the time with only Mummy for company. If I suggested going out, she'd feel too ill to be left. I brought a boy back once, years ago, and she nearly

255

had a heart attack.' She stopped. 'How old do you think I am?'

Eileen stared at the pretty, unlined face. 'About twenty-five, I reckon.'

'I'm nearly thirty and I've never even *kissed* a man. Isn't that terrible?'

'It's not exactly the end of the world,' Eileen said brusquely. Peggy's problems, real though they may be, seemed trivial compared to her own. She felt uncomfortable when Peggy lapsed into silence, clearly hurt at the put-down.

'Was I rabbiting on too much? I'm sorry,' she said after a while. 'It's just that Ted told me about your husband and little boy. I think he was scared I'd put my foot in it. I thought if I did all the talking it would take your mind off things. I must have sounded awfully selfish under the circumstances, concerned only with my own foolish affairs.'

Oh, God! Eileen instantly felt ashamed and full of contrition. It was *her* that should be sorry. Last night she'd been dead upset because Edna didn't talk to her, and she'd nearly bitten Peggy's head off for talking too much!

She apologised for being so short-tempered. 'Don't take any notice of me, luv,' she said. 'I don't know what I want or where I am at the moment. I'm afraid I'll have to ask you to put up with me until I've sorted me head out.'

Peggy smiled warmly. 'Just tell me to shut up in future. I'll understand.'

'You shouldn't have to. In fact, you'd have been better off with someone single like yourself.' They seemed to be two women whose experience of life couldn't possibly have been more different.

'I prefer someone older like you,' Peggy said

comfortably. 'I'm the oldest in the hostel, most of the girls are in their teens. Anyway, there's Horace hard at work. Now you'll discover what it's really like to be a land girl.'

They'd arrived at the edge of a massive field where the recently ploughed black soil was tipped with ice and covered with turnip-like vegetables. A very old man wearing a balaclava helmet and a shabby overcoat was bent double on the furthest side. He looked up as they approached and nodded amiably when Eileen was introduced. She noticed his uncovered hands were badly twisted, the knuckles swollen to twice the normal size with rheumatism.

'Horace has worked on farms for over sixty years,' Peggy said in awe. 'I don't know how he stands it.'

The old man's incredibly wizened face creased into a gentle smile. 'There's no job better than working with Mother Nature. A man comes face to face with his maker every day when he tends the soil.'

Peggy made a face at Eileen over the bent, rather dignified figure of the old man. 'He's a bit touched,' she said later. 'When he's not on the farm, he's in church, thanking God for letting him work for a pittance all his life for Mr Kinnear and others like him.'

'Poor ould thing. On the other hand, he seems happy, and I suppose that's all that matters.'

'Perhaps. I'll show you what's to be done with this horrible sugar beet.'

Once the tops of the beets had been removed with a sharp knife, they were thrown into a barrow and wheeled to the edge of the field, where they were tipped in a heap for Ted or Horace to collect in the cart.

Kate Thomas had warned her it would be entirely different from Dunnings; the work was back-breaking and much harder. Eileen thought fondly about the factory and her old workmates as she toiled away, remembering the repartee and joking intimacy. She wondered who'd been made overseer now she'd left. She hadn't seen any of the girls since the Friday night they'd been in and out to look at the red sky over Liverpool during the first of those terrible raids. Incredibly, that was less than a month ago.

At one o'clock, Peggy sang, 'It's dinner time.'

Eileen got painfully to her feet. 'Jaysus! I'll never straighten me back out again.' She began to walk towards the farm, but noticed Peggy had begun to undo the buckles on her haversack. 'Aren't we going back for our dinner?'

'It's too far. We eat on the spot.'

'But what about the lavatory?' She'd felt the urge to go for some time, but had been waiting for the dinner break. 'Are we expected to do that on the spot?'

Peggy replied, grinning broadly, 'I'm afraid we are. Either that or the nearest hedge.'

'Jaysus, Mary and Joseph! Me belly could bust before I'd go in the open air.'

'You'll get used to it,' Peggy assured her. 'Haven't you brought sandwiches?'

'No.'

'I'll give you half of mine, and you can share my tea. You'd better remind Ted that you're supposed to have a packed lunch. After all, they take half our measly twenty-five bob a week for bed and board.'

She opened a parcel wrapped in greaseproof paper and offered Eileen a sandwich.

Eileen looked at the sandwich warily. 'I don't want to appear ungrateful, but what the hell is it?'

'Ghastly, isn't it? It's beetroot, which soaks right through the bread. It's all they seem to give us at the hostel.'

They munched in silence for a while. Horace, sitting some distance away, seemed to be eating a raw onion. It was even colder sitting still than working and the damp sacks they'd been kneeling on began to seep through their backsides.

'We must be mad,' Peggy said with a giggle, 'sitting in a frozen field in the middle of January eating beetroot sandwiches and having to pee in the hedge. All the girls have decided they must be mad.'

'Are you sorry you joined?' Eileen asked curiously.

Peggy shook her head emphatically. 'We might be mad, but none of us are the least bit sorry. It's so much more worthwhile than our old jobs. We're doing our bit, you see. As for me, I feel free for the first time in my life. Mind you, we're too tired at night to do anything except throw ourselves into bed once we've eaten, but at weekends there's all sorts of dances and things to do.' She sighed blissfully. 'Despite everything, I've never been so happy.'

'I'm glad,' said Eileen.

'What about you? D'you think you'll stick it out?'

'Oh, I'll stick it out whatever happens,' Eileen assured her. Unlike the other girls, she'd already been doing a worthwhile job, but her inspiration for joining the Land Army was quite different. The tedious hard work, the icy cold, her freezing room, Edna's unfriendly attitude, all these took her mind off the things that really mattered. She didn't care what job she was given to do or how many hours it took to do it, she'd take it all in her stride and stick it out until, hopefully, the pain inside her lessened, and, as Conor Kinnear had predicted, she'd learn to live again.

*   *   *

Eileen was about to go into the next stall, but found Ted already there. 'You nearly got through half this morning, and I'd already started by the time you came.' He chuckled. 'You'll be better than me at this before you know it, and I'll be out of a job.'

'It seems easy once you get the hang of it,' she said.

Just then, Peggy arrived on her bike and was curtly despatched to collect the eggs and have them ready for the man from the Min of Ag when he called later in the morning.

'Why don't you go indoors and start on breakfast,' Ted said to Eileen as Peggy collected a bucket and trudged away. 'I won't be a minute.'

'I'll wait for you,' she said hastily. She always tried to avoid being alone with Edna. She watched Ted's expert fingers as he worked away underneath the cow.

'What's this one called?' he asked.

'Maud.'

'Come into the garden, Maud,' he warbled. He always seemed much more cheerful outside the house than in. He glanced in her direction and she smiled. 'Y'know,' he said, 'the way Edna acts, it's nothing personal.'

'I guessed that much.'

'She's had a lot of disappointments in her life and she took them hard, too hard.'

'Lots of people have disappointments,' Eileen felt bound to say, though didn't add they don't usually take it out on everyone else.

'Aye, that's true, but I suppose they affect different folk in different ways.'

'I suppose.'

Ted began to pour the milk into metal churns. One would be placed outside the gate to be collected along with the eggs, the other delivered to local customers as soon as he'd had breakfast. 'How's your back?' he asked.

Eileen made a face. 'Bent.'

'It looks straight enough to me.'

'It feels bent.' She was convinced her spine would remain curved for the rest of her life.

He screwed the top on the second churn and gave it a satisfied slap. 'Come on, let's get something to eat.'

*   *   *

She sometimes wondered if she could have stood it under normal circumstances; the mind-numbing, finger-numbing work, the sheer tedium of much of it. The worst job of all was clearing the land which had turned to scrub. One patch in particular, adjacent to the marshes, was virtually a swamp, and she and Peggy waded into the thick stagnant water to drag out rotting trees and other rubbish. One day they came across the skeleton of some other

261

farmer's sheep. In no time, the stinking, freezing water would spill over the tops of their boots and they would be soaked for the remainder of the day. It was a wonder to Eileen they didn't catch pneumonia. Instead, apart from numerous aches and pains, they both decided they felt unusually healthy.

'At least we're doing this particular job in winter,' Peggy said cheerfully. 'Imagine what it would be like in the hot weather! The insects would bite us to death.'

Eileen admired Peggy enormously for her stoical, uncomplaining willingness to tackle everything, despite the fact the results were usually met with churlish criticism from Ted. She would hold up her once-white hands, hands which had done no more than manipulate the keys on a typewriter until recently, which were now red and sore, a mass of blisters and scratches, the nails grimy and broken.

'Just look at these!' she would crow. 'Mummy would have a fit if she could see them.'

War, decided Eileen, brought out the very best in most people.

There were days when it rained, but no matter how heavy the downpour, they still had to work, and the rain would run down their necks and they would feel damp all over. On other days, it snowed, yet still they worked. According to Ted, it was an unusually mild winter, and both women tried not to think what it would be like if the weather had been worse.

It was the sheer inevitability of farmwork that Eileen found particularly daunting. How on earth could people like Ted and Horace spend their entire lives planting things at a certain time, pulling them up at a certain time, terrified there'd be too much rain or too much sun or not enough of either? The same old thing year after year after year, a sort of uncertain and precarious renewal, knowing exactly what you would be doing in May or July or September, not just in 1941, but in five years' time or ten. There was always something that had to be done—ploughing, sewing, reaping—then the whole thing would start all over again, like a never-ending circle.

*   *   *

Laura Kinnear arrived at the farmhouse, windswept and shabby, on Eileen's first Saturday there. 'Have you got anything to do?'

'Nothing all weekend, apart from Mass tomorrow morning.' Eileen had been wondering how to fill the two free days. Originally, she had planned on taking long walks, perhaps venturing even further than she'd done before, but felt bone weary, too tired to walk an inch, too tired even to stand. On the other hand, she didn't fancy spending the whole time in her room. Ideally, she would have liked to sit in the warm kitchen listening to the wireless, but that was out of the question. Ted rarely seemed to be in the house except for meals. He disappeared every night as soon as he'd eaten.

'I thought you might be feeling a bit lost,' Laura said, which surprised Eileen, as she'd imagined the woman to be entirely unaware of her existence. She couldn't remember them speaking, apart from being introduced, when she'd stayed at the house. 'Conor's back in Cambridge,' Laura continued, 'the children are back at boarding school or university or the Army. The house is dead. I sometimes wish there was a place for me to go to. I wondered, would you like to join our sewing circle? It's the Women's Voluntary Service, actually, the WVS. We always meet on Saturday afternoons, New members are very welcome.'

'I'd love to help, but I'm not much good at sewing.'

'Then you can stuff palliasses or something. Don't worry, we'll find something for you to do.'

Eileen wasn't sure whether Laura was merely being kind or genuinely wanted assistance. She hoped it was the latter. Either way, it seemed churlish to refuse. She agreed to go and was told to be ready at two o'clock. The afternoon was spent in a delightful stately home stuffing straw into palliasses made from flour bags.

'They're for the evacuees,' an elderly lady, the home's owner, informed her. 'Poor little things, some of them are so unhappy they still keep wetting the bed. Do you have any children, dear?'

Eileen had known the question was bound to be asked someday, though had never been able to work out what she would reply.

'Yes,' she said, 'I have a little boy of six, his name is Tony.' Then she moved away, just in case the old lady asked where Tony was.

CHAPTER TWELVE

Eileen had been living on the farm less than a week when the letters began to arrive from home. She seemed to get at least one every day; from her dad, from Kate Thomas, from several of her Pearl Street neighbours. Apparently, after a lull over New Year, the raids had begun again, but although some were heavy, none were as bad as those before Christmas. There was a long funny letter from the girls at Dunnings relaying all the latest dirty jokes and including love from the entire workshop. Lil had been offered the job of overseer but had turned it down and Mona Dewar had been appointed, much to Doris's disgust as she felt the job should be hers.

Sheila had some good news: Sean had begun his training as an airframe fitter, 'which means he'll remain safely on the ground, thank goodness, even though it mightn't be in this country'. There was a PS: 'You'll never believe this, but Brenda Mahon's got a sort of boyfriend. He's a bus conductor, but don't mention it if you write to anyone, as no one else knows except me and that Carrie woman.'

Another letter arrived from Sheila before Eileen had a chance to reply to the first, this time enclosing an envelope addressed to 16 Pearl Street. Eileen recognised Nick's untidy scrawl immediately. Sheila had written on the back, 'The girl from your house, Alice Scully, brought this over this morning.'

'I've felt so hopeless since Christmas,' Nick complained, and she imagined his dark handsome face twisted bitterly as he wrote. 'Please write back straight away and assure me you love me. Please say we'll be together one day. It's all I live for. It's all that keeps me going throughout this damn bloody war.'

Eileen sighed. She felt equally hopeless, and, remembering the promise she'd made to Nick on Christmas Day, wondered if the time would ever come when the promise would be kept. She put the letter to one side and opened the one from Jacob Singerman which had arrived in the same post.

He'd been to see *Goodbye, Mr Chips*, though he'd had to stand in a queue which was longer than for his weekly rations. 'The whole country wants to go to the pictures nowadays to escape from the horrors of war. Even if you are killed, as several were in the Gaiety and the Ritz, what a way to die, with one's eyes fixed on Laraine Day or Greta Garbo! As for the film, it was rather sad. All in all, I think I prefer a musical. I kept hoping Robert Donat would burst into song, or at least give us a tapdance.' Snowy, he went on, was becoming more agile by the minute. 'He can jump on the mantelpiece and sits there making faces at me. I wonder why I never thought of having a cat before. He's such good company and keeps me amused all day long.'

'Because it took you all your time to keep your own belly half-full, let alone having a cat to feed as well,' Eileen said to herself. There was a letter from Ruth in the same envelope. Dilys Evans was enormous and her time must surely be near. 'She's determined not to keep the baby, so as I know nothing about how you go about such things, I shall get in touch with Miss Thomas as you suggested.' She assured Eileen there was nothing to worry about. Dilys was absolutely fine.

*   *   *

Ruth Singerman got off the tram at Spellow Lane feeling more than a little weary. It wasn't that she was physically tired, but calling on Dilys, which she'd done every single day since Christmas, was becoming a trial. Ruth would be accosted by the landlady on the way in and again on the way out. Was there nowhere else Dilys could go, no one else who would take her? She was driving the whole house mad with her noisy, hysterical behaviour.

'It'll be over soon,' Ruth would assure her patiently. The woman would then demand to know where Dilys intended to live when the baby arrived. 'If you've got somewhere lined up, why can't she go there now?' But Ruth had no idea what plans Dilys had for herself once the baby had been born and taken, Ruth supposed, to an orphanage. The girl was too busy bemoaning her fate, cursing herself for being 'sinful, just like me mam said', to consider her future.

Ruth opened the door of the off-licence and the landlady appeared immediately in response to the bell. 'Oh, it's you,' she said coldly. 'I thought it might be. Well, the girl's gone. She left this afternoon.'

'Gone!' Ruth felt her jaw drop. 'Gone where?'

'I've no idea, she wouldn't say.' The woman looked at Ruth with a mixture of contempt and indignation. 'You've got a nerve, telling us she was married. We had quite a little talk today and she told us she didn't have a husband. I would never have taken her in if I'd known the truth.'

Ruth's anger rose. 'You have no idea what the truth is,' she snapped as she went over to the door. There was no need to kowtow to the woman any more. 'You should be ashamed of yourself, throwing the girl out when her baby could be born any minute. I suppose you call yourself a Christian!'

The woman flushed. 'What do you take me for?

267

I didn't throw her out. I merely told her to find somewhere else and she immediately said she had a place to go. Anyroad, what's it got to do with you? You're not a relative.'

'I'm not a Christian, either, but I know where my duty lies when a young unmarried girl needs help.' It sounded rather pious, Ruth thought as she slammed the door and began to walk back towards the tram stop, particularly in view of the fact she'd been only too keen to have Dilys dumped in a home when she'd first discovered she was pregnant, but she'd grown fond of the girl over the last few months, though there were times when she could be intensely irritating. She felt worried sick throughout the journey home. Where on earth had Dilys gone and what would Eileen Costello say if she knew what had happened? She'd let both of them down, Ruth thought miserably. It had been wrong just to let Dilys rot away in that gloomy room. She should have spent more time with her, but she'd always been only too selfishly eager to escape from the poor girl's endless weeping. She supposed it was even more selfish to wish the whole affair would be soon be over; that Dilys would have her baby and continue with her life and Ruth would be left with nothing else to do except go to work, look after her father, and save for America.

Her mind was still consumed with worry over the whereabouts of Dilys when she opened the door of the house and realised there was no need to worry any more. Dilys was in the living room, nursing the white kitten and chatting happily away to Jacob.

'Hallo, Ruth,' she said as if nothing untoward had happened. 'I thought you wouldn't mind me coming. That woman, the landlady, turned out to

268

be dead horrible. She said I had to find somewhere else to live and where else could I go but here? Anyroad, I never thought much of that room and me money had run out, so I had no more left to pay the rent.'

Ruth glanced at Jacob, who merely rolled his eyes. He looked as if he was enjoying himself. Of course, he always loved a bit of excitement. She felt cross with the pair of them.

'I can sleep in your bed again, can't I?' Dilys said. 'It was ever so comfortable.'

Ruth stared wordlessly at the spotty, bulging girl who had taken over her armchair, had designs on her bed and seemed to have perked up considerably since she'd seen her yesterday. So far, Dilys had taken everything Ruth had done completely for granted. Ruth remembered Leah and Simon had been exactly the same. Children and young people seemed to think that grown-ups existed purely for their convenience. Probably Ruth herself had been the same, expecting sacrifices from her father as a matter of course. She felt slightly uneasy when she realised that she'd probably taken the place of Ellis in Dilys' eyes. Quite unintentionally and very unwillingly, she'd become a surrogate mother to the girl. Under the circumstances, she supposed wearily, it was only natural she would want to be with the person she thought cared for her, now that the time approached for her to have the baby.

Thinking of Ellis, she asked, 'Does your mother know you're here?'

'Oh, no,' Dilys said quickly. 'You won't tell her, will you? I'll keep very quiet.'

Jacob put a finger to his lips and looked

269

mysterious. 'We won't say a word, will we, Ruth?'

'No, but someone's bound to find out sooner or later.'

'It won't be for long,' Dilys said serenely.

She'd better have a word with Sheila Reilly, Ruth thought, and find out where Bootle women had their babies. Liverpool Maternity Hospital, where Dilys had been due to go, was now too far away.

The girl winced and clutched her stomach. 'I think I'll go to bed, if you don't mind,' she said. 'I feel dead tired. I walked most of the way home as I didn't have enough for the whole fare.'

Ruth felt stricken with guilt, though it was scarcely her fault, and her heart impulsively went out to the girl. 'I'll make you a hot-water bottle,' she offered, 'and a cup of cocoa.'

Dilys was already in bed by the time Ruth went upstairs, leaning comfortably back against the headboard. She wore a threadbare nightdress—the flowered pattern had almost disappeared, it had been washed so many times. The gas light had been turned full on.

'Ta,' she said as the stone bottle was tucked under the clothes against her. She grabbed Ruth's hand as she straightened the eiderdown. 'It's awful nice being home,' she said.

'It's nice having you,' Ruth said briskly.

Dilys seemed unwilling to let go of her hand. 'You've been dead kind. I don't know what I would have done without you.'

Somewhat unwillingly, Ruth sat on the edge of the bed and put her other hand over that of the girl's plump one. 'You'd have managed, somehow. Anyway, it's Eileen Costello you should really thank. It was her idea to look after you. As for me, I could have been much kinder.' She should have brought the girl back weeks ago, she realised with compunction, even if it meant giving up her bed. She looked so much happier and relaxed now she was 'home'. In an effort to salve her conscience, she said, 'I'll buy a pretty nightdress tomorrow for you to wear in hospital.'

'I won't need one.' Dilys looked at her, wide-eyed and utterly trusting. 'What's going to happen to me baby?'

'Someone else will take care of it. Isn't that what you want?'

'I suppose so.'

'There's a lady, a friend of Eileen's, who's coming to see me later in the week. She promised to look into it for me.'

'Will it go in an orphanage?'

'Either that or be adopted,' Ruth said, guessing.

'There was a girl in school who lived in an orphanage. She was dead miserable most of the time. We became best friends.' Dilys put her free hand on her stomach. 'It kicks sometimes, you know, or turns over ever so slowly, like a somersault.' She giggled. 'Maybe it's going to be one of them acrobats when it grows up.'

'Maybe.'

To Ruth's horror, tears began to run down the girl's pudgy cheeks, but not the wild, angry tears she was used to seeing. The tears were those of a woman, an unhappy woman. 'I love it, really,' she whispered, 'but I'd never feel right about it once it was born. I'd only go blaming it for things it hadn't done and calling it sinful.'

'Try not to think about it.' Ruth squeezed her

271

hand. 'Instead, think about what you're going to do after the baby's born. You've got your whole life ahead of you.'

Dilys cheered up immediately. 'I'm going to join the WRENs. I'll be sixteen soon, but I'll tell them I'm older. That woman, the landlady, thought I was going on for twenty. I'll write and tell you how I'm getting on, shall I?'

Ruth said reluctantly, 'If you want,' then, remembering she was the only person in the world the girl could correspond with, she added brightly, 'I'll be really interested to know how you get on.'

'You will?'

'Of course I will!' Ruth replied with as much sincerity as she could muster. 'I shall always feel concerned about you.'

She could almost have cried when she saw the pathetic, gratified expression on the girl's face. What a hypocrite I am, she thought fiercely. Even worse, was the fact she needed to *be* a hypocrite. Eileen Costello would have said all these things quite naturally, and what's more, she would have meant them! She removed her hands. 'It's about time you went to sleep,' she said softly. 'Come on, lie down and I'll tuck you in.'

Dilys slid down the bed and snuggled under the clothes. 'Thanks, Ruth, for everything.'

'Shall I turn the light completely off or would you like it left low?'

'Off, please.'

'Goodnight, I'll see you in the morning.'

Ruth had her hand on the door, ready to leave, when Dilys said in a scarcely audible voice, 'Ruth?'

'Yes?' Ruth's knuckles tightened on the door and she paused before adding, 'Love?'

272

'I want *you* to have the baby!'

'*What?*'

'You're the nicest person I've ever known and I can't stand the thought of it going in an orphanage.'

Ruth clutched the door, speechless for the moment. After a while, she managed to say, 'That's completely out of the question, Dilys.'

'Promise you'll think about it.'

'I'll think about it,' Ruth said, but only as a means of escape. She'd no intention of thinking about it for a single second. She ran downstairs, shaken, and found her father in the kitchen, where he was peeling potatoes. The white kitten was rubbing itself against his ankles, hoping for a titbit.

'I'm making you some corned beef hash. Dilys ate your stew.'

'I don't feel the least bit hungry, Dad. A cup of tea will do me.'

'What's the matter?' He looked at her with concern. 'You look as if you've seen a ghost or something.'

'Nothing.' Ruth went into the living room to get away from his worried gaze. She was still shaking, and felt a rush of unreasonable anger at the girl upstairs. What a thing to ask! 'I suppose I'm a bit worried about Dilys.'

'She seems fine, quite content,' he called. 'When's the baby due?'

'God knows,' Ruth said flatly. Today was the first of February. 'Any minute, I reckon.'

'Let's hope it doesn't arrive in the middle of a raid!' He came in chuckling, carrying two cups of tea.

'Knowing you, you probably hope it will.

273

Anything for a bit of drama.'

His eyes lit up. 'It would be just like the pictures, wouldn't it? Bombs falling, sirens blaring, and Dilys upstairs in labour in the Bette Davis part.'

'Don't, Dad!' Ruth shuddered, but he'd managed to calm her down with his nonsense. 'There've been no raids for a week or two, anyway.' After a spurt of quite heavy bombing during the middle of January, the remainder of the month had been quiet. 'Perhaps Hitler's given up.'

'That's what everybody says when there's a lull, but it always begins again when we least expect it.'

Ruth remembered his words when the air-raid siren wailed out its sinister warning as she lay wide awake on the sofa in the parlour. The sofa was too short and too hard and there wasn't enough bedding to keep warm. She stretched her legs out of the blanket for a while to ease the ache in her knees and waited for the German planes to arrive. They came eventually, but not for long, and if any bombs were dropped, they must have been a long way away from Bootle because there were no explosions nearby. The All Clear sounded after about half an hour.

'Perhaps that was merely a reminder to keep us on our toes,' she muttered as she tried to get comfortable. She dozed off eventually, but came to with a start, not sure whether it was minutes or hours later, convinced she'd heard someone cry out loud. She lay there, listening intently, and wishing she'd thought to bring the clock in with her, at least she'd know the time, but the cry was not repeated. It was deathly quiet in the street outside, so it must still be the middle of the night. Perhaps the cry, if there had been one, had come from Dilys? If so,

274

Ruth had better make sure she was all right. It would be a relief to get off the sofa for a while.

She crept upstairs so as not to disturb her father, and her heart almost turned over when she heard the sound of whimpering coming from the rear bedroom. She began to panic. What on earth was she supposed to do if the baby was on its way? She knocked softly on the door and opened it. The room, like the whole house, was in total blackness.

'Are you all right, Dilys?' she whispered.

Dilys' voice sounded quite normal as she replied, 'I'm fine.'

'You were making a noise. Are you crying?'

'I was probably dreaming.'

'Would you like me to sit with you for a while?'

'No, ta, I'd sooner go back to sleep.' She sounded faintly impatient.

'Are you sure?'

'Absolutely.'

'Goodnight again.'

Ruth returned to the sofa, curled up under the blanket, and when she awoke, shadowy daylight glimmered around the edges of the blackout curtains. She flexed her aching muscles, put her dressing gown on and went into the living room to light the fire. To her surprise, the fire was already blazing away and the kettle on the hob just beginning to boil. Her father was about to make a pot of tea. He looked tired, but greeted her in his usual cheerful manner.

'Morning, love.'

'What are you doing up so early?'

'I couldn't sleep. I don't know why, but I felt on edge all night. There were all sorts of spirits dancing around the house determined to keep me

275

awake. Snowy felt them, too. He kept nudging me with his nose.'

Ruth laughed. 'Nice spirits or nasty ones?'

He thought for a while before replying. 'Restless spirits, I think. Then I could have sworn I heard the front door close about six o'clock, but I told myself I was an old man whose hearing was getting as defective as his eyes.'

'The front door close?' Ruth frowned.

'Yes, but I probably imagined . . .' His voice faded when he saw the horrified expression on his daughter's face. 'Dilys! I'd forgotten all about her.'

Ruth was already bounding up the stairs two at a time. Had she gone into labour and decided to make her own way to a hospital? She would almost certainly know where to go. Or had she seen through Ruth's pretence of being a caring person and gone elsewhere? I *was* fond of her, Ruth thought desperately, I really was. But I was terrified we would become close. I don't want to feel close to anyone, never, never again.

'Dilys!' she shouted as she burst into the bedroom. She yanked the curtains back with both hands.

The bed was empty. Dilys had gone.

Ruth leaned against the window, groaning. She covered her face with her hands.

'What's happened?' Jacob shouted.

'She's gone, Dad. She's gone.' Perhaps it was still all right. Perhaps Dilys was even now lying safely in a hospital waiting to give birth, but why hadn't she woken Ruth? And here was me, Ruth thought brokenly, assuming she looked upon me as a mother!

She went over to the wardrobe. She'd get

276

dressed and go in search of Dilys. Somehow, she had to find the girl.

Ruth was about to reach for a frock when, out of the corner of her eye, she noticed the eiderdown move. It moved the barest fraction, up, then down. The movement was followed by a noise, a faint, almost imperceptible gurgle. Scarcely able to breathe, Ruth approached the bed and pulled the covers back.

The baby was wrapped in a bloody sheet, and as soon as the heavy bedclothes were removed, it began to flail its arms and legs and the sheet fell away. It was a plump, fair-haired boy.

'Aah!' Ruth felt as if the sound had been dredged up from the very pit of her stomach and a pain as fierce and strong as any felt when she'd given birth herself swept over her. 'Aah!' she cried again.

She reached down and touched the baby's shoulder and, as if conscious of the touch, he flailed his sturdy arms and legs even harder. She picked him up and cradled him in her arms and a range of emotions rushed through her that left her reeling, though she could never remember afterwards what they were. She began to cry, to weep uncontrollably, though she'd never cried, not once, since the day Benjy had hanged himself and her children had gone away. It was as if the agony of losing them was being purged from her body.

'What's the matter?' Jacob began to climb the stairs. 'My dear girl, what's wrong?'

He came panting into the bedroom, his face fearful, but stopped short when he saw what Ruth was holding.

Ruth went towards him, still weeping. 'We've got

277

a baby, Dad! See, we've got a little boy.'

*   *   *

'He's beautiful,' Sheila Reilly marvelled. 'He must be all of nine pounds. And you say she had him during the night without making a sound?'

'Scarcely a sound.'

Ruth was in the Reillys' noisy, chaotic house, where she'd gone in the hope of borrowing a bottle and teat, and one or two items of baby clothes until the shops opened and she could buy them for herself, assuming Sheila still had the things to borrow. 'I'd already bought Dilys a few odds and ends, but there's no rubber pants or nappies, and I hadn't got round to a shawl.'

'I keep all me baby clothes,' Sheila assured her, 'though some are so old they were bought for Dominic, me first. Cal and me intend to have more kids once this bloody war's over.' She chucked the baby under the chin and Ruth regarded the action jealously. Seeing as Sheila had provided the bottle and the teat, she hadn't liked to argue when she'd insisted on feeding the baby with warm water and sugar.

'I'll buy a tin of baby milk later,' Ruth said. She was amazed at how normal and matter-of-fact her voice sounded, whilst her mind remained a turmoil of emotion.

'Evap's the best. There's no lumps and it doesn't upset the baby's stomach like that powdered stuff.' Sheila laughed. 'He's a tough little bugger, isn't he? Just look at the way he's kicking!' The baby's legs were punching Sheila's thighs. 'What's going to happen to him?'

278

Two boys came into the room before Ruth could answer, both dressed for school. 'Where's Siobhan?' demanded Sheila. 'Siobhan!' she yelled. 'Are you ready? Dominic and Niall are about to leave.' Two other children, a boy and a girl, were playing underneath the table, and a tiny girl was clinging to Sheila's leg watching the baby being fed with great interest. Every now and then she squeezed his toes, much to Ruth's alarm.

'I'm sorry to have come at such an inconvenient time,' she murmured.

'It's not inconvenient, not at all,' Sheila said dismissively. 'Anyroad, I don't often have the chance to hold a baby which is only a few hours old, though he seems more like a week, he's so big and lively.'

'It's terrible, but I can't really remember what mine were like.' It had all seemed like a dream at the time, and there'd been nurses in the maternity home to do everything for her.

Siobhan appeared and Sheila buttoned the girl's coat with her free hand. 'You'll get your death of cold, going out like that,' she scolded. The house quietened down somewhat after the older children left.

The baby drained his bottle and Sheila hoisted him over her shoulder where he seemed to crouch, looking oddly masculine in his long white flannel gown. She began to rub his broad back. 'What's going to happen to him?' she asked again.

Ruth didn't answer immediately. She looked down at her hands and noticed her fingers were knotted tightly together. 'Dilys wanted me to have him,' she said.

The little girl climbed onto Sheila's knee and

began to rub the baby's back along with her mother, and it gave a mighty burp. 'You clever little chap!' Sheila said delightedly. 'That was all due to you, Mary, luv. You'll make a dead good mam when you grow up.'

'Can we keep him, Mam?' a voice asked from under the table.

'No, luv. He belongs to someone else.'

'Do you think they'll let me have him?' As soon as she'd set eyes on the baby, Ruth knew she had to keep him. She'd even had the strangest feeling that he was already hers, that he had nothing to do with Dilys.

'Who's "they"?'

'The authorities that deal with such matters, adoption societies or whatever they're called.'

Sheila looked puzzled. 'What's it got to do with them? If Dilys said you were to have him, then you should. There's a woman in Garnet Street who brought up another woman's baby when she had a girl and not the boy she really wanted, and one of me mates from school lived with her grandma right from when she was born. All you need to do is get him registered, that's all.'

Ruth shook her head. 'I want it to be official. I couldn't bear it if someone took him off me in a few months' time.'

She would be heartbroken enough if he was taken from her now. With a flash of illumination that left her reeling, she knew that was why Dilys had bravely struggled through the birth, alone and virtually silent in the dark, so Ruth would find the baby in her own bed and want to keep it. In hospital, it might have been whisked away in a stranger's arms. The poor girl had been told what to expect and knew when she went to bed she was in labour. What was it she'd said when Ruth offered to buy a nightdress? 'I won't need one.' Perhaps, you never know, she'd felt contractions in Spellow Lane and deliberately had herself thrown out so she'd have an excuse to come back to Pearl Street, drawn instinctively to Ruth, the only person who cared. No, she couldn't possibly let someone else have Dilys' baby.

'What about Ellis? She's his grandmother,' she said.

Sheila snorted rudely. She lifted the baby off her shoulder where he'd gone to sleep and stared at his grumpy, old man's face. 'If there was a chance of Ellis getting her hands on this lovely little bugger, I'd kidnap him meself,' she said flatly. 'She won't want anything to do with him, I know that for sure. Here, take him back, and I'll make us all a cup of tea.'

Ruth stretched out her arms eagerly for her baby.

*　　*　　*

In February, the entire country decided that as far as the war went, things were definitely looking up. Morale, though never low, began to soar. Lloyds of London, it was reported, were laying odds of five to two that peace and victory would be theirs by June that year, and at last it looked as if the marauding, murderous U-boats were being brought under control. Tobruk was taken by the British and Australians, and Mussolini was being hammered into the African ground. In Ethiopia, which had been conquered by Italy in 1936, the exiled

Emperor Haile Selassie was brought back by the British whilst they continued to drive the enemy out. Italy, it seemed, was beginning to fall apart.

What did it matter then, with victory on the horizon, that there wasn't enough meat to fill your rations, or the greengrocers had hardly any vegetables, except potatoes, and even less fruit, and the sweetshops stayed closed for days for lack of sweets to sell?

'We shall pull through,' Winston Churchill assured the people, 'we cannot tell when or how, but we shall come through. None of us has any doubts whatever.'

*   *   *

In Pearl Street, Kate Thomas went to see Ruth Singerman as promised. She was astounded to find Dilys gone, and the baby being held firmly in the arms of a beautiful woman with shining eyes and dark red hair who looked rather like a Madonna as she stared down at the child. It was the first time Ruth and Kate had met.

After initial exclamations of awe and wonder at his size and strong build, Kate Thomas asked, 'Has he been checked by a doctor?'

'Of course. I took him to be examined straight away,' said Ruth. 'The doctor said he's a perfectly healthy baby and beautifully formed.'

'And you wish to keep him?'

'That's what Dilys wanted,' Ruth said firmly. She was conscious of the baby's heart beating close to her own.

'Well, I see no harm in that, but what about your job? I take it you won't be able to give up work?'

Ruth found the woman's manner rather officious and overbearing, but Eileen had already warned her not to take any notice. 'She's upper-class and used to bossing people about and giving orders. Underneath, she's all heart and anxious to help.'

She replied, 'No, I need the money more than ever now, but Sheila Reilly—that's Eileen's sister— has offered to look after him while I'm at work. She's longing to get her hands on a baby. And my father will take him for walks. Sheila's promised to lend me a pram.'

'You seem to have everything quite nicely sorted out.'

Miss Thomas chucked the baby under the chin. 'What do you intend to call him?'

'Michael,' Ruth replied. The name had come to her out of the blue and held no connotations or memories of people she had known in the past.

'As this is Liverpool, everyone will call him Mike or Mick or even Micky.'

'My father's already pointed that out, but I shall call him Michael, nothing else.'

'You don't need my help, after all,' Kate smiled. 'Everything's perfectly fine.'

'Not really.' Ruth looked at the woman anxiously. 'I want to adopt him. I want him to be officially mine.' She stroked the baby's cheek. 'Have you any idea what I should do?'

Kate looked dubious. 'I don't know much about these things, but I think the powers that be like children to go to married couples. I've no idea how they would regard a single woman.'

'But I can try, can't I?' Ruth said eagerly.

'I wouldn't if I were you.' Kate looked even more dubious. 'I'd advise against getting in touch
283

with anyone in authority. You know what some of these people are like, little tinpot Hitlers, if you'll pardon the comparison. Once they know you have the baby, they might start waving the big stick and take him away, even if it means the poor little thing being dumped in an orphanage. Frankly, I'd keep quiet about it.' Her earnest little face split into a wide grin. 'Either that, or get married. That would be the best thing of all.'

*   *   *

Something else happened in February, though scarcely of world-shattering importance. It mattered only to one person, but to that person, it felt like a milestone that she'd never thought she'd pass.

Eileen Costello was accepted into the Women's Land Army and moved into the hostel, a dilapidated old vicarage, with Peggy Wilson and eighteen other land girls, where the warden, Mrs Bunce, a moody but good-natured woman, kept them strictly in line. Eileen didn't care about curfews; she didn't even mind the appalling food, so different from that supplied by Edna. She knew straight away she would like it; the atmosphere was carefree and full of fun, just like Dunnings, though here the girls came from all walks of life, stretching right across the social sphere. They slept four to a room, and the backgrounds of the three women Eileen shared with couldn't have been more different. Gillian Mitchell, intense and studious, had just finished university when the war started, and had a BA (Hons) degree in Biology, whereas Val Hanrahan, just eighteen, was the only

284

experienced farmworker in the place, having been born on a farm in County Antrim. Pam Jones, very tall and as thin as a lath, had never worked before. She was a quiet girl, who'd married a midshipman in the Royal Navy just before Christmas, and she spent most of the time writing long letters to her new husband.

All the girls had adapted to their new environment with remarkable, cheerful stoicism. They made a joke out of their aches and pains, and the appalling conditions under which they worked.

The thing that happened, the milestone, occurred on Eileen's second night there, when Gillian removed a Wellington boot and a mouse came scurrying out and disappeared through a hole in the skirting board.

Gillian screamed blue murder, despite the fact, as she assured them later, she'd examined many a mouse under a microscope during her course at university, but the others, the mouse by now in a place where it could do no harm to three girls who worked every day with creatures immeasurably bigger and more dangerous, fell about with helpless laughter, including Eileen Costello, much to her astonishment when the laughter had subsided.

Later that night, she wrote to Nick, an affectionate letter in which she suggested they meet. 'Can you get a weekend's leave? You could stay in the village pub. I'd love to see you.'

She'd never stop mourning Tony, she knew that, but perhaps she was beginning to learn to live with it.

CHAPTER THIRTEEN

Brenda Mahon smiled cynically when she noticed the letter on the mat was from Xavier. His letters were becoming more frequent and more frantic ever since she'd stopped sending money. 'It's awful hard managing on seven bob a week,' he complained. 'What's happening down there? Has the dressmaking dried up or something?'

She still wrote to him regularly every Sunday, friendly little letters that she didn't mean a word of, which completely ignored his pleas for cash. In fact, she didn't even mention money, and imagined how frustrated he must feel when he opened the envelope and a postal order for thirty bob or more didn't drop out as it used to and there was no explanation as to why.

It wasn't until a couple of hours later that she bothered to read the letter and when she did, she felt herself grow faint. Xavier had a few days' leave beginning on 10 March. He was coming home!

'Bloody hell!' she screamed. She tried to remember today's date, but couldn't even remember the month. Since Carrie turned up, life was nothing but a lazy meaningless blur. In the end, she had to nip along to Sheila Reilly's to take a look at her calendar where she discovered today was Friday, March 7, which meant Xavier would arrive on Monday. He'd given no indication of the time.

Brenda ran home and hastily lit a fag to calm her nerves. 'Bloody hell!' she said again.

'Whassa' matter?' asked Sonny, who was playing

with a feather duster.

'Your dad's intending to put in an appearance,' she told him.

Brenda was on tenterhooks all day long waiting for Carrie to come home so she could break the news. Not that she got on all that well with Carrie lately. Relations had turned frosty since New Year's Eve. It seemed as if the dance had reminded Carrie there were other men in the world as well as Xavier, and she was out on a date almost every night. She'd dash in, yellower than ever, plaster another layer of make-up over the one she'd put on that morning, change her frock, then dash out again to meet her latest feller.

'Why don't you come with me?' she asked Brenda regularly. It seemed that Tom or Dick or Harry had a mate and they could make a foursome.

'I don't want to,' Brenda would answer sourly. It was her own fault the atmosphere had changed. She no longer felt even vaguely happy as she wallowed in the pigsty that had become her home. The truth was, she felt jealous of Carrie. She knew darned well the mate wouldn't want her. His face would be bound to drop when plain old Brenda Mahon turned up. 'Anyroad, I'm already married, aren't I?' she said once. 'Not like you.'

'What's that supposed to mean?' Carrie demanded.

Brenda didn't know what she meant. She didn't know anything nowadays. She was merely the dressmaker who lived downstairs whose entire life had been turned upside down. Some days she hated Carrie and other days she admired her tough, sparky spirit. Then there were times when she wanted Xavier back more than anything in the world, and times when she could have killed him. Why did he take a second wife? What had Brenda done wrong or not done right to make him go off and marry someone else? You never know, she thought on the blackest days, he might have a third wife by now, a Scots girl called Flora Macdonald or something, who wore a tartan dress for the wedding. Xavier would really fancy himself in a kilt.

'Seeing as how you're so bleedin' virtuous,' Carrie sneered on one occasion, 'what are you doing with Vince?'

'He's just a friend.'

'Huh!'

But Brenda felt too confused and depressed to argue.

Vince had turned up at the beginning of January. 'I bet you're missing something,' he said when Brenda opened the door to his knock. She stared for a long time at the rather ugly young man, neatly dressed in a belted gabardine mackintosh and tweed cap, before recognising him as the conductor on the bus on New Year's Eve. It was the thick glasses that did it.

'Not that I've noticed,' she said.

He produced something bright green out of his pocket. 'Your evening bag! I put it in Lost Property, but when no one turned up to claim it, I thought I'd better bring it round. I felt sure it would be you. If I remember right, your dress was the same colour.'

Brenda gasped. 'It's got me identity card in! I hadn't noticed it was missing. It's not like a proper bag, the sort I keep me purse in.' She recalled shoving it in her pocket, but it must have gone down between the back of the seat instead.

'That's how I knew where you lived.'

'It's dead kind of you.' She felt quite overcome. 'Ta, very much. Did you come much out of your way to get here?'

'From Smithdown Road, but I go for free on the bus.'

Brenda had no idea where Smithdown Road was, but knew it wasn't local. It seemed mean not to offer him a cup of tea, but, as usual, the place was like a midden. She wondered which was worse: not to ask him in, or to let him see the dustbin in which she now lived? 'Would you like a cup of tea?' she enquired, deciding on the former and hoping he'd refuse.

Instead, he said eagerly, 'Well, I never say no to a cuppa.'

'I'm afraid it's all in a bit of a state. I haven't had time to tidy up this morning.'

When they went into the living room, she hastily removed an empty gin bottle and two glasses off the table, and picked up some of the litter off the floor. Sonny began to wail when she took away the empty cornflake box he appeared to be eating. She gave him one of Monica's dolls and he immediately began to screw the head off.

'Sit down,' she said, emptying a chair of dirty clothes.

'I suppose I'd better introduce meself. I'm Vincent McLoughlin, Vince for short. I already know your name from your idenity card. Brenda, isn't it?'

'That's right.' She fetched a kettle of water and threw a few more cobs of coal on the dying fire. It was a bind having to remember to keep the fire stoked up.

'That's a fine looking little chap,' said Vince, nodding at Sonny who was chewing the doll's ear.

'He's not mine,' Brenda said quickly. 'He belongs to me friend. I only look after him while she's at work. I've two girls, meself, Monica and Muriel. They're both at school. Me husband's in the Army,' she added, just in case he got any ideas. She could have sworn he looked slightly disappointed and wasn't sure whether to feel flattered or not.

'I'm not married meself. I was courting for five years, but we broke up right before the wedding.'

'I'm sorry.'

'Don't be. It was a mutual decision. We decided we weren't right for each other, after all.'

Well, you certainly took your time about it, Brenda thought. 'It was dead nice of you to come all this way with me bag,' she said.

'Think nothing of it. I reckoned one of these days you'd be looking for your identity card and you'd never remember where you lost it.'

'You're probably right.' She would probably have thought Sonny had eaten it.

'When you got on me bus on New Year's Eve, I couldn't make out if you were dead upset or angry.'

'I think I was a bit of both. I'd been to a dance at the Orrell Park. It was me first dance and I hated it. I'll never go to another.' It had been thoroughly degrading, standing there like a pill garlic waiting to be asked onto the floor, then bored witless by having to make stupid conversation. Though not as degrading as having your husband marry another woman when he was still married to you. Brenda began to feel confused again as she thought about

290

the uncertain future. She sighed.

'What's the matter, luv?' Vince asked.

'I'm sorry. There's days when everything seems to get on top of me,' she said.

'It must be dead rotten, with your husband in the Army and two kids to look after, as well your friend's,' he said sympathetically.

'It's not that, it's . . . oh, nothing!' She'd no intention of revealing her private affairs, but she'd managed fine without Xavier, better than most women would, with a good business of her own. She was used to being without him—he was away most nights of the week long before he joined the Army. 'With Carrie,' a little voice reminded her.

'The kettle's boiling.' Vince interrupted her chain of thought. 'Would you like me to make the tea?'

'No, ta. I'll do it.' She'd sooner die before she'd let him into the back kitchen, which was the filthiest room in the house.

Vince stayed for more than an hour, most of which time was spent explaining how the raids were playing havoc with his timetable, and he was fed up with passengers complaining the bus was late. When he got up to leave, he asked if he could come again. 'Just for a cup of tea and a chat, like.'

Brenda agreed because he was easy to get on with and didn't seem to notice the place being in such a state. She guessed he liked her, which did her ego a mite of good under the circumstances, and if he ever made a move she decided she'd slap him down pretty quick.

Since then, he'd begun to turn up regularly, and all they did was talk about this and that, mainly bus routes and timetables. Carrie had been there on a

291

few occasions, but Vince didn't seem the least bit interested, despite the fact she sat with her skirt halfway up her smooth yellow thighs which did Brenda's ego even more good.

Brenda read Xavier's letter for the umpteenth time and wondered if she should tidy up, because if so, she should start now. It would take days to return the house to some sort of order. She decided she couldn't be bothered. Let him see the state he had reduced her to! In fact, it was a pity he wouldn't be home on Sunday for Monica's Confirmation, to witness his daughter being confirmed in a cheap white taffeta frock, the first shop-bought frock her girls had ever worn. Although Brenda had meant to make it herself, she just never seemed to get round to it. She recalled miserably that the girls' First Holy Communion dresses had been subjected to much lavish praise from the nuns at St Joan of Arc's and much envy from the other girls' mams.

'Oh, *bugger*!' she said aloud.

'Bugger!' Sonny echoed from the floor.

The girls came home from school soon afterwards, Muriel in tears. 'Me knickers fell down in the playground,' she sobbed. 'Sister Cecilia said the elastic's gone.'

'Jaysus!' said Brenda, feeling guilty. 'I'll mend them later.'

'Sister Cecilia said they were dirty, too.'

'I'll find you a clean pair for tomorrer,' Brenda promised, wondering where. She felt terrible about neglecting her girls so woefully. In fact, she'd met one of the lay teachers in church a few Sundays ago who'd asked, 'Is everything all right at home, Mrs Mahon?'

'Everything's fine,' Brenda replied, avoiding the woman's eyes.

'It's just that your girls aren't doing nearly so well at school as they used to.'

'They're probably missing their dad,' said Brenda, though that didn't account for the grubby, creased frocks the girls wore lately, their unpolished shoes and dirty socks, and the fact they went to bed at all hours, so were late for school more often than not.

'I suppose I'd better make the tea,' Brenda said, as she reluctantly got out of the chair. 'On the other hand, Monica, perhaps you could pop round to the chippie for me. I don't feel much like cooking today.'

*   *   *

'Strike a bleedin' light,' Carrie said when she came home and read Xavier's letter. The frosty atmosphere had quickly melted as the women became united against their common enemy, Xavier Mahon. 'What the hell do we do now?'

'Can you take the day off?' asked Brenda. 'I'd like both of us to be here when he arrives. When Carrie nodded, she went on, 'It's his face I can't wait to see, the expression on his face when he claps eyes on us together.' It was what had kept her going through the last few months. She began to cry, 'Oh, God, Carrie, I don't half hate him.'

'I know you do, gal,' Carrie said gruffly.

'But I don't half love him, an' all.'

'I know that, too,' said Carrie.

*   *   *

Carrie had been swilling gin and orange down like nobody's business all day, but Brenda held back on the drink, wanting to keep a clear head for when Xavier arrived. It was gone seven, which meant Carrie had lost a whole day's pay for nothing. 'Perhaps he decided to get off the train and get married on the way,' she suggested at one point. 'Will he come in the front way or the back?'

'It depends whether he's got his key or not. It could be either way.' Brenda felt a nerve twitch in her cheek and her palms felt hot and sweaty. The kids were making a terrible noise in the parlour. 'I think I'll make another cup of tea,' she said.

She'd just turned the tap on, when she heard the latch go on the backyard door and shot back into the living room.

'He's coming!'

The two women stared at each other, round-eyed with excitement, as the back door opened and Xavier Mahon came in. Brenda's stomach fluttered. He looked like a film star in his uniform.

'Hallo, luv!' He threw his kitbag on the floor and took a step towards her—then he noticed Carrie, and froze. His perfectly shaped jaw seem to drop several inches as realisation dawned that he'd been found out.

The women waited expectantly. Brenda had always wondered what his first words would be.

But Xavier said nothing. Instead, his eyes rolled upwards, his knees buckled and he collapsed dramatically on the floor.

Neither woman moved. They both stared wordlessly at the prone figure of Xavier, but after a while, Carrie started to giggle. Brenda wasn't sure whether to pick the handsome head up and cradle it in her arms, or give it a good kick.

He lay there, completely still, for a good five minutes, but jumped when a particularly loud crash came from the parlour, and Carrie giggled again. Slowly, almost reluctantly, he opened his eyes.

'What happened?' he asked pathetically.

'You pretended to faint, darlin',' Carrie said. 'I wonder why?'

Xavier sat up and leaned against the sideboard. 'That was a dirty trick to play on a feller,' he said indignantly.

Brenda and Carrie burst out laughing at his sheer nerve. 'Well, you should know about dirty tricks, being an expert,' Carrie hooted.

'I can explain,' Xavier said with a touch of desperation.

Carrie folded her yellow arms. 'We're listening.'

*   *   *

He'd acted badly, he knew that, but it was only because he was trying to do his best by both women. He was sorry he'd been unfaithful to Brenda, but once Sonny was on the way he felt he had to stand by Carrie and marrying her was the only way he knew how. He was sorry, more sorry than mere words could put it, but begged their forgiveness, nevertheless.

The three children came in whilst their dad was in the middle of this long, rambling vindication, none exactly overwhelmed to see him there. He'd always been too wrapped up in himself to pay much attention to the girls, Brenda recalled, though it was a bit late in the day to realise that. She scarcely opened her mouth all night, but left it to Carrie to ask the questions and lay the blame, and generally put their husband through the wringer.

It was nearly midnight, the children had put themselves to bed, and Xavier was still making excuses, when Carrie stubbed her umpteenth cigarette out and said scornfully, 'I'm off. I have to be up at the crack of dawn. I've no intention of losing another day's pay tomorrow.'

'I'll come with you,' Brenda said quickly. The two women had shared the double bed upstairs ever since Carrie came.

'What about me?' Xavier demanded.

'What about you?' Carrie leered. 'Would you like to join us in the middle?'

Xavier had the grace to look uncomfortable. 'Where am I going to kip?'

'You'll just have to sleep on the settee in the parlour,' Brenda said shortly. 'You'll find some bedding in the airing cupboard. At least, you might.' She hadn't been in the airing cupboard for weeks.

'What d'you think?' Carrie asked when they were in bed.

'I don't know what to think.'

'Me, neither.' Carrie turned over, and a few minutes later she began to snore.

Brenda lay wide awake for what seemed like hours, more confused than she'd ever been before. Her head ached and her cheek was twitching violently. She could hear Xavier moving about downstairs. Could she bring herself to take him back? Did she *want* him back? Did Xavier want *her*? There was no way of telling what Xavier wanted, not with both Brenda and Carrie there.

296

Perhaps it was time she had a few words with him alone.

She got stealthily out of bed so as not to disturb Carrie, and slipped into the pretty dressing gown she'd made herself in the days when she didn't have a care in the world.

Xavier was sitting gloomily in the armchair, staring into the dying fire. 'Hallo, luv,' he said warily when she went in. She wondered if he would rather it was Carrie who'd appeared.

Brenda nodded curtly as she sat down. 'Hallo, Xavier.'

'I couldn't get to sleep on that settee.'

'I don't doubt it.'

Suddenly, he burst into tears. 'I've made a right ould mess of things, haven't I?'

'That you have,' said Brenda. She felt moved by the tears, but made no sign of it.

'Oh, luv!' He stumbled across the room, fell at her feet and clutched her knees and began sobbing wildly in her lap. 'Can you forgive me? Can you ever forgive me?'

Brenda felt as if her body were being wrenched in two. She stretched out her hands and held them, poised and trembling, over his head. If she touched him, he would assume he was forgiven, and she wasn't sure if she was ready to forgive him, not yet, or even at all.

'Jaysus!' he wept. 'When I think of the way you've suffered, I could kill meself, I really could. I couldn't explain properly, not with that Carrie here, but she's an awful woman, Bren, dead awful.'

'I quite like her,' Brenda said stiffly. 'She seems nice.'

'I used to like her, too.' Xavier looked up, his

dark smouldering eyes red with weeping. Brenda, still undecided, let her hands fall on the arms of the chair. 'But once you get to know her, she's anything but nice. As soon as she found herself expecting Sonny, she threatened to set her brothers on me if we didn't get wed. You should see them, Bren, great hulking monsters the pair of them. They worked in Billingsgate fish market before they were called up. I had no option, luv. You know I'd never do anything to hurt you if I could avoid it.'

The tick in Brenda's cheek began to lessen. 'That doesn't alter the fact you slept with her,' she said. It was an effort to keep her voice cold. 'Or did she threaten you with her brothers if you refused?'

He began to cry again. 'Oh, I'm a terrible weak person.' He beat his chest with his small fists. 'May God forgive me. There's only been one woman for me, Bren, and that's you! There'll never be another Carrie, luv. It'll be you, and only you, from now on. Please forgive me,' he cried pitifully. *'Please!'*

He sank his head back onto her knees, and she felt his arms begin to inch up her legs to her hips, her waist, until they were tightly clamped around her. Brenda held her breath. All she had to do was lean towards him!

'What's to become of Carrie and Sonny?' she asked.

'I'll get the cash together tomorrer and send them back to London. Perhaps I can pawn me hats. Once the war's over, I'll have to support Sonny. That seems only the right and proper thing to do,' he finished virtuously.

'And you'll never see them no more?'

'As if I would, Bren!'

Brenda let out a long, shuddering breath. 'In

that case, I forgive you, Xavier.' But if he ever did anything like this again . . .

'Oh, Bren!'

She slid off the chair into his arms and, by the time Brenda returned to bed half an hour later, the headache and the tic in her cheek had completely disappeared.

* * *

There was a thud, and Brenda woke up with a start out of the first deep and relaxing sleep she'd had in months. 'What's going on?' she muttered.

'Sorry, gal, I was trying not to wake you.' Carrie seemed to be struggling with something in the corner of the room. 'I was just getting me suitcase down, that's all.'

'Your suitcase! Why? I thought you were going to work today.'

'I've decided to go back to London, instead.'

'What time is it?' Brenda sat up and rubbed her eyes.

'Six o'clock.'

Brenda felt muddled, but then she'd rarely felt anything else for months. 'Has Xavier had a word with you already?'

'What d'you mean?' Carrie asked sharply.

'What d'you mean, what do I mean?'

'Just a minute.' Carrie lit the gas mantle and turned it low. She sat on the edge of the bed, and Brenda saw she already had her coat on. 'What d'you mean, has Xavier had a word with me already?' she demanded.

'Well,' Brenda stammered, not wishing to hurt Carrie's feelings and appear to crow because it was she, Brenda, whom Xavier wanted, 'it's just that I went downstairs in the middle of the night and me and Xavier had, well, we had a little chat, like, and he thought it would be best if you and Sonny went back to London, that's all. I didn't think he'd say anything till tonight when you got home from work. Unless—is this all your own idea?' Perhaps Carrie had seen the writing on the wall and decided to return to London of her own accord.

'No,' Carrie said briefly. 'I woke up early, and Xavier had a word with me, just like you thought. I didn't realise you and he had already had a talk. He's been a busy little bee tonight, hasn't he?' She reached in her pocket for her ciggies. 'Want one?'

'No, ta. I think I'll stop smoking from now on. With you not here, there won't be the temptation.'

'It's a terrible drain on the pocket.' Carrie threw back her pretty head and emitted a long drawn-out puff of smoke. She looked very sad.

Brenda reached out impulsively and squeezed her shoulder. 'I'm sorry, girl. I'll miss you something awful. I hope you don't feel too upset, like.'

'I'll miss you, too, Bren.' Her gruff voice broke. 'And don't worry about me. I'm not upset at all.'

There was something wrong! The alarm bells Brenda had first heard when Carrie put in an appearance last November began to ring again and the sound was ominous. Why wasn't Carrie mad? Why was she taking it all so calmly and not using her wide and colourful vocabulary to curse Xavier to high heaven and beyond?

Brenda chewed her lip thoughtfully and gradually everything fell into place. 'You weren't going to tell me, were you?'

'No, gal,' Carrie said gently.

'He hasn't broken off with you at all!'

Carrie didn't answer for a long while. When she did, her voice was low and subdued. 'He suggested next time he was on leave he'd come and see me and Sonny in London.'

'And I wouldn't have known anything about it?'

Carrie shook her head.

If Brenda thought she'd been angry before, it was as nothing to the anger she felt now. This time, it wasn't just her cheek, but her entire body that began to twitch. 'Some friend you turned out to be,' she spat. 'Xavier intended to carry on double-crossing me, but this time, there'd be the two of you at it!'

'Christ Almighty, gal, what d'you take me for?' Carrie flung her cigarette across the room into the empty fireplace. 'I told Xavier to go and piss up his kilt.'

'You did what!'

'You heard. And I gave him a black eye, an' all. He's probably still bathing it.'

Every shred of Brenda's anger dissipated. 'You're much stronger than me,' she said, ashamed, 'I took him back. I took him back like a shot. Not only that, I insisted he never see you again.'

'Well, that's only natural. I'd probably have done the same if he was *my* husband. Not only that, you love him. I did once, but not any more. And, unlike you, I know a bit about men. Once bitten, twice shy, as they say.'

'I think I'll have that fag now,' said Brenda.

Carrie lit two cigarettes and poked one in Brenda's mouth. 'Here you are, gal. I wish I hadn't woke you up. You'd never have been any the wiser if I'd just disappeared, would you?'

'Actually, Carrie, I feel a bit hurt at the idea of you sneaking off without telling me, without even saying goodbye.'

'It seemed the best thing to do,' Carrie said sagely. 'It ain't often in my life I do nice things, but I'd never hurt you, Bren, not ever. I wanted you to think everything was tickety-boo with Xavier.' She looked at Brenda sideways. 'You never know, it could be with me out of the way.'

'No.' Brenda shook her head and there was an air of finality about it. 'I could never trust him again. He's shot his bolt as far as I'm concerned.'

'You don't sound very upset.'

'I'm too angry, I suppose. I'll feel upset later. By the way,' Brenda asked curiously, 'did he say horrible things about me?'

'He didn't mention you hardly.' Carrie examined her nails. 'What did he have to say about me?'

'Not much,' Brenda lied. 'I suppose he likes us both, that's the problem.'

'*His* problem!'

They both began to laugh till tears ran down their cheeks. 'He'll hear us,' Brenda spluttered eventually.

'We've been talking for ages. He probably already realises the cat's out of the bag.' Carrie got up and began to stuff her clothes in the suitcase. 'I'll wake up Sonny in a minute, then we'll be off.'

'You're not still going!'

Carrie stopped packing and looked at Brenda seriously. 'I think it's best, Bren, don't you? I think we should both start again, separately, without Xavier.'

'I suppose so.' Carrie was right. They couldn't

stay together, united in their hatred of a man who wasn't worth the candle.

'I'll get another factory job,' Carrie said chirpily. 'I'll find someone to look after Sonny. As for you, you should be able to manage on the money from the Army. You could take up dressmaking again. That dance frock you made for me's the nicest one I ever had.'

Brenda shook her head. 'I'll never sew another stitch,' she vowed.

'There!' Carrie clicked the shabby suitcase shut. 'Now, shall we go downstairs together and have it out with Xavier? Or would you sooner do it on your own?'

'I'd sooner we did it together.'

But when they went downstairs, Xavier had gone.

*   *   *

Carrie left soon afterwards, with Sonny in the girls' old pushchair, which had been second-hand when Brenda bought it and looked as if it had come out of a museum. 'Still, it's better than carrying him. He weighs a bleedin' ton,' Carrie said, as pleased as punch. 'I can fold it up and put it on the luggage rack on the train.'

Brenda felt far more upset over losing Carrie than losing Xavier. She'd even grown fond of Sonny, and could have cried when the the little chap was being strapped into the pushchair, and she realised she'd never see him again. Monica and Muriel, who'd got up to see them off, both burst into tears.

'Well, cheerio, gal.'

'Tara, Carrie.'

They all waved until Carrie turned the corner of the street. Brenda went back indoors and made the girls a good breakfast for the first time in months, and even ironed their frocks for school.

It wasn't until the girls had gone, and the house seemed particularly quiet, that she had a good cry. She found a single ciggie in a packet which Carrie had left on the mantelpiece and smoked it.

'That's it!' she said, when she threw the stub on the fire.

Then Brenda put her hands on her hips, took a good look around the filthy room, and began to tidy up.

CHAPTER FOURTEEN

It was a crisp, slightly blustery day with a definite touch of spring in the air. Great white clouds rolled majestically across the blue sky, obliterating the brilliant golden sun from time to time.

Sean Doyle came whistling round the corner of Pearl Street, a swing in his step and a smile on his face. He loved the RAF, he was popular with his new mates, and even the Flight Sergeant liked him. Not only that, the uniform suited him no end, which meant girls threw themselves in his direction with even more enthusiasm than they'd done when he was in civvies. Now, thought Sean happily, he was home on leave for the first time since Christmas and everyone would make a fuss of him: his dad, his sisters and all the pals he'd left behind. He'd take one of his old girlfriends to the pictures tonight, and a different one tomorrow. He knew that any one of them would drop everything the minute he showed his face. His little world was perfect, but then it always was.

Being only half past two, he knew his dad would be at work, so he didn't bother going home. He fancied a bit of grub, so made straight for his sister Sheila's house. To his disappointment, there was no one there when he let himself in. Sheila must have taken the kids to that clinic place, or perhaps there was something going on at church. He closed the door and crossed over the street to Eileen's, where he drew the key through the letter box and opened the door.

He was taken aback when he went into the living room and found a strange young girl ironing a pillowcase on his sister's table. There was a tall clothes maiden in front of the fire, on which more snow-white clothes were drying. The mantelpiece was crammed with statues and there was a big wooden crucifix in the middle.

'Who are you?' the girl asked coldly, without looking the least bit put out. 'Don't you know it's manners to knock before you come into someone's house?'

Sean, accustomed to being welcomed with open arms wherever he went, sat down suddenly.

'It's also rude to sit down before you're asked,' the girl said even more coldly.

'Where's . . . where's our Eileen?' Sean actually stammered for the first time in his life.

She placed the pillowcase on a pile already ironed and reached for another. 'D'you mean Mrs Costello?'

'That's right.'

'She's in Norfolk, isn't she, in the Land Army. She's been there for months.'

'Christ, is she?' Sean never bothered to read the numerous letters his caring family wrote him. There'd been letters from Eileen, but he hadn't even noticed the postmark.

'Don't swear,' the girl said brusquely. 'You haven't answered me first question. Who are you?'

'I'm Sean Doyle, Eileen's brother. What are you doing in her house?'

'What are you doing in *our* house?' the girl countered, reaching for another pillowcase. She ironed swiftly, like a machine.

'Looking for our Eileen.'

'Well, you're looking in the wrong direction, aren't you? She's miles and miles away. We've rented the house while our old one's being put right. We were bombed out before Christmas. I'm surprised you didn't know.'

'I'd forgotten,' Sean lied, not wanting the girl to think his family didn't keep him informed on all matters of importance. He smiled brilliantly, rather aggrieved that the girl hadn't immediately fallen for his obvious charm as girls usually did. He stared at her. She looked about seventeen and was rather a pale, insipid little thing with a tiny face and huge grey eyes. Her honey-coloured hair curled in wispy feathers onto her slender white neck. She was dressed very plainly, in a brown frock which was far too long, which meant he couldn't see her legs when he peeped around the table. Her sleeves were rolled up, revealing arms as thin as sticks. It was hard to believe she had the strength to pick up the big black iron she was manoeuvring so briskly. He felt even more aggrieved that someone so ordinary didn't look at all flattered at having him in her house.

'I'm sorry I barged in like that,' he said warmly, curling the corner of his mouth upwards, something which was usually enough to knock any normal girl flat out.

'And so you should be!'

She remained remarkably unimpressed by the smile and the curled mouth. Sean scented a challenge. He leaned forward in the chair, caught her grey eyes, and asked, 'What can I do to make amends?'

'You can sod off, for one thing.'

She couldn't possibly mean it! 'Would you like to come to the pictures tonight?' he said coaxingly. 'I've got forty-eight hours' leave.'

'No, ta. I've too much to do.'

Sean blinked, flabbergasted. It was the first time in his life a girl had turned him down. She picked up a sheet and began to fold it ready for ironing. 'Here, let me give you a hand.' The sheet was about ten times bigger than she was. He jumped up and took two corners. 'Which way do you want it?'

'In a square, ta. Y'can make yourself useful and fetch in the fresh iron off the stove. Put this one in its place.'

Anxious to help for some strange reason he couldn't quite identify, Sean went into the kitchen with the iron and brought the hot one back. The girl spat on it with gusto and began to iron the sheet.

'What's your name?' Sean asked. It was a new experience to talk to a girl who wasn't fawning all over him and he felt intrigued. Another thing, the more he stared at her, the more appealing she

307

became in his eyes. She was almost ethereal, like a pretty moth which would crumble to pieces if touched. Yet despite the fact there was scarcely anything of her, she was getting through the ironing with the strength and determination of a woman twice her size.

'I don't see as how it's any of your business, but as you don't seem to have any intention of sodding off as I suggested, I'll tell you. It's Alice Scully.'

'D'you belong to a big family, Alice?' He reckoned she must, considering all the bedding around.

Alice tossed her tiny delicate head, and the gesture made Sean catch his breath. 'You're not half nosy, Sean Doyle,' she said haughtily, 'but since you've asked, I do. There's me mam—she's upstairs in bed, she's not been at all well in a long while. Then there's our Tommy, he's training to be a plumber.' She paused and looked at Sean expectantly, and he realised he was supposed to look impressed.

'That's a fine trade to have,' Sean said heartily, impressed out of all proportion.

'It is that,' she said proudly. 'Me other four brothers and sisters are still at school.'

'What about your dad?'

'He died a long time ago,' she said flatly. 'He was killed on the docks, God bless him.' She crossed herself.

'Me dad works on the docks.' Sean hoped this might be a good mark in his favour and apparently it was.

'I know.' She nodded. 'Jack Doyle fought long and hard to get compensation for me dad. He got us twenty-five pounds in the end, which was a

308

blessing, 'cos me mam had already taken to her bed by then and I was still at school.'

'Is there anything else I can to do help?' Sean asked eagerly, keen to follow in his dad's footsteps and get in Alice's good books.

'No, ta. Oh, I don't know.' She paused, placed the iron on an upturned plate and put a finger on her tiny, pointed chin. 'Perhaps y'could help bring the washing in from the bathroom. I leave the stained stuff soaking in the bath, and it's a bit heavy to carry into the back kitchen for the boiler. Y'can give me a hand with that, if you like.'

'Anything,' vowed Sean. He noticed she scarcely came up to his shoulder as he followed her through the back kitchen, where more washing was drying on a rack, and out into the bathroom Francis had installed not long before he died. He also noticed she was limping badly, and when he looked down, he saw she wore boots, and the sole and heel of one was at least three inches thicker than the other. He hadn't realised she was a cripple. Instead of being repelled, as he might have been less than an hour ago, he felt his heart contract, not with pity, but something else, a sort of gnawing ache, a feeling he'd never experienced before.

'It's like a palace this house, compared with our place in Miller's Bridge, what with the bathroom and a proper stove and all,' Alice said in an awed voice. 'I hate the idea of having to move back.'

'Perhaps our Eileen will stay in Norfolk,' Sean suggested. He rather liked the idea of Alice living so close to home.

'No.' Alice shook her head. 'She'll want to come back once she's got over losing her husband and her little boy. Now, if you wouldn't mind lifting that thick coverlet into this bowl and fetching it into the house? Though you'd better take your coat off, else you'll get the sleeves of your nice smart uniform all wet.'

'Why are you doing washing today, anyroad?' Sean asked as he took off his jacket, rolled up the sleeves of his blue shirt, and began to struggle with the coverlet, which weighed a ton.

She was watching him worriedly, as if scared he'd tear something. 'What's wrong with today?'

'Well, it's not Monday, is it? I thought people only did their washing on a Monday.'

'I do washing every day.' She laughed for the first time and her little face lit up like a star. 'This lot's not ours! None of our sheets are as fine as this. I take washing in.'

'You mean you have to go through this procedure every day?' Sean was shocked.

'Except Sundays. I never work on the Sabbath Day, it's not right.'

'But that's not fair!' Sean burst out.

'I don't see anything unfair about it,' Alice said reasonably. 'We've got to eat, and I can't go out to work and leave me mam upstairs by herself all day, can I?'

'I don't suppose so.' But it still seemed unfair, Sean thought resentfully. It wasn't right, a little thing like her having to lug loads of washing round the house every single day except Sundays. 'Where does it all come from?' he asked.

'There's these posh ladies up on Merton Road who haven't got the time or the inclination to keep their bedclothes clean on their own, so they pay someone else to do it, in other words, me. I go up that way with a freshly laundered load every

310

morning, and collect another load off one of me other ladies.'

'How much do they pay you?' Sean's heart contracted again as he imagined the tiny form staggering all the way to Merton Road with piles of washing.

'You're a nosy bugger, Sean Doyle,' she sniffed. He recalled she'd told him off for swearing. 'If you must know, I get twopence for a sheet, three farthings for a bolster case and a ha'penny for a pillowcase. I'll charge threepence for that coverlet, it's dead heavy.'

'Jaysus!' gasped Sean. 'That's daylight robbery.' Slave labour, his dad would have called it.

'Mebbe,' Alice said complacently, 'but it keeps our bellies full. Which reminds me, there's some blind scouse cooking in the oven. I'd better turn it down, else it might get dry by the time the kids get home. We've always run out of meat by Thursday,' she explained as she turned the gas down on the oven. 'Our Colette buys the rations on a Saturday when she's home from school.'

Sean was struggling to get the coverlet into Eileen's boiler. He managed to squeeze it in and Alice covered it with water and lit the gas jet underneath. 'It's dead nice working with modern equipment,' she murmured. 'The boiler in our old house came out of the ark.' She put her hands on her narrow hips. 'That's a great help, ta. Now, I suppose I'd better get on with the ironing.'

'Don't you ever stop for a cup of tea?' asked Sean. His sisters seemed to stop work for a cuppa at least once an hour.

'I haven't got time. I want to get this lot done and have the table cleared ready for when the kids arrive home.'

'I'll do the ironing, while you make the tea,' Sean offered impulsively. 'Seems to me you're entitled to a rest.'

Alice looked amused. 'Have you ever done any ironing before? You don't exactly look the type who looks after himself.'

'I have, as a matter of fact,' Sean said, hurt. It had come as a bit of a shock to find he was supposed to do his own washing and ironing in the RAF, though there was quite a lot of stuff in his kitbag which he'd brought home for one of his sisters to do.

She didn't look particularly grateful for the offer. 'In that case,' she said, 'I'll take the opportunity to put me feet up for five minutes. I'll put the kettle on.'

'Have you got enough milk and tea, like? If not, I'll get some from our Sheila's.'

'You'll do no such thing!' Alice said in high dudgeon. 'I can look after me own visitors, thank you very much.'

'I didn't want to make you short, that's all.'

'That's why I take in washing, isn't it, so we don't go short. Do you take sugar?'

'No,' said Sean, who normally took two heaped spoons, three if he could get away with it.

A few minutes later, Alice appeared with a cup of tea which she took upstairs. He heard the murmur of voices, then she reappeared. 'Me mam's dead pleased you're here,' she said. 'She thinks the world of Jack Doyle after he fought so hard for compensation for me dad.'

'Me dad's always doing things like that,' said Sean, though it was something he'd scarcely

312

thought about before.

'Well, come on,' she said sharply. 'Get on with that ironing, else it won't be done in time. You'll have to drink your tea standing up, won't you?'

'Yes, Alice,' Sean said meekly. She sat down with a deep sigh. 'Oh, this is grand, I feel like one of me ladies up on Merton Road.'

'This iron's dead heavy,' Sean complained after a while. His arm was already aching and he'd only been working a few minutes.

'Y'need a heavy iron to get the creases out. Press really hard.'

'I am, I am.' He grinned to himself as he imagined what his mates back at camp would think if they could see him. He'd told them he was going to dig up a few old girlfriends and take them out on the town. Instead, he was doing ironing for this little pale butterfly of a girl who didn't seem the least bit grateful.

'What are you smiling about?' asked Alice.

'I didn't realise I was.'

There was silence for a while and Sean's arm began to throb quite painfully. How on earth did she keep it up, hour after hour, day after day? He tried to iron with his left hand for a change, but couldn't manage it and almost scorched a sheet in the process. He glanced quickly at Alice to see if she'd noticed—but Alice had fallen asleep.

She was sitting in the armchair, looking tiny and very vulnerable, with her chin resting on her shoulder and a half-full mug of tea clutched precariously to her chest. Sean put the iron down and gently removed the mug. He stood there for a moment, hovering protectively and wishing there was something else he could do. It was the oddest

313

sensation, this feeling of almost painful anxiety for another person. Until that point in his life, Sean was used to being the object of other people's concern. As there seemed to be nothing more he could do, he took the cup into the kitchen, lifted the lid of the boiler and gave the coverlet a stir. It had started to boil nicely, so he went back to his ironing.

He'd just finished, when he heard the latch go on the back door and four children came in. Alice woke up.

'Have I been asleep?' She stood up, flustered and slightly flushed. 'I've never done that during the day before.'

The children regarded Sean curiously. Two boys and two girls, as thin and undernourished as their elder sister, the youngest of whom seemed to be about eight. They were neatly dressed in clothes that had been patched and darned in numerous places.

'Don't stand there gawping,' Alice said sharply. 'This is Sean, and he's been helping with the washing. Now, wash your hands the lot o'yis, ready for your tea.'

'Are you in the RAF?' one of the boys asked in awe.

'I am that,' Sean announced proudly. 'I've nearly finished me training, then I'll be an airframe fitter and work on them big aeroplanes, Lancasters and Wellingtons, when they come back from dropping bombs on Germany.' He said this more to impress Alice, who hadn't asked a single question about himself since he arrived.

'That sounds very responsible,' Alice said, much to his satisfaction.

'Oh, it is, dead responsible.' Sean looked grim. 'They'll be sending me to Lincolnshire soon.'

'Lincolnshire! Where's that?'

'I dunno,' Sean said vaguely. 'Somewhere in England.'

Alice began to bustle around setting the table. 'D'you want some scouse?' she asked. 'There's enough to go round.'

'No, ta, me sister'll have a meal ready for me.' In fact, no one was expecting him and his belly had already begun to think his throat was cut, but there was no way Sean was prepared to take food out of the mouths of the Scully family. 'D'you want me to fetch the rest of the sheets in out of the bath? And that coverlet should be done by now.'

'If you don't mind, but don't you think you'd better be getting back to your sister? She'll be wondering where on earth you've got to.'

'She won't mind.'

It was well past seven o'clock when Sean reeled, exhausted, over to Sheila's, by which time, he'd put the coverlet through the mangle several times, spread it over the rack in the back kitchen, and also ironed a few more sheets. Somehow, he wasn't quite sure what came over him, he promised to help Alice take the finished washing along to Merton Road the following morning, and collect another load from somewhere else.

Alice seemed amused when he offered. 'I leave early, seven at the latest,' she said. 'I need to be back to get the kids off to school.'

'That's all right. I'm used to getting up early in the RAF.'

Sheila looked astonished when Sean walked into the living room carrying his uniform jacket and

315

with his sleeves rolled up. He threw himself into a chair and muttered, 'Phew!'

'I wasn't expecting you, luv!' she cried. 'Where the hell have you been, anyroad?' His blue shirt was damp and his coal-black hair was plastered to his head.

'I've been helping Alice Scully with the washing.'

'You've *what*?' She'd never known him wash so much as a handkerchief when he was home.

He leaned forward, eyes blazing. 'You know, Sheil, it's not a bit fair. In fact, I think I'll have a word with me Dad about it. She gets twopence for a sheet, and three farthings for a bolster case. Have you seen her? There's nowt to her. You could knock her over with a feather if you'd a mind.'

Sheila stared uneasily at her brother. This was a Sean she'd never seen before, and she felt more than a little alarmed at the fervour in his voice, the angry expression on his normally placid features. 'She seems a nice girl,' Sheila said, adding, she wasn't sure why, 'but you know her dad's dead and her mam's got cancer. I don't think the poor woman's long for this world.'

'Alice said she was ill.' Sean hadn't the faintest idea what cancer was.

'And Alice is a cripple.'

Sean shrugged. 'What's that got to do with things?'

'Their place in Miller's Bridge is nearly ready to go back to. It's nowt but a tenement and they're dead mean, those places. There's no parlour and no boxroom. Lord knows where they all slept without a boxroom.'

'I don't know why you're telling me this.' Sean shook his head irritably. 'Y'know, the iron weighs a ton. It took me all me time to lift it. Yet Alice irons for hours on end. You should see her arms, Sheil. They're no bigger than this.' He made a circle with his thumb and first finger.

Sheila ignored him. 'As for Alice,' she went on convinced in her heart she was wasting her time, but hoping there was still an opportunity to put her little brother off, 'those kids are a real credit to her, but there's no way she'll leave them till they're old enough to fend for themselves. Anyone who takes on Alice takes on the entire family at the same time.'

'They're nice kids,' said Sean, very grown up. 'Ever so well behaved.' He couldn't understand what his sister was going on about and decided it was time to change the subject. 'Is there any grub, Sheil? I'm starving.'

'Would you like some sausage and mash?' The sausages were for tomorrow's tea, but she'd go without herself and just have a bit of fried potato.

'That would be the gear,' Sean said.

As she passed him on her way into the back kitchen, Sheila clasped her brother's face fiercely in both hands and kissed him on the forehead. 'What's that for?' he asked, surprised.

'That's for nothing.' Sheila brushed a tear from her eye as she left the room. 'After you've finished eating, you can put your feet up and listen to the wireless. Our Eileen lent me hers before she went away.'

'I can't,' said Sean. 'I want to go home and get to bed early. I promised to help Alice carry the washing along to Merton Road tomorrer morning.'

He was lost, Sheila realised with a pang. All of them had high hopes for Sean, but although he didn't know it yet, he'd fallen for a little crippled girl who would shortly be an orphan and had five younger brothers and sisters to care for. A few months ago, he'd been a lad without a single care in the world. Now he was in the RAF, and, if Alice Scully would have him, apparently willing to take upon himself the liability of a ready-made family.

After Sean had gone, Sheila got out a writing pad and began a letter to her sister. 'Prepare yourself for a shock, Sis,' she wrote. 'I think our Sean's in love . . .'

CHAPTER FIFTEEN

The countryside was beginning to turn the palest shade of green. The black bushes, the black trees, all were covered with tiny buds which seemed to get greener and fuller by the day. Grass sprouted in the dank smelly ditches, and the shoots of wild flowers skirted the hedgerows which were also starting to burst into life, not just with the first flush of pink and white blossom; freshly built birds' nests were already cradled in their topmost branches and the rustle of tiny animals came from between the tight, impenetrable roots. The long, flat Norfolk roads had dried in the lukewarm sun, and seemingly endless rows of vegetables thrust through the now soft soil of the neatly furrowed fields.

Spring had arrived!

The birds sang gaily, a welcome dawn chorus, as Eileen Costello and Peggy Wilson cycled to work through this remarkable and heartlifting reawakening. War would never prevent nature from treading its inevitable course. The birds were still singing when they rode home, and it was always difficult, no matter how tired they felt, not to join in and sing with them.

It was Friday, always a special day, because the weekend stretched ahead and weekends were always enjoyable. On Friday nights, even though everyone at the hostel felt particularly weary after five whole days of hard, unremitting work, they all went to a pub and drank cheap cider, which was all they could afford on their twelve and six a week, and got slightly drunk and sang even more. They'd already been banned from one pub for rowdy behaviour.

'Are you seeing Phil tomorrow?' Eileen asked as they rode side by side. Peggy was madly in love for the third time.

'I'm not sure. Some of the girls are going to a dance in Norwich. I thought I might go there, rather than the camp.'

Everyone from the hostel went dancing on a Saturday, usually to the nearby RAF camp, and Eileen went with them rather than stay in by herself. For some reason none of them could quite understand, the land girls were looked upon with particular favour by the servicemen and were always the first to be asked to dance, much to the chagrin of the local girls, who eyed them enviously all night. It was awfully difficult, for Eileen and a few other girls who had husbands or regular boyfriends, to avoid being taken home, where a goodnight kiss and a request for another date was almost inevitable. She hadn't the slightest intention of becoming involved with another man. Nick was expected as soon as he could get a forty-eight-hour weekend pass. 'You must only come on a weekend,' she wrote. 'It's useless during the week. I'm out at work twelve hours a day and fit for nothing by the time I've cycled home. Anyroad, the warden locks the door at ten o'clock, so we'd only have a couple of hours together.'

'I thought you really liked Phil,' she said to Peggy. 'The other day you said you couldn't wait to see him again.' As far as she could remember, this was 'it'!

'I do like him, more than like him, I suppose. But you know that first chap I went out with, the one called Hugh from Broadstairs?'

'I remember. He seemed nice.'

'He was,' Peggy said briefly. 'He's also dead! His plane crashlanded somewhere in France and the entire crew were killed.'

Eileen's bicycle veered wildly. 'Oh, no!'

'So,' Peggy said flatly, 'I've decided the best thing to do is not get involved. From now on, I'm never going out with the same chap twice.'

'Unfortunately, life doesn't always work out like that. Some feller might turn up and you won't be able to help yourself. You'll be in love before you know it.'

Peggy laughed. 'It's ironic, isn't it? I've got chaps falling over themselves to go out with me, which is something I've only dreamt of before, and I'm terrified of falling in love in case they get killed.'

'Perhaps you should only go out with the horrible ones!'

They arrived at the farm, where Edna was already at work in the front garden. Since the weather had improved, she seemed to be there all day, digging and weeding and pruning the plants already there and planting new ones. She didn't look up when they alighted from their bikes and began to push through the heavy five-barred gate, but then Edna never acknowledged them. There was something strange about her today, Eileen thought. As she knelt, her back to them, her broad shoulders were heaving.

'Are you all right, Edna?' Eileen called, convinced the woman was crying, but as expected, there was no reply. She made her way into the cowshed; milking was always her first job of the day—and her favourite. Ted deliberately left it for her to do. The cows were almost ready to calve. She hadn't realised they were pregnant when she first came, and couldn't wait to see the babies which were due very shortly.

'Good morning, Norma.' She rubbed the soft moist nose. 'There's some fine fresh grass outside for you today.'

Ted arrived the minute she'd finished, to take the churn out to the gate for the Ministry to collect later. 'Is Edna all right?' Eileen enquired. 'She looked dead upset when we arrived. I'm sure she was crying.'

'She'll get over it,' Ted said briefly.

'Get over what?' Eileen pressed.

He looked slightly impatient as he replied, 'I had to get rid of them dratted kittens. If we kept every kitten that had been born in the house, there'd be bloody thousands by now.'

'Oh, Ted, they were really pretty!' She immediately thought of Snowy. The six kittens had been born in February, three tortoiseshell, a ginger, and the twins, as Eileen referred to them, two with

321

identical black and white patches. Now six weeks old, they were delightful, and Eileen and Peggy had wasted far too much time playing with them in the farmyard. 'What did you do with them?'

'I drownded them. She wouldn't let me do it when they were first born. She always lets herself get fond of them, then there's hell to play.'

'Couldn't you have given them away?'

'Who wants a kitten round here?' Ted said disdainfully. 'There's kittens being born and drownded almost every day.'

'Poor Edna!'

'She'll get over it,' Ted said again. 'Now, it's about time those cows went out to pasture.'

Eileen's heart went out to the poor unhappy woman who didn't appear to have a single friend in the whole world. In fact, the episode so upset her— she kept thinking of the kittens being thrust under water and struggling for their lives—that, unusually for her, she felt quite sick and brought her breakfast up when she and Peggy were on their way to finish clearing the ditches of dead leaves. If left, they'd start to smell and attract rats when the summer heat arrived.

Later in the morning, Peggy said suddenly, 'I think I might see Phil tomorrow night, after all.'

'What brought about the change of heart?'

Peggy shrugged. 'I don't know, really. I'm sure he liked me as much as I liked him, and it seems really selfish to let him down just in case he's killed. How does that poem go—'tis better to have loved and lost than never to have loved at all.'

'I don't know, luv. I've never heard it before, but I suppose it's good advice when you think about it.'

The following afternoon, Laura Kinnear drove Eileen home from her Saturday stint at the WVS. She'd not exactly joined, the Land Army was more than enough to keep her busy, but once a week she helped with some activity or other. The day had been spent sorting through waste paper and cardboard and tying it into neat bundles. Eileen's hands were sore with pulling the coarse string, but they were so often sore she scarcely noticed.

'Are you feeling better now?' Laura asked. 'You looked frightful when I picked you up this morning.'

'I'm fine,' Eileen said cheerfully. 'Like I said, I'd just brought me breakfast up. It must be the beetroot. We get given beetroot with darn near everything. I won't eat it any more.'

The car stopped at a crossroads and Laura waited for a tractor to go by. Eileen recognised they were in the tiny village where she'd bought the postcard for her dad when she first came. The passenger window was wide open and she could hear shrill screams coming from a cottage nearby. Neat and well tended, it was set well back from the road and half a dozen children were playing in the long front garden. A tyre on a rope was suspended from a tree and they were fighting for possession. A tall buxom woman with a mass of luxuriant blonde hair and an equally buxom baby on one arm came to the front door and shouted at them to keep quiet.

'I always think she looks like Mother Nature,' Laura Kinnear murmured, 'or Mother Earth.'

Two more children, smaller than the others,

came running out of the front door and joined the struggle for the tyre. The woman gave up shouting and threw back her head and laughed. Even though they were fifty feet or more away, Eileen could see her teeth were an almost startling white. She was outstanding in her way, beautifully vivid and alive.

'Who is she?'

'That's Violet Warren, Ted's woman.'

'Ted!' exclaimed Eileen, startled. 'Our Ted, you mean Ted off the farm?'

'That's right, Ted off the farm.'

'What about the children?'

'They're Ted's, ten altogether. The eldest, Tommy, joined the Army recently.'

Eileen gasped, nonplussed. 'But what about Edna?'

'This all happened before Conor bought the farm,' Laura explained, 'but apparently when Ted and Edna first married, she had as many miscarriages as Violet has since had children. I think she took one baby full-term, but it died after a few hours.'

'Jaysus! Poor Edna! So Ted just upped and got himself another woman?'

Laura nodded. 'That was twenty years ago. He spends more of his free time with Violet than he does with his wife. Rumour has it they keep hoping Edna will leave so they can move into the farmhouse.'

'Can't Conor do anything about it?' Eileen said heatedly. 'Give Ted the sack, for instance, and take on another manager?'

'What would happen to Edna then?' asked Laura, shrugging. 'At least she's got a home. Anyway, you know Conor, he finds it rather amusing, all part of the rich pageant of life.'

'Why didn't you tell me this before?'

'Because it seemed like gossiping. I hate gossipy women. I only told you now because we happened to see Violet. It might help you understand why Edna's the way she is.'

*   *   *

'It's your turn to climb the ladder,' said Peggy.

'No, it's not. It's yours.'

'Are you positive? I'm sure it was me who went up last time when we were trimming hedges.'

'It was definitely me,' Eileen assured her. 'If I remember right, you had hysterics halfway up and we had to fetch Ted to help you down, so I went up instead. What was it you claimed you had? Verty something.'

'Vertigo. I'm terrified of heights.'

They stood either side of the ladder which was propped against the barn. The barn was currently empty, but several tiles had become dislodged from the roof and had to be put back in place before the building could be used for storage.

Peggy was close to tears. 'I'm prepared to clean the pigsties out with my bare hands if necessary. I'd even have a go at shoeing the horses if Ted asked, and I'll be midwife to the cows. But going up a ladder, Eileen! Honestly, I don't think I can do it.'

Eileen stared at the ladder which she was convinced stretched upwards for miles. I'm not too keen on it meself,' she said dubiously. 'This is much bigger than the one we did the hedges with.'

'Much, much bigger!'

'Perhaps we should fetch Ted and tell him we

325

can't do it.'

'That's a good idea,' Peggy said eagerly.

'But then, he'd only rant on about bloody women having to turn to men for the difficult jobs.'

'What should we do, then?'

'I suppose I'd better have a go,' Eileen said reluctantly.

'I'll hold it really firmly, I promise.'

'You better bloody had!' Eileen began to climb the ladder warily and the further she climbed, the more it seemed to sway. 'Are you sure you've got hold of it? she called.

'Don't look down,' Peggy said sharply. 'I'm holding it as tightly as I can.'

Eileen reached the roof. To her dismay, at least twenty, perhaps thirty, tiles were out of place, several having slid down into the gutter—and she was supposed to crawl around the hazardous slope putting them back! Even getting off the ladder onto the roof seemed dangerous. To her intense horror, her head began to swim.

'Jaysus!' she muttered.

'What's the matter?'

'I feel terrible dizzy. I think I'm going to faint. I'm definitely going to be sick. Oh, Jaysus!'

'You're moving the ladder!' Peggy screamed, as Eileen retched into the gutter. 'Come on down.'

But Eileen had her arms around the ladder, holding onto it for dear life, as she struggled to prevent herself from lapsing into unconsciousness.

'Come on, move this foot.' Eileen felt a hand on the heel of her right boot, tugging until the foot was lowered onto the rung below, then her left boot, her right again. She still kept her arms tightly round the wooden frame and slid downwards as

326

her feet were moved. She had no idea how far down she was, when the dizziness refused to be contained another minute, and her toe slid off the next rung and she fell backwards. It was Peggy who cushioned her fall. Peggy, who, despite her terror of heights, had climbed the hated ladder to help her down.

But Eileen didn't discover this until much later. When she came to, she was lying in a strange room and a blurred figure was kneeling beside her bathing her forehead with a damp cloth. She blinked in an effort to clear her head and was astonished when the figure turned out to be Edna. They were in the farmhouse, in a room where Eileen had never been before, which looked like a parlour.

'How do you feel?' Edna asked. She moved away and sat in a chair.

Eileen didn't answer straight away as she tried to work out how she felt. 'Still a bit dizzy,' she said eventually. 'And a bit sore.'

'You've no bones broken, but there's quite a lot of bruising to your hips. The vet said you'll be all right.' The woman spoke in a slow, stilted way, as if she wasn't used to talking much. For the first time since Eileen met her, the expression on her raw-boned face was relatively friendly, almost kind.

'The vet!'

'He was on the next farm. Ted always prefers the vet to the doctor. He came over straight away when he got the message. Fortunately, he said the baby's come to no harm.'

Eileen's body seemed to freeze all over. 'I'm sorry, what did you just say?'

'Your baby hasn't come to any harm.'

'Me *baby*!'

Edna's little slate grey eyes widened in shock. 'Didn't you know?'

Eileen shook her head. 'No,' she whispered. She'd had no periods since Christmas, but had thought it was the shock of losing Tony. When Calum Reilly had gone missing at the beginning of the war, Sheila hadn't had periods for months, not until Cal was discovered safe and sound. She laid her hands on her stomach. She was carrying Nick's baby, the result of their brief lovemaking on that wretched Christmas Day. 'Make love to me,' she'd said, and it had been so sudden, taken him very much by surprise. He'd always made sure she wouldn't fall pregnant before. 'You don't think I'd want to bring a baby into a world like this,' he said once when she suggested it in the days when she thought she'd never see Francis again and she and Nick would always be together. But now it seemed he had!

'You're going to keep it, aren't you?'

She'd almost forgotten Edna was there. 'Of course!' She already felt different, actually joyful, at the knowledge there was a new life growing within her.

Edna looked down at her hands and began to rub her stubby thumbs together. 'Ted told me about your husband. I thought, with him being dead, you might want to get rid of the poor little thing.'

'I wouldn't dream of it,' Eileen said fervently.

'That's good.' Edna nodded approvingly. 'I think killing babies is the worst crime in the world. I suppose you'll be leaving the Land Army, won't you?' she asked casually.

328

'It would be irresponsible to do anything else. If I'd known what I know now, I would never have climbed that bloody ladder.'

'It's just that, if you're stuck for somewhere to live, there's plenty of room here. Not only that . . .' Edna looked at the ceiling, then at the floor, then directly at Eileen, ' . . . if you wanted to go back in the Land Army afterwards, I could always look after the baby for you. If that's what you want, of course,' she added awkwardly.

Poor Edna! Poor, poor Edna. 'That's the kindest offer anyone could possibly make,' Eileen said as gently as she could, 'but the truth is, luv, I've got me own house in Liverpool and all me family live close by.'

All of a sudden, she couldn't wait to get back home.

'I see,' said Edna.

*   *   *

Peggy came to see her at lunchtime. She was almost as bruised as Eileen, and the vet had taken a good look at her, too. 'I felt ever so embarrassed. I kept wondering if he was looking at me as a cow or a woman. It wouldn't have been so bad if he hadn't been so goodlooking. In fact, he asked me for a date.'

'Then he definitely wasn't looking at you as a cow! Did you accept?'

'I thought I might as well,' Peggy said blithely. 'You're not half heavy, Eileen. It was like a ton of bricks falling on top of me.'

'That's 'cos there's two of us.'

'What do you mean?'

329

'I'm expecting a baby!'

Peggy's face changed expression several times before she said, 'Are you pleased?'

'Of course I am.'

'I thought, what with the circumstances . . .'

'I'm pleased,' Eileen assured her.

'In that case, it's wonderful news. Congratulations! Do you want a boy or a girl?'

'A girl,' Eileen said instantly. She didn't want a boy to replace Tony, not yet. 'I shall call her Nicola.'

'That's a pretty name. What made you think of it?'

'I don't know. It just came to me.'

Ted arrived in a bad temper to say he was taking them and their bikes back to the hostel in his truck. 'The vet said it would be wise if you both had the rest of the day off,' he grumbled.

'I won't be coming back,' Eileen said shortly. 'I expect the vet'll have told you why.' She was glad she wouldn't be seeing Ted again. After what Laura Kinnear had told her on Saturday, she doubted if she could bring herself to be civil to the man again.

Ted stomped away, muttering something about having to train another bloody land girl, and Eileen sought out Edna to say goodbye.

The woman was in the kitchen. She looked up when Eileen came in, her face blank. 'I thought you'd like these. I made them all myself.' The kitchen table was full of babyclothes: little knitted cardigans and leggings and matching hoods, a beautiful crocheted shawl, several embroidered gowns, booties—an entire layette, all white, made with love and in anticipation of the family Edna had never had.

'They're lovely, Edna.' Eileen felt touched, but knew she'd never use a single item. She wasn't prepared to dress her child in clothes made for dead babies. She'd give them to a hospital, where they'd be put to good use by women less fortunate than herself.

Edna began to wrap the clothes in tissue paper and put them in a carrier bag. 'I should have given them away a long time ago. They've just been lying in a drawer upstairs.'

'Thanks very much.' Eileen took the bag. 'I'll write to you, shall I? Send you a picture of the baby when it's born?'

'If you like.' Edna turned away and began to run water in the sink. When Eileen said, 'Goodbye,' she didn't even answer.

*   *   *

There was a telegram waiting for Eileen when she got back to the hostel, and her heart fluttered because the dreaded orange envelopes more often than not contained bad news.

But not this time! Nick had finally managed to get a forty-eight-hour pass, and would be arriving on Friday night.

*   *   *

He was the only passenger to get off the train, and Eileen felt her heart turn over in a way she'd never thought it would again at the sight of the tall rangy figure in the blue-grey uniform. She ran towards him and he opened his arms, caught her, and

331

twirled her round till her feet left the ground.

'We meet again,' he murmured, before kissing her, long and hard and urgent. He let her go and stood, his arms on her shoulders, looking into her eyes. 'You look beautiful.' He shook his head, as if bemused. 'In fact, you look dazzling.'

Eileen linked his arm as they began to walk away. 'What did you expect me to look like?'

'I don't know, a little older, maybe, rather sad.'

She laughed. 'Older! It's only just over three months since we last met. And I was sad until I got the telegram. That's why I look dazzling, because you're here!'

He caught her mood, as he always did. 'Are you ready to be made love to?'

'More ready than I've ever been before!'

*   *   *

The bedroom in the hotel where Nick had booked was completely without adornment. There were no pictures, no ornaments, just plain beige wallpaper, a wardrobe, a chest of drawers and a double bed.

Nick locked the door and caught Eileen from behind. 'Take your clothes off!' he whispered.

She pulled away, turned, and looked at him tauntingly. 'Take them off for me!'

'Aah!' He sank his head into her neck and began to undo the fasteners on the back of her lilac frock. His hands slid down her body and the frock fell to the floor. Eileen kicked it to one side as Nick pulled down the straps of her petticoat and bra. He cupped her breasts in his long, lean hands, and she gasped when his thumbs began to press against her nipples.

'You're dead slow. You've lost the knack,' she teased.

Nick whooped. He picked her up and threw her on the bed, where he began to drag away the rest of her clothes. He paused, shocked. 'Where did you get these bruises?' he asked sharply.

'I fell off a ladder, but hang the bruises, Nick. They don't hurt.'

He kissed the bruises better even though they didn't hurt, and stroked her thighs, stroked and touched and kissed her body all over. Then he got undressed himself and Eileen watched greedily, taking in his gleaming brown limbs, every lovely bit of him.

He straddled her, and knelt there, poised and ready, and looking deep into her eyes. 'I've missed you. I've missed you more than I can ever find the words to describe. You're everything to me, darling. You know that, don't you?'

Eileen nodded breathlessly, but her body was at a fever pitch of anticipation. 'You talk too much,' she said impatiently.

She almost screamed with sheer uninhibited pleasure when he entered her, and clapped her hand over her mouth in case there were people in the next room who could hear. When the almost unbearable climax came, she screamed again, but by this time she didn't care.

Nick groaned and flopped down beside her. 'You wear me out,' he complained as he nuzzled her ear.

'In that case, we'd best not do it again,' she said lazily.

'At least not for another half hour.'

'I'd love a cup of tea.'

He propped his head on his elbow and looked

333

down at her. 'Some things never change! Aren't you going to have a post-coital cigarette?'

She frowned. 'You know I always smoked Capstan.'

He burst out laughing, but to her annoyance, refused to explain the reason why.

'Anyroad, I've stopped smoking,' she said huffily. 'You never seem to have time on the farm, and when you do, they're always wet.'

'Are you annoyed with me already?'

'Yes!'

He cupped her chin in his hand and bent and kissed her. Eileen felt as if she would melt right through the bed.

'Are you still annoyed?'

'Even more.'

'How long must I do this before you're not?'

'All night, all weekend, until you have to leave.'

'The things a man does for a woman!'

Then they were making love again, slowly this time, less urgently, but with a deep, whole-hearted satisfaction that left them both exhausted. Nick actually began to doze after a few minutes, and she realised with a pang that he'd probably been worn out when he arrived. There'd been no time to talk about themselves, but she knew from his letters he flew across to the continent every day—she didn't ask, because she didn't want to know, what he did there—but there was little time for sleep between one mission and the next. She slipped out of bed and began to get dressed. If she didn't have a cup of tea soon, she'd die of thirst. Whilst downstairs, she'd ask what time dinner was; they wouldn't want to waste time looking for somewhere to eat, not when there were far more important things to do!

Nick opened his eyes. 'Where are you off to?'

'In search of a pot of tea.'

'I might have known,' he grumbled. 'I think you prefer tea to me.'

'It's your fault I'm thirsty.'

He patted the bed. 'Come here a minute.'

'No. I don't want to take me dress off again, Nick. The hooks and eyes take ages to fasten.'

'I want to talk, that's all.'

She sat out of reach on the edge of the bed. 'What about?'

'Remember that hotel we stayed at in London?'

'As if I could forget!' She began to hum *We'll Meet Again*, and they looked into each other's eyes and laughed.

'I can get leave at Easter. Would the Land Army let you off?' Before she could reply, he went on. 'It could be our honeymoon, a real one this time. In other words, Mrs Costello, for the umpteenth time, will you marry me?'

They didn't touch. 'Yes, Nick,' she said softly. They could marry in a church now she was a widow, not a registry office as they'd planned before. The room seemed to dance before her eyes. It was possible, more than possible, even likely, that the future held out hope of happiness, after all. She'd been waiting for the right moment to tell him about the baby and this seemed to be it. 'I won't be in the Land Army by Easter,' she said. 'In fact, I've already left. I'm going back to Bootle. Me bags are packed and I'm coming with you on the train as far as London.'

'But I thought you loved the Land Army?' he said, astounded.

'I do, but something more important's come up.'

335

She looked at him, suddenly shy. 'I'm having a baby, Nick. I only found out the other day.'

She expected him to look overjoyed. Instead, a look of terrible sadness came over his face as he gestured tiredly around the room, at her, at the bed. 'So, that's what this was all about?'

Eileen felt an unpleasant niggle in her stomach. 'I haven't the faintest idea what you're talking about.'

'It was all about softening me up,' he said in the same hard voice he'd used when he'd accused her of letting him down by staying with Francis. 'You knew I'd bring up the subject of marriage the minute we met. Okay, my dear, we'll get married. I love you so much, I just don't care about . . .' He put his hands over his face. 'Jesus Christ!' he said brokenly.

'Don't care about what?' Her heart had begun to thump unnaturally loud.

Nick looked at her accusingly and said, 'You swore you'd never sleep with Francis!'

So that was it! Eileen began to search for her shoes which had been kicked so carelessly across the floor less than an hour ago in the heat of passion. She found the shoes and put them on and picked up her bag.

'Goodbye, Nick,' she said in a voice like ice.

His jaw fell. 'Where are you going?'

'It's nowt to do with you where I go, not any more.'

'But, Eileen . . .' He was close to tears, but then she was herself.

She paused at the half-open door, more angry than she'd ever been in her life, but what a shame the anger was directed at Nick, the man she loved.

'I've never lied to you, Nick. Me and Francis slept in separate rooms when he came home.' Now it was her turn to gesture around the room. 'This can't mean much to you, either, not if it seems to have completely slipped your mind we made love on Christmas Day. It's *your* baby, Nick. You'll be a father come September. Let's hope the baby grows up to trust people better than its dad.'

She slammed the door and began to walk along the corridor. The door opened and when she turned, Nick stood there, stark naked. 'Eileen!' he called desperately. 'I'm sorry. Come back, please, so we can talk.'

A woman was coming up the stairs. Eileen shook her head. 'There's no point. I've said everything I want to say.'

He made a move towards her and she laughed. 'You'd better not come another step, Nick, else you might get arrested and end up spending the night in jail.'

CHAPTER SIXTEEN

'So,' Jack Doyle said, 'you're back!'

'Seems like it.' It felt rather weird, thought Eileen, as she sat in the living room of her old house. The place seemed very small and cramped and dark, and she kept expecting the walls to close in on her. Through the window, the houses in the street behind seemed much nearer than they'd done before. She was worried she might never get used to it again, or Bootle, after the wide open spaces of Norfolk. Worst of all, there was no sign of

Tony; no clothes, no toys, nothing to indicate her son had ever lived. She wasn't sure if it mightn't have been better if the things were still there.

'Sheila said we weren't to expect you till Sunday night. I was surprised to hear you were home.'

'I decided to come yesterday, instead. I spent the night in London, and caught an early train. It wasn't so crowded, and we weren't delayed too much.' Last night, Friday, she'd rushed back to the hostel from the hotel, said a quick, tearful goodbye to the girls, and left hurriedly, in case Nick tried to catch up with her.

'How d'you feel?' her dad asked.

'Peculiar, and the house feels peculiar, too.'

'You'll soon feel at home,' he said warmly. 'The Scullys only left last week.'

'I know. I got Sheila's letter the day I left. You were lucky, Dad. I was intending to plonk meself on you if they'd still been here.'

'I wouldn't have minded. It seems very quiet without our Sean.'

Eileen glanced around the room. 'It all looks very clean. Nothing's changed a bit.'

'George Ransome brought over the bits and pieces he was storing, and Sheila put everything back in place. That Scully girl scrubbed the place from top to bottom the day they left.'

Eileen looked at him, eyebrows raised. 'That Scully girl?'

Jack Doyle flushed. 'Well, she's nice enough, Alice. Looks as if butter wouldn't melt in her mouth, but underneath she's as hard as bloody nails.'

'I suppose she's had to be,' Eileen said reasonably. 'She sounds like the salt of the earth,

338

looking after five younger brothers and sisters and bringing in the bulk of the money at the same time. Not only that, she's got her mam ill. According to Sheila, Mrs Scully's not long for this world. I'm surprised at you, Dad. I would have thought Alice is the sort of person you'd admire.'

He nodded. 'I do. And I agree with every word you said. I hate to have to admit it, but I'm prejudiced. I just don't want our Sean hooked with her, that's all.'

'It might do him good, a bit of responsibility.'

'It might do him harm, an' all. He's had no life. He's not long eighteen, yet if he takes up with Alice permanent, it'll be more than a bit of responsibility he'll have to cope with. He'll have a ready-made family, and if he can't get another house, Miller's Bridge is a terrible place to live.'

Eileen laughed. 'I hate to say it, Dad, but you actually sound snobbish, as if Alice Scully's not good enough for our Sean.'

He flushed again, deeper this time. 'It's not like that at all. But everyone likes the best for their children. They want them to be happy most of all, and I can't see our Sean being happy living in Miller's Bridge with Alice Scully and her family.'

'Well, there's nowt you can do about it,' Eileen chided. 'I hope you haven't said anything about this to Sean. It'll only make him stubborn if you do. Anyroad, does it look as if it's likely to be permanent?'

'According to Alice, she's already had two letters, which is two more than he ever wrote his dad,' Jack said sourly. 'But, still, you can never tell with our Sean. He's a flighty bugger, allus has been. It might just be a flash in the pan. In a few weeks' time he'll have taken up with someone else.'

Eileen folded her hands over her stomach. 'I suppose I'll be meeting this Alice pretty soon, and I can make me mind up for meself.'

Jack Doyle, only too glad to change the subject, noticed the protective gesture with her hands. It was something his late wife, Mollie, had done when she was expecting, long before her body showed any sign. 'What does Nick think about the baby?' he asked.

'He doesn't know,' Eileen said airily. She'd written to Sheila and her dad as soon as she'd found out she was pregnant, finding it easier to tell him, at least, in a letter. 'I think me and Nick had already reached the end of the road long before I found out I was having a baby.'

'You were never any good at lying.'

Eileen tossed her head, irritated. 'If you're not prepared to accept a lie, I'm not prepared to tell the truth. Anyroad, it's none of your business.'

'Suit yourself,' he shrugged. 'Though I can't keep up with you the last year or so. One minute it's Francis, next minute it's Nick, then it isn't Nick, and . . . I don't know, it's like the bloody Hokey-Kokey. It seems to me you're making a right ould mess of your life.'

'It wasn't me that dropped the bomb that killed our Tony!'

He stared at her, wishing he could disappear through the floor. Christ Almighty! What a terrible, tactless thing for him to say! Her eyes were bright with anger, yet at the same time, she looked unbearably sad. She was a fine looking woman altogether, his Eileen, and she appeared ten times better than when she'd gone away so wan and pale.

340

Although she'd lost some weight she looked healthy and there was a good colour to her creamy cheeks.

'I'm sorry, luv,' he said gruffly. He seemed to be making a right ould mess of things today. Perhaps it was time to change the subject yet again. He began to talk about something safe, his favourite topic, the war.

'I thought it was going to be all over by June,' Eileen said, after listening to a long tirade of complaints. Apparently, Hitler seemed unable to put a foot wrong, whereas we couldn't put one right. 'Not that I haven't heard *that* before. But people were putting money on it, if I recall.'

'Well, if they did, they wasted it,' Jack said bluntly. 'General Wavell made mincemeat out of the Italians in North Africa, but now the Germans have decided to put in an appearance, we've lost nearly everything we gained. They've got a new man, the Jerries, a General Rommell, and although I hate to admit it, he's a brilliant tactician. That's what the British need,' he finished in disgust. 'A few German generals.'

'Oh, Dad!'

She settled down, ready for an argument, feeling at last that she was really home. This was one of the things she'd missed when she was away, a good-natured discussion with her dad about the war, and she sensed he felt the same. But before they'd got much further, there was the sound of the key being drawn through the letter box, and Sheila Reilly came in carrying the most beautiful baby Eileen had ever seen.

'This is Micky Singerman,' Sheila said as proudly as if the baby were her own. 'I already told you, I look after him during the afternoons when Ruth's at work.'

'He's lovely!' breathed Eileen, holding out her arms. 'And so big! How old is he now?' The baby stared at her fixedly with his dark blue eyes and began to wave his arms and legs with vigour.

'He's only two months, but acts likes six. He's never still a minute. None of mine were so active at that age.'

'Nor was Tony.'

Sheila glanced quickly at her sister, but Eileen was still smiling at the baby.

'Well, I'll be off,' said Jack Doyle. He had no intention of listening to two women drooling over a baby.

'He's not a bit like Dilys,' Eileen said after Jack had gone. 'Has anyone heard from her, by the way?'

'Not a word. But he must have been a looker, the feller who ... you know. According to Mr Singerman,' Sheila giggled, 'he's the image of Ruth when she was a baby. He even got a photo out once to prove it. He's getting a bit muddled in his old age.'

'I must pop over to see him later on.' Eileen chucked the baby under the chin. 'Has Ruth done anything more about adopting him?'

Sheila shook her head. 'No, she's terrified of him being taken off her if she contacts anyone "in authority", as she calls it.'

'I don't know why she's so bothered. If Dilys wanted her to have the baby, that's all there is to it.'

'That's what I keep telling her, but she won't take any notice. She wants it all done properly, so

342

he's hers "on paper", I think she said. Dai Evans, being Micky's grandad, went with Ruth to have him registered, else she wouldn't have been able to get a ration book without a birth certificate.'

'I'm surprised Ellis would let Dai do such a thing.'

'Ellis doesn't know. Dai often pops in for a little visit on the quiet. It's beginning to get Ruth down. She's in ever such a funny mood lately, really happy because she's got Michael, but at the same time, she's an absolute bag of nerves.' Sheila stood up. 'Well, I'd better get home and make the tea. I just took all the kids for a long walk around North Park, then I dumped my lot at home. I just thought you'd like a peek at Micky Singerman.'

'I'll look after him for a little while, if you like, Sheil,' Eileen offered. 'Then you can get the tea ready in peace.'

'Peace! With six hungry children under me feet.'

'You know what I mean. Anyroad, I'd just like to cuddle him for a bit longer. Get a bit of practice in.' She felt reluctant to hand the baby back.

'If you like, luv. Bring him over in about half an hour and have your tea with us. I don't expect you've had time to get any rations in yet.'

Eileen had completely forgotten about food. 'I haven't, which reminds me, I didn't offer our dad a cup of tea, not that I had any to offer if I'd thought about it.'

'I'll lend you enough food to see you over the weekend, then you can get your own stuff in on Monday. Well, tara, Sis. I'll see you later. Oh, by the way,' Sheila called from the hallway, 'have you got your special ration book yet? Expectant mothers have a green one, which entitles them to all sorts of extras, including milk.'

'I need a doctor's certificate, and the only person I've seen so far is a vet! I'll sort it out next week.'

Sheila departed, and Eileen was left with Micky Singerman all to herself. His tiny fingers fascinated her, so perfectly formed, with little wrinkles around the knuckles, just like an adult's. She kissed his downy golden head. 'In six months' time, I'm going to have a little baby,' she told him, 'except mine will be a girl. You never know, the two of you might get married when you grow up.'

*   *   *

The tea dance in Reece's on Easter Saturday was particularly crowded. Ruth Singerman, seated at the piano, always found herself amused by the women who wore hats. There seemed to be more hats than usual today, and it was funny to see them bobbing around the floor, particularly the ones with feathers. Sometimes, in the middle of a complicated step, a hat would fall off and be kicked across the floor. All the women were smartly dressed, hat or no hat. Ruth had begun to feel rather drab lately, wearing only dresses that were over twenty years old, the rest brought up to date by a dressmaker she'd found in Marsh Lane. Perhaps it was time she bought one or two new outfits for work. She felt a little ashamed, turning up in the same old things month after month. On the other hand, she had less money in her pocket now there was another mouth to feed, and it was a while since she'd put anything in her bank account for America. If only Brenda Mahon would start dressmaking again, she thought wistfully, and would knock her up a few frocks really cheap.

A man dancing past winked at Ruth over the head of his partner, and she winked back. They were a married couple who came regularly and only danced with each other, so he wouldn't read anything into the gesture. It was only right and proper that the pianist should look happy and be friendly, but until recently, her attempts to appear sociable had been mechanical and forced. Since Michael had appeared on the scene, however, her responses had been genuine; she *was* happy, more happy than she'd ever believed possible considering what had happened over the last few years. At the same time, there was the worry that he might not stay hers.

When the interval arrived, Ruth finished *Two Sleepy People* with a flourish. She stayed where she was, and as people began to disperse to their tables or disappear to buy refreshments, she started to play Liszt's *Liebestraume*, one of her favourites. As the beautiful music began to flow through her fingers, Ruth forgot where she was for the moment, as she so often did during the interval. The people eating, talking and smoking in the background, seemed to fade into a grey mist, and she was in the sitting room in Ganz. The piano was situated close to the french windows, which were open, and the curtains were being lifted by a slight breeze. The scent of flowers wafted into the large, high-ceilinged room. A man was speaking to her. Benjy must be home . . .

'I said "hallo".'

Ruth came down to earth, rather exasperated, and ready to dismiss whoever it was as tactfully as she could. Men frequently approached her during

345

the break or after the dance was over to start a conversation which often ended with them asking if they could take her out.

There was something familiar about the tall, blond man who had spoken. Despite the fact the piano was on a dais, he was still tall enough to look down on her. It didn't take her long to recognise who it was. Matt Smith. No, Matthew Schmidt, she reminded herself. Matthew Schmidt, the German!

'Hallo,' she said curtly.

'I'm pleased to see you, too.' There was sarcasm in the deep voice, which held no trace of a foreign accent.

Ruth felt too angry to answer. She missed a note and took her fingers off the keys. Not sure what to do with her hands, she put them on her lap, and stared at the music on the stand in front of her. She rarely used music, knowing everything she usually played by heart, but today was the first time she'd played *A Nightingale Sang in Berkeley Square*.

'I wanted to talk to you,' Matt Smith said.

'Go ahead.' She hadn't much choice but to listen, she supposed, unless she was prepared to get up and walk away.

'Not here. Somewhere more private. Can I meet you afterwards?'

'I'd sooner not,' Ruth said coldly. 'I can't for the life of me imagine finding anything you have to say of interest.'

'You're very rude!' He actually had the nerve to sound quite hurt.

She glared at him. How dare he? He looked as angry as she felt as he glared back. She noticed two women sitting nearby were nudging each other as they eyed him up and down with obvious approval,

346

and she wondered if they realised he was Adolf Hitler's notion of a perfect specimen of German manhood. Ruth shrugged carelessly, 'So, I'm rude!'

Matt Smith turned to leave. There was a look of disgust on his almost perfect bronzed face. 'I thought we two might have something in common,' he said disdainfully. 'That's why I wanted to meet you before.'

Ruth knew she'd gone too far. She remembered the words of Jack Doyle on New Year's Eve, 'It's nowt but prejudice to damn the whole German race. Isn't that what we accuse them of when it comes to the Jews?'

Matt was already halfway across the floor. 'What is it we might have in common?' she called.

He stopped and merely turned his head. 'We've both lost everything,' he said.

Ruth sighed. 'All right. I'll meet you in the café downstairs as soon as the dance is over. But I can't stay long. I have to be home quickly for my little boy.'

He nodded. 'I'll be there.'

*   *   *

Ruth had never used the ground-floor restaurant at Reece's, though she had to walk through it to reach the stairs to the dancehall. It was big and lofty and painted cream. It had, she always thought, a slightly continental air.

Matthew Schmidt was sitting at a table in the furthest corner which was slightly shielded by a large potted plant. When Ruth approached, he stood up and courteously held her chair. 'Would you like tea or coffee?'

'Tea, please.'

He waved to the waitress, who came over and took the order. The girl quite unconsciously fluttered her eyelashes when he spoke. Ruth hadn't noticed before, but he was dressed well, in a grey suit and a blue and white striped shirt.

Whilst they waited for the tea to arrive, they chatted about the weather. It seemed quite warm for Easter, but then Easter was late this year. After all, it was almost the middle of April.

It was all terribly civilised, thought Ruth. It didn't seem possible that she was sitting in Reece's restaurant taking afternoon tea with a *German*!

The tea came and Ruth poured. 'Do you take sugar?'

'No, thanks, and no milk, either. I prefer lemon, but nobody, in Liverpool, at least, seems to have heard of tea with lemon before.'

He began to stir his tea, though there was nothing in it that needed stirring, and Ruth realised he was actually quite nervous. When he picked up the white cup, it looked ridiculously small and delicate in his large hands.

'I know you're in a hurry, and I'll be as quick as I can, but there are a few things I'd like to explain.'

'Go ahead,' Ruth said flippantly.

He put the cup down with a bang, and his blue eyes flashed. 'This is not going to be the least bit funny, I can assure you.'

'I'm sorry.'

'I want to be truthful, so there's one thing I must tell you first. I was once a member of the Hitler Youth.'

Ruth recoiled. '*What*!' She pushed her cup away and would have got up and left, there and then, in utter disgust, if he hadn't reached across and held her arm to prevent her going.

'It was 1930 and I was only eighteen,' he said quickly. 'I wasn't in for long. The blinkers soon dropped from my eyes, and the minute I realised what was actually going on, I left.'

'What did you join then, the SS?' She relaxed in her seat, but couldn't resist the barb, though instead of looking hurt, he smiled.

'No,' he said. 'I went to university and quietly studied languages, English and French, for four years. Afterwards, I joined the Communist Party, not so much out of ideology, but because they seemed to provide the main opposition to the Nazis, fighting pitched battles with the storm troopers on the streets. My parents were horrified. They both looked upon Hitler as some sort of god.'

The idea of Hitler being regarded as a god by anyone sane was so ludicrous that Ruth looked at him uncomprehendingly.

He made a funny little movement with his mouth. 'I know it sounds crazy, but you don't know what Germany was like for many years after the First World War. Unemployment was rife, our currency worthless—there were literally trillions of marks to the dollar and people were pushing their wages home in wheelbarrows. Living conditions were appalling and there was crime everywhere— no one was safe on the streets. Adolf Hitler put everything right. He appeared to many as a saviour; someone who would make our country great again.'

'But not to you?' Ruth asked suspiciously.

'Not to me, not to a lot of people. But even those who could see what he was doing, they said and did nothing. They kept their heads down, closed their eyes and let him carry on. It was safer that way. As long as they had a job and a roof over their heads, they didn't care what horrors were being perpetrated in their name.' He laughed sardonically. 'In the 1933 election, ninety-two per cent of the electorate voted for the Nazi list for the Reichstag. Even in Dachau concentration camp, most of the inmates voted for the party that had put them there.'

'Dachau! You mean there were concentration camps so long ago?'

'There were at least fifty, all run by the *Totenkopfverbaende*, the Death's-Head units, sadists and brutal murders one and all. Dachau is where my wife died in 1937,' he said in a thin, expressionless voice. 'Maria was whipped to death.'

'I'm so sorry,' she whispered. Jack Doyle had already told her some of this, but she'd closed her ears, just as the people of Germany had closed their eyes. She didn't want to hear because he was a German, and no excuses could be made on their behalf. 'What had she done, your wife?'

'She was a Communist and a teacher, like me. Though, like me, she kept her affiliation secret. It was insanity to do otherwise. We worked underground, arranged for speakers for other like-minded groups, produced a little anti-Nazi newspaper which we distributed on the streets, helped smuggle people the Nazis were after out of the country . . .'

'What sort of people?' Ruth asked.

'People like us, the ones who had been found out: agitators, trade unionists, pastors and priests who refused to swear an oath of allegiance to almighty Hitler. And, of course, Jews.'

But only the sensible Jews, Ruth thought bleakly, the ones who'd seen the bloody writing on the wall and taken notice. The rest, like her and Benjy, and millions of others, refused to believe the evidence of their eyes and escape to safety. What did it matter if you had to start again in another country with nothing? At least you were alive and living in dignity. Though it was easy to take this view with hindsight, Ruth thought ruefully.

'We didn't realise,' Matt was saying, 'that we'd been infiltrated, that we had an *agent provocateur* in our midst. One night, our meeting was raided and everyone was dragged away, including Maria. A month later, they were all dead. Before you ask why I wasn't with them, I was at home. I had *die Grippe*—what is it called in English? Influenza.'

'I'm so sorry,' Ruth said again.

'So am I,' he said bitterly. 'Sorry I was ill, sorry I didn't have the courage to give myself up and die with her. Instead, I went underground. A few months later, it was the turn of another group to spirit me out of the country. I came to England, where I was granted political asylum.'

Suddenly, a burst of raucous laughter came from a table nearby, and Ruth came down to earth with a start. A group of women were sitting there whom she recognised from the dance. She wondered what they'd think, the women, the other people taking afternoon tea and coffee in the restaurant, if they knew the conversation she was having with this man?

'Did you come straight to Liverpool?' she asked.

He shook his head. 'I changed my name to Smith by Deed Poll and got a job in Croydon as a language teacher, though the staff knew my nationality. They didn't seem to mind, not even when the war began. I'd made my feelings about Hitler pretty clear by then.' He cocked his head sideways and said thoughtfully, 'I suppose I should have been happy, or at least grateful I'd survived, but instead, I felt dead inside. Without Hitler to fight, I'd lost my reason for living—they wouldn't let me join the British forces, although I tried. Nothing seemed to matter any more. I'd also lost Maria, and my family had long since preferred to think I didn't exist.'

Ruth nodded. 'I felt the same, though I had my father. If it hadn't been for him, I doubt if I would have seen a reason for living, either.' Except the chance, the faint chance, that Leah and Simon were still alive.

Matt said with a quiet air of triumph, 'I said we two might have something in common.'

'So you did!' His handsome looks did him a disservice, she decided. Men as attractive as he was were often conceited and usually aware of the effect they had on women, yet he seemed entirely oblivious to the appreciative looks he was getting from the women on the next table, the ones who'd just laughed. He must have been very brave to have stood up to Hitler, one of the very few who had. She felt almost sick with shame when she remembered the way she'd spoken to him. He was a hero, and she'd treated him like dirt. She realised an apology was in order, and duly proffered one.

'I lumped all Germans together, I'm sorry. I thought you were all the same.'

'That's understandable,' he said generously. 'Jack Doyle told me about your husband and children, but it was partly my own fault. It was foolish to click my heels and address you in German the first time we met. I thought you might find the heel-clicking amusing, and I was anxious for a conversation. Despite everything, I miss my old language.'

Ruth shuddered. 'I never want to speak German again for as long as I live.'

'Is there any more tea?'

She'd forgotten to add the hot water to the pot. 'It won't be very warm.'

'It doesn't matter. As long as it's wet, as they say here.'

'What brought you to Liverpool?' she asked as she refilled the cups. Furthermore, what was he doing working on the docks when he was a teacher?

He smiled ruefully. She'd already noticed the smile never reached his eyes. 'It's where the boat docks from the Isle of Man.'

She stared at him, perplexed. 'What's the Isle of Man got to do with it?'

'That's where I was interned,' he said tightly.

Ruth vaguely remembered that was something else Jack Doyle had mentioned, but she'd felt so angry that night she'd not taken in properly all he'd said.

Matt appeared to be looking at some point above her, his face inscrutable. She sensed an unfathomable rage. 'After all I'd been through,' he muttered, almost to himself, 'losing Maria, risking my life and being bundled out of my country like a criminal, the British authorities decided I was an alien, an enemy, and put me in an internment camp with people most of whom were as innocent as myself.'

Neither spoke for a long time. Matt seemed to have forgotten all about her. He remained staring at a spot above her head.

'How long were you there?' Ruth asked eventually.

'Six months. When various people found out where I was they wrote and complained. I was one of those that helped them escape, they said. So, after a great deal of huffing and puffing on the part of those on high, they let me out.' He shrugged, still enraged. 'I landed in Liverpool. I had no wish to return to teaching. I had no wish to do anything, but I had to live, so I took the first job that turned up, on the docks.' He looked down at his cup, still full of tea. 'Why did I ask for more? I haven't touched this. Never mind.' He swallowed the drink in one gulp. 'You know, Ruth, it's ironic, in a way. I'd be far more use to my old country where I am now, reporting on shipping movements, than I ever was as a teacher.'

Why was he was telling her all this? Did he merely feel the need to confide in someone and, for some strange reason, think she was the appropriate person? She'd almost forgotten about Michael. Sheila Reilly would have deposited him with Jacob by now. Ruth pretended to look across the tables out of the window whilst she searched for a clock, though no matter how late it was, she doubted if she could bring herself to make an excuse and leave, not whilst Matt Smith was unburdening his soul.

Perhaps her dilemma showed on her face. He said, 'I suppose you're wondering where this is all leading?'

'Well . . .'

'I wanted you to know everything about me before . . .' He paused and smiled, and this time the smile actually reached his eyes and his face was transformed.

'Before what?' asked Ruth.

'Before I ask you to marry me!'

CHAPTER SEVENTEEN

It was one of those rarest of moments, a moment when everything fell completely quiet. As if a spell had been cast over them, people stopped talking, dishes stopped rattling and the restaurant was silent. Ruth felt convinced Matt's words had been audible to the entire room, rendering everyone as dumbstruck as she was herself. Then somebody laughed and, all of a sudden, conversation began again and the babble was almost deafening.

'Actually,' Matt said thoughtfully, 'I'd sooner put it another way; before I suggest we get married, which is a different thing altogether. It makes it seem more of a mutual decision, rather than a proposal.'

'Is this some sort of a joke?' Ruth said eventually.

'It would be a pretty lousy joke if it were.'

'But it's crazy. The whole thing's completely crazy. I can't believe it's not a joke.' Perhaps it was April Fool's Day? But that was long past. She began to fumble for her gloves, her bag. Almost in tears with embarrassment and irritation and the conviction she was being made a fool of, she again got up to leave, but once again Matt reached out and clasped her arm firmly to prevent her.

'It's not a joke, Ruth, I assure you,' he said brusquely, 'but you want to adopt a baby and you need a husband. Jack Doyle told me.'

She could have killed Jacob on the spot if he'd been there. He was nothing but an old gossip, telling everyone about her affairs. And Jack Doyle wasn't much better, nor Matt Smith, come to that. Yet men were always ridiculing women for gossiping.

'It's a stupid idea,' she said flatly. 'As if I'd marry someone I scarcely knew.'

Matt actually had the nerve to look impatient. 'It wouldn't be a real marriage, naturally. There'll never be another woman for me after Maria. I would expect nothing from you, and all you'll get from me is my name, my status as a husband, a father for your child. We can divorce as soon as the adoption papers have been signed, or we can stay married if that suits you better. It would be entirely up to you.'

'And what makes you so saintly?' She still felt convinced it was some sort of cruel jest. 'There must be something in it for you.'

He frowned deeply, and after a while gave an almost imperceptible nod. 'You're right, there is. I hadn't thought about it before, but I would feel of some use on this earth. I feel no use at all at the moment.'

'You're much younger than me. I'm forty-one.'

He spread his hands, palms upwards, in a gesture that reminded her a little of Jacob. 'I'm thirty-two, but what does that matter?'

She supposed it didn't matter at all under the

circumstances. 'Why would staying married suit me better?'

'Jack told me you were saving to go to America in search of your children. I wouldn't mind visiting America myself, and it might be sensible, and easier, to go together. I have dozens of contacts in the States, mainly refugee groups: religious, political, national.'

'Is there anything about me you don't know?' she said irritably.

'I doubt it. Everyone seems to know everything about everybody in Liverpool. I have a terrible job myself, fending people off with lies.'

'I know what you mean,' she said drily. 'Where would we live if we were married?'

'Where we're living now. Nothing would change, except your name.'

'I would never want . . . I mean, I couldn't bear to . . .' She paused, embarrassed.

'Neither would I!' Matt Smith said emphatically.

Ruth put her elbows on the table and sank her chin into her hands. The whole thing made sense in a crazy sort of way. After all, she had nothing to lose and an awful lot to gain. It would be a married couple applying to adopt Michael, and according to Kate Thomas that would be the best possible thing. But even so, it was a tremendous step to take, marrying a man who was almost a complete stranger.

She shook her head. 'No,' she said firmly. 'It's kind of you to offer, more than kind, but I'm afraid the answer's no.

*   *   *

Eileen Costello was sitting with Jacob when Ruth arrived home, Michael fast asleep in her arms. Ruth seized him jealously. 'How's he been?' she asked.

'No trouble at all, except he's half kicked me to death. Going to be a footballer when he grows up, I reckon.'

'No, he's not. He's going to be a pianist.' Ruth hugged the baby fiercely. 'Are you all right, Dad?' Jacob was half asleep and hadn't even noticed she'd come in.

He blinked awake. 'Oh, it's you, love. I'd better get the tea ready.'

'It's all right, Dad. I'll do it in a minute.'

'I'll put the kettle on, at least.'

Ruth watched worriedly as he shuffled into the kitchen, noticing the way he grasped the table then the doorpost to keep his balance. 'He's not been so well lately. He has good days and bad. There are times when he's just like his old self, full of beans and mischief. Other times . . .'

'I've noticed.' Eileen had been shocked at the deterioration in the old man, not quite so much physically, but mentally. When she first turned up, he hadn't recognised her. Even now, it seemed to take an effort to remember who she was, and when he did, he kept asking about Tony. 'Where is he? It's a long time since we've played cards.'

'I'll be off,' she said. 'It was me who brought Michael home, and I thought it wise to stay till you got back, your dad being asleep like.' Ruth took exception to the baby being called Micky. 'By the way,' she said, aware she was about to drop a bombshell. 'Dai Evans called in not long ago. He wants to take Michael across the water to New

358

Brighton tomorrow. Ellis and Myfanwy have gone to Wales for the weekend.'

Ruth's reaction was even more shocked than Eileen had expected. 'He *what*?' Every scrap of colour drained from her face. She squeezed the baby so tightly in her arms that he began to whimper. Jacob came shuffling back with the kettle and placed it on the hob to boil. He sank into his chair and immediately began to doze.

'C'mon, girl, sit down a minute.' Eileen led Ruth to the other armchair. 'I'll make you a cup of tea once the water's boiled.'

Ruth was almost too choked up to speak. 'Is that how he put it?' she asked hoarsely. 'He didn't *ask* if he could take Michael, just said he *wanted* to, as if he had the right?'

'I suppose he did.' Eileen understood Ruth's distress, but tried to sound reasonable. 'After all, he is the baby's grandad.'

'Even so, he can't just demand to take Michael out whenever he feels like it.' Ruth was close to hysteria. 'Would Sheila let your dad take her children out if it didn't suit her?'

'No, girl, but you see, Sheila's their mam . . .'

'And I'm not Michael's! Oh!' Ruth began to unbutton Michael's matinee jacket with trembling fingers. 'I've got no rights, have I? Legally, he belongs more to Dai than he does to me.'

'What are you doing, luv?' asked Eileen.

'I don't know.' Ruth burst into tears. 'I don't know.'

'Dai only wants to take Michael to New Brighton. He won't be gone for long.'

'What if he gets drunk? He's always drunk. What if the pram goes over the side of the boat? The pram!' Ruth looked triumphant. 'That's it! I won't let him have the pram! I'll tell him if he wants to take Michael out he must find his own pram.'

'That's being silly, luv,' Eileen said gently. 'You don't want to start rubbing Dai up the wrong way. He's just fond of the baby, that's all. Michael's his first grandchild.'

'He's getting too fond. He sneaks in the back on his way to the pub almost every night and insists on picking Michael up, even when I've just got him to sleep. The other night, he came in again on his way home, drunk as a lord, and acted really maudlin. It was sickening.' Ruth wiped her cheeks with the corner of the baby's shawl and looked down at him, eyes red with weeping. 'I couldn't bear it if he was taken off me.'

'Frankly, Ruth, I think you're making a mountain out of a molehill.' Eileen didn't, actually. She would have acted exactly the same in Ruth's place, but felt it was best to try and calm the woman's fears.

Jacob started to snore, entirely unaware of the drama taking place in his living room, just as Snowy, now fully grown, sauntered in from the parlour. He jumped on Jacob's stomach and began to purr.

Ruth whispered, 'What if Dai gets so fond of Michael, he talks Ellis into having him?'

'You don't know Ellis, luv. There's not much chance of that.'

But Ruth scarcely heard. 'Grandparents would always be given preference when it comes right down to it.'

'Don't forget, luv, it was *you* who Dilys wanted to have her baby, so you should be given preference

360

over everybody else.'

'Yes, but there's only my word for that!'

'In that case, you'd better find out where Dilys is and get it in writing. Did she say where she was going?'

'She intended joining the WRENs. I suppose I could write to the Admiralty in London.'

'The WRENs'd never take her,' Eileen said bluntly. 'She's too bloody thick!'

'Then where is she?' Ruth cried frantically.

Eileen shrugged. 'God knows! I suppose you could still write. If she applied, they might still have her address. You could try the ATS and the WAAF, as well—not to mention the Land Army.'

'I'll write everywhere I can think of,' muttered Ruth.

'As for tomorrer, I know what to do,' Eileen said triumphantly. 'We'll go out early, all of us; Michael, Jacob, you and me. Then, if Dai comes round there'll be no one in. If he says anything later, tell him you'd already planned a day out. Once Ellis is back, he won't have an opportunity to ask for Michael again.'

'But you said Ellis had gone for the entire weekend. What about Monday? Dai might . . .'

'No he won't, because we won't be here. We'll stay away the entire weekend.'

'Where?' asked Ruth dazedly.

'Remember the cottage in Melling I went to at Christmas? It belongs to . . . to a sort of friend. He won't be there, and he won't mind us using it. We'll spend the weekend in Melling. I've been dying to go ever since I got back from Norfolk.'

*　　　*　　　*

361

Sheila decided to come with them when she heard the news, though only for the day. 'We'll all go to early Mass—no, we won't, we'll go to Mass in Melling,' she said delightedly. 'I love that little church. It'll make a nice change, and it's a real treat, going out on Easter Sunday.'

'We'll have to go by train, what with all the prams. It means changing trains at Kirkdale for one to Kirkby, then it's a bit of a walk through to Melling.'

'The kids'll love that.' She looked even more delighted. 'The little 'uns have never been on a train before.'

*   *   *

On Sunday morning, the rising sun was hazy in a milky blue sky when Eileen Costello opened the blackout curtains. It was going to be a lovely day, though the air felt slightly chilly.

'Ne'er cast a clout till May be out,' she murmured to herself as she put a cardigan on underneath her coat.

To her joy, her dad came out of Sheila's house when she called shortly afterwards with Ruth, Jacob and Michael already in tow.

'I thought I'd come and take a look at the garden,' he said gruffly. 'It's a shame to see all that land go to waste. After all, we're supposed to "Dig for Victory", aren't we?' He'd been to the cottage before, last summer, to help get it ready for when she and Nick moved in.

'That's right, Dad. Y'know, Nick would never mind if you tended the garden properly. You could

362

go as often as you wanted.'

'You seem to know an awful lot about what Nick would and wouldn't mind, considering you two have broken up!' he commented drily.

The children were almost delirious with excitement when they reached Kirkdale and discovered a steam train took them to Kirkby. It had little narrow compartments, when meant the party could have one all to themselves. They flung themselves backwards and forwards against the plush seats, but their grandad put his foot down when Dominic and Niall began to swing from the luggage rack.

'Sit down, the pair o'yis,' he snapped. 'Behave yourselves. You'll have people next door complaining the way you're carrying on.'

'But there isn't anyone next door, Grandad. The train's almost empty,' Niall pointed out.

'Do what your grandad says,' Sheila said sharply, 'else you'll have us all thrown off.'

Ruth Singerman sat in the corner, keeping Michael's head safely shielded from the boisterous children, determined that *he* would never behave so badly when he grew up, entirely forgetting that Simon had been much worse when he was Dominic and Niall's age. Jacob, wide awake—it was one of his good days—stared out of the window, fascinated.

'Countryside! See, Mary.' He picked up Sheila's youngest child and sat her on his knee. 'See, green fields and cows. I never dreamt there was countryside so close to home. In all the years I've lived in Bootle, I've never been this far out before.'

The cottage looked neglected and unlived-in. Ivy had begun to creep over the front door and the downstairs windows, and the inside smelt damp. Eileen lit the fire, whilst Sheila put the kettle on, and the children poured out of the back door, whooping with joy, closely followed by Jack Doyle, who couldn't wait to get started on the garden. When Eileen went into the back kitchen, he was already turning over the earth with an ancient spade from the outhouse, and Jacob was watching with interest.

'It might be warm enough to sit outside later on,' she said.

'I feel awful about Dai,' Ruth said when Eileen took her a cup of tea. 'I really over-reacted, didn't I? Perhaps I should have put a note through the door telling him we'd already arranged to go out.'

'He'll be taking advantage of Ellis being away and having a good lie-in to sleep off last night's beer. You never know, he might have forgotten all about New Brighton.'

'I hope so. He really loves Michael. I know I'm being selfish, but at the same time, I'm terrified he'll take him away.'

'Stop worrying!' Eileen chided. 'Where's Michael's bottle? I'll make it before we leave for Mass.'

'It's all right, I'll do it,' Ruth said quickly. 'I know exactly how much evap and water to put in.' If Eileen made Michael's bottle, she might want to feed him.

'There's plenty of water in the kettle. It's already boiled.'

'Will your father be going to church?' Ruth wanted a word in private with Jack Doyle.

Eileen burst out laughing. 'Not likely! Me dad's an atheist. He can only be persuaded to set foot

364

inside a church for a wedding or a funeral. Soon after me mam died, he tried to talk our Sheila and me out of going, but it was too late by then. We'd already been brainwashed, as he put it.'

Later, Michael asleep in the single bed upstairs, and Eileen and Sheila and the children having left for Mass, Ruth went down the garden to see Jack Doyle. Jacob was standing in the middle of the garden, his hands in his pockets, staring around in wonder.

Jack had already turned over a great expanse of earth, and numerous worms were frantically wriggling their way back into the darkness underneath. He nodded as Ruth approached, and said breathlessly, 'I think I'll have a row of beansticks by the wall, and the 'taters in that corner over there. Have you noticed the blossom on the apple tree? It's as pretty as a picture.'

'It's lovely,' agreed Ruth.

'I've wanted a garden all me life.' He pushed the spade into the earth with his foot and upturned a great clod of black earth. 'It's good soil this, rich, you can tell by the colour. That's 'cos it hasn't been used in a long time. It's not worn out like soil can get when it's been sown year after year.' He paused and leaned on the spade. There was sweat dripping from his brow, but he appeared to be in his element, and his rugged, usually rather dour face shone with enthusiasm. He glanced around the wild overgrown patch of ground with an air of satisfaction—there must have been at least an acre, Ruth thought, perhaps more. 'Oh, yes, I've always wanted a garden.'

'Can I ask you something?'

'Of course you can, luv. Ask away.'

'I need to get in touch with Matt Smith.'

He paused, before shoving the spade into the soil. 'Do you now!'

'I don't know where he lives.' Her rejection of his entirely unexpected proposal had seemed so final at the time, there'd seemed no need to ask for his address. But now, with Dai . . .

'His lodgings are in Southey Street, but I don't know the number. Next time I see him, I'll give him a message, shall I?'

'Please.'

Just then, the children came hurtling back into the garden. Having such a large space in which to play seemed to have sent them all a little wild.

Ruth went indoors, where, to her annoyance, she found Sheila Reilly nursing Michael.

'He was bawling his head off when we came in,' Sheila explained. 'I can never bear to hear a baby crying, so I picked him up.' She stood Michael on her knee and jogged him up and down. 'But you're all right, now, aren't you, you little bugger?'

'Here, let me take him.' Ruth almost snatched the baby away. Eileen and Sheila exchanged glances.

'She's too possessive by a mile,' Sheila whispered to her sister when they were in the back kitchen making dinner.

'I don't suppose she can help it. After all, she lost her other children. It must have seemed like a miracle, Michael turning up like that.'

'Even so,' Sheila wrinkled her nose, 'I'm good enough to look after him while she's at work, but not good enough to so much as touch him when she's not.'

Eileen nudged her sister sharply with her elbow.

366

'Stop moaning and get on with the dinner—and don't put any beetroot on mine, if you don't mind. I've had enough beetroot to last me the rest of me life.'

*   *   *

Dinner eaten, they sat in the sunny garden, though after a while, Sheila and Ruth decided it was too cold and went indoors. Jacob had found a large pair of kitchen scissors and under Jack's direction was busy pruning the thick bushes. Eileen began to break down the overturned earth with a hoe.

'You shouldn't be doing that in your condition!' her dad said sharply when she joined him at the bottom of the garden.

'Don't be silly, Dad,' she snorted. 'There's some women who've got to scrub and clean till they're virtually in labour. A little bit of hoeing won't do me any harm. Anyroad, I can't stand doing nothing. I used to hate it when Francis wouldn't let me go out to work and I was stuck at home all day once Tony went to school.' She could talk about Tony now, actually mention his name without a lump coming to her throat. 'In fact, I've joined the WVS.'

Jack Doyle grunted as he wiped his brow with his sleeve. 'The what?'

'The WVS, the Women's Voluntary Service. I was helping out a bit in Norfolk, now I've joined proper. After all, the baby's not due for five months. I've got to do something with meself till then.' She hadn't told them she was expecting—you could hardly tell, particularly if she wore her old tweed swagger coat. Anyroad, she couldn't see why

367

it should make any difference. Everyone was entitled to help with the war effort, pregnant or not!

'You're nowt but a bloody idiot, you!' Despite the insult, Jack found it difficult to keep the pride out of his voice. His girl seemed determined to do her bit.

'Eileen!' Sheila had come to the back door. She looked agitated. 'The telephone's ringing.'

'Well, pick it up and answer it,' Eileen called. She walked towards the house, her stomach churning. There was only one person it could be.

'Not likely! I'm too scared to touch it.'

'You're nowt but a bloody idiot, you!' Eileen said as she pushed past her sister.

'Ta, very much!' Sheila said tartly.

'That's all right. It's what our dad just called me.'

Sheila followed her into the hallway, where the telephone shrilled away. She watched as Eileen reached for the receiver. 'What are you waiting for?' Eileen hissed.

'I just wanted to see how it was done.'

'I'm not going to pick it up until you scarper.'

Sheila stuck out her tongue and disappeared into the living room, and Eileen picked up the receiver and said, 'Hallo.'

'Eileen! I had a feeling you'd be there. I called yesterday, just in case.' There was crackling on the line and his voice sounded very far away.

'Hallo, Nick.' She leaned against the wall, her mind a turmoil of emotions.

'Are you there alone?'

'No, there's all sorts of people with me; me Dad's busy in the garden. I hope you don't mind.'

'Why should I mind? I've said before, as far as

I'm concerned, the cottage is yours.' He paused. 'Darling, it wasn't final, was it, you walking out on me like that?'

'Of course it wasn't,' she said tiredly. It would never be final between her and Nick. She'd always known he'd call or write, or she would contact him.

'It was my fault,' he cried passionately. 'It's always my fault. We see each other so rarely, and when we do I want everything to be perfect . . .'

'It was perfect, Nick, until you . . . until you said what you did.' She couldn't bring herself to put his accusation into words.

'Oh, God!' he groaned. 'That was a terrible thing to say, but I wish you'd stayed long enough to let me apologise, put things right. You know, darling,' his voice lightened, 'perhaps what we should do is spend all our time making love. We've never had a single difference of opinion in bed.'

She imagined him grinning into the telephone at his end. 'But that's not possible, luv,' she reasoned. 'We've got to be able to live in the real world. Everything was fine when it was just the two of us—and Tony—but the minute Francis came back, it all fell apart, and it's never been the same since. I never thought it possible, Nick, but you don't trust me.'

'But I do, I do,' he moaned. 'I think we expect too much of each other. Christ, darling, if only you hadn't gone rushing off . . .'

'I should have stayed,' she grudgingly agreed. They would have had a blazing row, but at least everything would have been sorted out, instead of being left in a sort of limbo. He was right, she realised as a terrible feeling of guilt swept over her. She expected far too much of him. For nearly a

369

year he'd lived on a knife's edge, seeing his comrades killed or burnt beyond recognition. It was a miracle he was still alive, yet when they'd met, instead of providing the little interlude of love which he so richly deserved, she'd stalked out just because he'd said something she didn't like. If he ever said anything like that again, she'd merely laugh and make a joke of it.

Nick said eagerly, 'Am I forgiven?'

She put her left hand on the receiver and cradled it against her cheek as if it was his head. 'Only if you forgive me,' she said huskily.

There was distinct relief in his voice as he replied, 'Of course I do.'

Eileen heard a sharp rapping noise at his end of the line. 'What's that?'

'Someone wants to use the telephone. There's a great queue outside the box, so I'd better hurry.' His voice became urgent. 'How are you? I've written a million letters over the last few weeks and torn them up; they all seemed wrong.'

'Me too,' she whispered.

'Oh, darling! Did you really? You know, I even contemplated pretending to get lost and landing my plane near Liverpool so we could talk, but it wouldn't have washed.' He laughed nervously. 'I can't believe I'm going to be a father. We really should get married before the baby's born.'

Eileen didn't answer. If only she hadn't been so thin-skinned they would already be married. She closed her eyes and slid down the wall until she was sitting on the floor. If only, if only . . .

'The trouble is,' Nick was saying, 'I've no idea when I shall see you again. The squadron's being sent abroad, to North Africa. We're leaving tonight.'

'Oh, dear God, no!' she sobbed. 'I hate this bloody war. It mucks up everybody's lives.'

'If it hadn't been for the war, we would never have met,' he reminded her.

'Even so . . .' There was more rapping at his end, longer and louder than the time before.

'I'll have to ring off now, my dearest girl, else the queue will lynch me. Look after yourself—and our baby. I shall post you a big fat cheque tonight to buy everything you need—and book yourself into a first-class nursing home.' His voice broke, 'I love you, Eileen.'

There was a click at the other end and the line began to buzz.

'And I love you, Nick,' Eileen whispered. 'I really do.'

*   *   *

Kate Thomas turned up just as everyone had sat down to their tea. 'I had some work to catch up with at Dunnings, so I thought I'd take a chance on finding you here!'

'Come in the garden!' Eileen cried, delighted to see her. 'It'll be nice and peaceful out there for a while.'

It was too chilly to sit down, so they began to stroll around the edge of the lawn. 'I was so pleased when I got your letter telling me about the baby,' Kate said. 'You must be thrilled.'

'I am. It's like a miracle and the last thing I expected. The trouble is . . .' Eileen told her about Nick's phone call. 'I've been trying to act normally ever since, but me head's been buzzing, wondering

371

when we'll see each other again.'

Kate squeezed her arm. 'Still, I'm glad things have turned out the way they have. One of these days you and Nick will be together. You know, you're terribly brave, Eileen, a real fighter. You deserve happiness, you really do.'

'Who doesn't?'

'I can think of a few names!'

Eileen laughed. 'How's everyone at Dunnings?'

'Fine. Doris is a brunette at the moment, Pauline is courting, but apart from that, it's just the same.' Her little face beamed. 'I have some wonderful news of my own. Remember I told you I had a Christmas card from my eldest daughter, Celia? Well, she's joined the WAAF, and has just been sent to Chester, of all places. We met yesterday for the first time in six years!'

'Kate, I'm so glad,' Eileen said warmly. 'Y'know, if anyone's a fighter, it's you.'

'Most women are, I've found. It's only their physical strength that holds them back when compared to men.'

'How did you get on with Celia?'

Kate's brow creased. 'Things were a bit strained at first. I tried to explain, as tactfully as I could, why I'd left, but she loves her father and I didn't want to demolish him in her eyes. He has a mistress and Celia hinted he treats her rather badly. I just hope my girls will work things out for themselves in time.'

They paused in front of a freshly dug patch of earth in which a spade had been left jammed upright. 'Someone's been busy,' Kate remarked.

'It's me dad. Oh, by the way, Ruth's here, if you'd like a word.'

'How is she?'

Eileen paused before answering. 'A bit tense. I tell you what, come and have a cup of tea. I reckon they'll be finished their meal by now.'

'Thanks, though I can only stay a minute. I'd love to see your father. I've only met him the once, but I really liked him.'

'Did you now!' Eileen raised her eyebrows suggestively. 'You realise he's a widower, don't you? I wouldn't mind having you for a stepmother, Kate!'

'Get away with you!' Kate laughed, but, to Eileen's great surprise, her face turned bright red.

*　　　*　　　*

Kate stayed for much longer than a minute, talking mainly to Jack Doyle outside. Eileen hadn't realised she was a keen gardener. As soon as she'd gone, Sheila decided it was time they too left for home and Jacob said he would go with them. He was already worried Snowy had been left alone too long. 'It's been a lovely day and a real nice change,' Sheila said happily. 'The kids have really enjoyed themselves.'

Jacob nodded. 'And so have I, Eileen.'

'We must do it more often once the summer comes,' Eileen suggested.

Jack Doyle had to be dragged away from the garden. 'Don't forget you're firewatching tonight,' his younger daughter told him.

'I might come tomorrer after work,' he mused. 'In fact, I can come mornings, too, when I'm on late shift.' He rubbed his hands together. 'Just think, we can grow all our own vegetables—that

Kate woman is going to let me have some tomato plants—and even have our own fresh fruit. There's already strawberries and a couple of goosegog bushes . . .'

'C'mon, Dad.' Sheila grinned at her sister as she pushed him out of the door. 'At least a garden's a better place to spend your time than the King's Arms.'

'It seems a shame,' Eileen said to Ruth when she returned to the living room. 'He's fifty-two years old, yet all he's ever had is a window box till now. It's not much for a man to want, is it, a garden?'

But Ruth hadn't heard. Her entire attention seemed to be taken up with Michael as she nursed him to sleep. She'd scarcely had the baby out of her arms all day. When she became aware of Eileen's presence, she looked up and frowned. 'I hope they don't tell Dai Evans where we are. You never know, he might turn up.'

Eileen shook her head, annoyed. 'None of them would be so foolish. Anyroad, Dai could never find his way out here and Ellis is home tomorrer.' She began to fiddle with the wireless. 'I wonder if the batteries are all right? I'd like to know the latest news.' The wireless spluttered as she turned the knob. She eventually found some music. 'I think this is the Home Service.'

'Don't have it too loud, now. Michael's almost asleep.'

'You know, Ruth,' Eileen said carefully, 'it'd be far better if you just laid him down and let him go to sleep on his own. It's not as if he's crying. If he gets used to it, he'll be expecting to be nursed asleep every single night.'

'I wouldn't mind,' said Ruth.

*   *   *

Next morning, Eileen began to cut back the ivy creeping over the front of the cottage. There'd been enough to keep her awake without the sound of its irritating tap-tap against the windows all night long. As she clipped the trailing leaves, she noticed how thick the dust was on the panes underneath. She'd clean them before she left.

The gate clicked behind her, and for an awful moment she thought it might be an irate Dai Evans in search of his missing grandchild. Instead, a tall blond man with the appearance and grace of a Greek god was coming down the path.

'I'm not sure if I've found the right place.' He smiled, though she noticed the smile didn't reach his eyes. 'I'm looking for Ruth Singerman.'

'Just a minute.' Eileen went into the house. Ruth had actually put the baby down in his pram for once and was washing nappies in the back kitchen. 'There's someone to see you. He looks like a Hollywood film star. You've got me worked up into such a state, I thought it was Dai at first,' she complained.

Ruth gasped. 'Fancy him coming here! He must have met your dad last night. Where have you put him?'

'I left him at the front. I thought I should check with you first in case it was Dai in disguise, but it seems you were expecting him. Who is he?' Eileen asked.

'Just a man.'

'I can see that much for meself!'

Ruth removed her pinny and patted her hair.

375

She picked up Michael and adjusted his shawl around his face. 'I'll speak to Matt outside.'

Matt! As soon as Ruth closed the front door behind her, Eileen felt too overcome with curiosity to resist a peep through the lace curtains in the living room. Ruth had never mentioned anyone called Matt before.

She rather hoped they might throw themselves into each other's arms. Instead, they stood, facing each other, several feet apart . . .

*   *   *

'He's very handsome.' Matt nodded at the baby.

Ruth nodded. 'Very.' She cleared her throat. 'That proposal you made. I've changed my mind. I'd like to accept, after all.'

'That's fine by me,' he said lightly.

'What do we do now?'

'I'll find out how you go about getting a licence. It will be in a registry office, of course.'

'Of course,' agreed Ruth.

'I'll need some details: your date of birth, that sort of thing.'

'Perhaps you could come round to Pearl Street tomorrow night.' Ruth jerked her head at the cottage. 'It's a bit difficult here. Come late, after my father has gone to bed.'

'Right.'

There was an awkward silence. 'Would you like a cup of tea?' asked Ruth. 'We'll be making dinner soon. You're welcome to stay.'

'No, thanks. I'd sooner be off.'

Ruth was surprised at how disappointed she felt when he turned to leave. 'I'll see you tomorrow, then,' she called.

He paused at the gate. 'Tomorrow.'

CHAPTER EIGHTEEN

'That's our Eileen!'

The voice came from out of the eerie red darkness, from somewhere amongst the men queueing for their cup of hot soup. The voice throbbed with pride, as if the speaker had been almost moved to tears when he spotted her standing behind the counter of the mobile canteen which was parked outside the tall gates of the Gladstone Dock.

'Is that you, Dad?' she called.

'It is that, luv. Now, hurry up with that soup. Us lot have got a pang in our bellies. We've been working hard without a break for bloody hours.'

There was a burst of gruff laughter from the waiting men. 'So, you're one of Jack Doyle's girls? He's allus on about you and your Sean.' The face of the man at the front was streaked with dirt and his eyes were red-rimmed with tiredness. It was long past midnight and the men had been working since eight o'clock the previous morning. They should have finished their shift at four, but had stayed behind to unload an urgent shipload of ammunitions which had arrived that afternoon from the United States. There was the smell of sweat and dust, the sound of men sighing and the shuffling of feet. The entire atmosphere was one of total exhaustion, yet Eileen knew that each and every one of them would work until they dropped.

An air raid had finished about half an hour ago, short but brutal, as if the Luftwaffe had been keen to shed their lethal load as quickly as possible before returning home. She'd like to bet the men had ignored the raid and worked right through.

There was the usual after-raid activity: the urgent clang of fire engines, ambulances screaming by, people shouting, and every now and then there would be the thud of an explosion and everyone would duck. The docks had been hit, as usual—those between Pier Head and Sandon had taken the brunt of the high explosive bombs that night, and the sky was its usual lurid shade of red from the fires raging below. The queue that stretched before her was a blur of tired faces, tinged pink by the distant flames. The tall black silhouettes of cranes could be seen, bending and turning as the urgent cargo continued to be unloaded.

'Whatever me dad said, it was lies.' Eileen smiled. 'We're all quite nice, really.'

'I gathered that much. Are you the one that was in the Land Army?'

'Aye, that's me.'

'We heard all about the mouse in your welly.'

'It wasn't my welly,' she laughed. 'It was another girl's. I think I might have died if it were mine.' It was hard to imagine her dad telling these big tough dockers such trivial things out of her letters.

Surprisingly, the man reached forward and gripped her hand quite hard. 'I was sorry to hear about your little lad, luv. I lost me own grandson the same way.'

Eileen's face remained expressionless. 'Ta,' she said briefly.

Beside her, Mrs Hilda Barrett clapped her hands

378

impatiently and barked, 'Who's next?'

'Me, miss.' The next man meekly stepped forward for his soup and slice of bread and margarine.

'I think this slice has been margarined both sides,' Eileen remarked.

'I'm not surprised,' Hilda sniffed. 'If the good lord had expected us to see in the pitch darkness, he would have equipped us with a torch as well as eyes.'

It wasn't exactly pitch dark inside the van, but almost, and the two women worked as best as they could, more by feel than sight.

'I don't mind.' The man took the bread, and Hilda thundered, 'Next!'

'Reporting for duty, ma'am.' The man saluted smartly, clicked his heels and winked at Eileen.

Mrs Hilda Barrett frequently rubbed people up the wrong way with her autocratic manner. Scousers didn't have much time for people in authority, and Hilda exuded authority in abundance. Fortunately, she had a hide like a rhinoceros and rarely noticed when she was being mocked, and if she did, she didn't care. All Hilda Barrett wanted was to help with the war effort. 'I had no intention of pussyfooting around knitting or making cakes,' she said scathingly to Eileen when they first met. 'I wanted to do something I could really sink my teeth into. I took to driving the mobile canteen like a duck takes to water.'

A widow of some sixty years, her children long married and living elsewhere, every single day of the week, she drove to Bootle from the relative safety of her lovely house by Birkdale golf course to do her stint in the WVS. Her outsize green uniform was always immaculate, the shirt starched and ironed to perfection, but for some reason, she pulled her hat down around her ears in a way that reminded Eileen of one of the Marx brothers. But beneath Hilda's brusque sergeant-major manner and capacious bosom, there beat a heart of pure twenty-two-carat gold. Although Eileen had only joined two weeks ago, the pair had become instant friends. Before the war, neither would have found much in common other than that they were the same sex, but nowadays, class and age no longer mattered. Eileen had taken over from Hilda's previous partner who, by strange coincidence, had joined the Women's Land Army. Like Hilda, Eileen had no family commitments, no husband or children, nothing to keep her at home.

'Aye, aye, luv.' Jack Doyle had reached the front of the queue.

'Dad! I didn't half feel embarrassed, you shouting out like that!'

'I'm sorry, girl. It took me by surprise when I saw you, that's all.' He nodded in her direction and said to Hilda, 'You've got a jewel there.'

'Dad!' Eileen blushed.

'Every woman in the WVS is a jewel,' Hilda replied crisply. 'Including me!'

'You're doing a fine job, the pair o'yis.'

'I know,' said Hilda. 'And so are you, particularly tonight.'

'Aye,' Jack sighed, 'but it was a wrench missing out on the May Day do at the Labour Party.' He grinned at Hilda—Jack claimed he could recognise a Conservative if he was blindfolded. 'The comrades always have a drink and sing *The Red Flag* on the first of May to celebrate the Soviet revolution.'

Hilda ignored him. 'Next!' she bawled.

The next man leaned on the counter. 'Let's see! I'll have cod and chips, plenty of salt, a little sprinkling of vinegar, and a bottle of ginger ale, please.'

'You can have bread and soup. From there on, you'll just have to use your imagination.' Hilda allowed herself a glimmer of a smile. '*NEXT!*'

*   *   *

'Where to now?' Eileen asked as Hilda started up the van, the dockers having been fed and returned to work. They set off with the barest glimmer of light from the masked headlights on the road in front.

'To the nearest conflagration,' Hilda barked.

*   *   *

It was almost daylight by the time Eileen returned home, and she threw herself into bed, totally worn out. Scores of firemen, Civil Defence workers and ARP personnel had been fed, as well as several battered citizens who'd been found sheltering in shop doorways or wandering round, dazed, after being bombed out of their homes.

She lay in bed and listened to the sounds of the street waking up: Nelson's hooves clip-clopped over the cobbles as he and Mr Harrison set off with the first load of the day, doors slammed as people left for work and she heard the rattle of bottles, heralding the arrival of the milkman. It seemed strange, going to sleep just when everyone else was

381

getting up, but she preferred it this way. No matter how hard she tried, she couldn't get used to the place without Tony. Entering the house was the worst, when she kept expecting him to come running out to meet her, his cheek turned for a welcoming kiss.

*   *   *

The air raid siren shrieked forth that night at a quarter past ten, and it was twenty to three by the time the All Clear sounded. During those hours, it seemed as if all hell had broken loose. The incendiaries were dropped first, lighting fires throughout the city, and providing visual markers for the heavy explosive bombs that followed by the ton. The very earth shook as explosion followed explosion and, as its people were slaughtered and its buildings and houses were blown to smithereens, the entire city of Liverpool seemed to be gripped in an orgasm of sheer bloody horror.

Eileen and Hilda Barrett were sheltering in the cellar of a lock-up garage off Marsh Lane where the mobile canteen was parked when not in use, which was rarely. Hilda usually read a book whilst a raid was in progress, but she couldn't read tonight.

'I think this one's worse than December,' she remarked.

'Jaysus! I hope me sister's all right,' Eileen breathed. She thought about her dad, firewatching on the docks, and Sean, recently transferred to an air base in Lincolnshire. Then there was Nick! 'It's crazy,' she muttered. 'The world's gone mad.'

'And it's all due to one man,' Hilda mused. 'What a powerful personality he must have!'

They emerged when the All Clear went and Hilda drove the van through Bootle and down to the Dock Road, providing hot drinks and a bite to eat for all who needed it.

*   *   *

Eileen called on Sheila on her way home that morning, relieved to see Pearl Street still standing and not even a single window broken. Her sister came out of the back kitchen, looking tired. She flung her arms around Eileen. 'Jaysus, sis,' she said hoarsely. 'I've been worried sick about you all night. Have you seen our dad?'

'There was no one in when I called.'

Sheila crossed herself. 'I hope to God he's all right. I scarcely slept a wink last night, nor did the kids. Our Dominic was frightened for the first time. Until now, he thought the raids were fun, but it seemed to get through to him that we might be killed. He kept asking for Cal.'

'That's why I'm here, sis,' Eileen said briskly. 'I want you to pack your bags and get out to Melling in case there's another bad raid tonight. You know where the key is, under the stone by the front door. Take Brenda with you. Even if it's standing room only, it's better than being a sitting target here. I'll have a word with Ruth Singerman in a mo.'

Sheila needed little persuading. 'I'll go as soon as we've had our tea, before it gets dark.'

'I'd go sooner, if I were you. The roads are blocked and I'm not sure if there's many buses running. As for the trains, the overhead railway's down and Exchange Station's been hit. You might end up having to walk most of the way.'

383

Sheila looked dismayed. 'I didn't realise things were that bad! In that case, I'll start making me way some time this morning. Anyroad, the kids love playing in that garden. Are you coming with us?'

'No, sis, I can't. I've got a job to do.'

'You always seem to have a job to do of some sort.'

Eileen shrugged. 'That's the way me life seems to have gone lately, all topsy-turvy. If it weren't for Tony, I'd still be at Dunnings.'

'Eil?'

'Yes, luv?'

'You're not staying because . . .' Sheila paused, as if unable to find the right words. 'I mean, I hope you're not staying for the same reason you stayed after Tony died. You never said anything, but I know you were hoping you'd be killed so you could join him . . .'

Eileen shook her head. 'No, luv. I don't want to be killed, not any more.' She patted her stomach. 'I've got me little girl in here, haven't I? And there's Nick. One of these days we'll sort ourselves out and be together.' She shook her head again. 'No, sis. I don't want to die now.'

'Then why don't you come with us?' Sheila argued.

'I told you, I've got a job to do. I'll only be taking the same risk as the thousands of other people who'll be staying in Bootle—and Liverpool—tonight.'

Ruth Singerman was just as anxious as Sheila to go to the cottage, having spent the night under the stairs with Michael, terrified the house was about to collapse around her ears. But she had a

384

problem. 'It's Saturday. You'll probably think me stupid under the circumstances, but I wonder if there'll be a dance this afternoon? Lots of young servicemen turn up and I don't like to let them down.'

'I don't think you're stupid at all,' Eileen assured her. 'Life seems to go on, no matter what happens. People might feel more like dancing today than they've ever done before. The trouble is getting there.' She explained the situation regarding transport. 'There's a phone box on Marsh Lane, or at least there was until yesterday. Why don't you ring up and find out if the dance is still on? Sheila will take Michael to Melling if it is. Now, if you'll excuse me, I think I'll turn in before I fall asleep in the middle of the street.'

*   *   *

It was almost nine o'clock that night when Ruth turned up at the cottage. She was flushed, almost starry-eyed, and didn't even ask about Michael as soon as she came in. 'For the first time today, I really felt as if I was doing my bit!' she cried. 'Reece's was crowded, and everyone sang as well as danced. I had to play the last waltz half a dozen times and every time I finished, people either cried or cheered. The atmosphere was tremendous.'

'How did you get home?' asked Sheila. 'You're terrible late.'

'The same way as I went. I walked a bit and ran a bit. I caught a bus, until it could go no further, then caught a tram a few yards more. On the way here, a man gave me a lift from Aintree Racecourse, else I'd still be walking now.' Ruth threw herself onto the sofa. 'It was all really worthwhile.' Her face changed, became grave. 'But you should see the damage, Sheila. You could scarcely pass a street that hadn't been bombed.' She sighed. 'How's Michael?'

'Fast asleep in his pram. Me and Brenda managed to carry it upstairs. We're short of bed space, I'm afraid, there's so many of us here.'

'That's all right, then. Is there any tea going? I'll take a look at Michael later on.'

As Sheila filled the kettle, she reckoned hopefully that Hitler would probably leave them alone from now on. It had probably been a waste of time them coming to Melling. If so much damage had already been inflicted on Liverpool, what point was there in inflicting any more? She would never, if she lived to be a hundred, understand how killing little children like Tony Costello helped win a war.

*   *   *

Jacob Singerman had insisted on staying in the house where he had slept for nearly fifty years, in the bed where Rebecca had died giving birth to their only daughter.

'I'm not going,' he said stubbornly when Ruth pleaded with him to leave with Sheila. 'I'd be the only man there, for one thing, it would make me look like a coward.' He chuckled. 'Someone might send me a white feather.'

'Don't be silly, Dad. You're over eighty years old. No one expects you to be a hero.'

'I do,' Jacob said simply. 'I'm staying. No one, not even Adolf Hitler's going to turn me out of my own bed.'

It was almost half past ten when the siren went, and Jacob was already half asleep. He ignored the warning, as he always did, turned over, and covered his head with the clothes. Snowy, irritated at being disturbed, jumped off the bed, stretched, and jumped back again and snuggled into Jacob's back.

'Well, Snowy,' Jacob muttered after a short while, 'this is a raid and a half.' Last night's blitz paled into insignificance beside this one. He sat up, feeling agitated. 'It sounds as if they're trying to bomb Bootle out of existence.'

Snowy crawled into his arms, where he lay shivering. The cat was absolutely terrified of raids. Jacob stroked him, as the bombardment outside increased in ferocity, and he pondered over the evil that men did to each other. What need was there for this? What would Hitler do if he won? What possible gratification could he get out of bombing a country into submission? How could a man exist with so much implacable hatred directed against him? You'd think he would shrivel up and die, he was so utterly loathed throughout the entire world. What justice was there on the earth when one single person could inflict so much misery and mayhem on his fellow man?

Death and destruction rained down all around as the questions chased each other through Jacob's old brain. Every now and then, the house would groan, as if the bricks were shifting against each other.

It was such a wonderful world, Jacob mused; people could be very happy if left alone to get on with their lives, go to work, bring up their children without interference. Yet, always, *always*, some power-crazed individual would come along, some malign despot who wanted to take control.

'It's not fair, is it, Snowy?' He tickled the furry neck. 'It's just not fair.' There was silence for a miraculous second, and somewhere in Pearl Street a baby cried.

Michael!

Jacob was about to get out of bed when he remembered Michael was somewhere else, along with Ruth. At least they were all right, he thought with satisfaction, though he wasn't sure about Benjy or the other children, Simon and Leah. His brow creased as he tried to recall where they were, but couldn't, no matter how hard he tried. There was a thunderous explosion close by and he felt the house crack, as if it was about to split in two, followed by deafening noise downstairs, and something fell on the roof with an almighty crash and several slates slid off and landed in the street.

I don't mind dying, Jacob thought. I'm old, I've had a good life. Nevertheless, his heart began to drum and Snowy howled, leapt off the bed and shot out of the half-open door.

Across the road, Nelson whinnied frantically, and Jacob could hear the horse's hooves thudding against the stable door. He stumbled out of bed, calling, 'Snowy! Come here.'

It was strange, the landing and the hallway were lit by a bright red light. When he reached the top of the stairs, he saw the front door was no longer where it should be, but lying crookedly, still in one piece, on the stairs.

Something snapped in Jacob's brain. '*Tony*!'

The little boy had escaped, run out into the inferno, and *it was all Jacob's fault*!

'*TONY*!' he screamed, and somehow scrambled

over the front door and ran out into the street after the child he loved so dearly, just as a demented Nelson managed to demolish the stable door that was confining him to his own personal hell and came galloping out, whinnying like a demon, the whites of his eyes gleaming insanely. His owner followed, desperately trying to restrain him.

Nelson and Jacob hit each other head on, but to Nelson, the old man was merely the flimsiest of obstacles as he galloped off to freedom, and Jacob was trampled underneath the carthorse's massive hooves.

'Nelson! Jacob! Oh, Jesus Christ!' Mr Harrison stood in the middle of Pearl Street, his arms spread wide in despair. He looked up at the heavens, spilling death, and shook his fist. 'What do you think you're trying to do to us, you bastards!' he screamed. 'Whatever it is, you won't win. You can bomb us till kingdom come, you Jerry bastards, but I promise you, you won't win!'

*   *   *

'I wonder if there'll be any of Bootle left by the time this is over,' Eileen whispered as another explosion rent the earth, closely followed by another, then a third. A layer of dust flickered down from the ceiling and she coughed.

Hilda shook her head. She'd been rather subdued all night, not at all her usual buoyant self. 'God knows,' she said bleakly.

The dark, dank cellar was lit only by an oil lamp which Hilda herself had provided. The room, scarcely used except for storage, smelt musty, and held only a few empty wooden boxes on which they both sat. There was no way to make a drink, except by going upstairs into the garage and lighting the urn in the mobile canteen, which neither felt inclined to do under the circumstances. Hilda had brought a flask of coffee which had long gone.

'I'll buy one of those flasks tomorrer,' Eileen said. 'It doesn't seem fair, me drinking half your coffee every night.'

'You can't get flasks for love nor money, just like you can't get hot-water bottles or clocks and a million other things.'

'Bloody war!' Eileen snorted. 'In that case, I'll bring a bottle of lemonade.' She wriggled this way and that, trying to get comfortable on the box, and settled back, leaning against the wall, her hands settled on her stomach.

'Why have you got your hands like that?' Hilda demanded. 'I used to do that when . . .' Her face showed a mixture of concern and downright anger. 'Are you pregnant?'

It seemed useless to deny the fact. 'Yes,' Eileen said flatly.

'You silly, irresponsible girl!' Hilda spluttered. 'You should have gone to Melling with your sister. It's outrageous for someone in your condition to be taking unnecessary risks.'

'Well, if I'm taking unnecessary risks, so are you!' Eileen countered heatedly.

'Don't be stupid, girl,' Hilda snapped. 'You know what I mean.'

Eileen didn't answer. She knew exactly what Hilda meant. There'd been times during the night when it seemed as if the world was being blown to pieces and she'd wished she was with Sheila and the other women who had fled to safety, not for her

390

own sake, not for Nick's, but for her baby's. She'd already lost one child and she didn't want to lose another.

As if reading her thoughts, Hilda said in a more gentle tone, 'It's not fair on the baby, and it's not fair on your husband. Oh!' She made an anguished face. 'I'm sorry, Eileen, I forgot about your husband.'

'Actually,' Eileen threw back her head and looked Hilda straight in the eye, 'it's not me husband's baby. It's someone else's. We're going to get married one day, me and Nick.'

She could die any minute, and she wasn't going to die and leave Hilda believing a lie. One day very soon, she'd have to tell the street about the baby—she'd noticed Aggie Donovan's already curious glances, and was aware of the speculative gossip going on behind her back. They'd all assume she was carrying Francis's baby, and she wouldn't disabuse them. Francis was dead. What did it matter what people thought? She had to continue living in Pearl Street, and there would be consternation and much unpleasantness, if she told the truth. But right now . . .

'I see!' Hilda's voice was totally expressionless.

The two women were silent for a while. A bomb screamed earthwards, and Hilda put a broad arm around Eileen's shoulders and they huddled together until the bomb found its target. Dust fell all over them, like the finest snow, as the blast shook the building.

'They say if you can hear it screaming, it's not meant for you,' Hilda said.

'I've always thought that a bit stupid. After all, you'd have to be dead before you can prove it

391

wrong.'

Hilda laughed. She left her arm where it was, and said in a girlish voice, entirely different from her usual bellow, 'You know, I had an affair once!'

'Never!' Eileen gaped. 'You look far too respectable to have an affair.'

'As a matter of fact, so do you! But it's nothing to do with respectability, is it? The most respectable people in the world can fall in love quite out of the blue.'

'Was it during the last war?' Eileen asked curiously.

'No, it wasn't.' There was a dreamy look on Hilda's usually stern features. 'It was 1929. I was almost fifty at the time and already a grandmother. He was an accountant and had been sent to my husband's office to audit the books. Ralph brought him home to dinner and we just . . . I can't think of the word.'

'Clicked?' Eileen suggested.

'That's it, clicked! Until then, I'd thought myself happily married, and I still think that in a sort of way, but with Peter, it was a different thing altogether, as if . . .' she giggled, ' . . . as if bolts of lightning were passing to and fro between us.'

'Did you . . . you know?' A stick of bombs fell, one after the other with deadly regularity, but neither woman seemed to notice.

'Of course we did!' Hilda said indignantly. 'I said I had an affair, didn't I? We didn't pussyfoot around. We met in his hotel room every afternoon for three days. Then he went back to his wife, and I went back to Ralph—not that I'd ever left in person.'

'It sounds as if it was dead romantic,' Eileen

breathed.

'It was, and it's something I've never told a living soul before, but there've been a few times tonight when I've felt as if I was about to meet my maker, and it was rather nice to confide in someone for the first time.' Hilda squeezed Eileen's shoulders. 'Now, this Nick. I want to know all about him. Where did you meet?'

'Well,' Eileen began, 'it was Christmas. I was in this café in Southport, and . . .'

*   *   *

It was quiet in the cottage. All that could be heard was the soft sound of breathing. Sheila Reilly, curled up in an armchair fully dressed, hadn't managed to sleep any more that night than she'd done the night before. She got up and peered at the clock on the mantelpiece—half past four, yet still the bloody battle raged over Liverpool. She could hear the dull thuds in the distance and every now and then tried to convince herself the sounds were growing fewer, but in her heart she knew they weren't.

Ruth stirred in the other armchair. They'd tossed a coin for where to sleep and Brenda had won the settee. Sheila crept out of the room, opened the front door and went into the garden. It was a lovely night, beautifully clear and the moon was crisp and sharply defined. The birds, or perhaps it was some other creatures, were rustling in the hedges.

But, Jaysus! The sky was redder than ever. She said a prayer, for everyone in Liverpool and the rest of the country, and for the German civilians being killed by British bombs . . .

'Sheila?'

'Who's that?'

'It's Ruth. I couldn't sleep.'

'Nor could I.'

Ruth stood beside her, looking in the same direction. 'I hope my father is all right.'

'Aye.' It was no use offering platitudes, saying, 'Of course he'll be all right.' Instead, Sheila nodded. 'I hope so, too,' she said.

They stood together silently for a long time, each woman preoccupied with her own thoughts. Then Ruth shoved her hands in the pockets of her cardigan and said casually, 'I've got something to tell you. I'm getting married on Saturday.'

Sheila's jaw dropped. She forgot, for the moment, all her various worries. 'Y'what?'

'I'm getting married.'

'Who to?' It seemed a funny question to ask, 'Who to?', when you saw someone almost every single day of the week and they'd never even mentioned a man's name, let alone been seen with one.

'Matt Smith. He's a friend of your father's.'

'Matt Smith! I remember him, he's dead goodlooking—me dad brought him to our house on New Year's Eve. You're a canny bugger, Ruth Singerman,' Sheila said incredulously. 'I didn't know you two were going out!'

'He started coming to Reece's,' Ruth lied. 'We got to know each other very well. It's not exactly the romance of the century,' she added hastily, in case people noticed they weren't all lovey-dovey the way newly married people usually were. 'We just decided to try and make a go of things together, that's all.' How had Matt put it? Like flotsam and jetsam thrown together on the shore. Although Matt hadn't intended it to be, Ruth thought it sounded rather romantic.

'Well, I hope you do—make a go of things, that is.' Sheila found it hard to keep the sympathy out of her voice. What a way to enter a marriage! Still, it took all sorts . . .

'I wondered if you'd pass the word round,' said Ruth. 'You know what the street's like. It'll be a registry office wedding, no guests, no reception, and I'd like people to know who Matt is when he moves in.' They'd decided it would be best if he slept in the box room, so they would have the same address and it would look authentic when she applied to adopt Michael legally.

'I'll pass the word round, don't worry.' Sheila could hardly wait. 'What does your dad have to say? I bet he's pleased.'

'I haven't told him yet. It's going to be a surprise,' Ruth said awkwardly. Every time she started to tell Jacob, the words died in her throat. He could see through her like no other person. The old gossip may well have told Jack Doyle she needed a husband, but it had probably been said as a joke. He'd be distraught if he knew she and Matt were marrying out of convenience. On the other hand, she thought with a smile, she could put the blame on him. 'It's your fault, Dad. It was *you* who put the idea in Matt's head!'

'You know, luv,' Sheila Reilly said wistfully, 'it'd be a shame to go without a reception. Pearl Street loves a wedding. We could all club together and make a few sandwiches. If it's a nice day, we could set them out in the street . . .'

'Thanks all the same,' Ruth said quickly. 'But Matt doesn't want any fuss.' Funnily enough, she wouldn't have minded taking Sheila up on her offer. At odd moments, she even found herself looking forward to sharing the house with Matt.

'Oh, well, if you change your mind . . .'

'That's not likely.'

Sheila took a final look at the sky. 'It's a waste of time trying to go to sleep. I'll make a pot of tea.' As they began to go indoors, Sheila went on, 'I think I'll go to six o'clock Mass. I'll take the kids to a later one. I've a feeling today's the sort of day when it wouldn't hurt to go to Mass twice in one morning.'

They closed the door, just as the All Clear went, and the high-pitched drone had never been so welcome.

*　　　*　　　*

The whole of Merseyside, from Birkenhead and Wallasey, across the city and out as far as the town of Bootle, had merged into one vast raging inferno. From horizon to horizon, the heavens were a canopy of bloody crimson, shot here and there with a hint of orange from the flickering flames and darkened by clouds of swirling black smoke. The few barrage balloons that still remained looked pretty, like silvery-pink flowers thrusting upwards into the sky.

On the ground below, there was utter pandemonium. Fire engines and ambulances screeched this way and that on urgent errands of mercy, and the air was thick with ash and fluttering scraps of burning paper.

Shortly after the All Clear, Hilda and Eileen emerged from the garage into Marsh Lane with the canteen. The urn, operated by a gas canister in a cupboard underneath, was bubbling with freshly boiled water. The van's tyres crunched over millions of fragments of glass which covered the road like a carpet of diamonds. Hilda stopped the van a few yards out and they stared, horrified, at the utter devastation that confronted them.

Landmarks, places which Eileen had known all her life, had completely disappeared, had been turned overnight into vast brickfields emitting clouds of dust and flames, with girders and joists protruding crazily. A piano stood in the middle of the street that faced them, slightly skewed, but undamaged, as if ready for someone to sit down and play a tune. Which street was it? Eileen couldn't tell.

'This is inhuman,' she wept. 'It's nowt but sheer bloody carnage.' It was a scene from an unimaginable nightmare and she knew she would never forget it as long as she lived. Everywhere was lit by a sinister red light and no matter which way she looked there was nothing but havoc and broken houses, broken lives. Even the places that stood were blighted, with half their roofs gone and no windows left, the curtains hanging limply outside. As she watched, the front of a burning house seemed to bend outwards, almost in slow motion, and topple to the ground in a heap of bricks. Several men standing nearby jumped swiftly out of the way. Incredibly, one of them actually laughed.

In the midst of this chaos, the ARP and Civil Defence workers beavered away, a look of gritty determination on their tired faces, as they tried to rescue the people trapped underneath the rubble. Several ordinary civilians worked alongside them, desperately throwing chunks of masonry and bricks to one side. Eileen could hear a woman's terrified wail, 'Our Sally's down there. I've got to find our Sally.'

There was a shout, and a young boy was gently pulled out of the wreckage, placed on a stretcher and carried to an ambulance.

To the left of the van, two firemen were standing precariously on the top of the ruins of a house, their hoses directed through the windows of a shop Eileen knew well: a little sweet-shop and tobacconist's in which Tony used to spend his pocket money and which she herself had used as a child. The inside of the shop was burning as fiercely as a furnace, and she felt a searing sense of loss at the thought that the shop would never serve another customer.

It seemed as if she had been watching forever, but it must have been only a few seconds, because Hilda nudged her and said briskly, 'I think there are a few people here who might like a cup of tea, don't you?'

*   *   *

Daylight dawned. There might have been a sun behind the smoke and flames and dust that rose from Bootle that morning, but if so, it didn't shine on that first Sunday in May.

Many streets were blocked by rubble and impassable, Hilda found, as she took the canteen from one scene of devastation to the next. She would park as close as possible, and as the weary rescuers came for a cup of tea to quench their thirst, Eileen began to wonder if her town would ever function again. She'd no sooner had this thought, when she saw two young girls coming along the street; well made up and smartly dressed, they were obviously on their way to work, their gasmasks slung over their shoulders. Then a woman came out of the front door of a house that had been left relatively undamaged, a georgette scarf tied around her curlers, and began to brush her step. Even more incongruously, a milk cart arrived, bottles jangling, the blinkered horse, at least, entirely unaware of the devastation all around him. She realised that, no matter what happened, life would go on.

Mid-morning, they ran out of water, but when Hilda asked a Civil Defence worker where she could refill the boiler, to her consternation, she discovered there was no water to be had.

'The mains have been ruptured. There's no electricity or gas, either. He suggested I drive out as far as Waterloo to fill up.'

'Do you mind if I pop round to Pearl Street while you're gone?' Eileen asked. 'Someone said it'd been hit.'

'Of course I don't mind,' Hilda said. She was grimfaced and clearly fatigued, as was everybody, but showed no inclination to rest. 'In fact, Eileen, I'd sooner you didn't come back at all. I can always get someone else to help me out.' When Eileen began to protest, she said sternly, 'Remember our little talk last night?'

'I suppose you're right.'

'You're very brave, but you're also very foolhardy. Once you've been home, I suggest you immediately make your way to Melling and join your sister. Promise?'

Eileen nodded and gave a little smile. 'I promise.'

'Take care, dear.'

'You too, Hilda.'

So Eileen went back to Pearl Street, where she discovered Jacob Singerman was dead and there was a neat little space on one side of the street where her sister's house and the two adjacent ones had been.

*   *   *

It was almost biblical, the exodus of people from Liverpool early that evening. With prams and handcarts piled high with precious personal possessions, not to mention the most precious of all, their children, they began to leave the city in their thousands, heading towards the relative safety of the fields and villages outside. All they wanted was a good night's sleep and a few hours of safety from the raids.

Eileen walked alone, carrying only her shopping bag with a few clothes and a toothbrush. There was nothing in Pearl Street she cared about if she lost her house that night.

By the time she reached Melling, the sky was clear and the sun was shining. Birds sang in the trees and the water in the stream which ran alongside Dunnings gurgled merrily over the white stones. The gardens of the houses in the High Street were full of flowers, and children played Tick in the churchyard. It was a beautiful, peaceful spring evening, and war, and all the suffering it

400

brought with it, seemed a million miles away.

They were having their tea in the cottage.

'There you are!' Sheila breathed a sigh of relief when Eileen appeared. 'How's our dad? Have you seen him?'

'I haven't seen him, but he's okay, apart from a burnt hand. He'd been round to Pearl Street looking for me.' She'd tell Sheila about her house later, there was something more important to deal with first.

Ruth Singerman was giving Michael his bottle. She looked at Eileen, smiling anxiously. 'I suppose Jacob swore he slept through the whole thing?'

Eileen went over and knelt in front of Ruth's chair. 'I'm sorry, luv . . .'

*   *   *

That night, everyone in Liverpool held their breath as the clocks ticked towards midnight. It looked as if they were to be allowed a respite, time to catch their breath and catch up on their sleep. But at five to twelve, the unearthly wail of the siren blared forth, and they went wearily to their shelters, and the various Civil Defence workers squared their shoulders in readiness for the terror about to begin. If it was anything like last night, there'd be nothing of the city left to bomb by tomorrow . . .

The raids on Liverpool continued, though on Monday and Tuesday, Glasgow and Tyneside were the main recipients of the enemy bombs. On Wednesday, the Luftwaffe targeted Liverpool and Bootle yet again, to complete a week-long blitz. On that particular night, Marsh Lane Baths, which was being used as a temporary mortuary, received a direct hit. The bodies, including that of Jacob Singerman, were buried in a mass grave.

Jack Doyle, as brave as a man could be, felt convinced morale was at breaking point. There was just so much the human spirit could endure. He'd been into Liverpool to find the centre of the city reduced to little more than a wasteland, and the sight of so many beautiful old and treasured buildings, lost forever, had almost reduced him, a grown man, to tears.

'If this goes on much longer, we'll snap,' he said one night in the King's Arms, where the windows were boarded up and the only illumination came from candles on the bar, and according to Mack, the landlord, there wasn't enough ale to last the week out. To some, this was the unkindest cut of all.

Wild and totally unsubstantiated rumours circulated, not surprisingly when you considered the chaos in which people lived: without water, gas or electricity, without food and transport, without homes. Even worse, without the loved ones who'd been cruelly snatched from them during the seven nights of mayhem. It was said that martial law was about to be imposed, that the homeless had marched through the city waving white flags, that food riots had taken place.

All this proved to be untrue. The spirit of Liverpool may have been weakened, but the spirit was iron at the core and would never, never break.

Anyroad, miraculously, it was Hitler who decided he'd had enough and Wednesday night's raid turned out to be the last—for the time being.

CHAPTER NINETEEN

That May was perhaps the blackest period of the war so far, a time when Hitler seemed unstoppable and the terrifying realisation dawned that the victory that had so far seemed inevitable, might turn out not to be theirs.

British and Allied troops continued their retreat in the deserts of North Africa, and those sent in aid of Greece when Hitler invaded were humiliatingly driven out with the loss of their equipment. The troops withdrew to Crete, and with almost breathtaking audacity, Hitler invaded the island from the air. More than three thousand paratroopers dropped from the skies, in what was thought might be a dress rehearsal for the invasion of the British Isles. In an evacuation considered even more inglorious than Dunkirk, fifteen thousand troops were forced to withdraw again, this time to Egypt, leaving behind many thousands to become prisoners-of-war. In the ensuing chaos, three cruisers and six destroyers had been lost.

Whilst all this was going on, HMS *Hood* was sunk by the German pocket battleship *Bismarck* with the loss of thirteen hundred lives, a tragedy which somewhat overshadowed the subsequent sinking of the *Bismarck* itself.

There was minor jubilation when Rudolph Hess, Hitler's deputy, landed in Scotland, having fled from Nazi Germany alone. People hoped this was the first drip through the dam, that Hess knew the fight was lost and had decided to desert the sinking ship, but as they listened to their wirelesses or read their newspapers, it appeared Hess had come all this way just to complain about the food!

*   *   *

Most of the front doors in Pearl Street were wide open, and in order to get the best out of the sparkling June sunshine, several old people were sitting outside on their steps.

Since the May blitz, windows had been temporarily repaired with sheets of canvas, slates replaced and doors refitted—many doors had already been treated to a fresh coat of paint. Sewage no longer seeped up through the grids and ran in the gutter, and it was several days since anyone had seen one of the hundreds of rats which had been disturbed by the bombs. Water, gas and electricity had all been reconnected, so, really, there was no more need to eat in one of the British restaurants which had hurriedly been established after the blitz, except that at fivepence for breakfast, and eightpence for your dinner, the meals were definitely a bargain, and you saved on your rations at the same time.

You could almost pretend the street was back to normal, Eileen Costello thought as she stood in the bedroom, struggling vainly to fasten the buttons of her biggest frock, particularly if you ignored the ugly gap where Numbers 19 to 23 used to be.

Sheila had refused to remain in the cottage when she learnt she no longer had a house of her own. 'If you don't mind, Eil, I'd sooner move in with you. It's too noisy here.'

'Noisy!' gasped Eileen. 'That's the last word I'd use.'

404

'Well, there's the trees rustling all night long, for one thing,' Sheila explained. 'Then the birds start at the crack of dawn, followed by a cockerel not far away, which wakes up the dogs. They all make a helluva row between them. I suppose I'm used to the sounds in Pearl Street. Anyroad, I'd sooner live in Bootle than any place on earth.'

So, Aggie Donovan and George Ransome offered the loan of their spare beds, and Number 16 burst into life as Sheila Reilly moved in with her six children. The Reillys had lost everything they possessed, except their lives, so Sheila didn't complain.

'You must write to Nick and tell him that we'd all be dead if it weren't for the cottage,' she said to her sister. 'Just think, we would have been under the stairs, all seven of us, when that bomb fell . . .'

As soon as Sheila found another property, she would get a nine-pound grant from the Government to replace her lost furniture. In the meantime, Eileen made sure the family had a change of clothes off the second-hand rack at the WVS.

Eileen gave up trying to fasten the frock. Even if she got the buttons in the holes, they'd pop out if she dared so much as breathe. She sat on the edge of the bed and watched Dai Evans paint his front door exactly the same shade of green it had been before it had been torn off and thrown halfway up the stairs. Her dad had promised to paint hers as soon as he could find the time. She'd do it herself, but even the thought of the smell of paint made her feel slightly nauseous.

Watching Dai, she felt a surge of pride at the way everyone on Merseyside, the ordinary people as

405

well as those in charge, had collectively cocked a snook at Hitler, pulled themselves up by their rather frayed and tatty bootstraps, and begun the almost superhuman task of putting things to rights after the raids—though it would be years before the thousands of houses totally destroyed were re-built. Eileen still shuddered when she went down Marsh Lane and came face to face with the devastation wrought by the German bombs. There was scarcely a house left in Bootle that hadn't been damaged in some way—and the raids still continued. There'd been two bad nights at the end of May, but they were nothing compared to those at the beginning of the month.

Even the docks, battered, bruised and broken though they were, the waters clogged with sunken ships, had miraculously continued to function, so that the port of Liverpool had never closed.

A white cat came wandering along the street and began to sniff at the paint which Dai Evans had put on the doorstep. Eileen stiffened. Snowy! But when she looked properly, the cat had a black-tipped tail. Although several people, including Eileen, had searched, Snowy had never been seen again since the night Jacob Singerman had died, though Nelson had returned home of his own accord the following day. Dai aimed a kick in the cat's direction, which missed, and the animal shot down the entry beside the railway wall.

Eileen's eyes welled with tears when she thought about the old man who'd been such a dear friend. So many people had gone forever—the remains of five hundred and fifty had been buried in a brick vault at Anfield Cemetery—and even more had been seriously injured and would forever bear the scars of that week-long blitz.

'Are you all right, Eil?' Sheila called. 'You've been up there for ages.'

'I'm just thinking, that's all.'

'Mind you don't strain yourself!'

Eileen took a cardigan out of the drawer. Even that would scarcely stretch over the gaping hole where her frock refused to button. She seemed to have grown big all of a sudden.

'I'm just popping over to Brenda Mahon's for a minute,' she told Sheila when she went downstairs.

Brenda's front door was open to the brilliant sunshine. Eileen poked her head into the hallway. 'Are you there, Bren?' she yelled.

'I'm in the kitchen,' Brenda yelled back. 'Come on in, Eileen.'

Everything was as it used to be in Brenda's house, except there was no longer a photograph of Xavier Mahon on the wireless and the front room was as neat as the rest, the sewing machine having been relegated to a corner, where it remained, unused.

'I've just made an eggless sponge,' Brenda explained when Eileen appeared in the back kitchen doorway. 'If you use a spoonful of vinegar instead of an egg, it's supposed to rise just as well.'

'Does it work?' Eileen asked, interested.

'I dunno yet. It's still in the oven.'

'Let me know how it turns out and I'll make one tomorrer.'

'Okay, Eil.' Brenda licked her fingers. 'I was just scraping the bowl. Can I offer you a cup of Bovril? I'm afraid I've run out of tea.'

Eileen wrinkled her nose. 'No, ta. I always feel as if I'm drinking gravy. I came to ask a favour, actually, but I expect you'll send me away with a flea in me ear.'

'Try me,' Brenda said with a smile.

'I was wondering if you would run me up a couple of maternity smocks? Look at me!' She unbuttoned the cardigan and exposed the gap where the buttons wouldn't meet. 'This is me biggest frock and I've got nowt else that'll fit. I've kept me eye open in the WVS, but they've never had anything suitable. I thought, if I let the seams out of me old black skirt and put a patch in both sides, then two smocks will see me through till September.'

Brenda shook her head. 'I'm sorry, Eileen, but I'm just not in the mood for dressmaking.'

'You haven't been in the mood for months!'

'And I'm not likely to be, not ever!'

Brenda said this with such utter finality that Eileen reckoned it was no use arguing. Nevertheless, she said gently, 'You shouldn't let what Xavier said put you off, luv. It seems such a shame to let all your talent go to waste.'

'I know I shouldn't, but I just can't help it. Every time I go near my machine, it all comes back to me.' She was merely the dressmaker who lived downstairs and fancied him. 'A woman came yesterday I haven't seen for a couple of years, wanting a wedding dress and four bridesmaid's frocks, but I still said no.'

'Oh, well, never mind,' Eileen sighed. 'I'll just have to look around the shops. I wonder how many coupons they'll cost?' Clothes rationing had begun at the beginning of the month. She was a fool not to have bought them before, but had been reluctant to waste her savings—or the money Nick had

408

sent—on maternity clothes.

'Eil?'

'Yes, luv?'

'I wanted to ask . . .' Brenda wrinkled her face and looked slightly uncomfortable. 'I mean . . . Oh, never mind, it doesn't matter.'

'Go on, Bren,' Eileen urged.

'I was just wondering . . . would you like half the sponge when it's done?' Brenda said in a rush.

Eileen stared at the woman thoughtfully. 'No, ta,' she said eventually. 'It's very generous of you, but keep it for you and the girls.'

As she crossed the street to go home, Eileen wondered what it was that Brenda had *really* wanted to ask.

*   *   *

What Brenda was too embarrassed to ask Eileen was, how did she feel about spending the rest of her life without a man? Did Eileen have the same dead scary sensation as Brenda had, as if she was only half a person?

There were times when Brenda was terrified that Xavier might turn up and plead with her to take him back, and although she'd sworn she'd never touch him again with a barge pole, she might well take him because she couldn't bear the thought of being alone. It wasn't that she minded being by herself, she was used to it, even before Xavier was called up, but he was always there, in the background, someone to talk about to the neighbours or on the tram or in queues. She still talked about him now, as if nothing untoward had happened, as if he hadn't betrayed her with Carrie

Banks and probably half a dozen other women. But once the war was over and Xavier hadn't returned—Brenda crossed her fingers—who would she talk about then?

It wasn't the bed thing, either. Although it was nice whilst it lasted, she didn't miss it a bit. In fact, there'd been times when it had been a bit of a nuisance if she'd just dropped off to sleep.

Of course, there was always Vince. Brenda sighed. Vince worried her, too. In a moment of weakness, she'd told him about Xavier, and since then he kept demanding they move in together. Not in Pearl Street, of course, Brenda wouldn't have tolerated the thought for a single second, but on his side of town, where they could pretend they were married.

'It makes sense, luv,' Vince kept urging. 'We get on, don't we? We always have a lot to talk about.'

Well, Vince did. He bored her rigid going on about bus timetables, and a change of route became the sole topic of conversation for days. Yet she couldn't bring herself to stop him from popping in several times a week for a cup of tea, and she was frightened, really frightened, that ugly and boring though he might be, he was a man, and one of these days she'd agree to his proposal and move in with him, assuming she hadn't taken Xavier back first.

Brenda shuddered at the very notion she was willing to consider spending the rest of her life with a man she couldn't even bring herself to kiss!

She opened the oven. The sponge had risen, not so well as with an egg, but the surface was smooth and brown. She took it into the back kitchen to cool, rather glad Eileen hadn't agreed to the suggestion that she have half. The girls would go through the cake like a dose of salts when they came home from school. She also felt glad she hadn't asked that question. Eileen Costello and Brenda Mahon were as different as chalk from cheese. Once Eileen had the baby, she'd no doubt have a string of men running after her. Indeed, there'd been a rumour going round about a year ago that she was having an affair with someone in the RAF, though Sheila stoutly denied the whole thing. Everyone in the street was waiting to see when Eileen's baby was born. If it didn't arrive before the end of September, then it couldn't be Francis Costello's, which meant his wife had been up to more than digging fields when she was in the Land Army.

Brenda went into the parlour and stared at her dumpy reflection in the full-length mirror. If only she wasn't so damned *plain*! It just wasn't fair. She fluffed out her mousy brown hair, but it merely fell back against her scalp, as flat as a pancake. Maybe if she used a different shampoo, but it was hard enough to buy a shampoo of any sort nowadays.

The sight of the sewing machine in the corner only added to her sense of despair. It might be a good idea to pawn it, get the thing out of the way forever, instead of leaving it as a constant reminder of how she'd been betrayed. Anyroad, the few bob it would fetch would be more than useful. Things were a bit tight at the moment, as the allowance from the Army was scarcely enough to keep body and soul together. If she gave it a good polish . . .

She fetched a duster and a tin of beeswax and began to polish the heavily carved top which had the make SINGER attached to it on a little black

411

and gold enamelled plate. Brenda had always thought the name appropriate, as she often sang as she slid the material through and saw it emerging from the other side, the stitches satisfyingly neat and perfect. She removed the top for the first time since she'd made herself that horrible green frock for the dance on New Year's Eve, and the sun dancing through the parlour window caught the silver bobbin pin, the needle and the slide plate underneath, the gold paint on the curved black body of the machine; SINGER again, in big gleaming letters. Without thinking, she pressed the treadle with her foot and the needle flashed up and down and the shuttle shot back and forth with a quiet, well-oiled clatter.

Brenda caught her breath, and Xavier might as well never have existed, as a strange warm sensation swept through her body. It was almost as good, no better, than making love! She ran her hand up and down the smooth cast-iron body, and it was like caressing something live, a real person.

She was almost choking with excitement as she opened the door of the sideboard where she kept remnants of material, and began to fling them wildly on the sofa. By the time she'd removed the lot, pieces of cloth were spread all over the room: jewel-coloured velvet, stiff taffeta, soft silk so satisfying to touch, a length of chalk-striped suiting, a lovely piece of navy-blue linen, several pieces of cotton, both striped and gingham, which she'd bought to make frocks for the girls, numerous odds and ends of lace . . .

The pattern books were on the mantelpiece, full of Sonny's crayoned scribbles. When Brenda opened the Vogue, fingers trembling, it was like

412

greeting a crowd of old friends. She turned to Maternity. There were several smocks, and she could run up a couple for Eileen that very afternoon. Perhaps one in gingham for every day, and that piece of navy-blue linen with a cream lace collar for best. Brenda felt a bit guilty about the way she'd thought about Eileen earlier on. So what if she'd had an affair! Francis Costello had appeared to be the perfect husband, but then, who could have seemed more perfect that Xavier?

Men, Brenda thought in disgust, they were all the same!

She dragged the machine into the middle of the room, opened the drawer in which she kept her thread, and tut-tutted when she found several spools of cotton were grubby on the surface. She recalled how the children used to roll them to each other during the crazy upside-down period when Carrie had been there.

Half an hour later, the material had been cut out, and Brenda Mahon was singing at the top of her voice as she fed the navy-blue linen under the silver foot of her sewing machine.

*   *   *

Ruth knocked on the door of Jacob's old bedroom and Matt called, 'Yes?'

'I was wondering, would you like a cup of tea?'

'No, thank you.'

She hovered on the landing, and jumped when Matt suddenly opened the door. 'I'm sorry,' she murmured, though had no idea why she should apologise. It was, after all, *her* landing.

'I shall be going out in a minute,' Matt said. 'I'm

413

on duty with Jack Doyle, firewatching.'

'I know. I just thought you might like a drink before you went, that's all.'

'Perhaps a flask of something to take with me?' Matt suggested.

'Would coffee do, though I'm afraid it's that awful Camp stuff?'

'That would be fine,' Matt said politely.

Ruth hurried downstairs, feeling he'd asked just to stop her fussing, and he probably didn't want a drink at all. It was just like when she'd been a child and Jacob had insisted she put a scarf on in the winter, when a scarf was the last thing she wanted to wear.

Matt came down just as she was screwing the top on the flask. He was dressed as if for work, with a donkey jacket over his old clothes.

'Would you like some sandwiches?' she asked.

'No, thanks.'

'It would be no trouble.'

Matt smiled. 'I hate to say this, Ruth, but you're beginning to sound a little like my mother.'

'I'm sorry.' She sensed irritation behind the smile.

'That's all right. But if I want anything, I promise, on my heart, I'll ask.'

After Matt had gone, Ruth checked on Michael who was sleeping peacefully in the cot beside her bed. She watched him for a while, hoping he'd wake up so she could take him downstairs and nurse him, but the baby didn't stir.

Leaving the door half open, Ruth crept along the landing into Matt's room, something she often did when he was out. She knew she was prying, and felt ashamed. It was precisely the sort of thing she

414

detested in other people, the persistent curiosity about other people's lives, but Matt bothered her. Except for meals, he hardly ever sat downstairs, to talk or listen to the wireless, but spent all his time shut in this room. She realised it was unreasonable to expect otherwise, after all, the marriage had been made on the clear understanding that they expect nothing from each other, but she couldn't help feeling slightly hurt that he'd sooner be alone than in her company.

The room was exactly the same as when it had been Jacob's. Apart from a few books, Matt had added nothing to turn it into his own. But then he'd come to Pearl Street with only the working clothes he stood up in. The house in Southey Street where he'd lodged had been completely destroyed in the blitz, and he'd lost whatever few possessions he had. Although they'd both agreed the wedding was a mere formality, that there'd be no fuss, he'd had to buy clothes for the ceremony.

Ruth opened the wardrobe. Matt's new suit, a rough brown tweed hung neatly alongside Jacob's small collection of faded shirts and his one and only suit. Ruth ran her fingers along the collar of the shiny black jacket. Strange, but she hardly missed her father. In fact, the neighbours appeared more upset at his passing than she did. Although she'd grown to love him during the short time they'd been reunited, now he'd gone, it was as if they'd never come together again. When she thought about him, it was the Jacob of her childhood who came to mind.

She was about to close the wardrobe, but instead paused and, looking from left to right, as if worried someone were watching, she rooted through the pockets of Matt's suit to see what she could find.

Nothing, except for a handkerchief, which had been there when she looked the other day.

Ruth bit her lip, slammed the wardrobe door, and leaned against it, panting. What on earth had got into her lately? She was becoming obsessed with Matt. Although she'd affected sympathy, she'd actually felt glad when he told her Maria's photograph had been lost in the bombing, as well as her letters and the watch she'd given him on their wedding day.

'They were all together in a tin box,' he said. 'I searched through the rubble, but it was nowhere to be found. I wasn't even sure if I was looking in the right place.'

'Never mind, you have your memories,' Ruth said.

'That's right. No one can take them away, can they?' Then he'd gone upstairs and she hadn't seen him again for hours.

Ruth recalled that Jacob had once said something much the same. She sighed and noticed the cover of the bed was creased where Matt had been sitting. There was no chair in the room. She straightened it, then realised Matt might notice and gather she'd been in, so she sat on the bed to crease it again.

'What a fool I am!' she whispered. 'I'm falling in love with him.'

*   *   *

There was something about the Liverpool air, Matt Smith thought as he was on his way round to Jack Doyle's, particularly when it was sunny. It had a uniquely special quality, a sort of vivid brightness and a luminosity he'd never encountered before. He took a deep breath. No matter how low he felt, he always felt uplifted, even if only momentarily, when he walked through the streets of Bootle on a sunlit day.

Double summertime had been introduced recently, and despite the fact midnight was a mere hour away, it was still light. The fiery sun had just disappeared behind the roofs directly ahead, leaving the sky a magnificent vista of vivid purple slashed with green and gold.

He passed a bomb site, then another. He always felt terrible guilt when he saw the damage his fellow countrymen had inflicted on these generous, big-hearted people. Perhaps justice would have been served if he'd been at home when the bomb struck Southey Street and he'd been killed, along with his landlady and her two little girls.

But then he wouldn't have been there to marry Ruth!

Matt thought uncomfortably about their recent conversation. Ruth worried him, the way she fussed around pressing food and drink on him which he didn't want. It could be just his imagination, but he sensed she resented him spending all his time upstairs, as if she would have liked them to sit together like a proper married couple and discuss their day as he and Maria used to do. She seemed to have become a different person altogether from the cold, haughty woman he'd spoken to in Reece's. Perhaps it was only natural she'd want to look after him with her father so recently dead, offering to darn his socks and do his washing when he was only too happy, indeed preferred, to do all

417

these things for himself.

She was even worse with that poor baby. In fact, Matt thought uneasily, Ruth was almost certainly not fit to adopt Michael. The child was quite literally smothered with affection and scarcely out of her arms during the hours he was awake. It bordered on the unhealthy, the obsessive and possessive love for another woman's child. On the few occasions when Matt was left with Michael, he noticed his basically good-natured and sunny personality was beginning to change. He refused to lie quietly in his pram, which Matt felt sure was what babies were supposed to do, at least for some of the time, but bawled to be picked up and nursed.

Matt kicked at a stone and it landed with a little ping against a lamppost. Perhaps the way Ruth behaved with Michael was only natural, too. After all, her other children had disappeared, perhaps forever. Who could blame her for attaching herself so passionately to a child which had appeared in her life as if by magic? But if that was the case, Matt thought, feeling even more uneasy, so had *he*! What if she was re-creating for herself a family; first a child, then a husband?

'What the hell have I got myself into?' he cursed as he knocked on Jack Doyle's front door.

There were raised voices coming from inside. Jack called, 'Is that you, Matt?' and without waiting for a reply, 'Let yourself in.'

Matt drew the key through the letter box and went inside, where Jack and his eldest daughter, Eileen, appeared to be in the throes of a blazing row.

'You've no right to call him a hypocrite,' Eileen said heatedly. 'We're allies, now, just like he said.

What did you expect him to say?'

'Allies!' Jack was almost beside himself with rage. 'Allies! He hates Russia and he hates Communism and everything it stands for. He allus has and he allus will.'

Matt sat down and listened with interest. He wondered who the 'he' was, the subject of the argument.

'Frankly,' Eileen said icily, 'I haven't got much time for Russia meself. They invaded Poland at the same time as Germany did. Not only that, Russia and Germany signed a Non-Aggression Pact. Nevertheless, we've got to accept that things have changed. I mean, he couldn't very well refer to them as "Our former enemies", could he?'

'Huh! He could have apologised for all the things he said in the past.'

'Don't be stupid, Dad.'

'Has something happened?' Matt intervened nervously.

Jack turned on him so fiercely that Matt flinched, half expecting a blow. 'You bet your bloody life it has,' he spat. 'Germany's only gone and invaded Russia! It was on the wireless earlier on. What d'you think of *that*?'

Matt closed his eyes briefly. It seemed that Hitler's ambition knew no bounds, that he was intent on dominating the entire world. To Matt, it only meant more carnage, more cruelty, more wasted lives. He almost felt like apologising to Jack for what his country was doing, but then, Jack knew how he felt.

Instead, he said tiredly, 'Well, it didn't do Napoleon much good, did it?'

'What gets me,' Jack went on, 'is on the wireless

419

Churchill referred to Russia as "our great ally", the bloody hypocrite! He's been calling them every name under the sun for the last twenty-five years, ever since the Revolution. In fact, the entire establishment is anti-Communist. They wouldn't play the *Internationale* on the BBC when it was May Day.'

'But Churchill didn't have any choice, did he?' Eileen looked at Matt imploringly, as if anxious to get him on her side.

Matt had no intention of becoming involved in a family argument, though he privately thought Jack was being foolish. Winston Churchill was the best leader the country could possibly have, a fact Jack seemed to recognise most of the time, even if he couldn't hide his basic, long-held dislike. 'I'd sooner not take sides,' he said, smiling.

'Oh, well,' Eileen sighed. 'At least it means Hitler'll be preoccupied somewhere else, though I feel dead sorry for the ordinary Russian people, the same as I feel sorry for ordinary Germans.'

'I reckon the Führer's bitten off more than he can chew, taking on Russia,' Jack said ominously.

Matt felt that was something with which he could agree. He nodded. 'You're right, Jack. Let's hope he has.'

Suddenly, everything was back to normal. Eileen said, 'Would you like a cup of tea before I go, Dad?' as if they both had these sort of arguments quite frequently and neither appeared to hold a grudge.

'I wouldn't mind. How about you, Matt?'

'Please.'

Eileen got to her feet. 'I've made a sponge cake for me Dad and I was going to give him half to take

420

with him. Would you like the other half, luv?'

'That would be very nice, thank you.' Matt felt he could take things from these people, because they gave without wanting anything in return, unlike Ruth. Everytime he let Ruth do something for him, he felt as if he were making another small commitment, and the more he let her do, the more he let her give, he had the feeling that before he knew it, he would be committed fully. Anyway, he liked the Doyles. He liked being in Jack's house, and the one in Pearl Street in which Eileen lived with her sister and a crowd of children, where Jack had taken him once or twice. He watched Eileen Costello through the doorway of the back kitchen. She wore a red and white smock over her swelling stomach, and her long straight fair hair was held back with a wide red ribbon. She was humming underneath her breath as she put the dishes on a tray, the spoons on the saucers . . .

'Do you take sugar, Matt?' She turned and caught his eye.

'No, thanks.' He looked away, uncomfortably aware he'd been staring.

'That's a blessing. There's not much left and me dad takes two.'

The kettle boiled on the hob over the fire. Matt carried it out to the back kitchen.

'Ta, luv.' She took it off him, smiling, and Matt was conscious of the faint smell of lavender.

'Can I do anything else?'

'You can carry the teapot in. Me Dad likes the tea poured at the table. He says it tastes different that way.'

'It does!' Jack shouted from the next room.

She winked at Matt and said loudly, 'It's best to

humour him. He's quite likely to get in a terrible rage if he doesn't get his own way. He used to beat us something awful when we were kids.'

'Don't go saying things like that,' Jack growled. 'People might believe you.'

Matt and Eileen carried the tea things in between them. Matt returned to his seat and Eileen handed him his drink—he'd forgotten to mention he didn't take milk. He noticed the way her hair fell forward when she bent towards him, curling over her smooth cheeks in creamy swathes. Until tonight, he'd never realised how lovely she was. Jack had told him all about her. She was *eine Witwe*—think in English, think in English, he told himself—she was a widow who had lost her husband and son, her only child, six months ago. So many tragedies, Matt thought sadly: Eileen, Ruth, himself—he remembered his landlady and her two little girls . . .

'I've got something to show you!' Jack went out and returned with a bowl of strawberries. 'We picked them in the cottage this morning,' he said proudly. 'Have you ever seen strawberries that big before?'

'Never!' Matt affirmed, though they were only half as big as those his father used to grow. For a moment, the sight of the rich red fruit brought back memories of the farm where he'd grown up: his mother in the garden in her long cotton apron, his father tramping off to work and disappearing into the wet, early morning Bavarian mist.

'Our Eileen's going to make . . . what's it called, luv?'

'A flan.'

'A flan, that's it. A strawberry flan.' He thrust the

422

bowl at Matt. 'Take one.'

The fruit felt soft between Matt's fingers, though the taste was exactly as he remembered it. He wondered if they realised strawberries didn't keep. 'You're supposed to eat them straight away,' he said, 'otherwise they go off.'

'Do they now?' Jack looked down at the bowl. 'We've never had strawberries before, not even in peacetime. Well, I never! You learn something new every day.' He grinned at his daughter. 'In that case, we'd best eat them now. You can have one of them there flans already made next time we go to the cottage.'

'Perhaps you and Ruth would like to come out to Melling with us one Sunday,' Eileen suggested. 'You know where it is, don't you?'

It seemed incredible, now, that he hadn't given her a second glance the day he'd turned up at the cottage on Easter Monday to see Ruth, though he'd found her rather vulnerably appealing on the few occasions they'd met since, but had put this down to the situation she was in. As he watched, she tilted back her head, opened her mouth and dropped the strawberry in, as if determined to get all the enjoyment out of fruit as she could. Her bare arms had caught the sun and downy fair hairs were noticeable against the faint gold flesh . . .

Oh, God! Matt felt his entire body break out into a sweat as a long-forgotten feeling swept through him, a feeling he'd never thought he'd experience again after losing Maria. He'd felt convinced that part of him was dead forever. He began to panic, remembering Ruth, his wife, but told himself it was only temporary. Once the adoption was sorted out . . .

'Are you all right, Matt?' Jack said, concerned. 'You've turned quite red.'

Matt ran a finger around the collar of his jacket. 'It's hot in here,' he muttered.

'Oh, you should have taken your coat off!' Eileen turned accusingly on her father. 'You've no idea how to behave with visitors, Dad. You didn't ask for his coat when he came in.'

'It's all right. We'll have to be going soon.' The rest of the room became a blur and Matt was aware only of Eileen Costello, all pink and cream and red, as luscious at the strawberries her father had picked that morning. He felt perspiration trickle down the back of his neck, troubled by the ardour of his thoughts, worried that she could read his mind. If she as much as sensed what he was feeling, she would think him the biggest heel in the world; married less than two months, and already attracted to another woman. Matt told himself that one day soon he would be a single man again, free to get to know Eileen Costello better.

CHAPTER TWENTY

'Mind your manners!' Alice Scully reached out and slapped her sister sharply on the wrist. The little girl looked as if she were about to cry.

Eileen Costello smiled warmly at the child. 'They're lovely cakes, aren't they? I can't wait to have one meself.'

'She must learn to wait until she gets the say-so,' Alice said sternly. 'Manners maketh the man—or the woman.'

424

It was hard to believe that this little ethereal creature could be so strict, even heartless, Eileen thought. Alice Scully looked exactly as her dad had described her, as if butter wouldn't melt in her mouth, yet she kept her younger brothers and sisters in line with a will of iron.

Sean, home on leave from Lincolnshire for the first time in months, was staring at Alice with a silly, almost besotted, expression on his face. Eileen regarded him with a mixture of amusement and trepidation. This was the first time she'd met Alice and her family, and, like Sheila and her dad, she wasn't sure if she approved of the match.

'Where's the tablespoon for the jelly?' Alice snapped.

'I'll get it, luv.' Sean jumped to his feet.

'No, you don't. Our Tommy was supposed to set the table.' Alice glared at the eldest boy. 'Tommy, the big spoon, if you don't mind!'

As the boy meekly went into the back kitchen, Eileen glanced around the room. The Scullys occupied four rooms on the second and third floors of the tenement, which were reached by an iron staircase at the rear. Alice had obviously gone to great pains to make the place look nice. The windows sparkled, there was a vase of paper flowers on the sill, and the blackout curtains were freshly washed and ironed. Through the window, washing could be seen drying on the open-air landing. Everywhere was scrupulously clean and smelt strongly of a mixture of furniture polish and disinfectant, but Alice could do nothing to disguise the abject poverty in which she and her family lived. Eileen noticed the faded, damp-stained wallpaper was held up by drawing pins on the

425

outside corners and the bare floorboards were rotten in several places. There was scarcely any furniture, just the table, which had a piece of folded cardboard underneath one leg, and several rickety hardback chairs, none of which matched, yet, apart from the back kitchen, this was the room which served all the family's daily needs. There were no armchairs, not even a proper sideboard, merely a chest of very chipped and scratched drawers which had a well in the middle, as if it had once been a dressing table.

The five younger Scullys were as thin and underfed as Alice herself, yet their darned and patched clothes were immaculate, their faces scrubbed, the hair of the two little girls plaited painfully tight. The eldest boy, Tommy, who Eileen understood was at work, though you would have never have guessed, because he looked no more than twelve, wore a suit which was several sizes too big for him, as if it had once belonged to his late father. Alice's own brown wool frock hung loosely on her fragile frame, the material far too thick and heavy for such a warm summer's day.

Yet, despite all this, when Eileen and Sheila arrived, the table was heaped with food: two plates of wafer-thin tomato sandwiches cut into triangles, fairy cakes with a little piece of cherry on top of each, two jellies, one red and one green, decorated with hundreds and thousands, and a bowl of custard. Alice had clearly gone to enormous trouble to impress the two women who might become her sisters-in-law.

'Take your elbows off the table,' Alice snarled. For a moment, Eileen thought it was she who was being rebuked. She hastily removed her right arm,

426

but it turned out to be Tommy who had thoughtlessly relaxed for a moment to talk to Sean.

'Has everyone had enough butties?' asked Alice.

'Yes, ta, luv. They were really lovely,' Sheila said politely. 'Weren't they, Eileen?'

Eileen nodded. 'Very nice indeed.'

'Would you like a fairy cake?'

The children made a united grab for the cakes, but Alice turned on them with a face like thunder.

'You'd think you'd never had a bite to eat before.' She lashed out at the nearest child, one of the boys, and caught him around the ear. 'It's manners to let our guests help themselves first.'

Sheila caught her sister's eye and made a face, but Eileen pretended not to notice. She reckoned Sheila was glad she'd left her own kids at home with the neighbours, as their table manners were non-existent compared to the Scullys, who seemed unnaturally well-behaved.

'Y'can have a cake now,' Alice said when the two women had taken theirs, 'and eat them properly, like, else you'll get a clout.'

'Yes, Alice.'

The meal was gradually becoming torture. When the time came for the jelly and custard, Eileen was terrified one of the children would spill theirs on the clean cloth and Alice would lash out again. She began to wonder what on earth Sean, so good-natured and easy-going, could possibly see in this intolerant, ill-humoured little tartar.

'Well, I suppose we'd better be going . . .' Sheila stood up and pushed her chair back as soon as she'd finished, as if anxious to get away.

'Y'haven't had a cup of tea yet. Colette, put the kettle on.'

The girl trotted obediently into the back kitchen, and soon after, Alice followed, dragging her left foot as she went. When the tea arrived, Eileen noticed her own cup and saucer, as well as Sheila's, were new, as if bought specially for the occasion.

'Would you like me and Sheila to do the dishes, luv?' she asked when the tea was drunk.

'No, ta.' Alice looked indignant. 'It's the girls' job to do the washing up.'

'Is it all right if I pop upstairs for a few words with your mam? I've never met her, have I?'

Alice looked undecided. 'If you like,' she said eventually, 'though she's probably asleep. She nearly always is.'

The curtains were tightly drawn in the bedroom where Mrs Scully lay, and no amount of disinfectant could disguise the sickly smell of death that hung there. You could scarcely move in the room, which had a double bed in one corner, where no doubt Alice and her sisters slept, and a single one in another which was occupied by the frail form of the dying woman.

'Mam!' Alice knelt beside the bed and stroked her mother's forehead. 'You've got a visitor, Mam.'

Eileen found it difficult to believe this gentle girl with the soft voice was the same person they'd just had tea with. Her opinion of Alice Scully altered considerably for the better, though she still found it hard to accept the way she treated her brothers and sisters.

'It's Eileen Costello, Mam, Sean's sister.'

The vivid July sunlight shone like a halo around the edges of the blackout curtains, and Eileen could just about see the eyes of the woman on the bed slowly flicker open. Alice took a step back and

428

pushed Eileen forward.

'Are you Jack Doyle's girl?' Mrs Scully whispered. Her face resembled a skull, with the skin stretched sharply over the bones, translucent and as thin and fine as the softest silk. At first, Eileen thought the sunken eyes were sightless until the pupils caught her own.

'I am that,' she answered.

'He's a good man, the very best.'

'I know, luv.'

'I'm dead proud of the fact your Sean's taken up with our Alice.'

'Me dad's proud, too.' Eileen lied with utter conviction. 'Your Alice is one in a million.'

Mrs Scully nodded almost imperceptibly and, as if the effort was too much, her eyes closed and she turned her head away.

'She's gone to sleep again,' Alice said. 'I'll give her some jelly and custard next time she wakes up.'

*   *   *

'Just look at this place, it's dead scruffy!' Sheila said disgustedly when she and Eileen were outside. Several barefoot and only partially dressed children were playing in the gutter. Further down the road, two boys were chucking debris out of the broken window of one of a row of four partially demolished houses. They cheered each time something landed in the street outside with a thunderous crash. 'Come on, let's get out of here quick!' She grabbed her sister's arm. 'I thought that meal would never end. I was dreading those kids doing something else wrong and getting another clout off Alice.'

'I felt the same, but even so, she went to an awful lot of trouble.'

'I don't care,' Sheila said in a hard voice. 'Me heart sinks when I think of her getting her hooks into our Sean!'

'I reckon it's the other way round, and it's Sean trying to get his hooks into Alice. Did you see the daft way he kept looking at her?' Eileen laughed. 'I don't think our Sean will come to too much harm if he marries Alice Scully.'

*   *   *

'Can we go outside and play, Alice?'

Alice Scully stared desperately at the four little faces which were looking up at her expectantly. 'Only if you promise to keep your clothes clean for school tomorrer,' she said.

As the children raced for the back door, she screamed, 'There's no need to rush. Walk properly—and don't forget there's the dishes still to be washed.'

Tommy appeared to have settled down for a chat with Sean, whom he regarded as some sort of god. Alice jerked her head. 'Make yourself scarce, our Tommy. I want to talk to Sean.'

'But . . .' Tommy began indignantly.

Alice wasn't in the mood to argue. 'Sod off,' she barked.

Tommy said, with as much sarcasm as he dared, 'You mean I'm allowed to play out in me best suit?'

'Mind your tongue, Thomas Scully, else you'll feel the back of me hand where it'll hurt most. Just because you go to work . . .' Alice took a threatening limp towards him, and Tommy

430

scarpered pretty sharpish, pulling a face at his sister as he went.

'And keep clear of that Joey Kelly,' Alice called after him. 'If you come back smelling of tobacco, there'll be hell to play.'

'He's getting too much lip, that boy,' Alice sighed as Tommy's boots clattered down the iron staircase. She began to clear the table like a whirlwind.

'I thought you wanted to talk to me,' Sean said as she flew in and started stacking the dirty plates, one on top of the other.

She stopped, and Sean noticed her hands were trembling. Suddenly, without warning, she sat down at the table with her head in her arms and began to sob uncontrollably.

Alarmed, Sean sat beside her and put his arm around her thin shoulders. 'What's the matter, luv?'

'They didn't like me,' Alice wept. 'Your Sheila's never liked me, now your Eileen doesn't, either. Your dad hates me, too. It was a stupid idea to ask them to tea.'

'Don't be silly.' It was impossible for Sean to imagine anyone not liking Alice. 'Of course they liked you. What makes you think they didn't?'

'I could tell by the way they looked at me and the way they kept looking at each other,' Alice said despairingly. 'Oh, lord, Sean, I spent all yesterday cleaning the place from top to bottom. I washed the curtains and the tablecloth and all the towels. I even washed the bedding, which was a good thing as your Eileen asked to see me mam. Today, I've done nowt but cut sandwiches and make cakes and jellies. I even sent our Colette to church to light a penny candle to make the jellies set when it looked as if they mightn't.'

'Everywhere looked really nice, and the meal was first class, luv,' Sean assured her, but she appeared to take no notice.

'Those tomatoes were five shillings a pound,' she moaned, 'though I only bought a quarter, and the man in the Co-op wasn't a bit pleased when I only asked for an ounce of cooking cherries. I walked all the way to Paddy's Market last Friday to buy two cups and saucers, 'cos ours were all chipped. Y'see, I've never had anyone to tea before, this is the first time—and the last! Me nerves were at breaking point the whole meal through.'

Sean mentally tried to work out how many sheets and bolster cases she'd had to launder to buy everything, but was too upset by her tears to cope with the sum.

She looked up at him, and his heart turned over at the sight of her tear-stained face. 'D'you think they noticed the way I cut the butties?' she enquired plaintively. 'I saw one of me ladies do it that way, in triangles 'stead of squares, and I thought it looked dead posh.'

'I'm sure they did, luv.' Sean felt slightly guilty that he hadn't noticed himself.

'Your Eileen brought a sponge cake with her, as if we mightn't have enough food,' Alice sniffed, clearly offended, 'and Sheila gave me a quarter of margarine. You'd think we were dead poor or something.'

'People always do that since the war,' Sean explained, 'because they don't like using other people's rations.'

'Do they?' Alice looked at him anxiously. 'Are

you sure?'

'I'm positive.' Sean patted the pocket of his blue-grey battledress. 'I've brought you something, too.'

'A letter! Is it a letter?' She wiped her cheeks with her sleeve and her grey eyes lit up. 'I've still got all your letters. I keep them tied up with string underneath the bed.'

Sean kissed her tenderly on the lips. 'And I've kept yours.'

'I didn't think it was possible to write so many pages. I was never any good at writing at school, but when I asked one of me ladies how to spell a word, she gave me a thing called a dictionary, and I use it every time I do a letter.'

'Anyroad, this isn't a letter, it's something else.' Sean tapped his pocket again. 'D'you want to see?'

'Of course I do.'

Sean took a tiny box out of his battledress and opened it. A solitaire diamond ring nestled within the velvet centre.

Alice stared at the ring, round-eyed. 'What is it?'

'An engagement ring, of course,' Sean said smugly.

'How much did it cost?'

'Four pound, ten shillings. It was the smallest in the shop. I hope it fits.'

'*What!*'

'I told you, four pound ten.'

Sean felt the atmosphere in the room turn cold and Alice seemed to shrivel beside him. To his dismay, she stood up, knocking against him, and the box containing the ring flew across the room.

'You're nowt but an idiot, Sean Doyle,' she screamed in a fury. 'Four pound ten for a bleedin' ring. What is it they say, "a fool and his money are

433

soon parted"'?'

'But Alice . . .'

'Don't "but Alice" me. You need your head examined, you.' Her little body looked as if it might explode. She began to throw the remaining plates on top of each other, stopped, sat down and dropped her head in her arms again and began to cry even louder than before.

'Jaysus, Alice,' Sean complained. 'I can't keep up with you. I thought you'd be as pleased as Punch.'

'I am, I am,' she cried, distraught. 'Where is it? Oh, where is it? If it's gone down a crack between the floorboards, I'll kill meself.'

Sean retrieved the box. The ring remained safely tucked in the padded slit. 'Try it on.'

The ring slid easily over Alice's knuckle and rested, twinkling, on the third finger of her tiny left hand.

'It fits perfect,' she breathed. 'Oh, Sean, I'm sorry. I never thought I'd have an engagement ring, least of all one as nice as this! It was just when I thought of all the washing I'd have to do for four pound ten.'

'I know, luv.' Sean put his arms around her and she nestled close. He hadn't felt all that perturbed by the outburst. The Alice Scully who'd just recently dominated the tea table, was nothing like *his* Alice, who wrote him long tender letters every week; letters in which she seemed able to put down all the things she found hard to say in person as she struggled daily to keep the family together, to ensure they were clean and fed, and, her most ardent wish, that they grew up 'respectable', as she put it. She told him how scared she was for their future, that she was terrified her mam would die, or

434

the war would continue long enough for Tommy to be called up. And she told Sean how much she loved him, and that never, in a million years, had she thought someone like him would fall in love with her. It might not seem so to Eileen and Sheila, but the Scully family were bound together by a bond invisible to outsiders. The younger children might well be frightened of their older sister's sharp tongue and heavy hand, but Alice had to keep up a front and appear to be strong, and they knew, in their heart of hearts, that the blows meant nothing. They cared for Alice every bit as much as she cared for them.

He kissed her ear. 'You know what I think, Alice?'

'What, luv?'

'I think we should get married straight away.'

'But where will we live? I mean, there's no room here.'

'We can put a mattress on the floor in this room,' Sean said carelessly. 'We'll think of something, don't worry.'

Alice said cautiously, 'Don't you think we should wait till we're a bit older?'

'If I'm old enough to fight for me country,' Sean said bluntly, 'then I'm old enough to get married. Anyroad, the other day I discovered that married men's wives get an allowance—twenty-five bob a week, along with another seven off my pay. That means you'd get thirty-two bob all to yourself. Fact, looked at a certain way, luv, they'd actually be paying us to get married.'

'Never!' Thirty-two bob sounded a small fortune to Alice.

'It means you can give up doing other people's

washing.' It bothered him when he was away, thinking of her trailing up to Merton Road and back with loads of laundry, and he'd never forget the weight of the iron! To some, it might not seem a very romantic reason for getting married, but to Sean, it was the best reason on earth.

*   *   *

Late that same night, Jack Doyle came bursting into Number 16, where both his daughters were listening to the wireless. The children were fast asleep in bed.

'What's Churchill done now?' Eileen grinned when she saw his angry red face.

'It's nowt to do with Churchill. It's our Sean. He's just come home and told me he and Alice Scully are getting wed.'

'Oh, no!' Sheila wailed.

'My feelings exactly,' Jack snapped. 'What did you think of her?' he asked Eileen.

'She seemed all right to me,' Eileen said calmly. 'In fact, I don't know what all the fuss is about. Alice is a bit short-tempered—well, more than a bit,' she conceded when Sheila gave a contemptuous snort, 'but who can blame her when you consider what she has to put up with? Most girls would have put those little ones in an orphanage a long time ago.'

'Mebbe, but that doesn't make her a good wife for our Sean,' Jack argued.

'It doesn't make her a bad one, either.'

'What did you say to Sean?' Sheila asked.

'I managed to persuade him to put if off till Christmas, when he'll be nineteen. After all, he's only known the girl a few months. In the meantime, I'll look round for a better house just in case.'

'I don't suppose there's much harm in that,' Eileen said. 'I might pop round and see Alice tomorrer. I suppose it's time I got to know her proper.' It wasn't that she loved Sean any less than her dad and Sheila, but neither seemed aware of how shallow he was and entirely lacking in character, taking up with girls and dropping them without the least concern for their feelings. There'd been times when she envisaged him becoming another George Ransome: a lonely middle-aged man, the permanent bachelor, unable to sustain a relationship and making a fool of himself with a long succession of different women. She felt convinced that someone as strong as Alice Scully, together with all the responsibilities that came with her, would be the making of Sean Doyle.

CHAPTER TWENTY-ONE

Matt Smith dropped down onto the grass beside Eileen. 'Isn't it a glorious day?'

'Glorious,' Eileen agreed lazily.

She was leaning against the cottage wall. Her feet and long slim legs were bare, and the smooth skin gleamed softly in the sunshine. Her hands were clasped over her vastly extended stomach, as if protecting the child growing inside.

'It's lovely here.' Matt's gaze swept over the large garden. Jack Doyle had gradually brought about a sense of order. At least half of the lawn had been turned over to vegetables, and what remained had been neatly cut with the old rusty mower Jack had discovered in the outhouse and which Matt had helped to restore to working order. The bordering shrubs and bushes were bursting with flowers. A dark shadow had appeared in the far corner, gradually extending as the late afternoon sun crept across the grass. Beyond the apple tree, already full of tiny crab-like fruit, Jack was busy turning over a patch of earth for Brussels sprouts. Now and then the spade would hit a stone with a little clanging noise and Jack would swear aloud, but apart from that, he had the look of a man entirely contented with his lot, as if he would never be happier than with his feet in the earth, his hands on a spade, and surrounded by the green shoots of the vegetables he'd already planted.

The wireless was on inside the house, and the sound of Judy Garland singing *Somewhere Over the Rainbow* came through the open window.

'Have you seen the picture?'

Matt blinked. 'Sorry?' Eileen was looking at him. Her eyes were sad.

'The picture, *The Wizard of Oz*? We went to see it in London last year when it first came out. Tony, me little boy, was thrilled to bits. We marched all the way back to the hotel singing *Follow the Yellow Brick Road*.'

He shook his head. 'I haven't been to the cinema in ages.'

'You and Ruth should go some time. I suppose she's told you, her dad would have lived in the pictures if they'd let him. He went nearly every week.'

'She may have mentioned it.'

'S'funny,' Eileen mused, 'the way songs remind

you of people and places more than anything else. If they're still playing *Somewhere Over the Rainbow* in forty or fifty years' time, I shall always think of Tony.'

She lapsed into silence and Matt settled himself against the wall. The bricks felt hot against his back. It was strange, he thought, but summer Sundays felt exactly the same wherever you happened to be. The atmosphere was as he'd always remembered it: sounds more muted than usual, yet everything lit with brilliant clarity. He stared at the almost unbelievable perfection of the blossoms on a *Pfingstrose* bush nearby—he racked his brain for the English name, peony!—the dark red centres fading to the palest pink at their tips. A bird landed on the bush, opened its beak and began to sing its heart out.

'You wouldn't believe such a tiny thing could make such a lovely loud noise, would you? Eileen murmured. 'Mind you, they get on our Sheila's nerves, the birds.'

'Is that why she didn't come?' Matt asked.

'No. Dominic and Niall aren't feeling so well. I think they're coming down with something.

'Who does the place belong to?'

'A friend,' Eileen said vaguely.

'I'm surprised you don't live here permanently.'

'I nearly did once, last September, but then . . . Well, all sorts of things happened.' Eileen gave a little shrug. 'Anyroad, as soon as me baby's born and I'm on me feet again, I'm moving into the cottage for good. Our Sheila's taking on me house in Pearl Street, we've already arranged it with the landlord.'

'I shall be sorry to see you go,' Matt said. He

genuinely meant it. He'd miss her calling in on Ruth from time to time.

'Oh, you haven't seen the back of me, don't worry!' she grinned. 'I shall probably go home every other day. Not only that, now you've started giving me dad a hand in the garden, I'll be here to make you a nice cup of tea, won't I?'

Matt resolved he'd come with Jack at every available opportunity once Eileen Costello was ensconced in the cottage. He bent down to hide his face, plucking at a daisy which nestled in the grass, in case he hadn't quite hidden his feeling of pleasure at the idea of seeing more of her.

'Being here reminds me of my childhood,' he mumbled. 'The sounds and the smells. I was brought up on a farm.'

'I didn't know that! Whereabouts?' She looked at him with her big blue eyes, clearly interested.

'Croydon,' said Matt. 'Just outside Croydon.' He felt convinced that, of all the people he'd come to know since arriving in England, she would be the least shocked if he told her the truth. Perhaps, he thought, one day I will . . .

'That's a nice watch,' she said suddenly. 'Is it a new one? Me dad said you lost your watch in the raids.'

Matt bit his lip as he looked down at the watch on his wrist. It had a mother-of-pearl face and a leather strap. 'It's second-hand. Factories have more to do than turn out new watches when there's a war on. Ruth bought it for me.' He wasn't sure which emotion raged uppermost, anger or pity, when she had given him the watch; there was anger that she was trying to take the place of Maria, and pity because Ruth didn't deserve to be reduced to such a pathetic gesture.

'I suppose I'd better go back and give Jack a hand.' Matt got to his feet. 'I had to stop for a while. I got cramp in the back of me leg.'

'Would you like me to rub it for you?' she offered.

He glanced down at her quickly, but the expression on her fresh open face was entirely devoid of guile. With a pang, he realised she didn't look upon him sexually, as a man, but as another woman's husband. 'No, thanks,' he said. 'It's gone now.'

She giggled. 'Do you know what you just said?

Matt frowned, mystified. 'No. What did I just say?'

'You said you had cramp in the back of me leg, not *my* leg. You're becoming a real scouse, Matt. No one will recognise you when you go back to Croydon.'

'There's no reason for me ever to go back. I think I'd like to stay in Liverpool for the rest of my life—me life!' he corrected himself, and Eileen burst out laughing. She extended her arms towards him.

'Give us a hand, will you? I'll be stuck here forever if I have to get up by meself.'

He took her hands, which felt soft within his own, and pulled her upwards. Once upright, still laughing, she stumbled against him, and he grasped her shoulders to prevent her from falling.

'Ta.'

Their glances met, and, to Matt's dismay, perhaps she sensed the turmoil raging within him at the feel of her warm body beneath his hands because she flushed and looked away.

441

Ruth came out of the cottage at that moment and began to peg nappies on the line. She glanced at Eileen and Matt standing close together on the grass. 'I thought it best to wash them now,' she called. 'They'll dry much better here.'

After Ruth had gone inside, Eileen began to walk down the garden to where her father was working. 'Have you got any further with the adoption?' she asked Matt.

He wondered if she'd deliberately changed the subject to something which was personal to him and Ruth. He shook his head and tried to keep his voice steady as he replied, 'Hardly. We've applied to the County Court and they've appointed someone called a Guardian *ad litem*, but nothing further can be done without the mother's consent and there's no trace of Dilys Evans anywhere. Ruth has written to every conceivable body she can think of, but all we get is a negative reply or no reply at all. She seems to have disappeared into thin air.' He couldn't wait for it all to be sorted out so he could escape. The longer he stayed, the more he became a part of Ruth's fantasy family.

'It's a dead shame,' Eileen said sympathetically. 'Our Sheila was only saying the other day, Michael is the spitting image of you. You'd never guess you weren't his real dad, not in a million years.'

'I know,' said Matt. 'Ruth says the same thing all the time.'

Jack Doyle shoved his spade in the soil and leant on the handle when they reached him. 'I was just wondering how that pair of buggers were getting on in the North Atlantic?'

'Which pair of buggers is that, Dad?'

'Churchill and Roosevelt, a'course. They're

442

having a conference in the middle of the ocean. Didn't you hear the announcement on the BBC the other day? It was Clement Attlee himself who made it,' he said proudly. 'I reckon America will come in with us any minute now.'

'I only came to ask if you'd like a cup of tea, Dad, that's all,' Eileen said patiently. 'It's too nice a day to start talking about the war.'

'Huh! That's women all over,' Jack snorted amiably. 'The sun only has to come out and they forget there's a war on.'

'Maybe so, but if it were up to women, there wouldn't be a war to talk about, would there!'

*   *   *

'Me dad and Matt would like a cup of tea. How about you, luv?'

Eileen poked her head into the living room where Ruth was sitting on the settee, apparently staring into space. She'd turned the wireless off and Michael was lying beside her, clutching his feet with his hands. He turned his head at the sound of the strange voice and began to gurgle a welcome.

With some difficulty, Eileen knelt on the floor and rubbed her cheek against his chubby one. 'Aren't you the cleverest baby in the whole wide world?' she cooed. Michael gurgled agreement and pulled Eileen's nose. 'I wonder why people always speak to babies in such a stupid way?' she said.

'What were you and Matt talking about?'

The question took Eileen by surprise. Although Ruth's tone was pleasant, it seemed a strange thing to ask. 'This and that,' she replied. 'Nothing important. Why?'

443

'I was just wondering.'

Eileen sat on her heels and regarded the woman. Ruth appeared terribly strained. There was a pinched expression between her eyes and deep, drawn lines around her mouth. She'd also lost weight lately, and it didn't help that she'd started to use quite a lot of make-up: carmine lipstick which only exaggerated the downward curve of her lips and rouge which made clownish patches on her white face. As soon as Brenda Mahon had started sewing again, Ruth had ordered three frocks. She had one on today, a turquoise crepe-de-chine with little white flowers, yet it seemed to do nothing for her. In fact, the pretty colour only made her look sallow.

'Are you all right, luv?' Eileen asked, concerned.

'Just worried,' Ruth made a sweeping gesture with her hands, 'about everything.'

'Never mind. Dilys is bound to turn up some time.'

'I suppose so,' Ruth said dully.

Eileen went out to make the tea, feeling guilty that she'd been outside virtually the entire day, leaving Ruth, who didn't like the sun, indoors alone. The truth was, once Sheila had decided to give the cottage a miss, Eileen had been quite looking forward to a few hours of quiet contemplation, about Nick, her baby, the future. It was difficult to hear yourself think at home since the Reillys had moved in.

At first, it had just been Matt coming to help Dad with the garden, but then, at the last minute, Ruth had decided to come too . . .

Why, wondered Eileen, when she didn't like the sun, and never seemed particularly happy in the cottage? Now she thought about it, Ruth and Matt had scarcely exchanged two words all day, so she clearly hadn't come to keep him company.

As she set the cups out in a row and began to pour the milk, the baby turned a cartwheel in her stomach, and she winced, 'Ow!' It had become increasingly active lately, particularly when she was in bed at night. She remembered Matt preferred his tea without milk, so drank it herself, patted her stomach and murmured, 'That's for you!'

Matt! She could have sworn there was a look in his eyes when he helped her up, the same look she saw in Nick's eyes, a look that definitely shouldn't be there.

Jaysus! She liked Matt, though it was difficult to do otherwise because there was little to dislike. Despite his pleasant manner, he seemed empty of emotion and real feeling, but if she hadn't imagined the look, then she'd been wrong in her assessment.

Yet Ruth and Matt had only been married just over three months!

With concern mounting, she wondered if Ruth had noticed anything. Perhaps that was another reason why her nerves looked on the point of cracking, she was suspicious of Matt. She'd come into the garden, Eileen remembered, just as he was hauling her to her feet.

'Is the tea ready?' Ruth appeared, Michael on one arm.

'I was just about to pour it.'

'I'll take Matt's out to him.'

*   *   *

445

Ruth remained tightlipped and silent on the journey home. When they entered the house, Matt immediately went upstairs without a word and shut himself in his bedroom. He had no idea why Ruth was in such a bad mood, but sensed it was to do with him, that he'd done something wrong. He threw himself on the bed. The situation was becoming impossible.

Downstairs, Ruth was thinking exactly the same as she laid Michael in his basket. If things didn't sort themselves out soon, if she didn't hear from Dilys, if Matt didn't stop behaving as if she were invisible, she felt as if she could quite easily go mad.

She'd noticed the way Matt looked at Eileen Costello. In fact, she'd been aware for weeks of how well they got on. Matt never talked to her as he did to Eileen, and it was difficult to miss how his face lit up on the few occasions he'd come home and found her there. It was why she'd decided to go to Melling that day, as soon as she realised there would only be the three of them there.

Her hands shook as she filled the kettle for Michael's bottle. Eileen Costello was a single woman and she and Matt were the right age for each other . . .

Ruth placed the kettle on the hob and looked at herself in the mirror over the mantelpiece. She looked *terrible*! She rubbed the rouge off her cheeks with the back of her hand, then the lipstick. Her reflection improved, but only slightly. She still looked like a ghost, just less garish. She'd been trying to make herself attractive for Matt, when all she'd done was look ridiculous.

There was no sound from Matt upstairs. Ruth

remained, staring at herself in the mirror, feeling sick at heart, until the kettle boiled. Michael began to cry, but if she picked him up now, how could she make the bottle?

'Shush, love. Mummy won't be a minute.'

Panic-stricken, she rushed into the kitchen with the kettle, talking to the baby as she measured out the water, the evap.

'I won't be long, Michael,' she called desperately. 'Shush, now!'

She couldn't stand to hear her baby cry. Only bad mothers left their children to cry alone, and bad mothers didn't deserve to have children. Bad mothers should have their children taken away.

The boiling water spurted over the neck of the feeding bottle onto her hand and Ruth almost screamed in pain. Somehow, she managed to squeeze the teat on, and wrapped a nappy around her scalded hand.

Seconds later, clutching Michael, she sank into the easy chair, and he began to suck eagerly on the bottle.

'You'll have your mummy a nervous wreck,' she whispered, as she stroked his soft fair hair with her left hand.

The bottle was soon finished and Michael began to doze. Ruth felt too tired to move, and after a while felt her own eyes begin to close. Fortunately, it was too late for Dai to pay a visit. No doubt, he'd called when they were still out and would be in the King's Arms by now. She was almost asleep when there was a knock on the door and she dragged herself to her feet, laid Michael in the basket, and went to answer it. It couldn't be Dai, who always let himself in by the back way.

A plump young woman was standing outside. She wore a blue moygashel suit with a little veiled matching hat over one eye, and grinned when Ruth looked at her uncomprehendingly.

'You don't recognise me, do you?'

Ruth gasped. 'Dilys! I would never have known you. You look very grown-up—and what a lovely suit! It's terribly smart.' The girl's spots had completely gone and her skin looked fresh and clear. Her brown hair had recently been permed. 'Oh, am I glad to see you!' Ruth cried. 'Where on earth have you been? Come in, dear. Come in.' She was about to hug the girl, when a man, who'd been standing out of sight, appeared behind her.

Dilys said coyly, 'This is me husband, Reg. We only got married last week.'

'Married! Congratulations, both of you.' Ruth shook Reg's hand. He looked much older than Dilys, twice her age, at least. He was a dark, unsmiling man with thinning hair.

'This is the third time we've called today,' he said in a complaining voice. 'Have you been out somewhere?'

'We spent the day in the country,' Ruth explained, slightly taken aback by the inference she should remain at home just in case Dilys might decide to turn up out of the blue.

She stood aside to let them in. 'I've been trying to find out where you were for months, Dilys,' she said as she followed them down the hall. 'I must have written at least twenty letters.'

'I've been working in a café in Portsmouth,' Dilys began. Her tone changed. 'Oh!' she said softly.

By the time Ruth reached the living room, Dilys

448

was on her knees beside the basket on the floor. 'Is this him? Is this my baby? Look at him, Reg! Isn't he adorable?'

'He's called Michael,' Ruth said thinly, as a dreadful suspicion entered her mind. *My baby!* 'The reason I wanted to contact you, Dilys,' she said hurriedly, conscious that the words seemed thick on her lips, 'is that I'd like you to put in writing . . .'

But Dilys wasn't listening. 'Michael!' she breathed. 'Michael! It's a lovely name. In fact, it's a name I might have picked meself. Isn't he huge for six months, Reg?' She looked up at her husband, smilding childishly like the Dilys of old. 'Six months, one week, and two days. There's scarcely an hour passed since that I've not thought about him.'

She picked the baby up, and although he didn't wake, he seemed to snuggle comfortably against her breast as if he knew it was where he always should have been. Reg reached down and squeezed her shoulder. 'He's a fine little chap, love.'

Ruth watched, feeling as if the world were collapsing around her ears. *They'd come to take Michael away!* If they did, if they did—she tried to visualise a world without Michael, but couldn't, no matter how hard she tried. Once her child had gone, there wouldn't be a single reason left to stay alive.

'You've done a wonderful job, Ruth,' Dilys said gratefully. 'I knew my baby would be safe with you.'

'But, Dilys, you said . . .' Ruth stopped, unable to continue. She began to sway, and grasped the door to prevent herself from fainting. Neither Dilys or Reg noticed. They were only interested in the baby.

Reg suddenly seemed to remember Ruth was

there. He reached in his inside pocket and drew out a wallet. 'I'd like to compensate you for the expense you've had looking after Michael. Would ten pounds be enough?' He put the notes on the mantelpiece. 'We don't want any of his things, by the way. We've got all new stuff at home, and we brought enough clothes with us in the car.'

'Compensate me?' Ruth began to laugh hysterically. '*Compensate* me? You must be mad, both of you, if you think you can just walk in and take my child away.'

'He's not your child,' Dilys said pettishly. 'He's mine!' She looked uneasily at Reg as Ruth continued to laugh.

'*No!*' Ruth snatched the baby out of Dily's arms. 'He's mine! You gave him to me, remember?' She looked down tenderly at the sleeping baby. 'He's mine!'

'Now, look here!' Reg tried to drag the baby back.

'Mind you don't hurt him,' Dilys cried, and Ruth began to scream.

'*What's going on!*' Matt appeared in the doorway, looking angry and bewildered.

'Matt!' Ruth had forgotten all about him. 'Oh, Matt,' she sobbed, 'they've come for Michael. They're going to take him away from me.'

Matt was never quite sure what made him do it, but he went over and took Ruth in his arms. For better or worse, she was his wife and there was no way he would stand by and see her manhandled by a stranger. He held her trembling body, murmuring, 'Shush, now,' whilst the enormity of the situation sank in. What the hell would this do to her?

450

'And who's this?' The man who'd been struggling with Ruth was looking at Matt aggressively.

'This,' Matt said coldly, 'is Ruth's husband.'

Dilys gasped, 'I didn't know you were married, Ruth?'

'Well, she is. I suppose you're Dilys Evans.' Matt was conscious of Ruth sobbing quietly against his shoulder.

Even in the midst of the drama, Dilys managed to look coy. 'It's Dilys Harvey, actually. This is Reg, me husband.'

'They offered me ten pounds, Matt,' Ruth moaned. 'Ten pounds for my baby.'

'It's not your baby,' Reg began.

'Ten pounds?' Matt said sarcastically. 'Is that what you think Michael's worth? Where is it, the ten pounds?'

'On the mantelpiece.' Reg rubbed his forehead, as if everything was getting beyond him.

'Well, take it back if you don't mind. We neither want or need your ten pounds.'

Now it was Dilys's turn to burst into tears. 'But I want my baby,' she wailed. 'I want Michael.'

'There, love.' Reg put his arm around her shoulders. 'Don't take on so. You'll have him, don't worry.' He turned to Matt. 'If you don't give us that baby here and now, I'll fetch the police.'

'Matt!' Ruth screamed.

'Why don't we all sit down,' Matt suggested reasonably, though he felt anything but reasonable inside—he could have snapped the man's neck in two with pleasure, 'and talk this through like civilised people?' He gently manoeuvred Ruth into a chair. The other two sat down at the table, albeit reluctantly.

451

'Don't see that there's much to talk about,' Reg said churlishly.

There was silence for a few seconds. Dilys eyed Michael tearfully, as he still slept peacefully in Ruth's arms. Reg looked edgy and kept glancing worriedly at his young wife.

'Have you the remotest idea how cruel this is?' Matt said softly. 'You asked Ruth to have your baby, Dilys, and she did. She's taken care of him since the day he was born. In Ruth's eyes, Michael is *her* baby. Did you seriously think you could just turn up and snatch him out of her arms? Put yourself in her shoes. How would you feel if someone took away a child you thought was yours without a single moment's notice? Are you utterly devoid of feelings, the pair of you?' He found it hard to keep the contempt out of his voice.

'I only meant for her to look after him till I'd sorted meself out,' Dilys sniffed.

'No you didn't,' Ruth whispered. 'The whole time you were pregnant you swore you didn't want him. You called him "sinful".'

Dilys tossed her head. 'Well, I wasn't meself, was I?'

'Shush, love.' Reg had clearly been deeply affected by Matt's words and looked quite mortified. He put his hand on Dilys's arm. 'He's right. We should have written beforehand.'

'Dilys should have written a long time ago, if it was her intention to take Michael back,' Matt said.

'Why didn't you, love—write, that is?'

'Because I couldn't take care of him proper while I was single, and it never crossed me mind I'd get married, not till I met you, Reg.' Dilys looked shyly at Matt. 'We only met a month ago when he came into the café. It was what you call love at first sight.'

'She told me about the baby—about Michael,' Reg explained. 'It didn't bother me a bit about taking on another man's kid, but I'm afraid I didn't realise the situation was quite as it is.' He nodded uncomfortably in the direction of Ruth. 'I tell you what.' He stood up suddenly and pushed back his chair. 'We'll come back in a few weeks. Give the lady time to get used to the situation.'

'But, Reg, I want him now!' Dilys wailed.

'Well, you can't, love,' Reg said firmly. He looked squarely at Matt. 'She's got to have him, you realise that, don't you? I know it's cruel, like you said, and Dilys hasn't gone about it fair and proper—she told me she'd only left the baby with someone to be looked after, temporary as it were, not that she'd given him away. Even so, it's only justice that she gets the baby back.'

Matt glanced at Ruth. Her eyes were tight shut as she squeezed Michael's tiny body against her own. For an awful moment, he thought she might be squeezing the life out of him rather than hand him over to another woman.

'We'll be good parents, I promise,' Reg was saying. 'I've got my own shop, a draper's, so we're not short of a few bob. There's no need for the lady to worry about the way he's looked after.'

'Ruth,' Matt whispered, bending over her. 'Let Dilys have Michael.'

She opened her eyes, and he thought he'd never seen an expression so tragic and utterly devoid of hope. 'Must I?'

'Yes, you must.'

'Aah!' She uttered an anguished cry as she let

Dilys take the baby out of her arms, then left her arms there, empty and imploring. Michael woke up and smiled at the strange face staring down at him.

'It's best for you to take him now,' Matt said. He felt a sense of loss, not just for Ruth, but for himself. He hadn't realised how fond he'd grown of Michael. 'It would be nothing less than torture for Ruth to keep him, knowing it was only for a few weeks.'

Reg nodded in agreement. 'Whatever you say.'

Dilys laughed as she rocked the baby back and forth. 'Haven't you got a lovely smile?' she cooed.

'I think you should both go now,' Matt said quickly.

Reg glanced at Ruth. 'Perhaps we should. Come on, love.'

Dilys paused in the doorway. 'Thanks, Ruth, for everything.' But she might as well have spoken to the wall, because Ruth's face seemed to have turned to stone.

When they were outside, Reg said, 'I'm sorry about all that business before. I don't know what got into me. I suppose the thing uppermost in my mind was that I wanted my Dilys to be happy. I hope she soon gets over it, your wife.'

'I hope so, too,' Matt said as he closed the door.

*   *   *

He wouldn't have minded if she'd cried and wept, screamed out the anguish she must be feeling, but he couldn't bear the way she sat trance-like in the chair, her body like ice, her face frozen in an expression of utter despair.

'Ruth,' he pleaded for what must have been the
454

hundredth time. 'Please speak to me. Say something, please, Ruth.'

'What is there to say?'

At last! 'It's not the end, dear. What is it they say—"where there's life, there's hope".' He realised how trite and stupid the words sounded.

'There's no life for me, and there's no hope.'

'Ruth, you came through one terrible tragedy with flying colours, and you'll come through this, you'll see. Dilys will be a good mother to Michael, and although she behaved badly, he *is* her child.'

'I seem to be fated not to have children. At some stage, they are always taken from me.'

She began to cry and Matt felt relieved. Crying he could cope with. 'But Michael never was your child, Ruth,' he said gently. 'It was always on the cards that this might happen. You must have known that, somewhere deep down in your heart.'

'If I did, it never stopped me loving him as if he was my own.'

'I know. I'd become fond of him myself.' He'd already begun to miss the baby's presence. He was aware of the empty basket, the smell of milk, and noticed the empty bottle on the table. If it affected him so deeply, how must it affect Ruth?

She was still crying, deep racking sobs that seemed to tear through her body. Matt moved away and stood in front of the fire, clutching the mantelpiece. He stared into the flames and recalled the words he'd spoken in Reece's on the day he'd offered to marry her. 'I want to be of some use on this earth. I feel no use at all at the moment.'

He took a deep breath as he turned to the weeping woman, and for a moment, Eileen

Costello's lovely fresh face flashed before his eyes.

'Ruth,' he said, 'you're still young enough to have children. Why don't we start a family of our own?'

'What!' She stopped crying and looked at him, startled.

'After all, we're already married.'

He wasn't quite sure what reaction to expect. He thought she might be indignant at the suggestion, though in view of how she'd been acting over the last few weeks, she might be pleased. He was quite unprepared for the way she threw herself into his arms and began to kiss him passionately.

'Oh, Matt!' she breathed. 'There's nothing I'd like better. You're the only person in the world who can take the place of Michael. I love you, Matt. I've loved you for a long time.'

'And I love you,' Matt lied.

'Are you sure?' She clasped his face in her thin hands and stared at him intently.

Matt swallowed. 'I'm sure.'

'Then take me to bed, Matt.'

She began to drag him towards the door. Matt loosened her arms from around his neck. 'No, Ruth, not now. You don't know what you're doing, what you're saying.' She'd swung from bitterness and despair to delirium within a matter of seconds, and he knew it wasn't natural. Her eyes were fever bright in her haggard face, and even if he'd actually wanted to make love, he couldn't have done it. He said, 'I'd like you to think it over for a few days before we . . . Let's discuss it properly tomorrow.'

She looked disappointed. 'If that's what you want.'

'It's what I think is best, Ruth.'

'Shall we drink a toast?' She clapped her hands together like a child. 'There's still some rum left from Christmas.'

'I'd love a drink.' The idea was more than welcome, and it might help her sleep.

Ruth produced the rum and a couple of glasses from the sideboard. She swallowed hers in a single gulp. 'I think I'll go to bed now.'

'There's something I want to do first.'

Matt went upstairs and dismantled the baby's cot which was beside her bed, and put it in the boxroom. You never know, it might be used again, if he and Ruth . . .

As soon as she'd gone to bed, Matt finished off the rum, drinking straight from the bottle. After a while, he went upstairs and lay on the bed, fully clothed, staring at the ceiling. The nights were getting darker and you could barely see in the room. There was the sound of men's voices outside; the King's Arms must have let out and they'd all be standing on the corner of the street having a last minute jangle, as they called it, before they went home to their families. There was a burst of laughter, and he felt envious of the men who seemed to lead such uncomplicated lives compared to his own. What on earth was he doing here, in this little terraced house in Bootle, married to a woman he didn't love? He'd entered the situation quite freely, eyes wide open, yet never, in his wildest dreams, had he imagined it would turn out the way it had.

A woman called, 'Goodnight, Dad,' and he felt sure it was Eileen Costello, but when he got off the bed to look, the door of Number 16 was closed.

Shortly afterwards, the siren went, which it still

457

did from time to time, followed almost immediately by the All Clear. There'd been no raids during August. It must have been a false alarm.

Matt continued to lie there until it became dark. There was no moon that night and the blackness was total, as was the silence. Ruth must be fast asleep, thank goodness. For a brief moment, Matt considered making a quick getaway before she woke and the whole thing started up again, but the thought was rejected as fast as it came. She had no one except him, and although the marriage vows had meant nothing at the time, nevertheless he'd made them and he felt he owed her something. She was a good woman who'd had a rotten deal from life over the last few years.

The hours crept by. Matt had never felt less like sleep, yet he was on early shift tomorrow—no, today. Perhaps it might be a good idea to get undressed. He was about to get off the bed, when he heard footsteps on the landing and there was a knock on the bedroom door.

'Matt, are you awake?' Ruth called.

His heart sank and he wondered what she wanted. He dreaded another scene. 'Yes,' he said.

The door opened and she came in. 'I thought you might be. Do you mind if I put the light on?'

To his relief, she sounded quite calm. 'The curtains aren't drawn,' he warned.

'I'll see to it.'

She drew the curtains, turned the gas mantle on, and he saw she was, like him, still wearing the clothes she'd had on all day. She sat on the edge of the bed and smiled. 'I'm all right now,' she said.

Matt watched her, unsure what his reaction should be. What did she mean, she was all right

458

now?

Ruth shivered. 'It's cold in here.' She took Jacob's old overcoat from where it still hung behind the door and draped it round her shoulders. She pulled a wry face as she touched a worn cuff. 'I've been thinking about my father. You know, I'd scarcely noticed he was dead, I was so taken up with Michael.'

Her face was no longer haggard, the lines had smoothed out. In fact, her expression was as calm as her voice.

Matt continued to watch her warily, unsure as to whether this was merely another mood she'd swung into.

'Oh, Matt!' she said softly. 'You look absolutely terrified. I promise I'm not going to eat you. I've been lying on the bed all this time, just thinking: about my father, about Simon and Leah—I'd almost forgotten about my own children. The more I thought, the clearer everything became. I would have been a terrible mother to Michael. He'll be far better off with Dilys. I was trying to make up for all the things I'd done wrong with Simon and Leah. I thought, if I loved Michael hard enough and strong enough, then I'd never lose him the way I lost them.'

Matt felt his body sag with relief. She really was all right. 'I suppose it was only natural,' he said.

'And the way I behaved when Dilys came . . .'

He interrupted harshly, 'Don't be too hard on yourself, Ruth. Dilys Evans may be dim, and perhaps she didn't do it deliberately, but she used you quite ruthlessly in her own way.'

'Don't make excuses for me, Matt. I think I've been slowly going mad over the last few months.'

459

She looked at him. 'It wasn't just Michael, either. Benjy and I didn't get on well for years. I was trying to put it right through you, except that you wouldn't let me!'

'I think I realised it was something like that.'

'Poor Matt! I've really put you through the wringer, haven't I? I'm surprised you stayed.'

'It never crossed my mind to do otherwise.' Not until tonight.

'You're welcome to leave at any time. Tomorrow, if you wish.'

He looked at her dazedly. 'But what about, you know, before?'

She smiled. 'As if I would hold you to that! I feel embarrassed when I think about it. I told you, I'm all right, though I shall cry a lot over the next few days thinking about Michael. I already miss him terribly. But I don't love you, Matt, not now that I've come to my senses, and you don't love me, though it was good of you to pretend.'

'I wasn't . . .'

She put her hand on his arm. 'Yes, you were, Matt. I can't help but wonder why?'

Matt frowned and wondered why himself. 'You know,' he said, surprised, 'I think I was doing the same as you. I deserted Maria when she needed me most. I suppose I thought it would make up for what I did if I stuck by you.'

Ruth nodded. 'You didn't desert her, and I wasn't a bad mother to Simon and Leah. You're as bad as me, Matt, in your own way, both trying to put the past right in the present.'

'What will you do now?' Matt asked.

'I've thought about that, too. I shall keep on with Reece's—the pay's good and I quite enjoy it—and

460

become a piano teacher. I'll put an advert in the *Echo* next time I go into town. Quite a lot of people who know about these things will have heard of me. I had quite a good reputation in my day as a budding concert pianist. As soon as I have enough money, then I shall be off to America in search of Simon and Leah. Perhaps you can give me all those addresses you spoke of before I go.'

'I promised to come with you, didn't I?'

Ruth shrugged. 'It's up to you, Matt. I don't mind either way. As far as I'm concerned, you can leave tomorrow.' She laughed. 'I absolve you of all promises.'

Incredibly, Matt felt slightly hurt that now she was herself again he seemed to mean so little to her. 'We've only known each other a short time, but we've been through a lot together. Is that how you really feel?'

She thought a while. 'No, it's not. I like you very much, and I shall be sorry to see you go, very sorry, but I don't want you to feel under any obligation.'

'In that case, I'd sooner stay, if you don't mind.'

'I don't mind at all.'

'As I said once, we have a lot in common.'

Ruth nodded her head. 'That's right, and now we have even more, shared experiences, though not exactly pleasant. Which reminds me, did Dilys leave an address?'

Matt looked at her, frowning. 'No, and I don't think it would be a good idea to keep in touch.'

'It wasn't for me, but for Dai. I'd forgotten all about him. He'll be upset when he finds Michael's gone.'

'Reg Harvey has a draper's shop in Portsmouth. Dai Evans can easily find her if he really wants to.'

461

'I suppose so.' She stood up. 'I think I might be able to sleep now.' She turned the light out and looked through the curtains. 'It's getting light already.'

Matt groaned. 'I've got to go to work . . .' he looked at his watch, 'in two hours' time.'

'I'm sorry, it's all my fault. Would you like some cocoa?'

'I wouldn't mind, thanks,' he said, stretching. 'I don't think I shall bother sleeping myself, I doubt if I'd wake up in time. Perhaps it wouldn't be a bad idea if we bought an alarm clock?'

'Why don't you come downstairs? The BBC will be starting up shortly and I'll make breakfast. We'll have tea instead of cocoa.'

'That's not a bad idea.'

'I'll boil some water for you to get washed in.'

Ruth left. Matt put his hands behind his head and lay listening to the noises coming from downstairs: the fire was raked, the kettle filled, dishes rattled in the kitchen. He felt surprisingly contented. He heard the clip-clop of the horse's hooves on the cobbled street and the flutter of seagulls on the roof, followed by their ugly squawk. It reminded him of the bird singing its tiny heart out at the cottage, and it seemed incredible it had only happened twelve hours ago. He thought about Eileen Costello in her gingham smock, her hands resting on her stomach, her legs bare and gleaming in the sunshine, and instead of the rush of desire he always felt when she crossed his mind, there was nothing!

He sat upright on the bed, puzzled, and tried to untangle the ravel in his brain. Gradually, everything fell into place, and he realised he'd been fooling himself, telling himself he loved her when he didn't. It had merely been a way, in his mind at least, of extricating himself from Ruth's clutches. Eileen Costello was a lovely woman; they got on well together and he liked her very much, but that was all. Now that everything had been sorted out, he felt a strong desire to remain with Ruth; two lost souls who both knew all each other's secrets. What was it he'd said once which had amused her? They were 'like flotsam and jetsam thrown together on the shore!'

'Breakfast's ready, Matt!'

He got off the bed, bones aching. 'Coming, Ruth,' he called.

CHAPTER TWENTY-TWO

The baby hadn't moved for days. Perhaps it was dead, Eileen thought in a panic. She stroked her stomach through her nightdress, but could feel nothing except a hard lump. Her back started to ache and she groaned inwardly and considered turning over, but it was a major job, turning over in bed when you were eight-and-a-half-months pregnant. She felt unreasonably irritated with her sister, sleeping soundly beside her. The trouble was, Sheila kept such early hours and insisted Eileen came to bed with her.

'You need your sleep, someone in your condition.'

'I'm fed up with hearing that! You'd think I was the first woman in the world to have a baby,' Eileen complained.

'I wish I'd had someone to wait on me hand and foot each time I was expecting.'

'I don't want to be waited on hand and foot, thanks all the same. I want to *do* things. I feel full of energy.'

She'd never thought it possible, but her sister was actually beginning to get on her nerves. Sheila acted as if Number 16 was already hers. Eileen was shooed out of the kitchen, told to put her feet up, and not allowed to lift a finger, when she felt like spring-cleaning the house from top to bottom or beating the hell out of a cake.

'Still, she's only got me best interests at heart,' Eileen thought, 'even if she's killing me with kindness. It's probably me own fault, anyroad. I'm dead touchy at the moment.' She was quite likely to burst into tears at the drop of a hat.

Tomorrow, Cal would be home and perhaps Sheila's attention would be switched to him, though they still hadn't sorted out where Cal was to sleep, assuming that is he and Sheila slept together. All sorts of computations had been run through: the girls could sleep with Eileen, the boys could go in with the girls, the girls with the boys. Whichever way would cause disruption.

'I don't like the idea of you sleeping with three children, not in your condition,' Sheila said.

Neither did Eileen, whatever her condition, though she said nothing, and felt like an intruder in her own home.

Sheila folded her arms and pondered hard. 'I suppose Cal could kip down on the settee, and I'll come upstairs after . . .'

'After what?' Eileen asked innocently.

'After . . . you know.'

464

'I haven't the faintest idea what you're talking about.'

'Come off it, Sis! It sounds awfully practical though, put like that, not a bit romantic.'

'Perhaps I could sleep on the settee?' Eileen suggested. She'd never speak to her sister again if the offer was accepted.

'Don't be stupid!' Sheila said scathingly. 'As if I'd let you do that in your condition!'

And that was where the matter of Cal's sleeping arrangements rested for now.

Eileen raised herself on her elbow and glanced at the phosphorous figures on the alarm clock. Only a quarter past eleven! What person in their right mind went to bed at such an early hour when they didn't have to go to work next day? she thought indignantly. No wonder she had so much energy to spare. She was lying down, if not sleeping, for at least two hours more than she was used to.

Feeling a bit like a child doing something naughty, she threw the covers back and slithered awkwardly out of bed. She'd make herself a cup of warm milk and listen to the wireless.

Downstairs, she put the milk on the stove and re-read Nick's latest letter as she waited.

It's hot, hot, hot here, though things are far less dangerous than they were back home. Twenty of us take off on a mission, and believe it or not, twenty of us return, all safe and sound.

The post is very unreliable. I got nothing for a month, then three of your letters arrived all at once! I have since read all three at least a hundred times.

Maybe it's the heat, but I miss you more than

465

ever. I fantasise about us making love, kissing you, touching you all over . . . I feel sad that I won't see you bearing my child. Describe yourself! I imagine you looking like a beautiful hippopotamus. Eileen, my darling girl, I ache when I think of you. We must never forget what it's like being apart, such an awful, gnawing ache. Do you feel it, too? I know we'll row and perhaps say bitter things in the future, but we must try not to hurt each other ever again . . .

The milk began to simmer and Eileen folded the letter up and tucked it back in her handbag. If she read it through to the end she'd only cry. There was music on the Home Service, something classical which sounded very sad and romantic. She curled herself up in a chair as best she could and began to sip the milk as she thought about Nick. It seemed inconceivable that the day would come when the war would be over and they would live peacefully together in the cottage. She tried to imagine a normal day, waking up in Nick's arms, him going to work, Tony to school . . .

Oh, God! There were still times when she found it hard to believe her son was dead. She turned the wireless off, the music was too sad and made her want to weep for the things she'd lost and the things she'd missed.

'I'll turn it on again for the midnight bulletin,' she decided. 'Then I'll go back to bed.' She hadn't listened to the news all day and Ryan and Mary had made paper hats out of the *Daily Herald* before she'd had an opportunity to read it, which meant she hadn't a clue what was going in the world at the moment.

The Russians were suffering terribly, she knew that much. Stalin had adopted a 'scorched earth' policy, which meant the Germans might well take a town, but there was nothing left to take, everything had been destroyed in the wake of the retreating Russian Army. Last time she'd managed to catch the news, it had been announced that Kiev, the capital of the Ukraine, was about to fall.

Still, she thought, everyone at home was rallying round the Russians, raising funds and offering aid of every conceivable sort—the RAF was sending two 'Wings', whatever they were, and next week was 'Tanks for Russia' week—much to her dad's disgust.

'I'm not against the aid, of course not, but they wouldn't have given the Reds so much as a toy gun before, let alone a tank! They're nowt but bloody hypocrites, the lot of them. It's Russia this, and Russia that. Communism's suddenly become respectable, and Joseph Stalin has turned overnight into "Uncle Joe". The whole thing makes me sick.'

Eileen heard the back-yard door open and close and there was a tap on the living room window. It could only be her dad, hoping she'd be up. He'd probably come for a good old moan about something.

To her utter astonishment, it was her brother, Sean, outside.

'What on earth are you doing here?' she said, aghast. 'Come on in, luv. You look fair whacked out.'

Sean threw himself wearily into a chair. His face was pale and there were dark shadows underneath his eyes. 'Mrs Scully died last night,' he said.

Eileen looked down at him, frowning. 'How on

467

earth did you find out?' The news hadn't even reached Pearl Street yet.

'I got a telegram.'

'Did you now!' Eileen bit her lip and held her tongue. She felt sorry for Alice, but it seemed more than a little unreasonable to have fetched Sean all the way from Lincolnshire for something that had been on the cards a long time. 'Would you like something to eat?'

'I wouldn't mind a butty. I don't want nothing cooked, me belly's a bit upset.'

'All right, luv. I'll do you a bit of hot milk at the same time. We've plenty of milk at the moment, I get extra on me green ration book.'

Eileen went into the back kitchen, feeling angry. His belly was upset! Not surprising, seeing as he'd spent the day racing from one side of the country to the other. 'I'm surprised the RAF let you go,' she said. 'I thought you only got compassionate leave if it was a close relative who'd died.'

'That's why I didn't ask,' Sean said tiredly. 'I just upped and left when I got the telegram.'

'Oh, Sean!' Eileen gasped. She stopped cutting the bread and went to the doorway. 'You're not—what's it called, absent without leave?'

'AWOL, that's right,' Sean looked sulky. 'I had no choice. I had to be with Alice, didn't I?'

'No, you didn't, luv,' Eileen said indignantly. 'Alice had no right to send for you. She's stacks of neighbours who will help, and there's me! I call in every week or so.'

'That's what Alice said when I arrived. It wasn't her who sent the telegram, it was Tommy. She really laid into him in front of the neighbours.' Sean managed the glimmer of a smile. 'He'll be
468

turning up for work tomorrer with a big bruise on his chin. Y'see,' he explained, suddenly very grown up, 'Tommy looks on me as a dad. They all do, the little ones. I was the first person Tommy thought of when his mam died.'

'You were always a flighty bugger, our Sean, but you weren't at the girls when you were only four!' Eileen returned to the kitchen. 'So, Alice wasn't very pleased to see you, then?'

'Not in the least,' Sean said ruefully. 'She really blew her top. Then she flew at Tommy, and chucked me out! She said the sooner I got back to camp, the less trouble I'd be in.'

'Here you are, luv, here's your butty. I've done a few more to take back with you.'

'I don't need them yet, Eil. I thought I'd stay the night here. I daren't go round to me dad's, he'll kill me.'

'No, Sean.' Eileen shook her head firmly. 'Alice is right. The sooner you get back, the better. The minute you've drunk your milk and eaten your butty, you can sod off. Have you got enough money for your train fare?'

'I've scarcely got a penny. I hitched a lift all of the way home.'

'In that case, I'll give you a couple of quid. You can catch a train from Marsh Lane Station. It's not yet midnight, so they'll still be running.'

Sean looked at his sister anxiously. 'You won't tell me dad I've been back, will you?'

'Of course I won't, and I won't tell Sheila, either. Unless they hear it from someone else, it'll be a secret between the two of us.'

'Ta, Eil.'

She felt her heart contract as he rapidly ate the

469

food and then forced himself to stand. He was clearly exhausted. 'Oh, luv!' She pressed her cheek against his and said cautiously, 'This would never have happened if you'd taken up with a different sort of girl.'

'I know, Sis, but it's Alice I love,' Sean said simply.

Eileen nodded. 'So you do! As for going AWOL, or whatever it's called, as far as I'm concerned, I'm proud of you, Sean Doyle. I hope you don't get into too much trouble.' If the telegram had been a test, then Sean had passed with flying colours. Her little brother had become a man that day.

'I just wish Alice had been a bit more pleased to see me,' he said sadly.

So do I, Eileen thought. She said, 'She probably was, deep down. She's a good girl at heart, is Alice Scully. You'll do well with her.' She took his arm. 'C'mon, leave by the front way and I'll close the door quiet, like. Oh, and another thing, Sean,' she said when he was on the pavement. 'You're not to be scared of our dad any more. You're eighteen, you're getting married at Christmas, and you're fighting for your country. If Dad ever dares raise his voice to you again, then tell him to go to hell!'

For some reason Sean looked as if he was about to cry. 'All right, Eil,' he said.

She watched him till he turned the corner, looking stooped and old, then closed the door and burst into tears herself.

*   *   *

Next morning after breakfast, Eileen went round to the Scullys'. As soon as formal condolences had been offered in the presence of several neighbours who sat drinking tea and smoking around the table, Alice dragged Eileen into the back kitchen. Her huge grey eyes were anxious with worry. 'Did Sean turn up at your house last night?' she demanded, agitated.

'He did, too. I fed him, gave him some money and sent him on his way.'

'Was he all right? Oh, I'm terrible, me,' Alice wailed. 'I threw him out I was so annoyed, and as for our Tommy, I could have killed him!'

'I understand you nearly did!'

'Fancy sending a telegram like that! As if I couldn't have coped meself.' She thrust her tiny chin forward and said haughtily, 'I've no intention of being a burden, you know. That's what you're all worried about, isn't it?'

'I'm not worried a bit,' Eileen replied reasonably, 'though seeing as we're being straight with each other, I must say your temper bothers me. Poor Sean had been travelling all day and he was dead tired. I reckon a warmer welcome wouldn't have come amiss.'

Alice started to cry. 'No, it wouldn't, would it? If only last night could happen again, then I'd throw me arms around him, honest.'

'Never mind, luv.' Eileen patted the girl's shoulder. 'Please don't cry, else you'll have me crying with you. I'm in that sort of mood, I'm afraid. Anyroad, who am I to criticise? I've done the same thing meself before now, lost me temper, then been sorry when it was too late.' She'd walked out on Nick just because he said something tactless, and had regretted it ever since.

Alice stopped crying. 'Would you like to say tara

471

to me mam?' she sniffed. 'She's all laid out in the bedroom.'

Eileen nodded, though saying goodbye to a dead woman was the last thing she felt like doing at the moment.

*　　*　　*

When she got home, Pearl Street was full of children enjoying their last few days of freedom before they went back to school on Monday. Most of the boys were kicking a football against the railway wall, though a few clambered over the ruins of the three demolished houses and threw bricks at the walls that still remained. Aggie Donovan came out and shook her scrawny fist at them.

'I'll fetch that bloody Hitler to you if you don't sod off, the lot o'yis!' she screeched. 'Little buggers,' she said as Eileen waddled past. 'Don't know what sort of homes they come from.'

Eileen checked hastily to see if Dominic and Niall were there, but her nephews were playing football. The boys disappeared from the ruins, and as soon as Aggie slammed the door, they returned, whooping. The girls whizzed up and down the street with their skipping ropes or played hopscotch on the pavement.

'I used to love hopscotch when I was a little girl,' Eileen said wistfully. Siobhan and Caitlin had chalked the grid directly outside her house, or what used to be her house!

'Would you like a go, Auntie Eileen?'

'No, ta,' she grinned. 'I'd have a job picking the stone up, wouldn't I?' She thought nostalgically about her own school holidays. The weeks seemed

472

to stretch ahead into infinity when you first broke up in the summer, and going back was a bit like starting a life sentence. Nowadays, time seemed to flash by. It seemed like only yesterday that the holidays had started, yet it was nearly six weeks! Before you knew it, it would be Christmas and 1942!

'Me dad's home,' Caitlin called as Eileen was about to go inside.

'Hello, luv.' Calum Reilly kissed his sister-in-law on the cheek. 'You're a sight for sore eyes, I must say. When's the baby due?'

'In about ten days.'

'I bet you can't wait.'

Sheila emerged from the back kitchen, all starry-eyed and flushed. 'Cal's brought you a prezzie, Eil. Where is it, luv?'

'On the mantelpiece.'

'A scarf!' Eileen cried. 'Oh, it's lovely, Cal—and real silk, too! I love the colours.' She draped the pastel patterned scarf around her shoulders. 'It's ever so big, more like a shawl than a scarf.'

'Where've you been?' Sheila asked.

'Miller's Bridge. Mrs Scully died the other day.'

'God rest her soul, poor woman.' Sheila blessed herself. 'I'll buy a wreath and send it round.'

'Perhaps it would be best if you took it yourself, Sheil. It's about time you got to know Alice better. She's marrying Sean at Christmas, and from then on she'll be one of the family.'

'Aye, I suppose you're right.' Sheila nodded reluctantly.

'We'll take it together, luv,' Cal said. 'And I can introduce meself to this Alice.'

'As long as you promise to watch your manners,'

Sheila said grimly, 'else she's quite likely to give you a clout!'

'I'm gasping for a cuppa, Sis. Is there any tea made?'

'I've just put the kettle on. Now, come on, Eil, sit down and put your feet up. Move that stool over, Cal. You shouldn't have walked all the way to Miller's Bridge, not in your condition.'

'If you mention my condition again, Sheila Reilly, it's you that's likely to get the clout!'

*   *   *

Eileen gave a little sigh of satisfaction when she went into Brenda Mahon's parlour, where Brenda was bent over her sewing machine, her mouth full of pins. There were lengths of material strewn everywhere and the picture rail was hung with more garments than it had ever been before.

'It's nice seeing the place the way it used to be,' Eileen remarked. 'I really missed it when you stopped sewing all that time. Even when I wanted nothing made, I loved it in here. It always reminds me of Aladdin's cave.'

Brenda gave a little pleased nod. 'I hope you don't want nothing made at the moment, Eil,' she said through the pins, 'because I'm dead busy.'

Eileen began to wander around the room, examining the finished and half-finished clothes. 'I do, actually, but I'm not in any hurry. Remember that dress you made me, the lavender one with the high neck and long sleeves?'

'Of course I remember. In fact, I was just finishing the hem when Carrie Banks turned up. What about it?'

474

'I wondered if you could make another exactly the same in a different colour? I can't try it on, obviously, but if you went by the first, it's bound to fit once I've had the baby.'

Brenda frowned as she eased a sleeve into the bodice of a green brocade frock. 'Okay, though what about a V neck instead of high, just for a change, like?'

'Anything you say, Bren,' Eileen said easily. 'This is lovely! Did you make it?' The long red sleeveless dress hanging from the wall was lavishly decorated with silk embroidery and sequins down the front.

'Nah! I'm going to shorten it and make sleeves out of the piece I cut off, just so's it'll look different. I'm doing a lot of alterations lately,' Brenda said happily. 'Since coupons came in, all the posh women are having their old clothes re-modelled. I love turning old things into new.'

Eileen pointed to the green brocade draped over the machine. 'What's that you're making?'

'A dance dress, but you'll never guess, Eil, this is an old curtain. You wouldn't believe the things I'm given to make clothes from. See that length of wine silk on the settee? It's only a bedspread! And I'm going to turn those two old costumes hanging on the wall into one.'

'What's this?' Eileen picked up a round piece of cream felt with a brim of large pointed petals.

'What does it look like? It's a hat, of course.'

'Can I try it on?'

'If you like. It's not finished yet. It needs a little veil.'

Eileen tucked her hair behind her ears and placed the pillbox hat on the side of her head. 'What d'you think?'

Brenda regarded her thoughtfully. 'It looks dead nice. I got the idea in the middle of the night and I couldn't wait to get started this morning. I've never made a hat before. It's not for anyone in particular, like, just an experiment.'

'Where did you get the felt?'

Brenda grinned. 'It's Xavier's old fedora.'

'He'll kill you if he finds out!'

'Huh! Xavier can jump in the lake as far as I'm concerned.'

'D'you ever hear from him?' Eileen asked curiously.

'He writes from time to time, but I don't bother to open his letters. I just throw them straight onto the fire.'

'Good for you, girl!' Eileen said warmly. She looked at herself in the mirror, transferred the hat to the back of her head and asked casually, 'What about that Vince?'

Brenda frowned again as she turned the second sleeve. 'Who?'

'Vince, you know, your boyfriend.'

'He never was my boyfriend, Eil,' Brenda said indignantly. 'He was just a friend, that's all. Actually,' she leaned on the machine and rested her chin in her hand, 'now's I come to think of it, I haven't seen Vince in a while. He must have got fed up coming round and always finding me so busy.'

'Who needs men, eh?'

'You're dead right, Eil. Who needs 'em?' Brenda regarded Eileen exasperatedly as she began to root through the material on the settee. 'Is that all you've got to do? As I already said, I'm dead busy, and you're getting on me nerves, hovering round like a wasp. I feel as if I'd like to swat you.'

Eileen cleared a space and sat down with a deep sigh. Brenda winced as the settee creaked underneath her weight. 'To tell the truth, Bren,' she complained, 'I'm bored to tears and our Sheila won't let me do a bloody thing. I can't read a book or listen to the wireless, because it's like bedlam over there, the kids are in and out by the minute. Not only that, Cal arrived home this morning, and I don't half feel in the way. I don't know what to do with meself at the moment.'

'What about the WVS? I thought you still lent a hand there?'

'I did until recently. They suggested I gave it up for a while. Is there anything I can do for you?' she asked eagerly. 'Start on the dinner, or something?'

'You must be joking! Your Sheila would have a fit if I let you. I tell you what, why don't you go along to Stanley Road and buy the material for your frock? What colour did you fancy?'

'Can I have this hat?'

'If you like.'

Eileen was getting the distinct feeling she wasn't wanted and Brenda would have agreed to give her almost anything to get rid of her. 'I'll pay you for it, of course.'

'You can have it for free. I've got a bit of net somewhere.'

'In that case, I'd like me dress in cream as well, though I can't buy the stuff today, it's half day closing.'

'Take a bit of felt to match it when you do.' Brenda picked up the remains of the fedora off the floor. 'I didn't half enjoy cutting this to pieces. I might well do the same thing with the other ten.'

'Ta. Oh, by the way, will you make something

smart for our Sheila? She hasn't had anything new in years—and perhaps a frock each for the girls.'

'Of course I will, but Sheila hasn't mentioned anything about it.'

'That's 'cos I haven't told her yet. It's a surprise.'

*   *   *

Although Brenda didn't know it, she'd just been asked to make Eileen's wedding dress. Once finished, the dress would be hung in the wardrobe of the cottage where Eileen would be living in a few weeks' time, ready for when Nick came home and they got married.

Eileen stood outside Brenda's house wondering where to go next. She decided to call on Ruth Singerman, but no one answered when she knocked on the door, and she remembered, it being Wednesday, Ruth would be at Reece's.

'Damn!' Eileen muttered. 'I feel a bit like a waif and stray with no home to go to.' There was no one else she felt like talking to, and if she went home, Sheila would only insist she put her feet up and did nothing and she'd feel a bit like a wallflower with Cal there.

A football landed at her feet. She aimed a kick at it and missed. 'They wouldn't take me on at Everton, would they?' she said to the boy who collected it.

'Not bloody likely!' the boy said cheekily as he dribbled the ball around her feet.

'Don't swear,' she said automatically, but the boy was already out of earshot.

She thought about going to the matinee at the pictures, but she'd only cry if it was a sad film—she

478

could well cry if it was funny—and, anyroad, she'd never been to the pictures by herself before, and it would feel peculiar sitting all alone.

'I know! I'll go down the Docky!'

It must be almost a year to the day since she'd last wandered along the Dock Road and met Donnie Kennedy. Francis had just arrived home, and she remembered how utterly wretched she'd felt, thinking about how she'd let Nick down.

She crossed over to Number 16 and poked her head into the hall. 'I'm going down the Docky, Sis,' she yelled.

A muffled reply came from the parlour and she noticed the door was closed. 'Don't go too far now, luv, not in your condition.'

*   *   *

It was as if someone had removed the heart from the city and beaten it to a pulp, yet the heart stubbornly refused to die, refused to stop pumping the vital lifeblood to the body it had sustained for more than two centuries, and continued to throb and beat, gradually getting stronger, greater, and more vibrant than it had ever been before.

Eileen Costello's own heart swelled when she turned into the Dock Road, which seemed to be literally pulsating with people and traffic and noise in the tingling Liverpool sunshine. Funnel after funnel rose majestically above the remains of the great walls, and cranes turned to and fro, the enormous loads swinging precariously as they were loaded on or loaded off the ships.

Eileen smiled as she began to stroll in the direction of Liverpool. She walked past the gates of the Gladstone Dock, where she and Sheila used to wait for Dad when they were little. Life had seemed so uncomplicated in those days, though she supposed the grown-ups had a struggle to exist from day to day. She could scarcely remember the Great War, when her dad had fought in France, and wondered if the whole country had been turned as upside down as it was now. Everything, everybody, seemed to have been touched by the conflict in some way or other.

She passed a group of sailors wearing strange uniforms with big white floppy collars, rather girlish in their way. One of them made a huge circle with his arms and called something in a foreign language and his mates laughed. A man in front of her in a formal black suit and wearing a trilby, who was about to go inside a ship's chandler's, paused, his hand on the door.

'He said you were an adorable and magnificent mother!'

Eileen, embarrassed, muttered something incomprehensible in reply.

There were sailors everywhere, of all different nationalities and in the most peculiar get-ups. She paused and watched as a great horde of them came pouring out of Alexandra Dock looking around them excitedly, as if they'd only just arrived in Liverpool, the greatest port in the world. She felt as if she were standing at the very hub of the universe, the place where everything began and ended.

And then a voice whispered in her ear, 'Penny for them!'

'Nick!' she said faintly.

She turned abruptly, stumbling, and found herself caught up in a pair of strong, familiar arms, and there he was, looking down at her with his lovely brown eyes and grinning from ear to ear.

'Nick?' she said again. She grabbed his shoulders. There was actually real flesh and bone underneath her fingers. She had thought she was having hallucinations on top of everything else. 'You're real!' she breathed. 'I thought I was seeing things.'

'Oh, my love! My dearest girl, my darling Eileen.' He rocked her back and forth, regardless of the passers-by who were glancing with amused indulgence at the tall, handsome RAF officer embracing his very pregnant wife—well, somebody's wife. 'You look beautiful, big and very beautiful. I knew you would!'

'What on earth are you doing here?' she cried. 'Why didn't you let me know you were coming? How did you know where I was?'

He continued to hold her. 'Questions, questions,' he groaned. 'I fly all the way from North Africa and drive through the night to see my girl and all I get is questions. Aren't you pleased I'm here?'

'Of course, I am.' She began to cry. It was impossible to have been more pleased about anything. 'Of course I am.'

'There now, don't cry.' He wiped her face with his handkerchief. 'Come on, let's go home. When I arrived in Pearl Street, Sheila told me you'd gone to some mysterious place called "the Docky", so me and your brother-in-law set off post haste in search of you. Cal's gone to look the other way.' He began to lead her along the road, his arm around her shoulders.

'But what are you doing here?'

481

Her heart lifted at the thought he might be home for good, but it didn't lift for long. Nick replied, 'The Squadron's being sent to Russia in support of Uncle Joe.'

'Jaysus!' She stopped in her tracks. 'Oh, Jaysus, Nick. That's more dangerous than anything you've ever done before.'

'Not for me, it isn't,' he said boastfully. 'I lead a charmed life. I've made a pact with my maker and he's promised nothing will ever happen to Nick Stephens.'

'Don't pretend, luv,' she said gently.

His face became serious. 'We all pretend, darling. We have to. It's what keeps us going.' He kissed her softly on the lips. 'Anyway, we're taking off from Northolt tomorrow afternoon, which means we have about ten hours together. I have to leave at midnight.'

'Ten hours!' she breathed tremulously. 'There's not a lot we can do in ten hours, is there?'

'I can think of one thing straight away, but I don't suppose that's on at the moment.' He looked down at her vast stomach. 'However, there's something else we can do, possibly more important . . .' He paused and looked mysterious.

She dug him in the ribs with her elbow. 'Stop codding me, Nick. What is it?'

He waved a piece of paper in front of her face. 'We can get married! I've got a special licence.'

'What?' She stopped again and looked at him askance. His brown eyes were dancing and his face quite literally glowed with happiness. She thought she had never loved him so much as she did at that moment. As they stood stationary on the pavement, a horse and cart rattled past, people

482

jostled against them, and a ship's hooter sounded three times on the river. Eileen only half heard or half noticed the activity and the noises all around her. Time seemed to stand still, and all she was conscious of was the piece of white paper which Nick held in his hand. She had nothing to wear. There was no time to arrange a reception, but most importantly of all, it just wasn't done, getting married when you were eight-and-a-half-months pregnant. What on earth would the priest think? As for the neighbours, their tongues would wag for months.

'All right,' she said. What did all these things matter when compared to the look on her beloved Nick's face?

'Phew!' he said, relieved. 'I had a feeling you'd raise all sorts of objections. I was all prepared for a marathon argument, though there was no way I would have taken no for an answer.'

Eileen gave a long shuddering sigh, and Nick said with some concern, 'What's the matter, darling?'

'I feel all funny inside. I can't believe this is happening.'

'Well, it is, I can assure you. All the arrangements have been made. I've been rushing around like a mad thing since I arrived in Liverpool this morning.'

'You've been here since this morning?'

'I got the licence, and I've been to see the priest in that little church in Melling. The wedding's booked for four o'clock, which gives us,' he looked at his watch, 'two and a half hours. What shall we do till then?'

She looked at him, scandalised. 'What do you

mean, "what shall we do till then?" I've got to get ready.'

'But you look beautiful as you are!' Nick protested.

'I'm not getting married in this ould smock, I've got a decent one at home. And I've got to do me hair, change me stockings, get made up, look for a hat—there's a million things to do. In fact, we'd better get a move on.'

They met Cal on the way back. 'There you are!' he beamed.

Eileen waited until they were in the house before she made the announcement. 'Nick and me are getting married in Melling at four o'clock this afternoon!'

Sheila screamed. 'You can't! Not in your condition.'

'I can, and I am, Sheil, so don't waste your breath trying to stop me,' Eileen said in a voice that brooked no argument.

'Oh, all right, but I've got nothing to wear.'

'Neither have I, but it's not stopping me.'

'Jaysus, our Eileen,' Sheila complained. 'Trust you to spring something like this on us without a word of warning. Another thing, the larder's virtually bare. We were having snoek and cabbage for tea, which isn't exactly what you'd term wedding food.'

'But we don't need food,' Nick put in hastily. 'In fact, we don't need anything. There'll only be the two of us. The priest said he can provide two witnesses.'

'You must be joking!' Sheila looked at Nick as if he was mad. 'D'you seriously think I'd let me own sister get married all on her own? And what about me dad?' she demanded. 'He'll have a cob on for the rest of his life if he doesn't give her away.' She went to the front door and yelled, 'Dominic? Niall? One of you come in this minute.'

Niall came rushing in, 'What is it, Mam?'

'I want you to run down to the Docky as fast as you can and tell them on the gate that Jack Doyle's girl is getting married in Melling at four o'clock and they'll let him off early. You know which entrance, don't you?'

'Yes, Mam,' Niall said importantly.

'And don't tell anybody else,' Sheila shouted as he was halfway down the hall, 'We don't want the whole street knowing.' She looked Eileen up and down. 'Not with her looking the way she does.'

Cal said, 'What d'you say you and me go for a bevy, Nick?'

'Good idea.' Nick looked relieved. 'I was wondering how to make myself scarce for a while.'

'Tara, luv,' Sheila said absently as the men both left. 'Eileen, have you got any decent stockings?'

'I don't think I have, no,' Eileen answered, panic-stricken.

'Neither have I. I'll send our Siobhan round to Veronica's for a couple of pairs. What about flowers? You'd like a little posy, wouldn't you? I wouldn't mind a buttonhole meself—but what'll I pin it onto!' Sheila looked distraught. 'Jaysus, Sis, I've only got two frocks and one's as old as the hills and the other's second-hand. And I lost all me hats, except for that woolly one, in the blitz . . .'

'What about the pink costume I wore for Annie Poulson's wedding?'

'It'll never go near me. I'm much bigger round the hips than you are.'

'Me blue crêpe-de-chine, then, it's a bit fuller—it'd go well with me navy-blue beret.' Eileen remembered she'd ordered wedding outfits for all of them earlier in the day, but never mind, they'd do for when Sean and Alice got married.

'I'll try it on in a minute. How are we supposed to get out to Melling, the lot of us?' Sheila said, suddenly indignant. 'Why couldn't Nick have arranged it at St Joan of Arc's?'

'Because he thought there's be just the two of us,' Eileen explained patiently. 'But he's got a car. You and Cal can go in the back with me dad if he gets here on time.'

'But what about the kids? He can't fit six kids in an' all. They'll want to see their only auntie getting married.'

'Are you sure, Sheil? You're turning this into a great big do all of a sudden.'

'Well, people only get married once in their lives, don't they?'

'Not everyone, Sheil. This is me second time, remember?'

'Jaysus, I forgot.'

A voice called down the hall, 'Are you there, Eileen?'

'It's Aggie,' Sheila mouthed, making a face. 'Come on in, Aggie.'

Aggie Donovan came bustling in, her face shining with excitement. 'Well, you could have knocked me down with a feather when I heard the news. Getting married, eh? That's a bit sudden, isn't it, Eileen?'

'Who told you?' Sheila asked sharply,

'Your Niall did. He shouted it out to the whole street.'

'The little bugger!'

Aggie folded her arms on her chest and regarded Eileen with sly, curious eyes. 'I suppose it's that big RAF chap I saw walking down the road with Calum Reilly?

Eileen nodded numbly.

'I thought as much!' Aggie said with a satisfied look, as if she'd known all along there was something going on. 'Anyroad, luv, you don't need to worry about the food for the reception. I've started on a cake—I managed to get some sultanas last week, but it's a pity there won't be time to ice it—and Millie Harrison's doing some cheese sarnies. Paddy O'Hara's gone round to see if there's any biscuits in the shops—they can allus find him odds and ends, him being blind, like—and Brenda's making one of those eggless sponges.'

'But Aggie,' Eileen said faintly. 'We weren't going to have a reception, and it's all the way out in Melling.'

'I know, luv, but Millie said the buses run quite frequent. She reckons we can get there in plenty of time. Well, I'll love you and leave you for the moment. I expect you'll be dead busy getting ready over the next couple of hours.'

She left, and Eileen and Sheila looked at each other and burst out laughing. 'This street! I don't know how you can bring yourself to leave it!' Sheila said eventually. 'Well, I suppose we'd better get a move on. Your other smock needs ironing, for one thing, and I'd better try your blue frock on.'

*   *   *

Over the next hour, Pearl Street became a hive of

activity. Women went into one another's houses, their faces creased purposefully, borrowing a quarter of margarine or a cup of sugar or in search of a precious egg. Frocks were ironed, hats brushed, shoes cleaned and best jewellery given a spit and polish. May Kelly brought Eileen a bottle of whisky and eight Easter eggs which she hadn't managed to get rid of. She was quickly despatched to buy a posy of flowers and six buttonholes if they were available. Unfortunately, as she regretfully explained, flowers weren't available on the black market. Mack, the landlord of the King's Arms, offered a crate of beer at a reduced price.

'I'm sorry, Eileen, but I can't afford to give it free, like.'

'Thanks, Mack. I'll pay you later,' Eileen said, doing her best to sound grateful. Nick would do his nut when he came back and discovered there was going to be a full-blown reception after the wedding.

Brenda Mahon came just as Mack was leaving. 'You know that hat you liked, well I found a bit of cream net and tacked it on. It'll look lovely with your navy blue smock, if that's what you're wearing.'

'Oh, ta, Bren!' Eileen said gratefully. 'That means our Sheila can have me white straw boater.'

'Is there anything else you want?'

'Yes, there is, actually. Seeing as how we're having a bit of a do, like, perhaps you could stick a note through Ruth Singerman's door and tell her what's happening? She might like to come if she gets back in time.'

'Okay, Eileen.'

'Is that you, Brenda?' Sheila called downstairs.

'Can I borrow your pearl necklace?'

'Yes, but the stuff's started peeling off the beads at the back.'

'That doesn't matter, that part'll be under me collar.'

Gradually, the activity ceased, and everyone who was in Pearl Street that Wednesday afternoon left to catch the bus to Melling.

'I'll see you in church, luv?' Sheila hugged her sister. The blue frock was a bit too snug around her waist, but with the white boater on her brown curly hair and her face carefully made up for once, she looked remarkably like the comely, flirtatious young girl who'd married Calum Reilly nearly a decade before.

'Why don't you wait for Nick and Cal to come back and we'll all go in the car?' Eileen pleaded, suddenly frightened of being left alone.

'I'd sooner not trust the kids with anyone else on the buses. Anyroad, I've got to let all that lot in the cottage to lay out the food, haven't I? I'm not leaving Aggie free to poke around.'

'Sheil!' Eileen called just as her sister was leaving. 'Give Kate Thomas a ring when you get there.' When Sheila's face fell, she added, 'If you're too scared to use the telephone, I'm sure one of the kids'll work out how to do it. There's one of them directory things on the table under the phone.'

After Sheila had gone, Eileen powdered her nose and applied her lipstick. She combed her hair back smoothly, clipped on her pearl drop earrings and put the hat that had been made out of Xavier Mahon's fedora on the side of her head.

She stared at her pale reflection in the mirror. In an hour's time she would be Nick's wife, Mrs Nick

489

Stephens. She said the words aloud, 'Mrs Nick Stephens.'

'Oh, God, I'm going to cry!'

Fortunately, her dad came marching down the hall dressed in his best suit. 'Have you seen Nick and Calum?' he demanded.

'No, Dad. They've gone for a drink.'

'I know that, girl,' he said irritably. 'I meant, have you seen the state they're in? They're outside, pissed as lords, the pair of them.'

'Oh, no!'

Nick was leaning on the Kellys' windowsill, giggling uncontrollably. 'We decided to wet the baby's head in advance,' he hiccupped when he saw Eileen.

'You're a bloody idiot, you!' She did her best to keep a straight face. 'Look at the state you're in! Where's Calum?'

'Over there!'

Calum was standing on the pavement staring at the vacant space where Number 21 used to be. 'Me house has gone!' he called, his face a picture of bewilderment. 'It was there a few minutes ago, and now it's gone.'

'Oh, well!' Jack said indulgently. 'I suppose they're just letting off a bit of steam. I've never seen Cal drunk before, and life hasn't been exactly easy for the two of them over the last couple of years, has it?'

'You're not fit to drive a car,' Eileen said exasperatedly to Nick. 'Where is it, by the way?'

'There's a big black Humber parked around the corner,' Jack said.

Nick saluted. 'That, sir, is probably mine. I can't remember the colour when I borrowed it, nor do I

490

recall if it was a Humber. However, I know for certain I parked it around the corner.' He turned to Eileen. 'Are you suggesting I'm not fit to fly a car?'

'Go and splash your face this instant,' Eileen ordered. 'And you, too, Cal,' she shouted. 'We'll have to leave soon.'

'But how can I,' Cal looked on the verge of tears, 'when there's no sink?'

'There's a sink over here you can use. Come on!'

Nick was looking at Eileen, eyes half closed and a stupid grin on his face. 'We'd better do as she says,' he said out of the side of his mouth when Cal came wandering over looking lost and forlorn, 'else Lord knows what she might do to us. She's a fine looking woman, though, isn't she, if a trifle overweight?'

Eileen gave an exaggerated sigh of resignation. 'I'll skin you both alive, if you're not careful. It's a good job there's no neighbours about to witness this performance.'

'Don't worry, luv, I'll sort them out,' Jack Doyle said. 'Come on, Nick, there's a good lad. Don't forget, you're getting married at four o'clock this afternoon.'

CHAPTER TWENTY-THREE

It was the strangest wedding anyone in Pearl Street had ever witnessed: the bride with her belly fit to bust at any minute, the groom, a handsome officer in the RAF, with his collar askew and a silly smile on his face throughout the entire ceremony. Even the best man, Cal Reilly, didn't appear quite sure where he was, and the female organist looked at least a hundred and had to be prodded awake every time she was supposed to play. It was a wedding in a million, one they'd remember for as long as they lived, and they wished, oh, how they wished, they knew the truth behind it all . . .

The tiny sun-drenched church was almost full. Just as the bride was about to walk up the aisle on Jack Doyle's arm, a pile of strange women came pouring in and sat at the back, most of them dressed, believe it or not, in navy-blue overalls, which only added to the bizarreness of the occasion.

'What a pity Francis Costello isn't here to see it,' Aggie Donovan thought wistfully, entirely forgetting that if Francis had been there the wedding wouldn't have taken place. Just as the priest asked the question, 'Do you take this woman to be your lawfully wedded wife . . .' the air-raid siren sounded in the distance, and Aggie noticed Sheila Reilly's shoulders stiffen, and she remembered it was considered an unlucky omen for the siren to go when you were getting married. Still, that was probably a load of ould cobblers, Aggie decided.

Instead of answering, 'I do,' the bridegroom hiccupped, 'Yes, please.'

Aggie leaned forward and seized Sheila's arm. 'Is he a Catholic, Sheil?'

'He was lapsed,' Sheila whispered curtly back, 'until this morning.'

The children had been in the garden of the cottage and stripped every rose of its petals, so that when the newly married couple emerged from the church they were showered with rose petals. Eileen

Costello, no, Eileen Stephens, looked rather like a rose herself, everyone thought, all flushed and pink and creamy and a fraction overblown at the moment.

The women in overalls disappeared at that point, though Lord knows what it was they said to Eileen before they went, because they left her in a terrible state, virtually helpless with laughter, to such a degree someone had to rush inside the church in search of a chair and a glass of water.

They came pouring out of the churchyard, the entire crowd feeling infused with unnaturally high spirits, as if the oddness of the situation and its suddenness had evoked some rarely felt emotion, and marched up the High Street singing 'Here comes the bride, fifty inches wide'. People came out to their gates to watch. Eileen, who was arm in arm with Nick at the head of the unruly procession, protested vainly, 'Be quiet, you're making a show of us!'

The food was already laid out when they arrived at the cottage and six bottles of wine had miraculously appeared from somewhere. 'Perhaps Jesus sent it,' Siobhan said knowledgably, but it turned out later to be Jack Doyle's contribution towards his daughter's wedding.

'It smells dead lovely here,' Paddy O'Hara said, as everyone spilled out into the garden with their drink and sandwiches. 'Take me to a tree someone, I'd like to lean against it. I haven't leant against a tree with a mug of beer in me hand since I left Ireland when I was a lad.'

As soon as Paddy had been tanked up sufficiently, he was pressed to play his mouth organ and they all began to dance.

'Eileen!' Ruth Singerman found Eileen sitting exhausted on a deck chair. 'We've just arrived. Congratulations! I've brought you a present. I'm afraid there wasn't time to wrap it.'

'Jacob's musical box!' Eileen cried, delighted. She opened the little blue and pink enamelled box and *The Blue Danube* tinkled out. 'I always loved this, but how can you bear to give it away?'

'You were more of a daughter to Jacob than I was for a long time. I think he would have wanted you to have it.'

'He's probably up there, watching, y'know, his fingers itching to get at his ould piano!' Eileen clasped Ruth's hand. 'Ta, luv. I'll treasure it for as long as I live.' She looked at the woman keenly. Ruth had taken Michael's cruel removal far better than anyone would have expected and the loss seemed to have made her and Matt grow closer than they'd been before, though a keen observer might have noticed they seemed more like great friends than lovers. 'We've come through, haven't we, you and I?'

Ruth glanced at Matt, who was laughing at something Brenda Mahon had just said. He looked thoroughly at home. Perhaps he sensed Ruth was watching, because he smiled and waved. 'I think we have,' she said.

'Are you happy, luv?' Jack Doyle asked his daughter, though it was a silly question to ask. Her radiant face already told him the answer.

'What do you think, Dad?

He gave one of his rare smiles. 'I reckon you're happy. He's a fine lad is Nick—and Cal's the salt of the earth, too. Me daughters have both got good husbands. I'm a lucky man in that respect.' He

494

shook his head sadly. 'It's a pity about our Sean.'

Eileen seized his arm impatiently. 'Your son will have a good wife, Dad, I promise. Alice Scully will bring out the best in Sean.'

'Well, we'll just have to see about that, won't we? I see that Kate woman's here. I'd like a word with her about those tomato plants she gave me.'

Oh, yes, she was happy, Eileen thought as she watched him walk away, but there was one thing that would have made her happier. From time to time, she thought she saw a glimpse of Tony's fair head amongst the children chasing each other across the dappled grass. He'd always wanted to have Nick for a dad . . .

'What are you staring at?' Nick came up behind and put his hands on her shoulders.

'A little ghost.'

'That would have made it perfect, wouldn't it?'

Eileen nodded, sighing, 'Dead perfect.'

Paddy O'Hara began to play *The Wild Colonial Boy* on his mouth organ, and, tired of dancing, everyone sat down on the lawn and began to sing. The sun slipped behind a cloud and a gust of wind suddenly lashed the trees, dislodging a shower of leaves which floated lazily to the ground like red and gold butterflies. Eileen shivered.

'I hope it's not a rude question,' Nick said amiably, 'but what time are this lot likely to make themselves scarce?'

'You don't mind, do you?' She put her hand on his and looked up at him, worried. He'd envisaged a wedding with just the two of them there.

He squeezed her shoulders. 'I don't mind a bit. In fact, I've enjoyed myself tremendously. It's like belonging to a great big family.'

'Our Sheila's already started tidying up.' She could hear the clink of dishes being washed in the back kitchen and Siobhan and Caitlin had been despatched to all four corners of the garden in search of stray glasses. 'Me dad'll get rid of them all shortly. There's a bus at half past seven. Anyroad, it looks as if it might rain.'

'Will he get rid of himself at the same time? I'd like at least a few hours alone with my new wife.'

*   *   *

'So,' said Nick, 'we did it!'

'So we did.'

They stood facing each other from the far ends of the room. Everyone had gone, merrily drunk most of them, and the cottage felt abnormally quiet, though the wind had become a gale outside and the trees were rustling wildly. Birds sang and the sound seemed louder than usual, almost angry, as if they were cross at being disturbed or were trying to vie with the noise of the threshing branches.

Nick had removed his jacket earlier and rolled up his sleeves. His arms were a deep golden brown. He looked tired, Eileen thought with compunction. He'd been on the road all night, and had the journey back ahead of him. But then, every time they met he was tired.

'Would you like a little sleep?' she asked.

He grinned and her heart turned over. 'No, I bloody wouldn't! Come here!'

She stumbled towards him and they came together in the middle of the room. He caught her in his arms and they stood for a long time wrapped

496

together, not speaking.

'I don't want you to go,' she whispered after a while.

'Christ, I can't bear to leave you.' His voice broke.

'Oh, Nick! When will it be over? When will we all lead normal lives again?'

'I don't know, my darling, I don't know.'

They still stayed together, clasped in each other's arms. 'How much time have we got?' Eileen whispered.

'Not long. Shall we go upstairs?'

'Yes, please.'

They lay on the bed, Nick's arm across her belly. 'I think I can feel the baby's heart beating.'

'That's me! I'm throbbing all over.'

'It's you who should have the sleep,' he said tenderly. 'You must be exhausted after today.'

'I'm all right. I'll have nothing to do tomorrer, will I? Not like you.' She stroked his forehead and he closed his eyes. 'Mmm! That's nice,' he murmured.

He fell asleep eventually, as she guessed he might, and she lay watching his mobile face, his long lashes blinking from time to time as she continued to stroke his brow. His eyes had scarcely shut, when she began to feel very alone, despite his warm body next to hers.

'It's always going to be like this,' she thought, 'until he's home for good.' Outside, the birds were making a terrible racket and the trees were working themselves up into a rage. Through the windows, she could see leaves were no longer fluttering to the ground, but being blown crazily, first one way, then the other. Suddenly, it began to rain and the downpour thundered against the window until it rattled in its frame.

She didn't have to live here, in the cottage. She could stay in Pearl Street if she wanted, but she'd always known here was the place where she should be once she had the baby. She didn't need the street, not like Sheila. She needed peace and quiet, the solitude to dream of Nick and think of Tony and look after her new child.

A little nagging pain seemed to roll through her stomach, and she remembered she'd been too excited to eat during the reception, so it was ages since she'd had food. Still, Sheila had left sandwiches and cake downstairs for their supper. As soon as Nick woke up, she'd set the table, switch the wireless on, and they would eat the meal like an ordinary married couple.

She gasped as another pain rolled through her, this one slightly sharper than the first, and she wondered if there was enough milk to make a drink.

'I hope I'm not going to be sick,' she thought. She watched Nick sleeping. His mouth twitched and she longed to kiss it. They'd scarcely had any time alone together. Perhaps she should wake him up, but then, he had that long journey back . . .

'Ouch!' Another pain, even stronger than the others.

Nick said sleepily, 'Whassa matter?'

'I think the baby's on its way.' How stupid of her not to realise that the pains were contractions!

'*WHAT!*' He shot off the bed like a bullet and looked at her wild-eyed.

Eileen had been all set to panic herself, but reckoned one of them should remain clam. 'Don't

498

get in a flap, Nick,' she said tersely. 'Put the kettle on and make a cup of tea while I sort meself out.'

'Tea!' he yelled hysterically. 'How can you think of tea! Get in the car and I'll drive you to the nursing home this instant—I take it you've booked?'

'Of course I've booked. Oh, but me suitcase with all me things in is at home.'

'Sod your suitcase and get in the car!'

'Not until I've had a cup of tea,' she said stubbornly. Another contraction hit her and she gave a little scream. 'Oh, all right, forget about the tea, I'm coming!'

*　　　*　　　*

'Hold on, Mrs Costello, until we get you to the delivery room. It's only at the end of the corridor. Hold on another minute.'

'It's not Mrs Costello, it's Mrs Stephens,' Nick said, as he virtually ran down the corridor with the wheelchair, Eileen clutching the arms precariously.

'It was Costello when she booked,' the young nurse panted as she tried to keep up. 'Turn left here.'

'Well, it's Stephens now.'

'It doesn't matter,' Eileen cried. She'd been holding on for miles, ever since Aintree Racecourse when her waters had broken. Then she'd forgotten the number of the nursing home in Merton Road, and Nick had been forced to drive slowly through the howling wind, looking for the sign outside.

'I've got the number all safe and sound at home,' she groaned.

'A lot of good *that* is!' Nick swore.

She felt herself being lifted onto a table and her clothes were removed, and despite the agony she was in, she managed to say plaintively, 'Be careful with me new stockings.'

'All right, me darling. Spread your legs out, wide now.' An Irish voice, a jolly nurse, much older than the first one, with a red face that shone like an apple.

'As if I'd want to do anything else! Oh, Jaysus!' The worst contraction yet, as if her insides were being split asunder.

'Is Matron on her way?' the nurse asked.

'I've no idea,' Eileen screamed.

The younger nurse replied, 'She's coming.'

A woman in a dark blue dress with a white headdress like a nun's loomed into view. 'Is she ready to push yet?' she enquired in a voice like ice.

'I've been ready to push for bloody hours!'

'I'm sure so, Matron.'

'Then let her.'

'Come on, now, Mrs Stephens,' the Irish nurse said, 'Let's have a real good push!'

'Just try and stop me!' She screamed again and a wave of pain engulfed her as the tiny being she'd been nurturing for nine whole months slid out into the world. Then the pain stopped and Eileen sank back onto the pillow, feeling shattered and triumphant.

It was over!

She heard a slap and there was an almighty and indignant yell from the baby. The Irish nurse said, 'You have a lovely little boy, Mrs Costello, and he's got a fine pair of lungs on him, I must say.'

'It's not Costello,' Eileen whispered, 'It's

500

Stephens.'

*   *   *

'Are they always so ugly?' Nick was looking at her
in an awed way, as if she'd just done something
totally unique. It was several hours later; Eileen
had needed three stitches after the birth, and poor
Nick had been left to pace the corridor, nerve-
racked and impatient. She'd booked a single room,
so there were just the three of them, Eileen and
Nick and their baby.

'He's not ugly, he's beautiful,' she protested,
smiling. She forgot entirely she had wanted a girl.
'In fact, he's the image of you!'

Nick looked alarmed. 'Is he?'

'The spitting image. He's got your hair, see?' She
stroked the tight dark curls. 'And your mouth and
your nose.'

The baby was curled up, wide awake, like a white
ball in her arms. As they watched, he yawned
crookedly and waved his fists. Nick laughed. 'He's
got no manners. Why is he wearing a dress?'

'It's a nightgown, silly. Babies always wear them.'

'I've got a son!' Nick said incredulously. 'Can I
hold him?'

'Of course you can. Put your hand under his
neck.'

Nick took the baby gingerly. 'God! This feels
peculiar. My son!' He touched the tiny nose, the
mouth, the hands, with his finger. 'He's perfect!'
He smiled at Eileen. 'We've got a child! We're a
proper family.'

'I know, luv.'

Their eyes met and Eileen knew he was about to

say the words she'd been dreading. 'I have to go,' he sighed. 'It's long past midnight and I'm already late. I shall have to put my foot down the whole way.'

She wasn't sure if she could bear it. 'Be careful, promise?' she said, trying to sound matter-of-fact and sensible.

'I will. Here, take him back, our son, and look after him for me, won't you?' Eileen nodded wordlessly as she took the baby in her arms.

'He *is* beautiful.' She could tell Nick was doing his damnedest not to cry.

'Like you,' she said.

'Well, I'll be off now.' He bent and kissed her fiercely on the lips. 'Goodbye, my darling girl. Goodbye, son.' He stroked the curly head briefly.

'Goodbye, Nick.'

He stood at the doorway for several seconds, staring intently, as if he was trying to take in the picture of his wife and son and impress it permanently on his brain.

'We'll meet again, eh?'

He left, and Eileen lay there listening to the sound of his footsteps as they became fainter and fainter. She heard him go down the stairs, and a few seconds later, the front door closed. A car engine started up . . .

'Nick!'

Somehow, she managed to struggle out of bed, though she could hardly walk, the stitches hurt so much. She staggered to the window, clutching the baby, and pulled the curtains back.

The wind was still howling and the full yellow moon was veiled by dark clouds, so she could scarcely see the car as it crawled out of the drive into the road. Then the car stopped, and she knew that Nick had seen her at the window and was waving.

She waved back frantically. 'Goodbye, darling,' she cried. 'Goodbye, my darling Nick. I love you, I love you.' She held their son up to the window and shook his tiny hand in Nick's direction. 'Wave to your dad, there's a good boy.'

The car started up again. Within seconds, it had gone. Eileen pressed her face against the cold glass and felt a searing pain rip through her entire body, a pain far worse, far greater than anything she'd felt throughout the birth. She cried out loud, a cry of despair and loneliness and longing, a cry of terror. How could she get through the rest of her life without him?

The door opened and the matron came in. 'I thought I heard a noise . . .' She stopped, shocked to the core, when she saw Eileen at the window. 'Get back into bed this minute,' she snapped. 'You're not allowed on your feet for seven days. And look at these curtains! You'll have the warden after us.'

'He's gone!' Eileen said hopelessly. 'He's gone forever.'

The woman's face softened slightly as she closed the curtains. 'You'll feel better about things in the morning,' she said awkwardly, as if she wasn't used to being kind. She clapped her hands together briskly. 'Come on now, Mrs Costello, back into bed. I'll put baby down in the nursery.'

'It's Mrs Stephens.'

'But I thought . . .'

'I know, it was Costello, now it's Stephens.' Eileen winced as she tried to hoist her legs onto the bed. Matron tut-tutted, grabbed hold of her feet and swung them under the covers none too gently.

'That'll teach you not to get out of bed again!' she said tartly. 'Let me have baby and I'll tuck you in.'

Eileen handed her son to the woman with unconcealed reluctance. Matron's expression changed completely when she looked down at the baby in her arms. 'He's a lovely little boy.' She was actually smiling. 'What are you going to call him?'

'Nick.'

'Well, Nick Stephens, it's about time you went to bed.' She switched the light off. 'Goodnight, Mrs Stephens. I hope you sleep well.'

The door closed, and Eileen was left alone in the darkness.